Death's Redemption

MARIE HALL

T0382436

FOREVER
YOURS

New York Boston

This book is a work of fiction. Names, characters, places, and incidents are the product of the author's imagination or are used fictitiously. Any resemblance to actual events, locales, or persons, living or dead, is coincidental.

Copyright © 2014 by Linda Hall
Excerpt from *Death's Lover* copyright © 2013 by Linda Hall
Cover design by Elizabeth Turner
Cover photography by Craig White
Cover copyright © 2014 by Hachette Book Group, Inc.

All rights reserved. In accordance with the U.S. Copyright Act of 1976, the scanning, uploading, and electronic sharing of any part of this book without the permission of the publisher constitute unlawful piracy and theft of the author's intellectual property. If you would like to use material from the book (other than for review purposes), prior written permission must be obtained by contacting the publisher at permissions@hbgusa.com. Thank you for your support of the author's rights.

Forever Yours
Hachette Book Group
237 Park Avenue
New York, NY 10017
hachettebookgroup.com
twitter.com/foreverromance

First published as an ebook and as a print on demand: June 2014

Forever Yours is an imprint of Grand Central Publishing.
The Forever Yours name and logo are trademarks of Hachette Book Group, Inc.

The publisher is not responsible for websites (or their content) that are not owned by the publisher.

The Hachette Speakers Bureau provides a wide range of authors for speaking events. To find out more, go to www.hachettespeakersbureau.com or call (866) 376-6591.

ISBN: 978-1-4555-4989-4 (ebook edition)
ISBN: 978-1-4555-4991-7 (print on demand edition)

Death's Redemption

ALSO BY MARIE HALL

Death's Lover

To my husband, you are my pillar and my rock. I could never do half of what I do without you. I love you.

Death's Redemption

Prologue

Toccata and Fugue in D minor" echoed through the cave, the glow of candlelight flickered across the red stone walls. The man in a white lab coat wiped the blood off his brow as a sound drew his eyes to the doorway carved inside the rock.

"Well?" The voice of the black silhouette standing in shadow made the man in the lab coat cringe. The sound always reminded him of a knife blade running across glass.

Licking his front teeth, he tossed the bone saw upon the mutilated corpse of the woman the shadow had dragged to the dungeon only a few short hours ago.

She was hardly recognizable now as the sexy redhead with pale ivory skin. The shadow, and that was all the man ever knew of his nocturnal visitor, always brought him a body or two at least twice a fortnight.

He never questioned why, or if the bodies might stop appearing. He had need of them as well. There was a compulsion inside him, an insidious monster that enjoyed the sight of blood, of turning something beautiful into something even more. As a child he'd been obsessed with Frankenstein, creating perfection from the parts of many.

But the shadow wasn't like him. The shadow had a purpose, a purpose he did not share with the man. The shadow's only demand was that the eyes belonged to him, the rest the man could keep.

Nodding, he held the small glass jar in front of him. "I've extracted the eyes. This was"—he swallowed hard, sweaty fingers clenching by his pant leg because the thought of releasing this part of her was abhorrent to him—"the most beautiful specimen yet."

"Set them down." The shadow's arm moved, pointing in the direction of the lab table.

The man in the lab coat nodded, walked over to the table, and, with a final pat to the lid, turned and walked back to the dismembered body. He needed to get the limbs on ice before they began to rot.

His latest work of art would be one for the ages. This woman had been beyond compare in beauty. Such a shame that the shadow had killed her first; perhaps if he'd met her while she'd been alive he might have even let her live.

But it was too late now for such maudlin thoughts. She was gone, and her sacrifice would not go to waste.

The man was careful to not glance at the shadow as it slowly slinked its way inside. He'd tried once, to peek, to look upon the face of his benefactor, and had nearly paid the price for it.

Shadow had one rule: never look at it. Never try to engage—he'd learned that truth with a knife across his throat.

There'd been so much blood, his blood had dripped from between his fingers as he'd tried to staunch the wound. But the cut had been sure and deep, and all the man in the white lab coat knew was…the shadow had killed him. He'd died. He'd seen a vision of a dark, dark tunnel, felt his soul (or consciousness, or essence, whatever you wanted to call it) begin to drift, slip off into a black void of fury and sounds that still made his body tremble if he thought on it too long, when suddenly he was back. Gasping and sputtering for breath.

The shadow had somehow brought him back, had spared his life, but with a warning. Never look upon it again, to not even wonder who or what it was, because if he ever did he wouldn't come back the next time.

All the man in the lab coat had seen had been a pair of ruby-red eyes. If he'd seen anything else, he could no longer remember. The rest was lost to him forever.

If it was a demon feeding him these bodies he didn't know, and he didn't care. He would never wonder again.

There was a sound like the scraping of a lid being turned, and then a low, furious hiss. "This is not the one. That bitch gave me the specs. Told me what she would look like. She was wrong." It slammed its fist onto the table, causing the sensitive electronics and tools of his trade to jump almost a foot up in the air.

Licking his lips, the man whispered low, "Perhaps if you tell me what you're looking for, I could try to help. I might be of more service than just—"

A brush of fingers trailed along the back of his neck, making his skin tingle and shiver as if shards of ice had been rubbed against it. He shuddered, heart thumping hard in his chest.

"You work for me, butcher. You'd do well to remember that." The voice in his ear was a sonorous echo, making his veins throb and his eardrums spasm with a sharp burst of fiery pain.

Howling, he grabbed his ears, keeping his eyes peeled on the stone floor. Praying to god the shadow wouldn't decide his usefulness had come to an end.

"Get back to work. I'll bring another." And from the corner of his eye he watched as the shadow picked up the hand of the woman and brought it to its lips. He couldn't be sure, but it seemed to him as if it even kissed her fingertips. Then it released the hand and walked away.

The man didn't move until he was sure the shadow was gone. Running to his woman, he picked up her hand, a faint blue color now marring her fingertips. Rubbing at the fingers furiously, he tried to take the spot off, but neither scrubbing nor dipping the hand in alcohol eradicated it.

Furious, he tossed the half-open bottle of alcohol against the cave wall. It landed with a dull thud. The shadow had ruined her perfection, but he had no other choice than to use her; he was on a deadline.

His audience waited.

Chapter 1

They were coming.

Mila panted, sweat poured down her brow, her back. Her lungs burned with fire as she raced around the corner of the brick building, trying to lose herself in the labyrinth of alleyways that bisected the city like a giant tic-tac-toe square.

A glass shard wedged itself into the sole of her foot, but she barely even felt it. Somewhere along the way she'd lost her slippers. She couldn't recall how or when.

She'd been in bed, dead to the world, and then the dreams had come—nightmares really, visions of the future. Visions of futures were never a sure thing; there were so many different possibilities, so many different choices to be made that could affect the final outcome.

The one she'd seen was a future she couldn't hope to make sense of. The dream had involved half-living things and fangs and a man with long red hair and silver eyes that gleamed like liquid mercury in flame. She'd seen him before, brief flashes of the same man throughout the years, and one thing had always remained a constant: she'd wake with her body burning for the touch of his hand. With a moan she'd gripped the sheets, writhing as the dream man leaned into her, whispering words she couldn't understand but felt like a dark promise in her soul.

Then suddenly the image had shifted, and it'd shown her, lying in bed. She knew instantly she wasn't witnessing a vision of herself; the one thing her kind could never do was see their own future. But in a twisted, convoluted way, she was now, because what she was seeing wasn't a possible future, it was the *present* of someone headed her way.

Her silhouette was dark against the shape of the light mattress as lavender rays of moonlight spilled across her pale face. She watched the scenes through a set of eyes outside her window. Standing next to the head she now inhabited lingered three shadowy forms converging slowly on her house, their sharp, angular faces intensely serious as they drew near.

In the vision an owl hooted, echoing the same chilling cry outside her window. She not only watched the vision unfold, but heard it happening around her. Heart trapped in her throat, she listened as a pebble skidded across asphalt, then saw that it was actually not a pebble but a bottle cap left behind by a child at play earlier in the day.

She shivered, all traces of sleep fleeing in an instant. Mila sensed their eager anticipation for her death; it clung in the air like oily tendrils, making her breathing hitch and her body shudder with an immediate wash of adrenaline, hyperaware and knowing she had less than five minutes to flee.

Alert and in a near panic, she'd barely had time to grab a robe and slippers and slide awkwardly out the bathroom window, running down the narrow path that separated this gingerbread home from that of the neighbors. The only element of surprise she still had left to her was the knowledge that they didn't know she knew they were after her.

She'd known today that *they* would come. That she'd blown her cover, it was why she hadn't hidden out in her home. She'd broken into a neighbor's home she barely knew, a neighbor she'd sometimes waved *Hi* to on her way to work in the mornings. She'd hoped it would throw them off her scent, but obviously not. Tomorrow she would have been safe. The boat she'd chartered would have taken her far from here, from this city that now felt more like a tomb.

As raw fear pounded an unforgiving melody in her skull, she pumped her arms harder, cringing at the taste of adrenaline thick on her tongue.

There was only one chance to escape them. If she could just reach Club X, Lise would give her sanctuary. Mila knew that; she didn't know how she knew that, but she knew that Lise had power, had always sensed the frail-looking woman was more than she seemed.

Footsteps echoed behind her. Fleeing had only bought her a very slim head start. In her dreams the shadows moving toward her bore fangs—she knew what these monsters were; she'd lived in San Francisco long enough, been around the day the creatures had finally come out of hiding. They wanted her scared, wanted fear pumping through her veins; it was an aphrodisiac to them.

They could catch her, would probably catch her. Running was just prolonging the inevitable, but she couldn't stop, because stopping meant she'd given up, and Mila never gave up. Her gran and mum had raised her to fight, to be proud, and to know that a woman's worth didn't come from being fearless, but from being brave in the face of fear.

Her chest ached, her legs shook—she wouldn't last much longer. It was three in the morning, and there were few cabs out right now, but even taking a cab wasn't safe: she'd put others in danger. They'd stop at nothing to get their hands on her, and she wouldn't put anyone else's life on the line; her conscience wouldn't allow it. The vampires wanted her, and she knew why: because of her powers. But they didn't know the truth. They'd kill her for something they could never hope to understand, could never hope to harness.

Somewhere an alley cat screeched.

She'd always been so careful using her powers. Even before the monsters came out of hiding and showed the world that they were more than myths, her mum had told her to guard her powers with her life. To never show it to outsiders. To never speak of it to others. To pretend it did not exist.

She'd been so careful.

Until today at the bar, but she couldn't regret saving that little girl. She'd do it again.

The footsteps were getting louder; a whimper spilled from

her lips. Gaze frantically searching for any sign of escape, she spotted a dilapidated brownstone a few yards ahead. The windows were boarded up and crime scene tape was stretched across its doorless frame.

She'd seen that abandoned house before, in another dream. Below a metal grating was a secret entrance, a tunnel dug out decades ago to help smugglers move drugs. The tunnel led into the sewers; in the dream she'd crawled through it, finding a silver ladder affixed to the wall. The ladder led up to the street. A sewer main had busted a few days ago. City workers had been at the site, but the man responsible for replacing the manhole cover had gotten a call from his wife. She'd gone into early labor. He'd been careless and the cover wasn't on all the way. Which meant she could maybe push it off. The tunnel was barely ten yards from the entrance of Club X. The chance of safety was slim, but it was her only hope.

The breeze stirred, carrying the stench of the streets with it, along with the sound of a coat flapping, like the rustling movements of bat wings. Heart lodged in her throat, Mila dove inside the door, landing hard on her knees. Pain exploded in her joints and she had to bite down on her lip to keep from whimpering.

They were toying with her, like a cat with a mouse. A quiet sob tore through her throat as she scrabbled back to her feet. It was so dark in here, there were no lights, and the smells were terrible—the place was musty and squeaking with rat chatter. Trying not to think about any of that, she held her hands out in front of her and made her way toward the kitchen.

She didn't need to see to know where she was headed; the

map of the house had imprinted itself in her mind the moment she'd dreamt of it. Ten steps down the hall, turn right at the first door, and now she was in the kitchen.

Walk five steps forward and…her fingers grazed the outline of an old fifties-style fridge. Planting her back against the side of it, she shoved off the balls of her feet, working it back away from the wall. Exposing the metal grate hidden behind it, she was so close. A horrible grinding sound reverberated like a gunshot through the nearly empty room as she pushed at the fridge. She was being too loud, they would find her, but she didn't have a choice to go slower. It was now or never.

Almost there, almost there, I'm almost—

"Did you really think you could run, little mortal?" The strange male's voice was like ice, heating her flesh in an arctic embrace, breaking her out in a wash of goose bumps.

Squealing, she didn't have time to think, because hard hands dug into her shoulders and flipped her around. Flailing wildly, she raked her nails across something and then stomped down on its foot as hard as she could.

He hissed, then a fist connected with her jaw and all she could see was a halo of stars. Pain flared and throbbed through her skull as she sank to her knees.

"She's in here," the male called out, and that's when the other two shadows converged on her.

Reaching into her nightshirt, Mila yanked out her rosary. "Hail Mary, full of grace—"

A woman laughed then jerked her chin up. Something sharp bit into her skin and broke through it—nails, fangs, she didn't know for sure, but whatever it was it burned like holy fire and made her have to bite down on her tongue not to scream out—blood slid thick and warm down Mila's jaw, bringing a wafting metallic scent with it.

"You think your God can save you now? We've been looking for you a very long time, little seer. The time for running has ended. We want what you have." The woman's voice was like brittle glass raking across her ear canals, making her wince and squirm as she tried in vain to break free of the male's hold on her shoulder.

"I don't know what you're talking about." Mila's words came out short and choppy through clacking teeth.

This time the hands that touched her were gentle, gliding, and then they framed her face, forcing her to stare into the glowing blue-eyed gaze of the other male captor. The burn from his eyes highlighted his features, and she cringed. The man staring at her had half his face melted off; his lips were grotesque on the left side, looking almost like they were sliding slowly down. His skin was mottled and as pink a newborn rat's.

"Wait, Lucian," another male voice growled just before a hand clenched ahold of her captor's wrist. "We were hired. If this betrayal is discovered, we'll be—" He clenched his jaw, muscle in his cheeks straining, as if the words he was saying he didn't actually want to say.

For a brief second hope beat powerful wings in her chest. Maybe this wasn't the end after all. Maybe she'd still be spared…she'd find a way out of this mess. Maybe…

Her captor curled his upper lip. "Gabrielle, you'll unhand me or I swear you'll wish you never did what you just did. She is ours, we have her now, and *nothing* will induce me to let her go."

Gabrielle swallowed hard. It was difficult to make out his appearance; his face and body were hidden in the darkest shadows of the house. Narrowing her eyes, hoping she was looking directly at him, she shoved as much longing for her life into her eyes as possible.

Trying without words to tell him that she wanted to live, that they didn't need to do this, to please help her. But her savior never came.

"Forgive me, Lucian," he said, words hushed and trembling with a thin thread of fear.

Any last vestige of hope she'd had died an excruciating and painful death. Because with those words the fingers clamped onto Lucian's wrist let go. She was alone with the devil himself.

"We will get what we want, mortal." His voice shivered with raw power, and Mila understood there'd never been a chance of escape.

Fighting at this point was worthless. They were too strong for her. There was only one option left, and as much as she'd always hoped it would never come to that, she had no other choice. Holding her chin high, Mila sucked in sharp breaths and glowered at the monster holding her.

His thumb rubbed along her cheekbone; his one eye searched her face. The other was nothing but an empty socket. He smirked, the right side of his lips tilting up just slightly.

"This is what your kind has done to mine. You humans swore we were safe, and yet still you try to hunt us. But your powers"—his mouth parted and a sort of hungry gaze burned back at her, his breathing rose as if he were...sexually excited, which made her stomach turn—"your powers will level the playing field. I've decided you belong to me, not her. Never her. Not again."

She couldn't make heads of his rambling. Did he not want the female vampire to claim her? She didn't know, and frankly, she didn't care. "You don't understand. It's not what you—"

His nostrils flared and he clamped her lips shut forcefully, his long nail nicking her flesh, making air hiss between her teeth at the sharp burst of pain.

"You're done talking. We monsters have played your human games long enough. Now it's time for you to play ours. Vanity"—he looked at the feminine shadow standing beside them—"hold her legs."

Gran, I'm sorry. She squeezed her eyes shut. She'd screwed up bad at the pub. If it'd been anyone but a child, she never would have done it. She would have walked out the door. She would have turned her face to the side and pretended that the future she'd seen wasn't meant to be.

But it was too late for regrets.

There was only one way to take her powers, she only prayed to God they didn't know it. Opening her eyes, she plastered on a sneer and then, gathering every last dredge of courage remaining, she opened her mouth and spit on him.

The only way to save humanity now was to make sure they killed her.

Chapter 2

Frenzy heard the screams first before he smelled the stench of blood. Fire ripped down his left side, burned the flesh off his hand, turning it to nothing but bone. The bumping sound of a heartbeat in distress slammed into his consciousness.

Sucking in a sharp breath, sweat coating his frame, he gasped as he turned to look at the dilapidated buildings towering around him.

Thanks to Cian's betrayal of The Morrigan, the queen of the fae sithen, Frenzy had been forced back into reaping souls—a task he did not want. He hated humanity and all it represented.

The greedy corruption of their souls had nearly infected him once centuries ago. No, not nearly—it had poisoned him. A betrayal by one had turned him into a monster. Frenzy had become someone of dark legend, an avenging demon of death. It'd been a black time in his long life and many had died. For the sake of the world, The Morrigan had yanked him away from the humans, made him serve her whims only, and he'd slowly begun to heal.

Now she'd thrust him back into this world, and there were no words to describe the absolute agony of being permanently returned to a place he wanted to see burn to the ground. They all deserved to die and to be forced back into their lands; to have to carry out the duties of a grim reaper all over again made a fury burn through his soul.

The bones of his hand throbbed, made bile roil through his gut. The only way to ease the ache was to drag the soul to its resting place.

A black alley cat screeched, arching its back as it peered up at him with angry yellow eyes.

"Come here, kitty cat," Frenzy drawled, wiggling his finger at it, then laughing when it jumped behind a Dumpster and scampered off with its thick tail tucked between its legs.

Gods, he hated this world.

Following the stench of blood, he slowly made his way toward an abandoned building, in no hurry to get there. The maggot could wait a while longer; not like he/she/it was going anywhere any time soon.

Frenzy rolled his eyes as he continued to snap and crack the bones of his left wrist. As the screams raged down the mostly deserted alleyway, he gazed at the abandoned houses with wooden boards hammered against the windows and bullet holes riddling the walls. Humans. They destroyed all they touched.

Kicking a glass bottle hard enough to shatter it against a set of crumbling cement steps to alert whoever was snacking on whatever that someone was at present, he waited and listened.

"Did you hear that?" something snarled. The voice came from the house directly in front of him.

The house had at one point been painted robin's-egg blue, but now it was mostly just patches of paint interspersed with long slivers of ragged wood poking out. The door was gone, and yellow crime scene tape marked the entryway.

A man's voice growled. "Go check it out. We've come too far."

Frenzy rolled his eyes. What the hell had he walked into this time? Another rape, murder, mugging? Only more of the same crap as always.

He could just sit out here, drape himself in essence, and become invisible until they finished whatever the hell it was they were doing, but he was bored and all he wanted now was to get back home. This would be his final harvest of the night, then he'd tell Morrigan he was done. Period.

She could flay him, skin him, rip him limb from limb—frankly, he didn't care. But he was done being death's bitch.

With a loud sigh, he opted to get it over with quickly. "I'm outside, dumbasses," he growled.

Suddenly the voices grew hysterical.

"Get the hell away from here. She's ours," a deep masculine voice rumbled before a pair of bright blue eyes locked onto his from the doorway. Instantly the ripple of *other* pulsed against Frenzy's body. It took barely a second for him to peg the monster. Werewolf killings were much gorier; the creature standing before him was clean, which meant he was a vampire. His jacket and jeans were spotless, but Frenzy's nose was as good as any bloodhound's. There was blood soaking into the floorboards of the old house.

The vampire cracked his knuckles, taking an advancing step out the door. "I said go. She belongs to us."

Snorting, Frenzy nodded, making sure to keep his hands hidden inside his black leather jacket. "Yeah, sure, dip weed. Finish her up, whatever. I'm patient."

Leaning against the ramshackle house, he bent his knee and yawned.

The vampire full-on growled, making a sound like an angry pit bull in the back of his throat. "Vanity, get the hell out here," he called over his shoulder, never stopping his slow, menacing glide toward Frenzy.

"Seriously, man, go finish." Frenzy waved him on, still trying to appear at ease while the muscles in his legs began to reflexively tighten up. "I'll wait."

Another vampire joined the first one—this one a female, with short black hair and intense amethyst eyes. The two began a slow convergence on him and Frenzy might have laughed, if he weren't suddenly annoyed.

"I don't think you heard me the first time," the male spoke up again, opening his mouth wide to expose the long canine fangs.

"I'd listen to Gabrielle if I were you." Vanity's full red lips curved up at the corners as she eyed him slowly up and down. Her fingers began toying with the collar of her pristinely white shirt.

The sexual heat in her eyes was obvious; so was the bloodlust. Her irises were a deep, bloody red. She'd recently fed on the human still inside the house.

The wind kicked up then, dragging the scent of blood, but mixed in with it was the unmistakable odor of vampire hormone. It was metallic and spicy and tickled the inside of his nose.

Frenzy chuckled, pushing off the wall as Gabrielle came within five feet of him. Unlike Vanity, the electric-blue-mohawked male was definitely posturing, ready for a fight.

"You should have left when you had the chance."

If the chuckle was intended to terrify Frenzy, it missed the mark. "Really?" He shook his head. "You're really doing this? I told you to finish, I'm not gonna stop you."

Gabrielle narrowed his eyes, his jaw clicked, and then a second later his nostrils flared. "You're a faerie." He spat the name like it offended him. His grin was nothing but teeth. "Fairies aren't welcome 'round these parts."

Vanity straightened up and where there'd been heat in her eyes only seconds ago, now there was the flickering flame of pure hate. Suddenly there were knives in her hands and she was standing by Gabrielle and they both knew they were going to kill him.

At least that was the attitude they were giving off. Goddess, he hated how stupid *others* were sometimes. Did they really just assume because he was a "faerie" he was an easy mark?

Being a faerie wasn't very popular these days. Not after the Great Wars, not after the way his kind had nearly caused the rest of the supernatural world to go extinct. But he didn't care about any of that; whatever hatred they still held on to, that was their own drama. He was only here to pick up the pieces of their meal.

If they wanted to fight, well, then…He smiled, more than happy to oblige them.

"Look, c'mon." He held up his hands. "Can't we all just get along?"

"Don't worry, sexy," Vanity purred, "I promise you won't feel a thing." She licked her fangs.

He snorted. "Yeah, sure. One more chance, guys. I'd really rather not kill you tonight."

Not that he cared one way or another whether he killed them, but he'd like to not get dirty. He hated the stench of vampire blood. It was a noxious odor, much more metallic than the norm and usually always black. Why, he had no idea. But getting the stench out, not to mention the stains, it was hell.

Gabrielle pounced, hands outstretched and fangs ready to sink into his neck. Vanity was suddenly at his back, and he rolled his eyes.

Vampires moved fast, but death moved faster. In less than a blink, he had Gabrielle pinned up against the rotted wood, which was groaning as the board bent inward, threatening to snap in two at any moment.

Vanity stopped moving, looking between him and Gabrielle's face with eyes as wide as saucers. Gabrielle was clawing at Frenzy's wrist; thing of it was, his wrist was nothing but bone. He didn't feel a damn thing and just chuckled as the vampire's eyes began to slowly pop from their sockets with his efforts to take a breath.

"What the hell are you?" Vanity hissed, still holding her knives in both hands, but they were now hanging past her waist, and there was a definite trickle of fear sliding from her pores. It was a thick, greasy substance that made Frenzy gag.

Spitting to the side of Gabrielle's booted foot, trying to get the nauseating taste from his mouth, he grinned. "Impressed yet?"

Her black Chinese bob bounced around her face when she yelled, "Lucian!"

This was really getting old. Frenzy debated whether to spare Gabrielle's life or not, then decided it really didn't matter one way or another to him. He'd given the goth bastard a chance to finish his prey. He'd wanted the fight. So…

With a smile full of teeth, he inhaled deeply and then, blowing out, pushed a jet of death down Gabrielle's throat. A rim of frost first coated the vampire's lips, turning them a deep shade of arctic blue, moving slowly but relentlessly down his tongue, his throat, the icy grip of death traveling through every nerve, vein, and muscle.

Within seconds the hands grasping his own began to slacken, and a moment later the vampire dropped like a sack of stone, shattering into a thousand pieces when his body hit the pavement.

There was no soul to gather from within the pieces of vampire; the fanged freak had died long ago.

But before Frenzy had a chance to gather his thoughts, claws raked fire down his back, and now he was pissed. He'd been ready to let the vampires have their prey, ready to wait them out.

Roaring, he twirled on his heel. There was another vampire in front of him, but this one looked wrong. His face reminded Frenzy of melting wax, the way it slid down one side. But the eyes were a glowing shade of blue.

Something about the vampire seemed familiar. A nagging thread tried to worm its way through his consciousness. Something about the intense neon blue of those eyes…about the iris that looked more like a teardrop than a circle. He'd seen those eyes before. But then the vampire was shoving his fangs out like a serpent ready for the strike and Frenzy stopped thinking.

The incisors literally seemed to leak a fluid and there was a sickly sweet smell, almost like raw almonds.

Lucian kicked Frenzy straight in the gut, shoving him against the wall. Seeing her buddy kick his ass must have spurred Vanity into action, because she was back in the fray. Slashing and moving her knives in a dance that was as beautiful as it was deadly. He'd blink and a new cut would appear, almost like magic, she moved so fast. But they were shallow slices, not even enough to leave scars. Blood slicked down his arms and sides. He needed to end this tiresome charade now.

"I gave you"—Frenzy slammed his bony hand against Lucian's cheek, every vein in his face standing out in bright green relief against the lily-white starkness of his flesh—"a chance to escape."

The press of death's hand to the vampire's cold flesh instantly immobilized him, but the trance wouldn't last long: maybe thirty minutes or so. And there was also the brilliant little side effect that while he lay in a catatonic stupor, the vampire's entire body would feel as if it was boiling in liquid ice. That knowledge shouldn't make Frenzy smile. But it did.

Two down, one more bloodsucker to take care of. Pivoting just as her curved blade descended for yet another stab, Frenzy thrust his fist through Vanity's chest.

Her entire body jerked, spasmed on his arm that had gouged a large hole through her abdominal cavity. The blades clattered uselessly to the ground and he tsked.

Vanity's mouth opened and closed in an ugly pantomime of a suffocating fish. He shook his head.

"So tell me, vampire." He cocked his head, peering up at her unusually pretty violet eyes. "What was so damn important back there that you were willing to tangle with death to get it?"

Her nostrils flared and a slight tugging pulled at his lips as the knowledge that she now realized exactly who he was expressed itself in her pain-filled gaze.

"Ah yes, my little prickly petunia, I am a grim reaper. Perhaps you should have thought of that before attacking me, eh?"

Again she said nothing. Grabbing her jaw, he moved her face up and down. "The correct answer is yes, Frenzy, I should have thought of that. Well, no worries."

Yanking his fist out of her, he let her slip to the ground. Her fingers shook as she grabbed at the gaping hole, which had very little blood coming out of it. Obviously she hadn't fed enough back there. Vampires could not produce their own blood; much like a mosquito, they had to suck their sustenance out of others in order to pass as mostly human.

Which begged the question, if she wasn't feeding on the human who was still obviously inside the house, what had she been doing? Vampires weren't known to run in packs unless they were on the hunt.

Breath rattled from her lungs. "The woman is ours," she managed to finally wheeze out.

He shrugged. "I do not care at all what you do with the carcass. The soul, however, belongs to me. You know how this goes, mosquito. Just business."

"You can't leave me this way," she gasped.

"I can do whatever I want." His smile was pure poison. "But since you're asking so nicely…" Leaning in, he pressed his palm to the side of the house.

Every reaper had a talent for killing, but not all reapers killed the same. Some could transform their bodies into killing vapors, literally shooting themselves like an arrow into their prey and ripping them apart from the inside out. Frenzy's preferred style was much more romantic.

Using his free hand, he feathered his fingers across her cold marble skin. Hissing, she twisted her face to the side.

"Shall I kiss it better?" he whispered as the power of death filled him, stretched him until he vibrated with it. The cadence of his voice lulled her gaze back, ensnaring her. Entrancing her.

Frenzy had always been more of a lover than a fighter. Tipping her face up to his, her breathing ragged from the pain and a sexual wave of intense longing for his touch, she melted into his lips.

But touching him while ridden by death was like kissing a volt of lightning. His mouth tingled as his power transferred to her. Death's kiss sank its tentacles deep inside her, rushing through her veins, her pores.

She gasped, pulling away as her body began to freeze from the inside out. Already pale ivory skin turned an alarming shade of arctic blue, and then cracks slid in large grooves down her face, her neck, her arms.

"Good-bye, vampire. It's been swell." He gently flicked the tip of her nose, and she shattered like a pile of broken marble at his feet.

Sighing, he stood, refusing to acknowledge that the knife wounds in his sides and back actually hurt like a mother. He licked his teeth, kicked the still-catatonic Lucian in the gut, just because he felt like it, and followed the sounds of wet gurgling inside the house.

The smells were the first things to hit him. A blast of spring, the scent of newly turned soil and seedling sprouts. Humans smelled of this. The good ones anyway. The ones who went to the light.

Not that he considered any of them good; as far as he was concerned they all deserved to be thrown into the fiery pit that reeked of sulfur. But whatever, not his decision.

The squeaking chirp of mice and rats rang like a melody all around him, almost in sync with the wet rattle coming from a few feet in front of him.

"Bloody freaking vampires," he growled, fully expecting to find a partially dismembered human with barely a torso attached and full of fang marks. Vamps could be a lot like sharks when in a frenzy, ripping off and sucking clean. The myth that they killed with a love nibble was rarely the case.

He now knew why their eyes glowed. Vampires could only pass as human when they fed properly. Only by being the parasites that they were could they attain the rich shade of healthy, pinkened skin and the natural eye color of what they once knew when alive and mortal.

But when a vampire didn't feed, they began to resemble the monster of legend. The pale-faced, glowing-eyed freaks whose looks gave them away as something other than human.

The vampires he'd fought tonight had been half-starved. Maybe they didn't care to appear human because San Francisco was the one city in the world that allowed any monster, be it vampire or zombie, to roam free and unmolested. A vampire did not need to hide his truths if he did not wish to. There were even clubs where humans and vamps went to hook up for those few but rare mortals who enjoyed being a vampire's snack for the night.

Times were so different from when he'd first roamed Earth, and a part of him missed the day when mortals had sense enough to fear *others*, when they worshipped the beauty of nature and the fae. But those days would never return again. Humans had adapted, just as the monsters had.

The black inside the ramshackle house of crumbling wood did not hinder his ability to see. The walls were covered in scratch marks, profanity-laced phrases written upon them with red and black spray paint. Decaying leaves and used needles littered the floorboards.

More than likely the vamps had stumbled upon a user too doped up to realize the type of danger she'd been in to flee in time.

Moon filtered in through cracks in the paned kitchen window. The female was bathed in shadow and weakly clutching onto her white robe, now stained a deep shade of crimson.

Standing in the doorway, Frenzy took his time studying the pathetic creature. The vampire, likely Lucian, had done a number on her. Her legs were splayed apart in an unnatural position. The feet were pointing in the wrong direction, but not only the feet: the hips were no longer even aligned.

Her chest cavity had been cracked open. Not unlike what he'd done to Vanity, but unlike the walking dead, the woman before him was a mortal and her very essence pooled around her in a large band of red. Pale fingers clutched almost spasmodically against the edge of her robe.

What must have once been a stunning face was now ribboned open at both cheekbones, the eyelids having been sliced off. There wasn't much in death that offended him; death was simply a fact of life. He'd killed many in his long life—vampire, shifter, witch, and human. But the savagery of this attack made the muscle in his jaw tick. A strange sensation filled his limbs, one he was not used to feeling often.

The emotion was pity. Much as he despised the mortals, the act of violence against this woman was an atrocity. Kindness was not an emotion inherent in him. So as much as he felt…something, it didn't change what he'd come here to do.

"Look at me, mortal."

A horrible snuffling sound, like she was trying to draw breath through a ruptured nose, issued from between her cracked lips.

Her head began a slow roll in his direction.

"What in the hell did those vampires want with you, little one?"

Flexing his bony hand, he placed it over her broken form, ready to harvest the soul from her body, when a pair of eyes stole the very words from his tongue.

Eyes the color of sun-warmed honey, a golden brown so rare he'd only ever seen the likes of it once before. Jerking his hand away from her chest as if burned, he sat back on his heels.

"Who are you?" he growled, as a strange sort of numbness infiltrated his limbs and brain.

Adrianna was the name running like a mantra through his head. His Adrianna. The only woman in the world he'd ever loved, ever needed, wanted, desired, adored…

A horrible grinding sound emanated from her as her lips flopped open, as if she was trying to speak. Disbelief kept his feet rooted to the spot. He needed to finish this, to get away from her and the memories surfacing like a bitter friend.

But he couldn't look away; the vision of his Adrianna kept merging with the battered face of this nameless woman. She was gazing at him with pain and fear, with hope. But not the hope that he would save her; she wanted death. He read it clearly. Her eyes were shrouded, angry, and screaming at him to hurry. To end it now.

"Who are you?!" he roared, even in his fury careful not to touch her with the bones of his hand.

Her eyes kept boring into him, accusing him, but there was something else in her eyes: pain. She was shrouded in it and barely hanging on to any last vestige of sanity.

"Kill...me," she croaked.

Yes. Yes. Yes.

He moved his hand, circling her head.

"Cannot...become...that."

Her broken voice scraped his nerves, set his teeth on edge, made a blanket of fury creep like a shadow across his mind. Fury at her for reminding him of a long-dead ghost, fury at the vampires for destroying her the way they had.

"It's too late, mortal. You already are that. Me taking the soul will not negate it. They've envenomed you." And they'd gone to great lengths to do it. She was covered head to toe in bite wounds.

Her head shook painfully slowly. "Then finish," she gasped, body shuddering as she tried to speak around the pain, "what...they...started."

Her eyes rolled back, and he could think again, because she didn't look so much like his Adrianna anymore. She was just a woman, a nameless, faceless woman. A human who'd destroyed and hated and lied and cheated and stolen...She was the worst of all creation.

Flexing his fingers, he flung them over her chest, ready to harvest the pulsing blue orb that was her soul, when there was a blinding flash of light followed by the unmistakable sharp and biting scent of frost.

Shielding his eyes against the brilliance, he turned to the side, but knew instinctively who'd intruded.

"Lise?" He jumped to his feet when the light finally turned down.

Lise was always a surprise. None knew of her true form or who she really was, always referred to as the Ancient One. All he did know for a fact was that even The Morrigan had to do what the old battle-ax said, which in his book meant that she wasn't one to mess with.

Dressed in a gown of sparkling sheer white, she reminded him of the frost he still felt shivering through the air. Strange, luminescent eyes hooked his, making him wonder all over again what she was.

After what Lise had done with Cian, all of faedom wondered what she was and why she'd taken such an interest in death. He narrowed his eyes.

"To what do I owe this honor?"

Quirking a snowy brow, she simply shrugged. "Must I have to have a reason to visit?" A vein of ice skated across the floor with each step she took.

"Do not tell me you've taken an interest in me now, Ancient One," he said with a thread of sarcasm.

A prim and small smile curved the edges of her petal-pink lips. "And if I have?"

"Good goddess"—he cast his gaze heavenward for a brief moment—"I'm not in the market, so if you're trying to get me to play patty-cake with a human the way you did with Cian, I'm not interested."

She was no longer looking at him. Lise was studying the woman, whose breathing was now a faint wisp of air.

"She hasn't got long in this world."

"Obviously." He knelt again. "Which is why I'm here." Extending his hand, he made to snatch up the glowing blue orb that was her soul, but a surprisingly warm hand latched on to the bone of his finger.

Brows gathering into sharp slashes, he shook off Lise's hand, surprised to note her skin still gleamed, almost glowed, like moonlight was trapped and filtering through her pores from within.

"You should have fallen to your knees in agony from touching that." His tone was accusatory. What bothered him most wasn't that Lise was unaffected by his touch, but that none were immune to death. Especially not an *other*, as indestructible as they sometimes seemed. Everything died. It was the continued mystery of who Lise was, why she interfered in the lives of the reapers, and what she could possibly want with him that really irritated him most.

"Do not try to make sense of me, boy. You never will." There was no malice in her words, merely amusement.

It made his teeth gnash.

"You must not allow Mila to become a vampire or to be taken by one of them."

Now that the real purpose of her visit was revealed, he still found himself just as confused.

"O-kay. She is covered in bite wounds. The venom has spread through her system. Are you suggesting I drive a stake through her heart?" He pointed at her still body; the bump of her heart was barely discernible now. She had literally milliseconds before human death occurred, at which point she *would* become the walking dead.

Crossing her arms she pinned him with a glacier glare. "Thank you, Captain Obvious."

His lips twitched despite himself.

Then everything stopped. Literally halted. The squeak of mice, the hollow scraping of a door creaking open and shut in a gentle breeze. The world was quiet and still, except for him and Lise.

The human was no longer breathing, but she wasn't dead either. She was in stasis along with the rest of the world.

Lise wore a smug grin. "Now then, as I was saying, she must not become one of them."

"And how do you plan to stop the inevitable, Ancient One? Keep her catatonic for the rest of her life?"

She wrinkled her nose. "Of course not. I already thought of that, but it really doesn't work for my endgame."

Nodding, he leaned against a fridge that'd been partially moved away from the wall. "What is it with immortals and their endgames?"

"Like you're one to talk, reaper. And what were you planning to do? Hmm?" The whites of her eyes glowed as she tapped her finger against her chin. "Tell the queen you were through being master of death? Is that not an endgame? Though a minor one, still an endgame."

He remained silent, refusing to rise to the obvious baiting.

"We are all the same; we all have a goal in mind. My goal involves you and this woman."

"No." A swift shake of his head didn't stop her from nodding as if he'd agreed.

"Oh yes."

Pinching the bridge of his nose, Frenzy licked his front teeth, counting slowly to three before speaking. "I do not think you heard me correctly. I'm not in the market for an Eve, especially not a human one. Cian at least got a witch. This…" His nose curled as he pointed to the broken shell lying before them.

Rolling her eyes, she looked at him as if he were merely a bug under a microscope and not the creature in whose hands rested life or death. She had no fear of him whatsoever. It was rather novel, and slightly off-putting.

"Well, as you succinctly stated just moments ago, she's no longer really human, now is she?"

"What?" He winced, trying to make sense of her nonsense. "You just said she couldn't be allowed to become a vampire—"

"Yes. And?"

"Aaaannnd…" He dragged the word out as he rolled his wrist, looking to her for a cue, some sign that she might have realized she'd spoken in riddles, but she was giving him a wide-eyed, totally innocent stare. "You confuse me."

She laughed. "I confuse them all, do not worry. Now, you and I will get along just fine if you listen to everything I tell you to do."

"Even if I agreed to this, whatever it is, it doesn't mean that The Morrigan would. She nearly killed Cian last time and—"

"Yes, yes, I handled that one. The kitten has been declawed; you work for me now. An arrangement the queen and I have made, if you will."

"What?" He jerked off the fridge, glaring at her now. "When did this happen? I work for the—"

"Not really. No." Her smile was laced in sugar. "You work for me. Memos may not have been handed down yet, but ownership has been overturned. Now listen up because we haven't much time."

And just like that all humor vanished from her face; she was intensely serious. The air between them shivered with the rawness of her power, like getting caught outside during an electrical storm. Waves of heat and ice and suffocating magic gripped him so tight he could do nothing but take a stuttering breath around the sudden pounding of his heart.

"From the moment that I release time she will have half a second before death. She cannot become a vampire, which is why you will not take her soul."

"Lise"—he shook his head—"I have to take her soul. If I do not, my hand will remain this way indefinitely." The dry bone clacked together as he opened and closed his fist.

"Then it shall. You are death, Frenzy."

Trying to breathe around the suffocating anger choking him, he willed himself to calm. Raging at Lise would only get him killed, in a likely gory and horrific manner at that.

"Point being that if it remains bone I will have—"

"A minor inconvenience. Wear a glove, not that it will matter around her anyway. She will die."

Again with the riddles. Trying to rub the sudden tension headache creeping up the back of his neck, he sighed. "So she *is* going to die?"

"Of course, death." Her eyes bugged and she was staring at him as if he was beyond stupid.

Smothering the growl that desperately wanted out, he settled for taking a deep breath instead. "When she dies I must take her soul. That is the way of things in my world, Lise."

She shook her head. "Not this time. I will make it so that no matter how often you touch her, she will never suffer death's caress. She will be immune to your charms."

He frowned. Was that even possible? But with Lise he supposed anything was possible. There was so much about her that was a complete mystery. "What am I supposed to do with this human?"

"Guard her, protect her."

"No." There wasn't even a point in thinking it over. There was no way he'd be saddled with guarding a human being.

"And honestly, stop thinking of her as human. She will no longer be once I wake her up. But you'll have to teach her how to survive what she will soon become, and I doubt she's going to enjoy the transition much. She'll need your support."

Powerful as she was, Frenzy was certain it was her mind that'd cracked centuries ago and not his. "I don't think you heard me; I said no."

Taking a step closer, she peered up at him with those unsettling white eyes. The Morrigan could cast glamour like none he'd ever known before, but she had the type of magic that made whoever her prey was unable to look away. To become ensnared and entranced in her predatory gaze, even while she ripped you limb from limb.

Lise had it too, but this was so much more.

Unease moved through his body and again his heart fluxed, banging hard against the cage in his chest. Rubbing at it, unable to tear his gaze from hers, he knew he'd never really had a choice in the matter.

She might be approaching him as a matronly figure of sorts, but the power in her seemingly frail body was vast and far superior to his own. She'd never had any intention of making this a democratic decision.

"Are you done sassing me, reaper?"

The sweetness of her voice did not hide the edge of steel buried inside the words. This was an ancient, a being of such terrifying power that she would get what she wanted one way or another.

Nostrils flaring, knowing he was bested, he clipped his head.

"Good. You must take her to George."

His lip curled up. "George is an outcast."

She shrugged. "I've run through all scenarios, and it's really the only way. If I send her to Lootah, king of the shifter clans, his bite will reveal the truth of her, causing her to be in more danger than she is even now."

Truth of her?

What exactly was this human? Was that why Lise was taking such an interest? Because she was more than another mere mortal? Turning, he glanced back down at the body. She was still frozen, limbs distorted, face a repulsive mass of bruises and slits, and he couldn't fathom the importance of her.

"Vampires have obviously figured her out. They tasted her blood. They already know; in fact, you'll barely have a minute to escape before they return in bigger numbers."

"I put down all but one of them. And that one should still be stunned for a while yet."

She rolled her eyes. "Frenzy, how long has it been since you've been out in the world and not suckling at the queen's teat?"

He clamped his lips shut.

"The world has progressed, child. What you think you know about *others*, humans, all of it…it's all so very different now. The vampire was merely stunned, apart from the one you shared death's kiss with, of course. That one is definitely d-e-a-d." She laughed and then shrugged, as if not in the least bit bothered by the death of a vampire. "And the one who shattered too"—she flicked her wrist—"you really should have destroyed the leader. Getting a little sloppy in your old age, death."

Lise ran Club X, a club that catered to all *others*. Be you witch, vampire, shifter, demon…She was Switzerland in a city overrun by monsters; she did not judge and she did not take sides.

Usually.

But she seemed to be doing so now.

"What's in this for you?" His voice dipped, because trying to make sense of this thing was going to give him a massive headache.

"Balance. Order. Same as you, reaper. The powers she possesses, they must not be manipulated by any other. To prevent another Great War, you must protect this woman."

"By taking her to George?!" He couldn't hide the disbelief from his voice; a low chuckle spilled from him. "Is the bastard still hiding out in the same cave I found him in all those centuries ago?"

She nodded. "He is."

Snorting, he shook his head. Might be good to visit George. It'd been a millennium at least. But honestly, wasn't death better for the woman than what Lise was suggesting? It had to be.

"No, it's not," she said, obviously reading his thoughts. "Her role in history is vital. In fact, my sisters and I have considered grooming her for future duties, but we haven't had enough time to study her lineage. In order for us to have that time, she must be protected. There is none more powerful than death to perform that duty."

There was definitely more to the story than what Lise was sharing. He knew that. He also knew she wasn't likely to give him more than she had.

"Who is she?"

She shrugged. "Just a woman."

That was a lie of epic proportions and he knew it; if she'd really been just a woman Lise would have let him reap her soul a long time ago.

"And why must I be the one to see to her? Isn't there another reaper available? Tariq, or Aeidin? Anybody?"

"Feral" was the word that immediately came to mind when

her lips split into a wide grin and, licking her front teeth, she shook her head. "None have the history you do."

"Falling in love with a mortal? A mistake I will never make again."

"Oh no, my dear death." She slid her hand up his arm. "No, I mean the wake of destruction you left behind after her death. To protect this mortal, you'll have to channel that baser side of yourself."

Scrubbing his jaw, knowing how pointless it was to argue, but needing to try anyway, he said, "And it nearly killed me. I went mad, absolutely insane for a quarter century. The Morrigan had me chained and locked up for the safety of those around me. I cannot become that monster again."

Clamping her hand over the spot of his heart, she shook her head. "That was because you had no focus. No point of reference to keep you grounded. Mila is that. Make her your point and you'll own the beast."

"Why?" He grabbed her hand. "Why is she worth protecting? What could she possibly know or have that makes every monster want her? What is so dangerous about that woman?"

"There are some mysteries in life that must be discovered with time. Only then can you truly make sense of them."

"Meaning what exactly?"

"Meaning"—she held her hand out as a bright bolt of power crackled from her palm into Mila's prostate body—"you'll find out."

The bolt of power picked the woman up off the ground and she floated toward Frenzy on a glowing, crackling bed of lightening. Her amber eyes stared sightlessly at him, eyes so similar to Adrianna's.

"Take her in hand, Frenzy." Lise talked to him like a mother reprimanding a recalcitrant child.

"I've got her," he snarled, yanking the body into his chest. "So when you wake her up, how exactly do you plan to prevent the transformation from occurring? If she's got a nanosecond, this all seems rather pointless."

Face deadpan, she couldn't have said more clearly how much of a fool she thought him than if she'd spoken the words aloud. "Obviously she will remain in stasis until the moment she is given to George. Then and only then will she reanimate."

It was on the tip of his tongue to ask her how she'd know to unlock the woman from her current status of human popsicle, but he found he didn't really care one way or the other. Lise had yet to convince him that allowing a lone woman to die was really as dire as she was making it out to seem. Problem was, he barely knew the Ancient One; to have someone come and tell him that grave danger would fall upon the world if he let one pathetic human perish seemed a tad melodramatic.

"The moment I release time, the vampires will attack. They're right outside the door. They want their prize. You cannot let them have it. Do you hear me? No matter what." She leaned up on tiptoe, standing nose to nose with him now. "Ever. Should you fail, I'll kill you."

"As if that frightens me." He scoffed.

"Oh, death"—she laughed, patting his cheek before taking

a step back—"you foolish, foolish man. Find your soul again, reaper; it is your only chance."

The rushing howl of wind pierced his skull as the bubble of time she'd trapped them in evaporated. In the muddle, he stood locked in place and slightly disoriented. It took him a second to realize what he'd initially assumed to be wind was actually the cry of vampires converging.

"Shit!" he snarled and, turning his back on the group of six leaping in the air, he swiped his hand opening the portal between the here and there. With barely a second to spare, he stepped through with his *precious* cargo and sealed it shut.

Breathing hard, he stared at the woman, who still hadn't awakened. Lise had obviously kept her word.

He needed to talk with the queen, find out what was really going on. He'd known The Morrigan his entire life; that she would willingly hand over the reins of one of her most powerful elite to some stranger smacked of the ridiculous.

He felt the press of Mila's amber eyes. Though he knew she was not conscious, she did not see him, he felt it all the same. A mocking, scorn-filled gaze that seemed to scream at him, accuse him that he would fail as he'd always failed.

Turning Mila's head to the side, he cursed his pathetic bleeding heart and headed toward George's cave. The queen would just have to wait.

Chapter 3

Standing at the massive gray stone entrance that led deep into the belly of the earth, Frenzy adjusted the woman in his arms.

"Bloody hell," he bit out, taking the first step into the black bowels. The air reeked of the rotten stench of half-eaten carcasses. Curling his nose, he followed the jagged stairs that'd been cut out of rock farther and farther down into the bottomless abyss George called home.

Mila was getting heavy. He'd been carting her around the past thirty minutes, trying to dredge up the nearly forgotten memory of George's hidden lair. Frenzy had stumbled upon George in the early fifteenth century.

The things he'd seen that man do, the atrocities and sins he'd committed, would have been enough to make Jack the Ripper lose his lunch. As the years progressed, George had tamed.

Well, as tame as a lone wolf was capable of being, anyway.

A drop of rainwater leaking from between a crack in the

stone wall plopped onto his nose. Grunting, Frenzy wiped his nose against Mila's blood-caked neck.

"You'd better be worth this," he muttered.

After countless stairs he finally saw a break in the utter inky darkness—a faint flickering of reddish-gold candlelight.

"George," he called out loud enough to make the sound of his voice echo. George was hard of hearing, or at least he had been last time Frenzy had seen him. A pack of feral dogs had caught wind of his noxious odor and pounced, ripping off both ears before George had been able to fend them off.

Shifters could heal. Normally. But after George had been exiled from the pack, his ability to heal himself had dwindled down to almost nil. Most of the magic a shifter boasted came from the combined efforts of the pack. A lone wolf was truly at the mercy of the world.

Goddess, it was almost a crime what Lise was asking him to do to Mila. As much as he despised mortals, turning something into a hybrid was plain cruel. There were so few cases of hybrids he could recall, and most of them had died grisly deaths because it was never a sure thing what a hybrid would become. It would gain either the best traits of both creatures or the worst, and you could never know from the onset. The few he'd known of had died due to the madness that'd infiltrated their brains from the moment they'd woken.

Studying a hybrid was difficult because in order to create one the circumstances had to be just right. Once you were turned vampire, or shifter, or even zombie, that was all you could ever be. A hybrid was created right at the moment of death. When life hung precariously between the two, the infinitesimal period was the only time to have it happen. Which meant you had to have two willing and opposite monsters turn the kill at the exact same moment.

George's bite would come several minutes after the vampire's; granted, Lise had placed the woman in stasis, so perhaps there was still a chance that she was fresh enough to become the hybrid Lise required her to be.

If he had to guess why Lise wished it to be George who bit her, his guess was that unlike vampires, shifters still retained their souls. Meaning, while the "raw meat" obsession was strong in them, so was their desire to retain their humanity. They weren't mindless killers, unless, of course, in life they'd been soulless monsters to begin with.

A shuffling drag came at Frenzy from the left. Turning, he inclined his head at his old friend.

George stopped ten paces in front of him. The grizzled wolf looked nearly the same as he had last time Frenzy had been around him.

Most of his parts were where they should be. It looked like something had maybe taken a nibble off the tip of his hawkish nose, and his skin was a slightly grayish pallor, but that was to be expected when the shifter refused to go aboveground. Extremely pale blue eyes sat in a face that never failed to remind Frenzy of the priest George had once been. There was an open and honest look about the man that made a person instantly want to trust him. Frenzy had no way of knowing just how far the desiccation of George had advanced since last he'd seen him because the priest had covered his body in a monk's brown robe.

Shoving a lock of dull gray hair out of his eyes, George lifted a brow.

"Should I thank you for the offering?" His English lilt was still very much evident, as was the sibilance of his *s*. As long as Frenzy had known him George had always had a slight lisp.

The cave smelled strongly of elderberry and pine, thanks to the pine needles and berries scattered throughout the cave floor. Clearly the wolf was trying to mask the sickly sweet odor of his body from scavenging predators. Without a pack to help protect him, George was in a very vulnerable position.

"You should know, death, I don't eat humans anymore. I find them very gamey, if it's all the same to you. Though I thank you for your kindness."

Chuckling, Frenzy nodded. George had been a vegetarian when he'd first met him as a human all those years ago and had never eaten a human so far as he knew. Well, he was vegetarian by shifter standards—which basically meant he ate any meat that wasn't of the Homo sapiens variety. "I'll remember that." Searching the room for a bench or a chair, he shrugged Mila up in his arms. "I need to set her down."

Lifting an arm, George motioned farther back into the cave where the candlelight was the brightest.

"Follow me." And turning slowly on his heel, he began the painful-looking shuffle-step back.

Frenzy wasn't certain how many years, lifetimes, George had spent in this cave. From the moment he was ostracized George had hidden himself within the bowels of the earth, carving out a labyrinth of tunnels. It would be too easy to get lost down here, which was likely how the priest trapped his prey for later consumption.

Eventually they made it to what was clearly the wolf's true sanctuary. Where the actual entrance of the cave was only decorated with pine and berries, the back room felt homey. A large, handwoven rug lined the space. An ancient pockmarked desk sat in the corner with an enormous and melted beeswax candle dripping yellow wax off the edge onto the stone below.

A lumpy feather-stuffed mattress, room for one only, sat tucked within a narrow alcove, and the rest of the cavernous room was lined with rows and rows of books.

"I see you've not escaped the Middle Ages. But where did the collection of books come from?"

George's lips pulled up into what Frenzy could only assume was a facsimile of a smile—something the priest clearly hadn't done in ages, because it resembled more a canine's snarl than anything.

"I've collected over the years. Lay her on the bed." Sitting on the low stool, George pointed to his narrow bunk. "Who is that?"

Setting the still immobile Mila onto the cot, Frenzy shrugged. "I've no clue. Lise asked me to bring her to you."

Dusting off his hands, he turned to find George's brows creeping along his shaggy hairline.

"You look…" Frenzy pressed his lips tight. "Well."

Laughing, the sound reminding him of crumpling up a palm

full of dried leaves, George shook his head. "'Well' is not the word I'd use. I survive, that is all."

Browsing the rows of books, tracing the gold lettering along the spines, Frenzy shrugged. "I expected to find you nothing but a skeleton, how have you survived intact for so long?" He turned to stare at the man he'd once called friend.

"I keep to myself and do not engage in fights I know I cannot win."

"How do you eat? What do you eat?"

He chuckled and again, it sounded all wrong, made Frenzy grimace in response. "Without a pack my flesh is absurdly fragile, as you well know." He pointed at the holes in his head where his ears once were. "Once I lose it I can no longer regenerate it. I have no desire to walk around looking like one of you."

Frenzy snorted and waved the bones of his hand.

"I wait until prey enters the cave, loses itself inside, and slowly starves to death. Then I eat." Pale blue eyes flicked toward her body. "Why has Lise sent you to me?"

Doing a double shoulder shrug, Frenzy sighed. "I assume to bite her."

Tapping his fingers upon the desk, George didn't take his eyes off Mila. "I haven't seen a woman in centuries." His voice was thoughtful and low. Then his brows bunched. "Is she dead? She does not breathe."

Grabbing a book off the shelf titled *The Demise of Morality*, Frenzy flipped through what was clearly light reading material for the monk, the pages worn, as if read frequently through the ages. "She is not dead. She should be, but she is not. Lise placed her in stasis."

Eyes flickering down to the book in Frenzy's hand, George narrowed them thoughtfully. "Why?"

Losing interest quickly, Frenzy slapped it shut and shelved it. "No clue other than I am to be this human's guardian. From what, I haven't an idea."

Gingerly getting to his feet, George grabbed a small candle and a holder, lit it, and then ambled toward Mila, dragging the glow of his flame along her body, studying her intensely.

"She is covered in wounds. What are these, vampire bites?"

Nodding, Frenzy joined him. "Yes."

Placing a thumb against his lips, George shook his head. "Lise wants me to infect her? She's already infected."

Squeezing his eyes, rubbing the bridge of his nose, Frenzy sighed. "Exactly. I questioned the Ancient One over and over, but she's very insistent you infect her too."

"But there must be more to the story, no?" George asked thoughtfully. "Truth is I do not know whether my infection can take with her so envenomed. And if it does, what she could be. The double dose will turn her hybrid. It is possible she will not survive this. Does the Ancient One truly want her to die such a ghastly and horrid death?"

Flicking his fingers together, Frenzy shrugged again. "Which is why I'm here. If she comes back as some psychotic animal, we'll simply drive a stake through her heart and dismember her. That is the only way to incapacitate one of you, correct?"

"Not the stake, no." George shook his head. "But the dismemberment is correct, along with ripping out the heart and burning it in fire. However, you know how I feel about killing. I will not do it."

Gently clapping a hand onto George's shoulder, Frenzy nodded. "And that, my friend, is why you've survived this long. But do not worry, if it comes down to killing, I'll be the one."

Lips pressed thin, George knelt and drew Mila's hand into his own. "She is very cold. She feels dead already."

Swallowing hard, he licked his lips, and Frenzy didn't want to know whether the priest suddenly found himself hungry.

"She is not for food," Frenzy growled low.

"Of course, of course not. 'Tis only I haven't eaten in weeks and…" He swallowed again.

"Hell, George." Frenzy snatched her hand out of the priest's. "Do not eat her. Can I trust you to bite only?"

Rubbing his eyes, taking two deep breaths, George nodded. "Perhaps if you find me some meat aboveground first?"

Much as Frenzy never wanted to be saddled with the woman's care, she was his responsibility now and he'd be damned if any harm came to her on his watch.

"If you eat her, I will take you topside and throw you to the wolves. Do you understand me?"

Licking his lips, wringing his hands, George nodded. "Yes, but hurry."

"Damn you, priest." With a growl, Frenzy ripped open a fabric of time between the here and there. In less than a second he was aboveground, breathing in the nippy, fog-soaked air.

Buttery moonlight bathed the meadow. Trees towered to the sky, and in those trees the soft exhalations of sleeping squirrels stirred like a gentle breeze.

This was ridiculous, hunting for rodent in the dead of night while a woman he barely knew but was forced to protect was currently being guarded by a shifter that hadn't eaten in weeks...The gods were laughing.

Swiping a hand through the air, he landed on the nearest, fattest branch. He wasn't a hunter, had no desire to try for stealth. Opening his hand, he blew on it. Undulations of frost rolled off the bones like mist, moving from branch to branch with one purpose.

To kill.

The dull thud of carcasses dropping to the forest floor beat a constant rhythm. He'd raze the entire forest if he really wanted to. But a couple dozen squirrels was good enough.

Snapping the frost back to him, he gathered the rigored animals by their scruffy tails and quickly returned to his exiled acquaintance.

George was still kneeling over Mila, staring at her with a hard-edged intensity Frenzy had seen many times in his life. The look of a wild predator sizing up its prey.

"Step. Away," Frenzy growled.

A shudder rippled down the priests' spine. "*Ssso* hungry." The voice spilling from him in no way reminded Frenzy of the man he'd once known.

Dropping the rodents, Frenzy rushed George, hooking his fingers into his shoulder blades and yanking him away from her.

"There is food on the floor. Rip into it, do whatever you need to do, then get your head on straight, because we have a job to do, wolf. And if you can't do that I'll become the killer I'm so very good at being."

The echoing vibrations of heavy breathing was the only thing he heard. George could have fought him back; though a lone wolf was fragile in many ways, they were still killers, incredibly hard to restrain if they wanted to eat. Frenzy knew the only way he could stop George if the priest was determined to get at her was to dismember him. Which would well and truly destroy him.

A fate he did not actually want for his friend.

"Let me go." Sounding more like himself, Frenzy decided to give the monk a final chance and slowly peeled his hands off from the shifter's back.

Crossing his arms, he made George walk around him. Frenzy didn't turn, giving the wolf some modicum of respect, pretending not to hear the slurping and crunching, ripping and gnawing.

The monk had obviously gone without a food source for too long.

Finally the rabid sounds of eating died down. A second later George cleared his throat.

Lifting a brow, Frenzy turned. The priest had cleaned up well. There wasn't a trace of blood or gore; there wasn't even a trace of fur.

"You okay now? Can you handle this?"

Rubbing the corner of his mouth, he nodded. "Yes."

"Then let's hurry. I don't enjoy lugging around a corpse." Stepping aside, Frenzy spread his arm and waited for the priest to pass.

"You do understand that without the woman being awake the bite will not transmit."

That fact hadn't escaped Frenzy. He could only trust that Lise would work her superpowers as she'd promised.

Mila looked same as she had earlier: a mess of slashes and bites and almost unrecognizable as human.

Running his hand over the body, George shook his head. "However I bite her, her condition will remain."

"Meaning what?"

"Meaning"—he touched the tip of his nose—"I do not carry pack magic in my bite. She will not heal as a normal shifter would."

"Vampires heal, don't they?" Frenzy asked.

"They do"—he nodded slowly—"but she will be a hybrid. It is possible that she will not receive the ability to heal from them."

Licking his front teeth, he finally got it. "The tears and bites."

"Will stay. Unless we fix them first."

"And how do you propose to do that?"

Walking over to a large wooden chest in the corner of the room, he lifted the lid, rusty hinges groaning loud. Reaching in, he extracted a small round tin, then returned.

"We sew the wounds shut."

"The hell we do." Frenzy snorted, eyeing the ridiculously large bone needle and thread in the wolf's hand.

Mouth thinning, George lifted a brow. "It's either do this or stare at open wounds for the rest of her life."

Staring at the face of the woman, Frenzy snarled. "They've ruined her, George. Doing this seems pointless. She has no eyelids, we can't sew shut the bite marks…She won't thank us."

Huffing, George threaded the needle. "Move."

"What?"

"Move out of my light. I'm going to sew her cheeks shut."

Clenching his jaw, Frenzy shrugged. "Then by all means, monk, do what you can."

Nodding swiftly, George bent over and very gently inserted the needle into her cheek, falling into an easy and practiced rhythm.

It took less than ten minutes. Cocking his head, Frenzy studied the sharp planes of her cheekbones, the heart-shaped jawline, and concluded that at one point she must have been a beautiful woman.

Looking into those amber eyes, he wondered all over again why they were doing this. Mila hadn't wanted to come back; she'd wanted to die rather than become a vampire. What would she think if she knew that he was now asking a shifter to turn her into one of them?

He doubted she'd be happy.

Setting the needle down, George picked up her hand. "She's still in stasis." He shook her hand.

The priest turned to look at him, a question in his eyes.

"Lise," Frenzy muttered not knowing what else to do, "if you're hearing, the time is now."

The air quickened, tightened with sparks of raw power. Tingling and rolling across his skin like a burst of lightening. George hissed, shaking his head with a dazed look.

A large, indrawn breath gasped and rattled.

"Now!" Frenzy pointed at Mila. "Do it now."

Bringing her wrist to his mouth, George bit.

Chapter 4

Fire.

She was covered in it; it was rolling inside her, through her. Running down her arms, legs, pumping like a fiery fist through her heart. Mila wanted to scream, but when she opened her mouth, it was like someone had fused her vocal chords. All she could do was grunt and cry and wish like hell she'd just die already.

"Hold her down," a hard male voice grunted, and then two sets of hands clamped down on her arms.

Last thing she remembered was staring into a pair of silver eyes. Silver eyes that belonged to the man with fire in his hair, whose movements made her think of the rapacious glide of a panther, both deadly and graceful.

She'd begged him not to let her turn. Begged him. With what little strength she'd had left in her body, she'd told him to never let it happen.

But she felt the change happening, felt her blood bubbling,

frothing, evaporating inside her veins. Spasming, she screamed inside her brain.

The moment she turned, she'd drive a stake through her heart.

* * *

"What's happening to her?" Frenzy scowled, turning to George.

Holding up his hand, George nodded. "She's necrotizing. This is the process. If you can't handle it, then go someplace else."

From the moment George had bitten Mila, she'd begun the change. To the shifter's credit, he hadn't stayed on her long.

Her skin had slowly leached of color, turning from a muted pink to an ivory so pale it almost appeared tinted with shades of blue. The veins underneath stood out in bold relief, a vivid greenish blue, but as time continued they grew more and more pale.

The blood that'd been coating her face and neck was literally absorbing into the skin, which was starting to gleam like a freshwater pearl. Blond hair that'd appeared ashen before was doing something strange. Instead of color leaching out, it was growing bolder. Brighter. Shot through with veins of gold.

"What the hell is happening to her?"

George shook his head, his eyes roaming her face. "I told you I wasn't sure what would happen. She's been bitten by two sets of species."

Ripping the shredded section of shirt off her stomach, Frenzy pointed. "The bites are fading, and look at her eyes."

A thin film of translucent flesh grew over the eyes, gradually shifting from clear to the same odd grayish-pearl tone of the rest of her body.

"A lone wolf cannot regenerate."

Pulling her lips back, Frenzy touched the tip of his finger to her canine. "She obviously is. But look at this, it's not growing."

She didn't seem to be turning into a vampire; a vampire was useless without its fangs. But she was definitely regenerating, so did this mean that she'd be one of the rare viable hybrids?

Tracing the length of her sewn-up cheek, George shook his head. "This isn't healing."

Her mouth opened then, and a scream ripped out of her throat, followed by large amber-colored doe eyes turning to him with a hostile glare. The silence was almost eerie after that ear-splitting shriek.

"You," she hissed and sat up, clutching at the tatters of her shirt. Then her eyes landed on George, her chest heaved in and out, and her nostrils flared as panic scrawled a hard line across her brows.

But rather than freak out and scream again, she merely stared, the silence confounding Frenzy.

Whatever transformation was going to happen to the mortal seemed to have occurred. Her skin was alabaster smooth, and her nails were long and deadly sharp looking. The hair was supple and silky and falling like a billowy wave across her shoulders. He slowly tracked the length of her long, long thighs, the graceful lines of her calves, and the dainty, bare feet.

She was as beautiful now as she'd been damaged then. There was not a flaw on her, save for the sewn sections of her cheeks, reminding him of a macabre porcelain doll.

"I dreamt of you," she said, voice even and smooth. Apart from her outburst the moment she woke up, she was now the picture of composed calm.

George and Frenzy exchanged glances. Not sure what that meant or whether there was even any true meaning behind it, so much as a muddled brain still working through the "change," he choose to ignore the comment for now.

She lifted a brow, holding her hand up in front of her face. "So I'm a vampire now, right?" There was a small hitch to her voice, something that would barely be discernible to anyone without his ability to hear the scamper of mice ten miles downfield.

There was an absolute stillness to her body, not a wrinkle or a frown around her eyes or mouth. She hardly took a breath.

George shook his head. "Actually, no."

At the sound of his voice, she turned. She was measuring him, it was obvious by the way her eyes touched his cassock, moved across his face and hands. Frenzy was amazed she didn't rail or shiver, violently questioning who, what, when, where, or how? Maybe she was in shock.

Those haunting amber eyes were cold, hard, and unswerving.

"Why didn't you kill me?" she all but growled at Frenzy. "You have no idea what you've done." Gaze dropping to his bony hand for a split second, she whispered, "You should have killed me."

"Why?" It was George asking. "Who are you? Why has the Ancient One taken such an interest in you?"

All questions at the forefront of Frenzy's mind, but he'd been unable to voice them because he couldn't make her out. Most humans would be falling over themselves with gushy tears of joy that they lived, had a new lease on life. Instead she seemed not only pissed, but disappointed in him. The thought prickled.

"You don't seem shocked by this," he finally spoke up.

Violently yanking on a thread poking from her robe, she shook her head. "Should I be? I knew the second they found me it was done." Rubbing the bridge of her nose, she inhaled deeply and then paused. Frowning, she inhaled again. "I smell…dirt?" She sniffed again. "And acorns?"

George's brows dropped, gathering in a caterpillar bunch at the center of his forehead. Kneeling, he crept slowly forward, cocking his head to the side and studying her like one of his specimens.

"What?" she snapped at him.

"It's just that"—pausing, he glanced back at Frenzy briefly as an astonished question mark flitted through the film of his eyes—"you *feel* different."

"Different?" Her tone dropped, became deeper and richer.

"How are you?" George asked her, not bothering to answer her question.

Running her hands across her flat abdomen, down her thighs, and up her biceps, she shrugged. "I feel fine. Great, actually." But then her fingers touched the scars on her cheeks and she hissed. "What is this?"

Crossing his arms, Frenzy decided he was done with this game of fifty questions. "Enough. You want answers, so do we. Start with who you are."

Nostrils flaring, she jerked to her feet. Her movements were swift, so fast, she obviously hadn't been prepared for it. One second she was scooting off the bed, the next she was on the domed ceiling with her fingers driving through the stone, anchoring her firmly into place, looking much like a terrified house cat.

"Let go." George's accent thickened as he shambled slowly to beneath where she was clutching onto the roof and breathing heavy, panicky breaths.

A cascade of blond hair waved in front of them as she shook her head. "Give me a second." Her voice wavered, but again, it wasn't nearly as thready or panicked as it should have been.

When Frenzy killed the man responsible for taking his Adrianna's life he'd siphoned her last moments from his mind. She'd been pleading, crying huge, angry tears, and begging for her life. Screaming as the knife plunged over and over into her body, whispering with her dying breath for him to let her live.

This woman was doing none of those things. It unnerved him in ways he didn't want to analyze at the moment.

Taking a deep breath, her body tightened, and then she jumped gracefully to her feet. Licking her lips, she looked up at the ceiling before finally dusting her hands off on her pants.

"I'm thirsty," she said and then shuddered, her shoulders rolling and her mouth turning down as she glanced at her feet.

Holding up a hand, George shambled over to the corner of

the room where he'd kept his meat. Stooping, he retrieved the final squirrel and handed it to her.

A blank stare was all that met the gift. Then a hard swallow and licking of her lips. "I…"

Her fingers convulsed around the furry body.

"Do you want to drink from it?" Frenzy inquired.

Confused amber eyes met his, nodding softly, her lips thinned. "I want to…to—" Lifting the rodent to her nose, she inhaled deeply, and this time when she shuddered it didn't seem to be in revulsion: a moan as of pure ecstasy spilled out her throat. "Take it away." She held it back to George. "Get it away from me. I'm not hungry."

But it wasn't true, because the irises in her eyes were bleeding a deep shade of crimson. The hunger, that vampiric need for blood that was so all-consuming, had made itself manifest.

"Yes, you are." Pushing George's questing hand out of the way, Frenzy stepped around the monk, forcing Mila to look at him.

"I'm…not." The breathless tone of her voice filled with the raw shiver of desire, and he smirked.

Fluttering his bony fingers along her jawline, he quirked a brow, realizing instantly that Lise had not lied. He still sensed the effervescence of her soul pulsing against his fingers, but she was immune to his touch.

Her gaze was instantly drawn to his hand, but again, she said nothing. Irritated at his curiosity, he growled. "Your throat is spasming, so dry all you can think of is that wet warmth sliding down."

Grabbing ahold of her stomach, she shook her head. But it lacked heat.

"Can you see the red, creature?"

She licked her front teeth, tongue lingering along the blunt edge of her canine.

Taking the squirrel from her lax fingers, Frenzy used the bone of his hand like a saw, inserting a roughened edge into the animal's pelt, just enough to create a small tear. Enough for her to see the pink meat inside.

Closing her eyes, she turned her face to the side. Taking perverse pleasure in her obviously disgusted desire, he chuckled.

"It is here. For you. Must you be so difficult?"

"Difficult?" Snarling, she whipped around. "How dare you? Do you have any idea what you've done to me? Who I was? That I can feel these...these..." Dropping her eyes toward the red pelt with a mixture of revulsion and pure unadulterated need, she shook her head.

"Wants. Needs. Desires?" He took a step forward.

"Yes! These perversions," she cried with force. "I told you to kill me." Breath sawing raggedly through her lungs, she stood before him like a shieldmaiden ready to do battle.

An answering thrum of awareness, of her strange scent of sun-kissed raspberry and freshly turned leaves, the way she moved and pierced him with honeyed amber eyes flecked with crimson—it took seconds for Frenzy to note them all. Not wanting to, he mentally compared her to the only other woman in his life who'd ever made him this aware, and discovered that he liked the fire. Liked her heat. After years of feeling nothing but the drudgery of life, he laughed and the sound came from deep inside. Filled with the raw excitement of the unknown.

"You do not act surprised by me." He cocked his head.

Her nostrils flared and she crossed her arms, pointedly not looking at the squirrel he still held.

He took a step into her, just to test her, to see what she'd do. Whether she'd back up or stand her ground. He felt strangely delighted that she did neither. Planting her hands on his chest, she shoved him back hard using the supernatural strength inherent to her now. But she was a baby in monster years; her strength was nothing to his.

"What do you know?" he asked, tracing the curve of her jaw with bone.

Lifting her chin, body vibrating like a tuning fork, she snarled. "Damn you, grim reaper. I know enough to know that you should never have let me live. You stupid, dumb arsehole. I should have died tonight, and now everything's in peril."

* * *

Mila tried to ignore the slab of meat cooling in his bony hand, not sure which she was more disturbed by—the fact that she craved that squirrel like a junkie with his fix, or the fact that she was standing in front of a grim reaper. The reaper she'd dreamt of for the past three years.

He lifted a brow, and her heart thumped violently. While she'd known of each subset of supernatural baddies living and working in San Francisco, it was one thing to have book knowledge, and it was quite another to be confronted with one so...

Potent.

So...man.

He was Michelangelo's sculpture breathed to life; he was all that was male beauty. A strong square jaw with a light dusting of facial hair—eyes the color of liquid mercury that gazed at her with the intensity of a predator spotting prey, making her feel exposed, alive, incensed, desperate.

His hair was fire, like hot molten magma, falling to his shoulders. A patrician nose that made him seem both cold and aloof, except for the fact that he kept touching her with the bone of his fingers. Caressing the scar of her cheek so softly, tenderly. But doing it in such a way that she wasn't even sure he realized he was.

But the most arresting part of the reaper was how his eyes seemed to drink her in, how they'd roll across her body like a lover's touch, how they'd land on her face and stare deep into her own eyes. There was a mystery behind his gaze, a powerful urge to return his touch consumed her, filled her limbs, and made her fingers twitch by her sides.

Discombobulated, disgusted by her obsessive need to take that squirrel and greedily slurp it down, she jerked out of his reach and snarled. Her skin itched and her ears throbbed with too much noise.

Fifty paces ahead a cricket kept rubbing its back legs together, the booming vibrations of his hairy bristles scrubbing her ears raw. The shifter standing in the cassock before her kept gulping, glancing down at the carcass in the reaper's hand.

God, why was she still here? She should have been dead. She'd tried to escape, but the moment she'd realized the futility of it she'd given herself into the hands of the vampires, goading them to a blood frenzy because she'd known no matter what, they could never take her alive.

Her people had been tracking the murders for weeks. Piecing the puzzle together as best they could. Finding dead bodies and matching them to the missing victims days later, looking like macabre princesses the way they'd been laid out and displayed. It'd been obvious their limbs had been first sawed off, then reattached. Their faces painted bright in garish colors, and their bodies all dressed in ball gowns. Each woman had been threaded through with laces, turning her into a human marionette, and posed into positions of beauty. Some had worn ballerina shoes and been forced to pirouette, others had been draped in nothing but fur, looking like sex-kitten cadavers.

It'd been sick and twisted, but it hadn't been the worst of it. The worst was knowing no matter how many girls they found there'd always be one item missing.

Their eyes.

The killer's treasure. Or at least that was what the strike force thought.

Mila had known differently. Deep in her soul, her gut, she'd known why the eyes were missing.

She'd told no one else; only she and her kind knew the truth. Understood the significance of it. The bodies were incidental; the countless "Black Dahlias" hadn't been the true crime. That was the mask, the cover-up for the truth.

The truth was the killer had been searching her out.

Somehow she'd gotten sloppy, done something to alert the shadow to her whereabouts. Because the monster was out and he was hunting for her. She was the last of her clan. She didn't know the face or the name of the monster, but her ancestors had kept records of its misdeeds. The part it had played in the O'Fallen family history.

Mila was a seer. Meaning she could see the future. Meaning any creature to get their hands on her would seek to control her, to force her to use her powers to give them the upper hand within their subclave. If the vampires had taken her, and turned her as they'd attempted to do, she would have had no choice but to forever be their puppet. Forever pump them information to make them unbeatable. Knowing the future meant you could prevent and thwart any attack that came your way. In the wrong hands, Mila was a ticking time bomb.

People might believe or think that there were many future seers in the world; there were enough humans claiming to be the real deal. But it just wasn't so; the talent lay in the blood. You had to be born with the genes to do it, and the genes were dying out. It was what made her kind so desirable. Though human, she was a rare breed indeed.

"How did you know what I am?" the reaper growled, and the sound of it didn't scare her or make her want to cower.

In fact, it made her own animal come padding out of the deep recesses of her mind. "Did you *creatures*," she spat, "honestly believe humans wouldn't do our due diligence? Wouldn't learn the strengths and weaknesses of those out of the closet?"

Silver eyes narrowed into thin slits. "You know nothing of my kind."

She scoffed. "I know you belong to a class of filthy fae."

Nostrils flaring, he gave no other outward indication that her slur had disturbed him. "And what would you know of the fae?"

Lips twitching, she tapped her nails on her biceps. "I know that it was your lot that started the bloody Great Wars. That you're a covetous kind, petty and jealous. That a human life means nothing to you. You're close-minded, selfish, and so damn vain you think the world should prostrate itself before ye."

At the end her brogue came out. Anger always caused that. She was usually so good at hiding it, but just being in front of the smug bastard made her feel a level of violence she'd never felt before in her life. Hiding the thing was one of the few ways she had to successfully keep herself hidden while in plain sight.

Torn between her desire to rake her nails down his face or just slap the hell out of it, she curled her fingers inward instead and turned aside, only to stare into the slightly filmy eyes of her other captor.

"Lone wolf." She curled her nose. "You are so rare. In fact, I know of only one."

His irises flared.

Lifting a brow, she nodded. "Necrophilia is apparently perverse even to monsters. Who knew, right?" She tsked, and she knew she was acting like a bitch, but it was how she coped. Rather than give in to the fear and scream and cry, she became a shrew.

He shrugged, but she could tell she'd rattled him because his breathing had become suddenly erratic. "No, I suppose they don't." Scratching softly at the top of his wild mane of brown hair, he frowned, looking at her as if she were the strange one.

"What?" she snapped, at her wits' end.

"How do you know so much about…us?" The red-haired faerie said the words as if he loathed the idea of grouping himself into the *other* category.

Standing here now, before her, the man was so much more than her dreams had made him seen. She'd never been into redheads, finding the shade of hair usually accompanied a pale shade of flesh and several hundred freckles to boot. But the faerie was unlike any redhead she'd ever seen. Instead of a bright orange mop, his was supple and falling to his shoulder blades. The shade looked more like a deep crimson rather than the shade of carrot she was accustomed to.

A hard, square jaw was clenched tight as his gaze roamed hot across her face and then dropped down the column of her throat before running across her suddenly too tight chest.

His lips quirked and she realized she'd been not just staring, but pretty much drooling. Humiliation crept hot fingers up her cheeks and, clearing her throat, she pinned him with her haughtiest glare.

"You should have let me die," she hissed again, but this time not with any true anger. Her stomach was churning, her throat was burning, and she knew she was seconds away from bawling.

"You keep saying that. Trust me…" His deep, whiskey-roughened voice shivered across her body like the caress of a lover's touch, pulling things down low and making her blood pressure rise. "If I'd had my way you'd be pushing up daisies."

Shoulders twitching from holding herself so erect, she puffed out a breath and planted her hands on her hips.

"Now answer. My. Question." His voice growled. Literally growled, echoing roughly through the cavernous room. A shot of heat pulsed through her blood. "Who are you? One last time to tell me the truth, human, before I decide you're not worth my time."

The shifter was silent as death, his filmy eyes drifting between the faerie and her. Damn that grim reaper, putting her in this position. If he'd only allowed her to die, none of this would be happening. To even contemplate breaking her oath, letting someone not of her own genus know who she really was, was blasphemous.

But the reality was she was no longer Homo sapiens. The red-headed bastard had let her become the thing she'd once helped to kill.

"I'm not mortal anymore, or have you forgotten?" Her upper lip curled. "Because of you I'm a vampire; because of you I'm no longer—"

"Well"—the monk held up a slightly gnarled finger—"that's not entirely true."

"What?" she and the grim reaper snapped at the same time—both turning on the now-cowering shifter.

Holding his hands up in a placating fashion, he curled his lips in an odd distortion of gums and teeth. A smile, maybe?

Pinching her brow, she shook her head. She didn't care to

hear anything they had to say; she should have died a while ago. Each second she lived, the more danger she was in. "Do you have a knife?"

The shifter frowned, clearly confused by her sudden change of subject. But not the reaper. Eyes widening, he stepped forward, clasping her forearms tight in his strong hands, and shook slightly. "Why? So you can stab it through your heart?"

She sucked in a sharp breath, and his smirk grew smug. "Think I don't know you, human? Your intentions are written all over your face. So tell me, why do you want to off yourself so badly?" His hot gaze made her body burn, tingle, and it was suddenly hard to breathe.

Blunt fingers traced the curve of her jaw, up and around the shell of her ear, before tugging on a blond lock. Mila could hardly think when he did that, when he touched her that way, looked at her like he wanted to eat her all up, reminding her of the faerie tales of old. He was the big bad wolf and she was his prey.

Swallowing hard, she licked her lips. "I'm a vampire. I've been sired. They...they can't know."

She couldn't believe it was her voice that sounded so breathy and sex-kittenish. It was so easy to believe the old stories about the fae now that she stood in front of one. How their beauty was as deadly as any blade, how a mortal (or immortal, as her case now was) could be beguiled and lost to the evil scheming of their cold, black hearts. How the faeries had turned brother against brother and sister against sister during the Great Wars, how they'd controlled and commanded armies of *others* to do their bidding, and all for one glance. One touch of their sexually charged flesh.

"Get off me." Forcing every last bit of will she had into those words, she ripped herself out of his grasp, rubbing her arms up and down to erase the memory of his hands on hers. "Don't ever touch me again."

"You're not sired." The priest cleared his throat, head bobbing up and down. "I understand now. Why Lise sent her to me. You're not sired."

Lise. The mention of the Ancient One's name sent a cold shiver down Mila's spine. She was the one being her people had never been able to learn much on. Other than the fact that she ran a club for the safe intermingling of the *others*, and that she was known to sometimes run interference between them in order to keep the balance and tenuous peace amongst species, her people hadn't been able to gather more intel on the woman. But Mila had always suspected that Lise was so much more than a moderator. It was why in Mila's hour of terror, hers was the first name that'd popped into her head.

"What do you mean, Lise? What does she have to do with me? And what do you mean I'm not sired?"

Licking his front teeth, the reaper swung the squirrel back and forth, and immediately the hunger she'd been able to pretend did not exist while she was furious at him came back with a vengeance.

Her body ached. Her bones hurt, the blood running through her veins pumped like thick sludge, making her aware of the gnawing, throbbing, spreading toxin through her blood. Her brain. All she could think of now was that squirrel. Ripping into it, feeling its blood soak down her throat, quenching the terrible, fiery ache spreading hot and quick. Tongue feeling three times its normal size, she licked her lips, internally raging at herself that she didn't drink blood. She would never drink blood.

"I offer a truce." The reaper's smile was laced with venom. "Food." Tipping the squirrel out until its tail brushed against the tip of her nose, a wicked gleam danced in his silver eyes as he brought it back to himself.

Throat aching, she groaned, balling her fingers tight to her side. "Food for what?" She growled, unable to stand the constant pendulum swing of the rodent in his hands.

"Facts." He shrugged. "Just answer some questions."

She was no longer human, therefore the vows she'd taken no longer applied. But to reveal who she'd worked for, what they'd done, could put the others at risk. On the heels of that thought came another. She was now one of the monsters she'd hunted in her past life. The irony did not escape her.

Feeling a terrible urge to cry, she gritted her teeth and nodded. "Fine. But then you give me that knife. Do we have a deal?"

Chapter 5

Staring at her outstretched hand, Frenzy didn't know whether to laugh or to smack it away. He couldn't believe this petite thing was making demands of him.

But he'd make the deal, because she didn't need to know he had no intentions of following through with it. Shaking her hand, he nodded. "Deal."

A visible shudder raced through her. "Good."

"Here." He tossed her the squirrel, his lips twitching when she snatched it out of the air, but instead of ripping into it the way any newly turned monster should have, she stared at the carcass with a look of both disdain and desperate longing.

As her pink tongue slid along her still-blunt incisors, Frenzy wondered which hunger was most prevalent—the need for meat or for blood.

"Monk," he boomed, causing George to jerk.

"What?" he stuttered.

"The lady obviously does not wish to appear crass in public.

Set a chair and table and whatever utensils you have so that she can hang on to the last dregs of her humanity."

Turning, George went to set up a table he probably rarely used himself.

"I'm fine." Her anger beat at him.

Smirking, Frenzy lifted his brows. "Truly? That why you're looking at the rodent like you want to rip its head off and tear into it, or toss it away like last week's garbage?"

Nose curling, she held it out by the tip of its tail, as far away from her nose as possible. "I don't want to eat."

"You say that." His gaze rolled across her white-knuckled grip. "And yet you're holding on to it so tight I doubt I could yank it from your cold, dead—"

Screaming, she threw the body of the animal against the farthest rock wall. "You're right, I *am* dead."

Snorting, he took a step toward her. "What's the matter, blondie? Afraid of the desires you feel now? Didn't you know tangling with a vampire might wind you up in just this situation?"

"I didn't tangle."

"Oh yeah"—his upper lip curled—"that's why I found you in a known crack house. What were you doing? Buying drugs?" He chuckled. "Don't tell me you were out for a late-night stroll through the Tenderloin, because we both know that's not the case. You don't walk on that side of town without knowing *exactly* why you're there."

From the corner of his eye, Frenzy saw George bend over to retrieve the badly broken body of the squirrel.

"You smug, arrogant faerie!"

Laughing, he grabbed both her wrists as she began flailing them at his face, pinning them tight to her side. "Yes, I think that part's been well established. How about you start telling us the truth? We've danced around this long enough. Why were you there?"

Her chest heaved up and down, whispering like a breath against his own, and though he didn't want to be affected by her touch, her smell, his entire body flared to life. His nerves tingled and he realized that though she infuriated him and made the beast inside stir, he didn't actually hate it.

In fact...

Her lips parted when he dragged a tendril of her luscious blond hair through his fingertips.

"Let me go," she whispered, but there was heat behind her words, and though her lips said one thing, her body betrayed her as she leaned farther into him.

A horrible smell rolled through the room. Realizing what he was about, Frenzy took a step back, feeling more discombobulated than he knew he should, dropping his arms from her immediately.

Charred flesh and singed hairs stunk up the cave. He was already annoyed, and the scent only ratcheted up his emotions. Frenzy curled his nose, glaring at George, who was rotating the body of the squirrel—which was now stuck on a spit—through flame.

Gagging, Mila tipped her face down. As bad as the smell was for him, it was likely magnified a thousandfold to her now–highly sensitive olfactory senses.

"Tell me, woman, or I'll toss you back to those vampires you suddenly seem so afraid of being sired to." Idle threat, but she didn't need to know it.

The way she looked at him made dormant emotions inside of him rise up from their long slumber. Emotions like humor, curiosity, and something darkly sensual.

"You know about me. About George." He jerked his head toward the old shifter, who was still doing something that looked a lot like cooking. "About the Great Wars. You're what? Twenty-four, twenty-five at best?"

"Thirty-two, you arse. I'm no child."

Thirty-two, that surprised him. Taking another long look at her, he studied the firmness of her skin, the rich gold of her hair, and her rosebud lips. When mortals became vampires, they didn't become suddenly modelesque beauties. However they looked in life, they'd now appear in death. That was why there was the occasional elder or child amongst the fangers' ranks. His lips quirked.

"Interesting." He grabbed her wrists, bringing her back to his side. He couldn't seem to help but want to touch her.

Face scrunching, she tried to yank out of his grip. She was a new monster; her strength was nowhere near the level of his, and by the sudden widening of her eyes, she now realized it.

Rubbing his thumb along her smooth inner wrist, he lowered his voice, easing his thigh between her legs. Not because he needed to do it to restrain her, but because he sensed that as much as she fought, she was not immune to him.

"Are we going to speak truth now? Or will I have to return

you to your sire? I got a good look at him. Blue eyes, melted face, long-ass fangs."

Her breathing hitched, and now instead of throbbing aware-ness, there was burning fear staring back at him from the depths of those exotically familiar amber eyes.

Releasing her wrist, he splayed his large hand against the base of her spine and pulled her farther into his body.

"You...you promised."

"I promised you nothing, babe."

"But...but you said, I tell you and you'll give me a kn—"

His smile was full of teeth. "But you've given me nothing. All you do is sit and bristle like a ruffled porcupine. So tell me, what's it going to be?"

Holding her so close, he felt the slight tremors coursing through her. Saw the way her big eyes held his look. She was ter-rified, but she wasn't going to back down. Frenzy wondered if her panic was preventing her from really seeing the truth.

She was terrified of being sired to a vampire. But George had already told her she wasn't. In her fury she'd obviously failed to register his words. But if she would just stop fighting a moment, she'd realize what was right in front of her.

Even her smell was different. Vampires smelled of traces of metal, of warm blood. Shifters smelled of warm earth, fallen leaves. Of the crisp scent of nature. She smelled of both. But maybe she wouldn't know that, since a human's sense of smell was pathetically limited, and though she'd obviously studied his kind, did the mortals know that each species carried their own scent? He doubted it.

George's bite had definitely infected her, and the way she'd been eyeing the rodent…it wasn't just for the blood that had now congealed inside its body.

It made him curious as to what she truly was. She was a very rare hybrid species; what were her limitations and strengths? He'd never heard of another vampire/shifter mix ever, since the two classes had a violent distaste for one another. What could she do? That was a mystery he desperately wanted to solve.

As she closed her eyes, he knew the fight had finally left her. Slumping in his arms, she nodded slowly. "You have to understand. This isn't easy for me. I took an oath and I took it seriously. Telling you, it breaks every promise I ever made."

Tucking a stray curl of hair behind her ear, he waited until her molten gaze met his before saying, "You died. That vow you made, it broke the moment it happened."

A loud scraping, like metal on metal, raked through his ears. George was moving a small fold-out table into the center of the room.

"Dinner is served." He spread his arms and, with a large smile, pointed at the charred remains of the body that no longer resembled a rodent so much as a black stick.

Grabbing two fold-out chairs, Frenzy jerked his chin to the one sitting in front of the blackened food. "Sit."

Swallowing hard, Mila pulled the chair out and took a seat. She delicately toyed with the tip of the black lump in front of her.

"Eat it," George whispered. "It's okay, I cooked it." His smile was full of crooked teeth.

"Clearly, it's been a while since last you cooked, old friend." Frenzy snorted.

Shrugging, the monk covered her hand with his own, his slightly bluer than hers. There were obvious differences between the two of them. Pale as she was, she still looked more alive than him. Not like a walking corpse full of veins and riddled with damage to the flesh.

Apart from the scars across her cheeks, she looked flawless. Frenzy's heart raced.

"As I've tried to tell you before," George said, "you are not sired. In fact, you are not even a vampire."

That statement caused her brows to drop. "What?" Holding out her wrists, she rubbed her fingers along the smoothness of her flesh, along the places on her body that had been most savaged while the vampires had been on her. "They bit me. Everywhere. They turned me." Touching one of her cheeks, she inhaled deeply. "They've ruined me."

Ruin was a matter of debate. The scars were nothing to Frenzy; he'd seen worse, and in fact it gave her a macabre appeal he found oddly exciting. The flaws on her intrigued him in a way that the classic perfection of his kind failed to do.

"They'll come looking for me. They'll find me."

"Without a sire bond, it will be next to impossible." Frenzy tapped his fingers on the table. "Why do the vampires want you?" he asked again, trying to be patient, but his patience was definitely beginning to wear thin.

Jaw clenching, he read the internal debate waging in her head as clearly as if she'd spoken it aloud. Whatever she'd done in her previous life, the brainwashing had been absolute. Even in death she didn't want to crack.

"Tell me how you know I'm not sired." Her voice trembled.

"No." He shook his head. "You first. No more games. Start talking."

Closing her eyes for a second, she nodded. "But you'll tell me what I need to know, right?"

Lifting a brow, he didn't answer.

With a defeated sigh, she began. "Do you know what the CIA is?"

George looked blank, but Frenzy nodded. "A branch of your government?"

Wiggling her hand, she nodded. "Yes. An elite branch and incredibly secret. I'm not CIA, but I'm the equivalent of them. CIA deals with human threats, terrorism, drug cartels, gangland type of things. I do too, but with monsters instead of humans."

He smiled, but it lacked warmth. "I've met Jack the Ripper, the Zodiac Killer—do not doubt that there are monsters within your kind as well."

"Obviously. But that's not the type of monster I was referring to." She huffed impatiently. "I'm talking about the *others*. You guys."

George cocked his head. "That is how you knew me on sight, and knew what Frenzy was?" He jerked his thumb at the reaper.

"Frenzy?" She said the name like a question, tasting it, sounding it out, and the way she did it made his pulse throb.

His name sounded good on her tongue. It'd been a long time since he'd indulged in the fantasy of being with a woman.

"Hmm." Amber eyes narrowed into shrewd slits. "Why does that name sound so familiar?"

Shrugging, he continued to drum his fingers on the tabletop. "So you are a sect of humans studying us?" Getting the topic back to what was important, refusing to be distracted again. "To what purpose?"

"Just because San Francisco opened its borders to you guys, doesn't mean that it's going to just let you run roughshod on them. From the moment your kind stepped out of the closet, we've been keeping tabs."

His gut told him they'd done more than just stay informed. "That's not all you did. Tell the truth." Setting his face into a hard, implacable mask, he stared her down, letting her know without words that he wasn't playing.

Shifting in her seat, she picked at the charred remains of her dinner in front of her. "Look, we did what we had to do."

"I haven't walked this earth in some time." Frenzy quirked a brow. "But I can tell that humans have grown more powerful. They have more knowledge of us than at any other point in history. How?"

Closing her eyes, a look of consternation flashed across her features. His question had hit a nerve and he couldn't help but wonder why.

"Hmm?" he prompted, forcing her to stare at him again. "How are they learning so much? You knew I was a reaper before you even saw my hand. You knew George wasn't merely a shifter, but that he was also a lone wolf—how?"

Scratching the back of her ear, she shrugged. "And this is why you found me as you did tonight. I'm very valuable."

Nodding slowly, he perused her for any telltale sign of anxiety. It was much harder to spot on the undead. Where a human would be sweating or visibly shaken, she was cool and still as only a walking corpse could be. "How?"

"How what?" Her eyes were wide and without guile. It seemed to him she was being as honest as she could be, but he needed to make certain.

"How did humans learn of us? You have knowledge. How much? It's not easy getting close to us. We tend to be a segregated bunch, preferring our own company as opposed to that of others. What did you do, little mortal? How did you get on the vampires' radar?" Flinging one question after another at her, he waited to spot the cue. The giveaway that he'd hit on a nerve, but her demeanor didn't falter.

"I'm a seer."

George whistled. "And now it all makes so much sense."

She nodded.

A seer was rare. Humans rarely held the gift; most of the gypsies and fortune-tellers he'd ever come across were nothing more than charlatans. The best he'd ever seen seemed to have a gut instinct when it came to reading a person's emotions and drawing assumptions based off them. But a true seer, that was a precious commodity many of his kind would kill to possess.

"I don't believe you." He licked his incisors. "The lines are rare and few; in fact, so rare there are only two."

"Aye, you bloody fool." She spat. "The O'Hares and the O'Fallens. Including me." Touching the spot above her heart, she raised a brow and his lips twitched, beguiled by the brogue that only seemed to come out when she was having a bout of temper.

The woman had spunk. He kind of liked it.

"If you are truly a seer, then you'd know to toss that knowledge around is tantamount to a death sentence. So what did you do, woman, to let those vampires in on the secret?" Frenzy asked.

"I'm aware of that. It's why I was so protected. Only very few within HPA knew who I really was, let alone that I even existed. I was perfect in keeping my secret; no one knew and that's the way it would have stayed, if not for what I did."

"And what is HPA exactly?" George interjected, lips twisting into a macabre version of a smile that showed slightly rotted teeth along the gum lines. For a four-hundred-plus-year-old lone wolf, he was miraculously well preserved. Without the pack magic to aid in regeneration, most loners died within their first century of excommunication.

Tucking a blond curl behind her ear, Mila wet her lips. "Human Protection Agency. HPA. Not the most creative acronym, but it got the point across."

"And mortals wonder why we can never take them seriously." Frenzy rolled his eyes at the absurd name. "So what exactly did you do? If you made it to thirty-two without alerting anyone before, you must have known better."

If she'd still been human he knew her cheeks would have pinkened. Notching her chin high, she gave him a withering look that caused his pulse to stir. "Look, I didn't pick the name.

Fact is, we're learning a lot about our backyard neighbors, most of it bad. You all may feel you have the final say on power structure, but Earth belongs to us, and we'll defend what's ours. As to what I did, it no longer matters. What matters is that my cover is forever blown."

Snorting, Frenzy shook his head. "'Us'? Dear girl, you are one of *us* now." He waved his thumb between them, intensely curious about what she'd done, but recognizing her show of temper to be nothing more than camouflage for embarrassment, he suffered a rare moment of sympathy and decided not to press that. She was right: what she'd done was inconsequential to the matter at hand.

Nostrils flaring, upper lip curling back, her look was savage and volatile. The air danced with the electric energy of her emotions.

"I'll never be one of you. Even if you don't kill me now, they will—they'll find me and take me out."

"The vampires?" Frenzy scoffed. "You can fend off a couple fangers now."

"I'm not talking about those parasites. I'm talking about HPA, about the shadow. Pick your poison. Either one will have a go at me."

Brows forming a question mark, Frenzy's lips thinned. "What do you mean?"

"Exactly what I said. HPA…because I know too much, I don't doubt they've already sicced a tracker on my arse." She shrugged as if that one were inconsequential. "As to the shadow, well…that is the seer's greatest enemy. The O'Hares and

O'Fallens never did learn of its origins; everything about the creature is steeped in mystery. The only thing I know to be fact is that it will not stop until it has consumed every last seer left."

"What? Why?" George's heavy lisp grew more pronounced, each word more a puff of breath than anything.

"I don't know."

Frenzy rubbed his jaw. "So are HPA and the shadow connected?"

She shrugged. "I doona know. But I doubt it. The creature has haunted my people down for centuries. It's why my life is a constant game of hide and seek. I never lay roots, and rarely stay in one place long enough for anyone to even learn my true name. It's the only way to escape it, to always stay one step ahead. I was doing fine, until recently. Did you hear of the Candyman killer?"

He frowned. "Candyman?"

"Aye." She nodded. "The killer leaving bodies of women contorted into grotesque positions with a candy ring on their ring finger?"

He had heard of something like that. "I may have. Why? What does this have to do with either the shadow or HPA?"

"Everything. It's why I was leaving the organization. I was set to flee again; if the vampires hadn't found me I'd have been gone tomorrow morning."

He frowned, still not connecting the dots.

Sighing, she tossed up her hands. "The bodies bore the shadow's killing stamp."

"And that was?"

Her lips thinned and he could read her indecision, that there was more to be said but she wasn't willing to say it.

Switching tactics, he approached from another angle. "How do you know it was the shadow? Are you implying the Candyman and the shadow are the same?"

"No, I'm not…" Her words trailed off before pinning him with a hard glare. "I've told you all I will about that. Make no doubt, the shadow will find me and it will take me out. So either give me a knife now or not. But it will kill me and you won't be able to stop it from happening."

This wasn't making sense. Did the woman have a death wish? Or was she speaking the truth? In all his years he'd never heard of a killing shadow. He was death; he should know of anything death-related, and yet the unmistakable quiver in her voice led him to realize that at the very least she believed what she was saying.

Her lips thinned and she turned her face to the side. Clearly she was done speaking, but he wasn't done asking.

"What did you do to make the vampires aware of you?" Yes, he said he wouldn't ask, but now with this shadow thing in the equation, maybe what she'd done was tied in after all.

She jutted her jaw out, something cold and raw flashing through her resinous gaze. "I did something I shouldn't have, betrayed years of silence and blending in by one stupid, stupid…" Sighing, staring heavenward, she shook her head. "It doesn't matter now."

Frenzy suspected that maybe it did. He was just about to badger her more about it, but George cut in first.

"But what I don't understand is why the vampires were trying to kill you. If you truly are a seer, and they knew that, why did they not keep you?"

Her smile was small and bitter. "Because there is only one part of me worth keeping; the rest is dispensable."

Finally he understood. Why she'd hesitated earlier and sealed her lips, looked away. Because it was her one weakness. "Your eyes." Frenzy waited until she turned that familiar gaze on him. The look in them heated every nerve ending inside him. So similar to Adrianna's, and yet, there was a hardness and rawness in these he'd never seen in his lover's.

Nodding as if reluctant to do so, she said, "Yes."

But something was nagging at him. Something he couldn't put his finger on. Things still weren't adding up completely. A seer was rare, exceedingly so. Such a gift was invaluable to whoever possessed it, and yet by her own admission, not only were the vampires coming for her, so was this shadow creature. Why? Keeping a seer seemed the better route than simply taking her eyes and hoping to make sense of the visions on your own. Without a seer to decipher the truth, reading the future was a lot like trying to watch a blurred satellite image.

"What aren't you telling me, Mila O'Fallen?"

Lips pouting prettily, she shook her head. "How do you know my name anyway? I never gave it to you." Rubbing her forehead, she seemed deflated, defeated. As if this was merely a change of subject but not an answer she was particularly keen on learning.

"Lise gave it to me," he said, intently studying her features. What was she keeping from him?

"Yeah."

He had no idea what that "yeah" was for. It was almost as if she wasn't even listening, not really.

"But why kill you? That smacks of counterintuitiveness," Frenzy blurted out with frustration. "A seer is vaunted, treasured. They should have done anything to take you."

"They were pumping me full of venom. I do honestly think their intention in the beginning was to take me, but I"—she twisted her lips—"I goaded them to a killing frenzy. It was my one hope of them not getting what they wanted from me. You don't technically need a seer around to see the future, so long as you have our eyes. Though it's definitely easier to keep us than to kill us. I'm pretty sure they didn't much care by the time I was done taunting them."

He snorted. That he could believe.

She poked at the squirrel, a heavy sigh spilling from her. "I hate to admit this, but I'm starving. Could I…" She swallowed. "Could I have a knife? Just to cut it up?"

"Use your fingers. You're no longer mortal, so stop trying to hang on to human conventions."

She hissed. "You think I don't know what sort of abomination I've become?" A stiff wind to blow through her hair and she'd remind him of Medusa with her poisonous locks.

Getting up, George walked over to a wooden shelf where he kept his plates and cutlery. "Sometimes hanging on to any vestige of our old selves helps to keep us sane." While his words were directed at Mila, his censorious gaze was directed at Frenzy.

Returning a moment later, he sat the sterling silver butter knife in front of her. Thanking the shifter, she took the knife in hand and tapped the body of the blackened meat.

Jerking his head to the side, George shambled off to a corner of the room, in clear invitation for Frenzy to join him.

After one last glance at her, Frenzy walked over. "What, monk?"

"I suspect she's lying."

Frenzy's lips thinned. "About which part? Are you claiming all she's said isn't the truth?" Because he didn't honestly believe it. Frenzy was pretty sure she'd told them mostly everything.

"No." George shook his head. "Most of it was true. HPA does indeed exist."

"If it exists, then why did you ask her what it was?"

Wringing his hands together, he sighed. "To test her. HPA is a human watch group, and they do learn about the society of *others*. They keep eyes and ears open on us and know much."

"And you know this how?" Frenzy growled, casting a quick glance at her. She was still tapping on the meat.

"I'm old; there isn't much for someone like me to do. I cannot live among the mortals, I'm a target on all sides. So much time on my hands, I learn things. I keep my ears and my eyes open. I first heard of HPA twenty years ago."

Rubbing the bridge of his brow, Frenzy shook his head. "Stop circling the wagons, George, and just spit it out."

"HPA are mainly watchers. Rarely do they involve themselves in our world. And only to investigate potential homicides directly related to the killing of mortals. I doubt very much they will come seeking her out to kill her as she implied. They seem to take a very hands-off approach. They're scholars, not killers."

"Then she is insane?" He looked back at her. She was no longer playing with her food, just gazing at it intently with a pent-up, glassy-eyed stare.

"No, I suspect she merely mentioned them to throw you off the true scent. I believe she plans to escape you at some point." The monk shook his head violently. "Her true threat comes from this shadow, and if I'm right, she's in serious danger."

Brows lowering, he frowned. "Why have I never learned of a shadow?"

Looking pointed, George growled. "Because you've kept yourself locked away in faerie land for so long you know little of the dangers living in this world now."

Second time tonight someone had told him that. First Lise, now George. Shoving his face to within inches of the monk's, he said in a low-pitched voice, "Then tell me."

"Irish folklore speaks of a beast born of the wild hunt."

Frenzy knew of the wild hunt; it was the faeries' equivalent of a wild, raucous party. A time when all fae, no matter how strong or weak, came together to revel in the wonder and splendor of faerie—when magic was powerful and potent. He'd run in the hunt for decades alongside his queen, reveling in the god-like power bestowed upon all during it.

"And what beast is this?"

"Its origins are hard to trace exactly, but the times I've seen it referred to in text, it's only ever called by two names. The shadow, or *drochturach*."

The wild hunt was a time of madness and chaos, birth, death, and magic. But Frenzy had never heard of this one.

"What does it do?"

"It finds and destroys seers. That is why they are so rare. The creature has been very thorough."

"So it kills them? Slices off their heads?" He ran his hand across his neck.

"Much worse." George swallowed convulsively. "It consumes them. Their physical bodies may die, but their souls stay forever trapped within it in a perpetual hell."

Grimacing, Frenzy wondered how he'd never learned or heard of this creature—this killing shadow.

"Not only that, but from what I've gathered, each death makes it stronger."

The possibilities were staggering. The potential for what it could be boggled his mind. "How many has it killed?"

George shrugged. "Stories vary. Some say ten, others three. I couldn't say for certain. All I can say is this creature is dangerous and unpredictable."

The pieces of the puzzle were slowly starting to come together: why Lise had been so insistent he keep Mila safe. Not because she had plans for Frenzy and Mila to become the next Romeo and Juliet, not even because she wanted to save her life. Mila was valuable. A rare treasure and a possession that even Lise would crave to own.

"Then I will just take her to faerie, keep her there for a—"

"No." George shook his head hard, adjusting his glasses on the bridge of his nose again. "The wards of faerie will not protect against this creature. It was born in your lands; there is no place it cannot go. Your only hope of keeping her safe is running, keeping low, and never letting her tap into her powers." He tapped his forehead. "Every time she uses them, it's like a dinner bell to the monster. It can track her off them."

Muscle in his jaw ticking, trying to make sense of all this information, Frenzy opened his mouth, ready to ask how the vampires were involved in all of this, when he heard a loud clatter and then a dull thud.

Turning on his heel, he spotted Mila slumped on the ground with the hilt of the knife poking up from her chest.

Chapter 6

Powerful hands gripped her shoulders, digging into muscle as they shook her violently.

"Stupid woman. Wake up!"

Frenzy's voice was rough and full of gravel. Moaning, she shook her head from side to side, groaning from the fiery ache spreading like acid through her chest.

The knife was ripped from her and she screamed, bending over double as the wound throbbed unmercifully.

"What the hell were you thinking?" He slapped her face, not as hard as he could have—more like he was trying to help her come to.

Swatting his hand off, she sat up and then glared at him, grabbing hold of her still-aching chest. "Why didn't I die? I stabbed myself through the heart. I should have died."

"You weren't a watcher, were you?" Silver eyes full of brimstone cut through her.

Rolling her lips inside her mouth, she refused to speak.

"Because if you were, you'd know stabbing a vampire through the heart only immobilizes them. It doesn't kill. To kill you need to rip the heart out and destroy it. Or give it death's kiss," he hissed.

Looking down at the red, angry wound in her chest, she watched, amazed, as right before her eyes the flesh and muscle began to knit itself back together. "I…I…" Squeezing her eyes shut, she shook her head. "I was a watcher. I just wasn't in the field."

"Damn you, woman," he growled, and the low timbre of it shivered down her spine, made her hot and achy in strange places. What was wrong with her? Why was she even thinking about how nice his voice sounded? The reaper looked like he wanted to strangle her himself. And why, because she'd tried killing herself?

Slapping his hand away, she scooted back on her heels. "Let me die. Kill me yourself. I don't care. But kill me. Please."

She cursed the fact that her voice broke just then.

"Why?" His face contorted into a frightful mask, giving his regal beauty a hard devilish bend, making her pulse race and her mouth dry. "Because you lied. Because it's not the humans coming out to find you. It's the *drochturach*. Isn't it? That's why you're so desperate to off yourself."

"No." She shook her head, tasting the adrenaline on the back of her tongue. "No."

"Yes," he spit out.

She shook her head harder.

His smile was cruel, showing off the canines of his teeth, the sharp pointed edges that made him look so much like the vampire he was not.

"I won't let you die. Want to know why, little baby vamppie?"

"No."

"Because I've suddenly realized just how precious you really are." Standing to his feet, he glowered down at her. "And you want to know something else? You're not a vampire, not really. You're a vampire/shifter hybrid. You're just about impossible to kill."

Something hot and wet shaded the corners of her eyes, making her vision blurry. "No. You're lying!"

He laughed. "Am I?"

What did that even mean? The possibilities rolled through her mind in fast forward. She'd never heard of a mixed breed, let alone what he claimed she was. "I…I…"

"Get up and get yourself together. You and I are taking a little trip."

"Where?"

Spinning on his heels, he walked back to the monk still standing in the corner, and that's when her tears fell. She knew she was in trouble and there was no way out of this.

Their heads were bent and they were whispering furiously back and forth to each other. Her hearing was ten times what it'd been when she'd been alive, so she could hear the gentle scraping of claws on stone as rats and other vermin scampered through cave tunnels. The constant drip of water echoed like thunder all around her. It should have been easy to make out what they were saying so she could decipher the meaning behind the curious looks they kept passing her way. But they were supernatural beings themselves and likely knew how to keep their thoughts hidden.

A sick sort of feeling began to gnaw its way through her belly, twisting her up in knots. The monk was a shifter. It hadn't escaped her notice that while he looked nothing like the typical werewolves she'd seen in movies, he definitely didn't look human either. The film over his eyes reminded her of the dull sheen a fish got after sitting on ice for three days. His skin was so bluish gray that if it weren't for the fact that he was actually talking, he'd pass for a corpse. Not to mention the fact that the tip of his nose looked as if it'd been bitten off. He was missing a large portion of one ear and he was exceedingly careful with how he handled things. He moved slowly, methodically, as if making certain he didn't trip or tumble over something.

Lone wolves didn't heal well. She knew that much, and yet she had. Maybe they were lying; maybe she wasn't really a shifter. Because the thought of being a vampire was bad enough, but being a shifter on top of it—it made her want to vomit.

But the thought that she hadn't died, she hadn't even gone immobile from the knife wound bothered her. Because a blow to the heart for a vampire meant they were as good as dead. It completely paralyzed them, gave their killers enough time to regroup and shove the stake all the way through. Aside from the fact that the stabbing had hurt like hell, she hadn't gone catatonic.

"Let's go." Frenzy was back in her face, mercurial eyes glaring hard at her.

Setting her jaw, she wrapped her arms around her legs. Yanking her by the hand, he forced her to her feet. "Where are you taking me?" she asked, trying in vain to tug out of his grasp.

"You're still not telling me everything, and if I'm going to guard you, I have to know it all. There is only one place to learn it."

Fear clamped ahold of her soul. Mila had pretty much fibbed and blustered her way through his interrogation. Truth was, she'd been a part of HPA only peripherally. They'd contacted her when her services were needed, but up until the point of the Candyman, she hadn't been around the task force much. All the knowledge she'd gained of the creatures hadn't come from studying up on them through fieldwork. It'd been passed down from one generation of O'Fallens to another, down the family tree.

Frenzy's barrage of questions had distracted and rattled her enough that she'd finally blurted out the truth of the shadow. The mere fact that he'd just called it *drochturach* meant either he or George had figured out what it really was. And if he knew that, then he also knew there was only one place in the world he'd find the rest of the answers he needed.

Faerie.

"If you're thinking about taking me to your home, no!" She held up her hands, taking slow steps back. "I canna go there."

Looking at her like she was a curiosity he couldn't make sense of, Frenzy's lips thinned. "And why not?"

"I'm an O'Fallen."

His brows formed a question mark. "I already know that."

"No, I don't think you do." She sighed. "My bloodline is ambrosia to a fae. One whiff of me and they'll try to enslave me, make me their own. The power inside me, it's potent, especially on fae soil, and they'll know that."

He didn't move. She looked at George, hoping that maybe he could back her up on this. "Tell him, monk. It's true. You know it is."

"George?" Frenzy didn't take his eyes off her, the look so pointedly heated that it was all she could do to remember to take a breath.

"It's true," the priest said, English accent much more pronounced. "The girl cannot go. She steps a foot on fae soil and she'll never leave."

"And I should let them keep her," Frenzy growled.

"No." Her nostrils flared. Staying in faerie was the absolute worst thing that could ever happen to her. Faerie wasn't what the tales made it out to seem.

As beautiful as the light court was, the night court was equally as terrifying. She could not know who would find her first, and honestly neither option appealed. Because they would both want what she had. That was why the shadow was after her. The shadow had been after her line for centuries. The creature was obsessed, mad with lust for a taste of her power.

Ironic as it was, her best chance of survival (at least for the time being, until she could convince Frenzy to figure out some way to take her life) was to stay with him. Because though he was fae, he was also death. In his own way he had the gift of sight and did not covet hers. Which meant he was safe. Terrible option though it was, it was the only one available.

"George, you watch her." Frenzy patted the wolf on the back, then, staring down his nose at Mila, said, "Don't let her do anything stupid while I'm gone."

He swiped his bony hand through the air, opening up a fabric in time before them. Mila's jaw dropped. She'd always heard of their ability to bend time and space to their will, but the tear in time was almost too beautiful for words: a spiraling helix of shimmering blue and dusted silver that grew from a pinprick to a large gaping veil. Standing there before the rift, his flame-red hair billowing behind him, he appeared frightening and powerful, and again she wondered why her dreams had revealed him to her.

Visions were never a certain thing; there were so many variables, so many different choices to be made to decide an exact and true path. But he'd been in her dreams for so long, what was Frenzy to her? Could he actually save her? Was it possible that death could bring hope?

From one blink to the next, he was gone. Leaving her alone with George.

"Monk?" she said softly.

Turning toward her, he nodded. "Hmm?"

"You have to help me die."

* * *

Choppy waves and salty air smacked Frenzy in the face the

moment he stepped onto Alcatraz Island. Covering himself in glamour to remain hidden from the milling tourists, he ran toward the ancient tree, the nearest entrance to his sithen, imbued with enough faerie magic to act as a portal between earth and his home.

Chanting the blessing beneath his breath, he stood and waited for the tree to open her doorway. The ancient oak shuddered, groaning loudly as a knot on the trunk transformed from mere wood to a man-sized hole. Mortals could not see what happened; the tree was enchanted to only appear as a tree to those not of faerie blood. The gaping darkness beckoned. The instant he stepped inside, the entrance sealed shut. A heartbeat later he was back in faerie and breathing deeply, letting the natural beauty and serenity of his lands ease the tension from his shoulders.

Frothy sea foam splashed his face. A cool hint of frost licked at his nose. Even in faerie it was close to winter. Jack's kiss lay heavy on the land. Hawthorns and berries spun their scent through the rolling winds that rang with the clear, angelic choir of sylphs flying through the spun-cotton clouds.

Above him a crimson-eyed crow perched on a dead branch watched his every move. The queen knew he was back. Badb and Nemain were her eyes and ears throughout all of faerie.

"Badb, tell The Morrigan that I have arrived and wish an audience."

With a loud caw, the enormous crow flew toward the spiraling black steeple of the castle off in the distance. After a millennium of living at the queen's palace, he knew how much she hated surprises. And after what Cian had done, following protocol seemed like the wise thing to do.

The skies, which had been white when he'd first stepped through, now began to gather, turning gray and black around the edges. Lightning struck patches of earth around him.

This was new. Clearly The Morrigan wasn't the only one aware of his coming, but so was the earth god, Dagda—The Morrigan's consort. Normally her male counterpart was known for being calm, or at least calmer than the queen herself, but clearly his mood indicated that was not the case today.

The castle was bustling when he entered. No one seemed uptight; in fact the mood was electric and rowdy. There was laughter and revelry, and maidens and warriors mingled, doing what lovers do.

Ignoring them all, Frenzy headed deeper into the labyrinth of the keep. Into the heart of it, where the consort and queen lived. The door to their chamber opened the moment he came to within a foot of it.

The queen was dressed in shadow, swathed in it. It veiled her body in a smoky, ephemeral draping from her neck to her toes. Her skin was polished ivory, gleaming with shades of mother-of-pearl. The black strands of her hair curled enticingly around her heart-shaped face, giving her a more youthful appearance than typical. She was the most beautiful woman in all the world. Deep red eyes stared at him intensely. Whenever the queen used her crows to "watch," her eyes would match theirs, and right now they had the same cold, dead stare of her prized birds. Her fury was palpable; it was a stench in his nostrils.

She did not move, or even breathe. She sat still as a pillar of marble, just staring at him from her throne of crystal clear glass. Dagda sat beside her. His burnished skin was a stark difference from the queen's, and brown hair came to rest just above the collar of his golden robe. Rich sable eyes sparkled with light, but it was a ruse Frenzy knew well—because the king controlled the elements, and outside the castle, it raged.

"Welcome, Frenzy." The queen's voice was cultured, full, and throaty, which made him shiver with an uncomfortable desire to either possess, or be possessed by her. But it was always thus with the queen, she commanded desire, reverence, and respect, even while you cursed her to a bloody and vile death.

Inclining his head, he waited for one or the other to speak first.

He didn't have long to wait.

"So tell me, where is the girl?" The Morrigan lifted a fine black brow as her ruby lips turned into a slight sneer.

"She is on Earth."

"We see that," Dagda said so softly Frenzy had to strain to hear. "Why?"

Schooling his features to remain impassive, Frenzy spread his hands. "She is of the O'Fallen line and therefore cannot safely cross into our lands."

The moment he said it, he understood why the queen and her consort were giving him the look that said they wanted his blood.

Mila hadn't lied, and how he'd not figured it out sooner was beyond him. Her powers must be strong indeed for the queen and king to notice. It wasn't mere curiosity making them ask this question; their lust at the thought of collecting a seer was a tangible presence. It snaked through the air like the sparks of hot metal beating metal.

Hissing, The Morrigan stood. "You're no fool, Frenzy. Never have been. We want the girl."

Suddenly the floor beneath them grumbled, rolling like a shifty tide. There was a bright snap of intense white light, and when it cleared, Lise stood a little to the left of him. Again she'd come in her crone guise, skin sagging and liver-spotted, hair a snowy white and gathered high up on her head. But there was a regality about her that even the great Morrigan could not compete with.

"She is not yours to take, queen of the fae." The sound of her voice was like cracking thunder.

The queen shuddered, then righted her chin and gazed down haughtily. "Why put something so precious in the hands of death? Give her over to me. I shall protect her, guard her. Keep her safe."

Lise laughed, the sound harsh and grating. "Ha! Do you truly think I'd ever fall for your lies?"

Nostrils flaring, it was the only outward sign that the queen was angered by the Ancient One. Her smile was bright and benevolent and so fake Frenzy almost choked on his tongue.

The band of a hurricane had nothing on the queen's fury. It brushed against him like cold, terrible barbs, made him cringe with the need to take a step back. Dagda remained immobile, neither coming to his queen's defense nor speaking up on the side of Lise.

All knew of the deal the consort had struck with Cian many months ago. Often the queen and her consort did battle on opposite sides. It was no secret of the queen's hatred of Lise, or that Dagda had actively thwarted The Morrigan's plans for the first grim reaper in fae recorded history to abandon his post so that he could take up with his witchy lover.

"If you've given her over to Frenzy's hands, then she must have been captured and killed. Correct?" The Morrigan's lips twitched.

"That is none of your concern." Lise's voice dripped honey, but beneath that honey was steel. The Ancient One would not cower, not even to the queen of air and darkness.

Licking her lips, the queen sat once more, crossing her legs and shrugging. "True enough, old one. No difference to me whatsoever."

As she narrowed her eyes, the air in the room suddenly felt thicker, cloyingly so. Like trying to take in oxygen through water, making it hard to breathe.

"You do not go after the girl. Or I shall come after you."

Snorting, The Morrigan turned her eyes up to the ceiling. "If she steps foot in faerie, she is mine. 'Tis the only sure way to keep her safeguarded."

The Morrigan rarely let her brogue show, not because, like Mila, she felt she had anything to hide, but more because she found the burr repugnant and not befitting a queen of her stature. That she was doing so told Frenzy she wanted Mila badly. Very badly indeed.

"You told me to guard her?" Frenzy turned toward Lise, who nodded and smiled.

"Aye, I did. You must keep her safe."

"From what? The shadow?"

A dreamy sort of expression crossed the Ancient One's face. "From herself. She is her own worst enemy."

"And yet you trust a grim reaper with the task?" The Morrigan's laughter shivered through the air like the ringing of demonic bells. "Ironic."

Nose crinkling, Lise deigned not to answer the obvious goading by the queen.

"What can you tell me of the shadow? Of her enemies?" he asked softly.

The room became suddenly, unnaturally quiet. As if both consort and queen waited on bated breath to hear Lise's response.

Her mouth twisted. "I told you not to come here. Did I not, death?"

His jaw flexed. Why was she saying this? He had a responsibility to his queen, to her consort. He wasn't Cian and would never be. He had no intention of flying solo and pissing off his entire race just to win the hand of one previously mortal woman. He'd done that before, and it'd nearly cost him everything. He'd learned one simple truth from that time. It hadn't been worth it then, and it wasn't worth it now.

"Because she is my queen. It is my duty." He bit out the words, holding his head high. Daring her to deny it.

The Morrigan's lips twitched with obvious satisfaction.

"Be careful to whom you show such blind fealty." Lise's words were sharp and quick.

The queen exhaled an angry breath. "He does still belong to me. I don't care what you did with Cian. Frenzy is loyal and always shall be. Are you not, my dear reaper?"

A blur of shadow passed in front of his face and then the queen was there, standing before him. Gazing down at him with her star-filled, jewel-like eyes. Her scent of clover and spring filled his head, his heart.

"Aye, my queen."

Snorting, Lise crossed her arms. "Pathetic. Me? I think not, Queenie. Do ye always enthrall those who surround you? I wonder what you'd do if any one of them ever saw you for what you really were? Oh, wait." She smiled sweetly. "One did, did he not? And as I recall you very nearly had him eviscerated."

"Be gone from my presence, hag." Flicking long, daggerlike claws in the Ancient One's direction, The Morrigan excused her.

"I think I made my position quite clear with you before, Queen," Lise bit out. "You are not to trifle with what is mine. And death, in all its incarnations, belongs to me."

Haughty disdain flashed across the queen's face.

But Lise obviously chose to ignore it. Turning toward Frenzy, she lifted her brows and, scanning the memory of the conversation, he tried to answer the last question she'd asked. "You did tell me not to come. I told you I must."

A happy sound came from their left.

"I cannot think with her in the room." Holding her palm out in the direction of the thrones, Lise froze time. Just as she had the first time they'd met.

Frenzy chuckled, eyeing the frozen form of his queen. "She will not be happy with you."

"*I* am not happy with *you*." Her words were loud and shrill. "There are reasons why I told you to stay away from the queen. Reasons that involve that woman. You must guard her at all cost."

"But you told me nothing—"

"I told you enough!" The great room boomed with the rumble of thunder. "You are an immortal. An old one. Could you not figure it out?"

"What?" he snarled, beginning to become vexed by her attitude.

"The queen and consort both want her. All of faerie will want her. The only one immune to the compulsion to obtain her is death. In the wrong hands, she is a weapon of mass destruction. To know the future. To see it, to wield it like a blade." She curled her fingers inward. "'Tis a power many would kill to possess."

Scratching the corner of his jaw, he eyed the queen. "But surely—"

"I know what you're going to say." Lise held up a hand to stay his words. "Neither queen nor consort are omniscient. They are old and very wise, but they cannot read the futures. They cannot know each conceivable outcome to every situation. Mila must be protected, for the good of all."

"So you pawn her off on me?"

Her smile was knowing. "Do you want me to take her to another? To Astrid, or Genesis, perhaps?"

Thinking of the flaxen-haired fae with eyes of pure gold made his gut hot and tight. There was no love lost between Frenzy and Genesis; the two of them were now nearly mortal enemies.

"You would give her to him? To that psychotic—"

Her lips twitched. "Of course not, that's why I sent you to her first. But if you choose not to accept the task, then I will have to find her another guardian. She must have a protector." Tilting her head forward, she lifted a brow.

Laughing, though the sound was wholly without humor, he shook his head. "Cian would have been perfect for this job."

Lise's thin, pink lips stretched. "Aye. That he would have. Though I think he's too attached to his mate to do this task properly."

Scrubbing a hand across his hair, Frenzy realized there was only one possible outcome for him to make. He could toss her off to Genesis, or maybe even Astrid, but not in good conscience. Genesis was a well-known misogynist and would just as likely rape her as he would kill her once she bored him. Astrid was only interested in coin, and the fact that Mila was a woman wouldn't sit well with the raven-haired beauty, one of a rare few female grim reapers.

There were other reapers, of course, but Lise was obviously making the point none so well suited as him. Which smacked of irony if he was the best choice.

"You like her. I can tell." She said it softly, and because she didn't seem to be mocking him, he didn't bother to deny it.

"I've not been forced to interact with a human for centuries. I've no idea how to do this."

"Then it's fortunate for you that she's no longer mortal. She's a *shampire*."

He snorted.

"Show her how to survive in our turbulent world, make her understand the severity of her plight."

Rolling his eyes, Frenzy could already picture this and didn't like what he was seeing. Lise wasn't saying it, but he knew she was suggesting he become a glorified babysitter. The thought irked. He was death, master of life. Being with Mila served no purpose.

She sighed. "I hear the thoughts in your head. Deny it to yourself all you want, Frenzy, but we both know you were considering hanging up your sickle after harvesting her soul. You no longer wished to be a reaper. I'm offering you a chance out."

Shaking his head, he said, "The queen would have—"

"Oh, please," she scoffed, "you think the queen would have rolled out the red carpet to you? Let you become her manservant?" Her blue eyes lit with raw anger. "No. We both know that's not what would have happened. She would have locked you away until you faded into the ether. You know it."

He wanted to deny it. Deny her. Tell her she didn't have a clue of what she said. But he couldn't, because the fact was, The Morrigan would have done that and more. She would have butchered him the way she had Cian. That's what he'd been prepared for. He'd known telling the queen he no longer wished to serve in death's capacity would have ended badly for him.

But to have to guard and protect a woman for eternity. Goddess, the thought was as a stench in his nostrils. A loner by nature, he'd never wanted a mate. There'd been a time, centuries ago, where he'd envisioned the impossible. But with Adrianna's death had gone the last shreds of his humanity. That was if a fae could even be accused of being humane.

Still, he could not deny Mila intrigued him and even occasionally made him laugh—a feat unto itself.

"Fine." He shuddered. "I'll do it. I'll guard her. But you have to tell me more about this shadow."

"As I told you before, Frenzy, I cannot tell you too much."

"Why?" he snapped.

"Because the telling can alter so many things. As Mila will tell you, no future is set in stone. There are so many different strings on the loom, so many possibilities. To tell you too much alters every possible outcome I've already seen."

Talking to Lise made him realize something. The Ancient One was also a seer. Which meant she knew of every possible outcome. But that wasn't what he wondered about.

"Did Mila know I was coming?"

"Yes."

"Does she know how this will end?"

"No." She laughed. "I've purposefully kept her in the dark about most of it."

Rubbing a hand across his whiskered jaw, he asked, "But if she's a seer, how can you change what she sees?"

Hearing this gave him a whole new level of healthy respect for the frail-looking woman standing before him.

"I may look like this. But I am so much more than I seem, death. Never forget it. And I'm not giving away trade secrets."

Pulse pounding, Frenzy wondered for a brief, crazy moment if Lise wasn't the only one of her kind. An ancient legend sprang to mind, one spoken of in many languages in many parts of the world. Of a group of immortals known as the fates, but the story at its core was of a group of women who encompassed the whole of the world—not just Earth, but infinity—within the palms of their hands.

How with one snip of a scissor they could snap the string off the loom of time and place. Of course, he'd always thought of it as myth.

Because in a world full of *others*, to think that the gods and goddesses might not only exist, but take an active role in one's life, was an unwelcomed thought.

"So even she knows nothing of her future?"

"No."

"Then how do we know we're getting it right?"

Her smile was serene. "You just will. Now." She looked over her shoulder. "If I've answered your questions sufficiently, it is time to get back to her."

"Why can't she simply die? Then we wouldn't have to worry about *others* trying to find her and enslave her."

"Because every life is precious, even a mere mortal's. Oh, and Frenzy…"

"Yes?"

"Do not come to The Morrigan again until it is time." She smiled sweetly.

When the last word was spoken, the translucent bubble they'd been encapsulated in ruptured. But instead of him turning toward a stunned Morrigan and Dagda, he found he'd been transported back to George's cave.

The sight that greeted him should have been one he'd expected, but he hadn't.

Chapter 7

Mila had her fingers curved downward in front of George's large, terrified face. "Give me a knife or I swear, I'll slice you into a million ribbons of flesh. I don't want to do this, George; I like you. But it's my choice whether I live or die, so give it to me."

She hadn't seen a rift in time; she hadn't heard Frenzy's return. But from one moment to the next she was standing in front of a cowering George, ready to do something so heinous she could hardly believe she could be so bloodthirsty, and the next she was being grabbed and shoved roughly in front of broad shoulders.

Mercurial eyes peered down at her, and in the stillness of the moment she was so very aware of Frenzy. Of his scent, like fresh rain and spring, the way his lips were a little fuller on the bottom. And he seemed just as aware of her as she was of him.

Taking a step farther into her space, he took up all her oxygen, and she could step back, she could stop *this*, whatever this was, if she really wanted to, so why wasn't she? She swallowed hard.

"I did not leave you here to terrify my friend. You're not killing yourself and if I have to knock that nonsense out of your head to make you believe it, trust me, I will. I've done far worse in my goddessforsaken life."

The way he growled, the possessive tone in his voice... It was crazy, but her body responded and she hated that.

Hated that he made a heart that should no longer be beating thump like a fist in her rib cage. Hated that her skin tingled where he'd last touched her, and that his spicy male scent made her insides run hot and cold.

"George, I apologize." He raked his eyes at his friend. "I'll return again."

And so saying, he banded an arm around her waist, yanked her tight to his side, and then tore open a rift in the veil of time—stepping through and dragging her along with him.

"Where are you taking me?" she hissed, trying to crawl up his body as the dizzying vertigo of nothing but a sea of stars spiraled and swirled around them.

His eyes were full of fury and fire; his hair almost seemed to glow, reminding her of the light from a lit cigarette in the dark.

Her head spun and her stomach heaved, cramping and clenching tight as the spinning spiral of the shifting tunnel continued ceaselessly.

Then something hard smacked her on the ass. "Ow!" she snapped, glaring daggers at him. "You hit me?"

He shoved his face into hers, and his warm breath sliding

along her bottom lip tasted of fire and cinnamon. "Threaten one of my few friends again and I swear I'll do it harder. You deserve more than just a swat."

Rubbing her tingling backside, she growled. "That wasn't a love tap, arsehole. I can still feel it throbbing."

"Good." His smile was all teeth, and again her traitorous body responded. Skin going tight with gooseflesh. "Maybe next time you'll think before you do something so stupid."

"Where are you taking me?" she huffed, wondering when this ride from hell would end, determined to ignore the fact that he'd basically called her an idiot.

"Away. From everybody. Apparently you're the supernatural's most wanted."

"Duh." She rolled her eyes. "I tried to tell you that. And I wasn't going to hurt George. Not really. He was nice. For a shifter. But I need to die and since you two pansy arses are too soft to do it, I figured the onus fell on me."

"Okay, one"—he held up a finger—"I'm not a pansy ass. Don't believe me, ask the vampires I neutered saving your mouthwatering derrière."

Huh? Was he being serious? Or just sarcastic? Did he find her attractive? And not that it should matter, because it absolutely did not, but it did make her stomach quiver and her thighs clench.

"And two," he continued on, completely unaware of what his slip of the tongue had done to her equilibrium, "stop trying to kill yourself. It's solving nothing other than pissing me off."

"Oh, excuse me." She patted her chest. "How horrible that

I'm pissing you off. Not like you just died, or became not one, but two"—she held up her fingers—"*others*, both in the same night. I'm sorry, what was I thinking?" Her laughter dripped irony.

Upper lip curling, he lifted her in his arms until they were nose to nose. "Stop feeling sorry for yourself."

And then he unceremoniously dumped her.

Startled, she yelped and couldn't understand why she was now staring at him eye to eye, except he was upside down. And that's when it dawned on her: he wasn't the one upside down, she was.

She was clutching onto the roof like a terrified cat.

Turning on his heel, he waved her away and then began to strip off his coat. It only took a second to realize that at some point during the fight he'd exited the spiraling vortex of doom and that now they were in a house or apartment of some sort.

The walls were painted a handsome smoky pearl gray. A California king–sized sleigh bed took up almost the entire room. A small night-light sat tucked away in a corner. The only other thing in the otherwise sparse room was a small fishbowl with a lone goldfish swimming lazily back and forth.

"You can stop clawing up my newly painted ceiling."

Her brows dipped. "This is your place?"

Mouth thinning, he didn't answer, simply walked to his closet and hung his jacket up.

Still not sure she should trust him, but knowing she looked as stupid as he was likely thinking her to be, she let go. Not used to the sudden catlike reflexes she'd recently acquired.

"Mind telling me why you jumped up there in the first place?"

Standing on the rich cherrywood floor, she looked around. "You scared me. I can't help how my body reacts now. You let me go; I thought I was going to fall."

"Don't." Sitting on the edge of his bed, he began unbuttoning his shirt.

Suddenly nervous again, she shifted on the balls of her feet. Darting quick glances around, into the stone-tiled bathroom at the lone white towel hanging off the towel rack, the white farmhouse sink. Getting a feel for the man.

Everything was sparse—just the bare necessities, and yet it was all elegantly appointed. His jewel-blue comforter was down—she could smell the feathers—and the gray sheets were obviously silk, judging by their obvious sheen.

"What the hell is your problem?" she grumped.

"You." He didn't grumble or sigh or even stare at her with hatred brimming in his cool silver eyes. He simply continued on with the business of undressing himself.

When he took off his shirt, she coughed and quickly looked away. But not before her photographic mind imprinted every groove and dip of muscle. The way his flesh bunched and gathered into tight ropes as he moved. The burnished hue of his skin. How he didn't just have six-pack abs, but the highly desired eight. She could probably bounce a quarter off it. And, hell, his pecs too.

She'd always had a thing for pecs. How tight and firm they were, how a man could flex and pop them when he worked out enough.

Mouth dry, and heat spiraling a hot, tight path down to the very center of her, she clenched her jaw. She was dead. Shouldn't she act dead? Not feel anymore? Not want? Shouldn't she be a mindless killing machine by now?

Desperate for a taste of blood and or meat? Gods, that was a disgusting thought.

And now that she thought of it, she did feel an ache burning in the back of her throat and gnawing at her stomach. Ugh.

Growling, she crossed her arms. "Will you stop that?"

"Stop what?"

Waving a hand in his direction, she said, "This. Undressing in front of me. Why'd you bring me to your place? What are we doing?"

"What does it look like?"

Forgetting herself, she turned toward him and her eyes bulged. "You're naked!"

"It's what one tends to do in their home when it's time to sleep," he growled, now beginning to visibly get upset. And it seemed the more upset he got, the harder he got.

His cock was long and quickly turning rigid. She tried to look away without seeming like it affected her, but she knew her eyes were enormous in her face and her heart was definitely doing a strange stuttering.

"Stop acting like such a virgin. This isn't for you."

Insulted, she whirled. "Oh, nice. So who is it for? That goldfish?" She stabbed a finger at the bowl.

"What the hell is your problem?" He jerked to his feet, coming at her. A very naked—correction, a very gloriously naked—man. "For reasons I can't make sense of, you've now become my problem. I have to figure out how to keep you safe from just about the entire dammed world and not choke the life out of your undead body while doing it."

Heat flooded her cheeks, and she wondered if it was possible to blush. There were so many things about being a vampire/shifter that she had no clue about. "Great, that makes two of us! Kill me, then." She offered up her neck, taking a step forward. "Do it—it will spare me tearing through this house to find a knife to do it myself."

Growling, he rubbed the bridge of his nose furiously. "I already told you, you can't kill yourself like that. You tried it once, it didn't work."

"Yeah"—she planted her hands on her hips—"that was because I thought I was only a vampire. This time I'll hack off my limbs if I have to."

His lips tilted. "You're so obsessed with killing yourself, you haven't even thought any of this through, have you?"

"I can't be allowed to live."

"I don't give two shits how you feel. You're not as precious as you think you are, Princess."

Frenzy's shoulder-length hair framing his purely masculine face, body looking like something Michelangelo would have wept over, Mila kept chanting to her brain over and over that Frenzy was fat, ugly, and soft around the middle. But the power of wishful thinking was simply *not* working tonight.

"I'll do whatever I have to." She glared, refusing to be cowed even though she seriously had a kinky urge to lick those rippled abs right about now.

Nostrils flaring, he laughed. "Fine." Storming out of the room, ass flexing with each strident step, she followed him as he marched into the kitchen.

She tried in vain to not admire the way his muscular thighs moved, how perfect his ass was. But it was a hopeless cause, so she just gave in to her voyeurism.

Yanking open a drawer, Frenzy pulled out an enormous meat cleaver and thrust it toward her. The wickedly huge blade came within inches of her. Instinct made her jump backward.

"Go on, then," he shouted. "Do it. Take it!" He shook it under her nose.

Her Irish temper had led her here. And here was never a good thing. It was known as being stuck between a rock and a hard place. She'd been so insistent on killing herself, mainly because she was just contrary that way: when someone told her no it just made her want to do it more.

But faced with that ginormous knife, she realized she didn't really want to do it. But she didn't want to tell him she'd changed her mind either. It was a lose/lose either way.

Snapping it out of his hands, she lifted a "so there" brow.

"Go on. Because I don't have time to deal with any more of your crap tonight."

Holding out her wrist, she placed the knife on top. "I will." She didn't move.

Crossing his arms, he spread his legs, and it was really hard for her to think when he so blatantly waved that "thing" around.

"Do it, then. But don't forget you have to cut off each limb, sever them at the base. Once that's done, take off your head. Then you'll have to scatter the limbs in such a way that one cannot find the other and then you'll have to burn it."

Her brows dropped. "I obviously can't do all that."

"Obviously." His lips quirked.

Heat gathered in her belly. "You're gonna have to help me."

"The hell I will. You want to off yourself, then do it. But stop wasting my time." And that said, he turned and walked back to his room.

She was an arse and she knew it. The worst possible humiliation was having to walk back into that room and admit defeat. Especially to him, that smug, arrogant bastard.

Staring at her wrist, she realized what a pointless, stupid thing this was. Mila didn't lose fights easily. She never had. Any battle she'd ever engaged in as a kid had been fierce because losing was never an option to an O'Fallen.

But she'd lost this fight. Standing here was now just delaying the inevitable walk of shame.

"Bloody hell," she hissed and tossed the cleaver into the sink with a loud clatter.

She walked back into that room ready to throw down and defend her obviously asinine position if only because the thought of letting Frenzy believe himself to be right made her want to go ballistic. What she did not expect was to see him spread-eagle on the bed. Snoring.

"What in the—"

Cracking open an eye, he growled, "There is one bed. No

couch in this apartment. Either we share or you sleep on the floor."

Lip curling with disbelief, she said, "I can't believe you'd even—"

Flapping his fingers at her in the worldwide sign of a man who was done listening to a yammering female, he sighed. "That's the way it is, O'Fallen. Bed or floor."

He had the nerve to close his eyes again.

Which only increased her fury by another notch. "Let me guess, you leave the toilet seat up too!"

If it wouldn't have made her look as petty as she knew it would, she might have actually stomped her foot just then.

When he didn't answer, she walked in farther. Seeing him lying there, nude as the day he was born, in no way trying to hide that part of his anatomy that clearly marked him male, she wanted to slap him.

Slap him because he obviously didn't give a crap about her. "If you don't want me around, then just get rid of me. You can do it. C'mon, death, are you a man or a mouse?"

There wasn't a man alive that could ignore an obvious jab at his manhood. Frenzy was no exception.

Jumping to his feet so quickly it literally startled her into jumping back a step, he was in her face. Handsome visage curled into one of not only anger, but disdain.

"You would love that, wouldn't you? Die the martyr? Does it give you a cheap thrill, vampire?" His long finger traced the column of her throat.

The touch was so gentle and delicate, so at odds with the violent wave of anger pulsating from him into her. Shivering, she stood still, wishing like hell she could just snap his finger off.

"Don't touch me."

His smile was pure rogue—two parts sensual, one part danger. She could feel the tension inside him, the coiling of emotions, the way his body shifted and moved, the way the air suddenly tasted charged, like a darkened sky a second before the storm. Everything inside her stilled. Death was just about as powerful as they came.

She'd not been with HPA long; most of what she'd learned concerning the *others* had been taught to her, handed down from generation to generation of O'Fallen women. Those with sight needed to understand that from the moment they'd been born they would always be on the run from those who wanted to possess what they did not own.

But what irritated her most wasn't her power to "see." It was the fact that when it came to her life, all she'd ever been able to see was darkness interspersed with fuzz. She could make out bits, but that was it.

Bits.

She'd seen Frenzy, but hadn't known what he was. She'd not seen that she would die last night (maybe it was last night; time seemed irrelevant now) and that she'd come back as a...a freak. A monster.

"It makes you crazy, doesn't it?" His low, throaty voice made her body ache in the most annoying places. She hadn't had a man in over a year, and being with one so virile wasn't helping matters.

Digging her nails into her thighs, she lifted her nose. "I don't know what you're talking about."

Full lips curved into a wicked smile, making her think terribly naughty thoughts. Like sucking on them, having them suck on her. His scent was driving her mad too.

She hated being a freak. Hated that she could smell the slide of sweat run out of his pores, how it teased her nose with a hint of sage and spice. Made her mind wander into the gutter, tread into places she'd vowed never to tread into again.

"The fact that you want me so damn bad."

Heart fluttering, panic flooded the back of her throat. "Get over yourself."

Either he was actually tired, or he refused to let her goad him. Turning his back on her, he walked casually back to his bed as if she hadn't ruffled his feathers just a second ago and, with a hop, landed on the mattress with his arms crossed behind his head and his eyes already closed.

"Just like that?" She snapped her fingers.

"Just like that, O'Fallen." He nodded, still not looking at her.

"God, you're infuriating!" She did stomp her foot then. "Do you realize having me here is like hugging a ticking time bomb? It'll find me; *then* what are you gonna do, Mr. Big and Bad?"

"Come to bed," he muttered, rolling over.

Realizing she'd been staring at him, she finally blinked. "I wish you'd put some clothes on."

Growling, he rolled over. "You want me in clothes?"

"Yes!"

"Do you?" He reminded her a little of her neighbor's pit bull growing up. The way his lip was curled back and how he was visibly vibrating.

Her gran had always told her she pushed things too far thanks to her stubborn Irish temper and that one day she'd get bit. She had been bit—it hadn't stopped her then, and it wouldn't stop her now.

"No." He laughed and she bristled.

"Is that the way it's gonna be with us, then? You say no, I say okay?" she asked in a low, heated whisper, because if she said it any louder she'd scream and act like a raving banshee.

Giving her that wicked smile of his again, he didn't say another word. But he didn't have to.

"Chauvinistic pig," she spat. "If I'm such a nuisance, why'd ye save me, then?" Mila had worked hard at softening the hard brogue, and slipping up was a sure sign she was seconds from completely losing her head.

"O'Fallen—"

"It's bloody Mila!"

"We've discussed this. That matter is settled and closed. I want sleep. If you don't stop talking, I'll make you."

"Oh yeah?" Her laughter lacked humor. "And just how do ye plan to do it?"

"Like this." It was all the warning he gave her.

She knew she moved fast; she felt the vertigo of it each time she jumped. But what Frenzy did, it wasn't just fast. He literally vanished from one second to the next.

Somehow she wound up not on the bed, or even on the floor, but over his lap, ass up.

"What the bloody hell is this?" she roared, kicking her legs at him, but his strength was absolute and unyielding.

"This is me giving you one last chance to stop now before I take this to the next level of foreplay."

It was on the tip of her tongue to demand he release her, but now his hand was framing her rear and she couldn't believe how hot it felt through the fabric of her jeans. How rough and coarse the blue jeans felt against her sensitized skin, how the way he glided it softly from one side to the other made her breathing stutter and pulse rocket.

Shuddering, she inhaled weakly, completely at his mercy. And she wasn't one bit sorry for how he made her feel, or even ashamed of these emotions. Frenzy was hot. Period. She might deny it to him, but never to herself. She'd wanted him to touch her this way from the moment she'd woken up in that shifter's cave.

"It's not even a challenge with you," he growled.

That did it. It was one thing to want to scratch an itch; she was here, they might as well. Two consenting adults, nothing wrong with that. But to toss her emotions away the way he just had, to make her seem…pathetic…

She slapped him. And it didn't matter that she was bent over the way she'd been; there was strength in her body now and she used all of it. She laughed when he cursed and dumped her to the ground. His face bore a bright red welt now.

"O death, where is your sting?" She laughed and for the first time in hours forgot herself, forgot that she was wanted by every last freaking immortal on earth, be it faerie, shadow, or otherwise. Forgot that if she'd had her way, she'd be pushing up daisies, not sitting here mocking someone who two days ago would have made her pee her pants to meet in person.

"Woman." Burrowing fingers through his fiery locks, he glared at her.

It was kind of fun knowing she could goad him this way. Because even though he was the grim reaper, she wasn't scared to die.

"I know what you're doing and this isn't going to work. You can make me angry all you want, I will not kill you."

Rolling her eyes, she stood.

"There are worse things than dying." His teeth looked vicious in his face when he smiled that way.

"Yeah, like being stuck here with you. Do you even have a plan?" She glared back.

"Other than putting duct tape on your mouth, you mean?" His eyes sparked with something, something she couldn't quite name.

It was dark and seductive, and made her body ache and crave and need and...

"I can't stay here with you. I just can't. If you're not going to kill me, then take me to Ireland, where I'd planned to go already."

Shaking his head, he rolled over, yanking the covers over him, finally.

Too hard to think when he was naked.

"It's too dangerous."

Clenching her fists, she realized trading barbs was likely to get her nowhere with him. So maybe being sweet would be the way to winning him over.

"Please." And just to further sweeten the deal, she smiled.

Suddenly the lights in the room dimmed. Startled, she jerked, expecting to find a phantom or boogeyman crawling through a window.

"I did it. Settle down," he said in that gravelly voice of his that always made her feel like her skin was too tight on her body.

Brows lowering, she turned to him. "How?"

He tapped his forehead.

"What, with your thoughts?"

When he didn't immediately answer she took that to mean a "yes."

"You can do that?"

Narrowing sexy bedroom eyes, he cocked his head. "I thought you said you knew all about us."

"I might have been bluffing. A little."

This time when he smiled it wasn't all teeth, it was a slow, sensuous curl of lips. Made her chest feel suddenly tight, the room a little too warm. Shouldn't these very human feelings have vanished after the change? She couldn't understand why she was acting this way.

She'd never been this big of a horndog in life. Mila had enjoyed sex, more so with certain partners than with others, but now it was all she could seem to think about. She closed her eyes, needing to stop looking at him so much. Maybe that would help.

"Do you have any family left?"

Eyes snapping open, she couldn't believe her ears. "I have a great-uncle." Just saying the word brought a pang of homesickness so swift and strong it very nearly brought her to tears. It'd been too long since last she'd seen home.

"Why'd you leave?" He asked it quietly, and she wondered at the sudden shift in his mood.

Was he actually contemplating it? Had she finally figured him out?

Realizing she was getting somewhere, she smiled wistfully. "To keep me safe. Ireland was too full of those who knew me, who'd sell me out for a bit of coin and brew. But," she was quick to add, "I've no plans to return to the old village. I plan to lose myself in Dublin, blend in with the masses."

His silver eyes were dark in the night, but she felt the press of them, even separated as they were. Trying to ignore the ragged beat of her heart, or the fact that he was still very naked and she was totally turned on, she swallowed.

"And yet you joined HPA, practically ensuring you'd get caught?" His deep voice shivered across her heated flesh.

Hmm…maybe he wasn't quite falling for the sweet, naïve Mila. Straightening her spine, she decided to just be honest.

"I screwed up, okay? I did something and knew the second I did it, I shouldn't have."

If he was curious as to what it was she'd done, he didn't ask. "Hide in plain sight, that it?"

Planting her hands on her hips, she defied him to tell her she was stupid. Idiotic. A dumb twit who'd obviously wanted to be found and have her soul consumed. She hadn't. Mila loved life. Loved who she'd been. The line of women she'd come from, it'd meant something. There was pride in it. Defending the line. Only she'd never gotten around to passing the line on.

She'd been killed before she could. She'd shamed the O'Fallen clan by not passing on the gift. The line had died with her and for that she'd be forever sorry. She'd not known she was running out of time, she'd always hoped there'd be more of it. That at any moment she would meet her Prince Charming. Would fall in love, make beautiful babies, and teach all she knew to the next generation.

"You're more than meets the eye, O'Fallen." Were her eyes deceiving her, or had he just smiled? And had he also complimented her? Because that seriously sounded like one.

"It's Mila," she corrected automatically. "Does that mean you'll take me back to my homeland?"

He snorted. "No. Do you take me for a fool? Think your smiles and charm would make me change my mind?"

Seeing red, she glowered. "What in the hell are you talking about?"

"Oh please"—he waved his hand down her body—"give me flirty glances, tease me, laugh with me. Tell me touching life stories and suddenly I'll forget that all you've been wanting since waking up is to find someone willing to kill you? Do you take me for a fool, woman?"

Sucking in a sharp breath, she barely refrained from jumping on him and clawing his eyes out.

"Odds are you likely know a killer in Dublin, or someplace close, who'll do the deed. No. You're not dying."

"Screw you, death," she sneered, because that hadn't been what she'd planned to do at all. All her life she'd promised that one day she'd return to her home, one day she'd step foot back on Irish soil and breathe in that clean Irish air. She'd died before she'd gotten to fulfill that promise.

"Fate's done a good enough job of that, thanks." Then the last light went off, throwing them into pitch darkness.

"That's it, then?" She tossed her hands up in the air. "Won't talk to me anymore? Just like that?" She snapped her fingers.

But he didn't say another word and she knew she'd lost that battle. Turning on her heel, she walked out the door, slamming it behind her as hard as possible. Hoping to even rip it off its hinges, but he must have built it to withstand the rigors of an immortal's strength, because all it did was slam loudly.

If she'd stayed in there another minute she would have lunged at him. And very likely would have lost. If only he were human—she was suddenly feeling murderous tendencies.

Her gran had also taught her something else, one lesson she'd actually taken to heart. Sometimes you might lose the battle, but that didn't mean you had to lose the war.

But right now, she was starving. As much as she kept trying to ignore her body's constant, and very painful, hunger pangs, it was obvious to her she needed food.

Since he wanted to sleep and she was so far from wanting that, she headed back into the kitchen, glaring at the knife in the sink one final time before heading to the fridge.

Normally rummaging around in someone else's house was something she wouldn't entertain; a home was a person's sanctuary. But A) Frenzy was no person, he was the devil incarnate, and B) he'd brought her here.

Opening the door, she studied the contents. Beer, some bread, a carton of eggs, half a gallon of skim milk. There were about three red apples in the crisper and a paper-wrapped block of cheese in the butter drawer.

None of which remotely piqued her interest.

Stomach feeling as if it was going to gnaw itself in half, she snatched up the cheese and bread. Not even bothering to warm it, grabbing a slice of bread and a hunk of cheese, she piled them together and took a huge bite.

Then she gasped as the food she chewed on tasted like rancid, spoiled milk. Gagging, she rushed to the sink and spit it out, stomach heaving as she tried to rid all traces of it from her tongue. Opening a cabinet, she grabbed a glass and filled it with water, swallowing three cupfuls before the rotten taste disappeared.

"Oh gods," she moaned, grabbing hold of her stomach as the knifing pain intensified. Vampires didn't eat solids. But shifters did. She'd seen them do it a time or two, except now when she thought of it, they were more about the red meat than dairy.

Going to the cabinets, she opened them, riffling through the dry goods. Looking for a bag of jerky—hell, even canned sardines sounded good right about now. Anything to get some protein in her body.

Hands starting to shake with desperation, because apart from a couple bags of flour and sugar, there was literally nothing she could eat in there. Vision going hazy, she realized she was starting to walk a little funny. Nearly stumbling over a corner kitchen rug, she grasped hold of the countertop and counted slowly to ten as the spots in her vision danced and swirled. Was this vertigo?

It felt almost like diabetic shock.

Heart racing, she fumbled and stumbled her way over to the small kitchen table, managing by some miracle to pull out a chair and plop into it. Mum had suffered type 1 diabetes her whole life. Once she'd seen her mum go into shock, and the sight of it had scared the crap out of her eight-year-old self.

It took all her effort just to glance down her body, to the hands lying useless in her lap. No matter how much she willed it, she literally couldn't move them.

And even around the darkness crowding her mind, she noted that her skin looked unnaturally pale, almost to the point of blue.

Just as she was noting that something was possibly very, very wrong with her, her heart stopped beating and blackness consumed her.

Chapter 8

He would die before admitting this to anyone, but Frenzy was struggling. Rolling onto his side, he punched his pillow and growled under his breath. The woman drove him crazy, brought out the ire and beast in him. He knew he was acting like the world's biggest prick with her, but he wasn't sure how to stop it. Because she was worming her way under his carefully crafted guard.

After Adrianna's murder he'd closed himself off. Emotions could kill—it was a lesson he'd learned the hard way. Her loss had very nearly destroyed him. After her death he'd gone mad, losing any shred of humanity he might have possessed, becoming a killer of legend. Decimating the local vampire coven down to mere dregs. Not because vampires had had anything to do with her death, but because they were there and he'd been in agony.

His chest ached as he rubbed at the spot over his heart, staring up at the ceiling. And then here comes Mila with her spun-gold hair and her soft Irish lilt and the emotions he'd thought he'd killed were coming out.

To see that knife in her today, he'd suffered a moment's panic so violent it'd nearly brought him to his knees. In physical form, she reminded him nothing of his sweet-tempered Adrianna, but there was a spunk to her, a breath of freshness that he couldn't seem to help but respond to.

Biting his lip, he tugged the sheets higher and then, with a growl, kicked them off. He was restless; he wanted to call her back here. Just being around her soothed him. Not that she'd likely think it. He'd been nothing but an asshole.

Sighing, he watched Lucky, his five-month-old goldfish, swim back and forth, and wondered what she was doing now. He should check on her, just to make sure she wasn't actually trying to kill herself. But he wasn't exactly ready to engage in a war of words with her again. Or to deal with the feelings she plucked out of him.

It was no longer a matter of him not wanting to kill her just to satisfy his duty; Mila was breathing life into his dreary, gray existence, and he craved more, like a junkie. Maybe he should try to be nicer to her, starting tomorrow. Make an effort to show her he wasn't really the jerk he was pretending to be.

But the thought of dropping the mask terrified him. The mask was what helped him survive; he'd become a man he hadn't once been because it'd been the only way for him to thrive without the constant reminder of all that he'd lost.

It was so much easier to make others hate you than to let anyone in. Because if they hated you, you knew where they stood, but if you invited them, then you'd always wonder if they felt the same.

Growling, he squeezed his eyes shut. He wasn't thinking about this shit anymore. The woman was making him soft and weak already. Lise should never have stuck them together. What had she been thinking?

It took him several hours to finally quiet the frenetic buzzing of his mind, but eventually he must have slept, because the next thing he knew he was rolling over and blinking open hazy eyes.

Frenzy couldn't remember the last time he'd felt so rested. Sunlight filtered in through his half-drawn blinds. Peeking around his room, he noted Mila was nowhere to be seen. But he smelled her earthy scent floating in from somewhere within his apartment, perhaps coming from the direction of the kitchen.

The wench was likely starving. He smiled thinking about her. Last night, the way she'd fought him, how soft and malleable she'd been in his arms when he'd petted her...goddess, it'd twisted him up inside.

He could try to deny it all he liked, but she intrigued him. Her fire, her spunk, the way she moved and smelled and how wild she got when angry. How her pale, iridescent skin would flush a faint pink. How human she still seemed in so many ways.

Rubbing his cheek, he snorted, remembering the sharp flare of pain. The way his body had tightened, his cock had grown hard—that hadn't happened to him in ages. She brought out his violence and his lust. It was only a matter of time before they either killed each other or had nasty, hot sex. He hoped for the latter, but figured it would likely be the former.

Neither of them had docile temperaments.

Stretching his arms above his head one last time, he jumped out of bed. Frenzy didn't need to sleep. None of the fae did, but he found he enjoyed the quiet, the meditative calm of just simply being still. It was when at rest that he could think best.

Last night when Mila grilled him on what he planned to do he hadn't answered—not out of spite, despite what she might think. Truth was, he didn't have a clue. Lise had given him no concrete plans on what protecting Mila actually entailed. He was as alone in this as she was.

Apart from George, who'd secluded himself away from all of humankind, he couldn't think of another monster who wouldn't betray his trust or worse to get at Mila. The queen and consort had shown their true colors last night. They were as interested in the her as everyone else.

Brushing his teeth, he took care of his bodily needs next and then dressed in no hurry to get back to her, perversely enjoying prolonging their reunion. Even after seven hours of rest he didn't really have a clue what their next move should be.

His apartment was only a temporary solution. None knew of its location, not even his queen. Frenzy had learned how to keep his personal life private thanks to Adrianna's death, a harsh lesson that living out in the open wasn't wise for someone like him. Since that night he'd learned to ward his homes with powerful magic.

Though his flat was in the heart of the business district, where hundreds of *others* roamed with impunity, they'd all feel a natural compulsion to give his place wide berth. It had cost a small fortune to get the crone to place the warding spell on it. She'd warned him that he wouldn't receive many visitors, but like every other member of his species, death was solitary by nature and he especially did not wish to mingle.

Fastening the final pearl button on his dove-gray silk shirt, he snatched up a pair of socks from his drawer and meandered toward the kitchen, frowning when he realized that apart from her smell letting him know she was still around somewhere, he heard no sounds. Not even the beating of a pulse.

No sounds of scraping chairs, glasses, or utensils on plates; there wasn't even an exhalation of breath. Suddenly alert, he cracked open the door and peeked inside.

The kitchen was as it always was. Frenzy was a minimalist in every sense of the word. He did not enjoy clutter, he preferred order to chaos. That was why everything from the appliances on the glossy Formica countertop to the refrigerator, the stove, even the floor tiles were white.

It took no time to find her sitting with her back to the door at the breakfast table. The way she sat so still, he wondered whether she'd fallen asleep attempting to raid the fridge during the night. But he had nothing in there for vampires or shifters. He wasn't much of a meat eater and would never require bloody cocktails to get him going.

"Wake up," he said. Walking up to the table, he toed at the back leg of her chair, determined that today he wouldn't be so harsh with her.

Instead of jumping, she dropped like a stone off the

side—smacking her face into the floor. Heart crowding his throat, he snatched her up, shaking her gently.

"Mila," he barked, noting the gray pallor to her cheeks and the veins now standing in bold relief. Her skin was dry too, like touching dehydrated corn husk. Her lips were cracked and oozing black. It took two seconds for his befuddled brain to figure out why.

She hadn't eaten a thing since turning two nights ago.

"Damn it, woman," he snarled.

Others were immortal and very nearly indestructible, but that didn't mean they couldn't go bat-shit crazy if they didn't take care of themselves. The longer she went without the sustenance her body needed, the more likely she'd suffer irreparable damage. She needed food in her quickly, needed to get her heart and blood pumping. Right now it was sitting like sludge in her veins. Not knowing whether the priority was blood or meat or both, he knew his only choice was getting her to a food source immediately.

"Mila," he whispered, not sure if it was a prayer or curse, then slashed a hand through the air, ripping open the fabric of time. Hauling her over his shoulder, he jumped inside, taking them to the only place he could think of.

Walking with her in the city was too much of a risk; there were creatures looking for her everywhere. She was too incapacitated to fend for herself, especially while he had her hanging off his back like a monkey.

No, he had to get her far away from the city. Which meant—stepping out of the tunnel, he inhaled the nutty aroma of sprouting wheat fields—he'd have to return to George's home.

But he couldn't let the lone wolf know they were there either. The longer he kept Mila around the monk's location, the more her scent would permeate, basically turning his bachelor's paradise into a homing beacon. George had managed to stay alive for so long by lying low; he wouldn't risk his friend's safety.

In and out. That's all they could afford.

"I hate to do this to you, O'Fallen," he said before releasing her and gently dropping her to the ground.

Last time he'd been hunting he'd caught squirrel. She hadn't touched any of it. So maybe rodent wasn't her thing.

A rustle of shrubbery caught his ear. Turning toward the noise, he spotted the fluffy tail of a rabbit burrowing in deep. Needing bigger game than that, he ignored it.

The sun was shining bright; there wasn't a single cloud in the sky and the trees were so wildly spaced that they didn't offer much coverage. Neck prickling with the need to get them quickly back to his warded home, he scented the air, quickly catching the musk of several different prey items.

The clean, icy scent of reptile. The nut-and-berries scent of bear. Fishy smell of hawk, the clover of more rabbit, and then finally the earthy gaminess of deer.

By his calculations the deer, a stag in musk, was a good mile off in the distance. He could drag her with him, but she'd slow him down, making it a sure bet he wouldn't be able to catch it.

There was only one option. Leave her. But not unprotected. He wasn't completely without skills. Unbuttoning his shirt, he yanked the tail out of his pants and then tore it off him. Bringing the dove-gray shirt to his mouth, he opened and exhaled.

After Adrianna's death and his subsequent years as a raving lunatic killing anything unfortunate enough to cross paths with him, he'd determined he'd never be weak again. Never allow anything or anyone to take what was rightfully his. He'd studied, taking centuries to master the limits of his powers. Learning there was so much more to being death than merely touching his skeletal hand to a mortal's chest.

He wasn't just pushing air onto his shirt, he was scenting it. Marking it like a predator. Lacing the very fabric of it with death's toxic kiss. Exuding a type of chemical bomb from his mouth, one that would kill anything that happened to graze it.

Because Mila was undead, the effects were harmless to her. Anything else would suffer hallucinations, seizures, vomiting, before the heart finally stopped beating. It would be a grisly way to go.

Laying it gently on top of her, he couldn't help but feather his finger across her delicate cheekbone. Her skin was so brittle and cold, and his heart ached to see her in this position. He debated whether to tell her he'd return soon, but he wasn't even sure she'd be able to hear him.

"Don't worry, little one, I'll come back very soon," he whispered before turning.

Each reaper had a unique and specialized gift only they had. His was speed—being able to move at the velocity of thought. Standing erect, he scanned the rolling hills, knowing he'd smell the deer before he actually saw it.

Gathering scent from the wind, he waited until he caught its trail again. Then he was off. Time jumping would be easiest, but not the most effective, as being within the tunnel would cut off his ability to scent it out.

The world was a blur of color, browns and blues and grays and greens all melding into one chaotic clash. Moving in between trees, he never stopped drawing lungfuls of air.

It was easy to follow; deer were generally stupid creatures, and though it could likely sense a predator's approach, it would never be able to outrun him. The animal was farther than he'd initially estimated. He'd easily run a mile by this point.

Hunters had likely overrun this place not so long ago, killing off many deer already. The one he'd tracked was the only one he smelled for miles in any direction. But soon the cool tang of water and freshly shorn grass had him veering to the right. Close now, he stopped, not wanting to spook the animal further. Able to make it out now, he noted it was a buck, only a few years old. There was still velvet on its antlers. Its head was high, its black nose in the air, and its eyes wide and alert.

The deer had to weigh almost two hundred pounds. Maybe a little too big for her, but he'd make steak out of whatever she didn't consume.

The next breath the deer took would be its last. Frenzy was upon it in less than a second, cracking its neck with a firm twist, watching as the beautiful creature dropped, lifeless, to the ground.

Wiping his mouth with the back of his hand, he inclined his head. All fae folk were in tune with nature and her children;

killing one wasn't sport. At least not for him. Needing to hurry back to her, he grabbed it by its midsection. Grunting under the weight of it.

He was a fast runner, but not with this thing on his back. Opening a rift in time, he brought the deer with him, returning to the clearing.

She was as he'd left her, eyes closed and not breathing. The grass she'd been on, which had once been lush and green, was now an ugly shade of yellowish brown. Beside her feet lay the rigored body of a garden snake.

Breathing a sigh of relief as he tossed the deer to the ground beside her, he picked up his shirt and put it back on.

"Wake up. I've brought you food."

Doing up the last button, he gently tapped her foot. But she still didn't move.

Kneeling, he pulled her to a semisitting position, leaning her torso and head against his chest.

"Wake up, woman," he said forcefully, and realized he was one again slipping into the douche bag role of his. Because he was angry at himself for the position she was now in. He should have forced her to eat yesterday, but he wasn't a vampire and knew little of what it meant to be a shifter. He'd never expected this to happen to her, and it was all his damn fault.

Rubbing his thumbs across her face, he whispered, "Come on, O'Fallen, wake up." He shook her a little, but all it did was cause her head to flop forward.

"Damn me to the gates of hell," he growled. He should have known better. He'd been told time and again how out of touch he truly was, and this was just another reminder of that truth.

Frenzy tried again, but not even a flicker of awareness crossed her face. "You have been such a pain in my ass," he growled, and then sighed. "And I'd be really pissed if you left me now." Then, dragging the carcass to him, he called the fire of transformation onto his hand.

He watched as the flesh turned to bone. He had no knife handy; his death hand was the best he was going to get out here. Sinking his fingers deep into the deer's neck, he flicked his wrist. Tearing it open, he prepared the meal for her to take easily.

"Now wake up." He shook her, trying to get her head to lull forward into the deer. But of course, it wouldn't be so easy. Grabbing the back of her skull with his free hand, he shoved her face-first into the blood bath pooling from the deer's neck. He didn't want to be so forceful with her, but she needed blood in her now. He'd ask her forgiveness later.

He began to worry when there was no movement, but a minute later he heard the faint sounds of swallowing.

"Yes, that's right, O'Fallen." A wave of relief engulfed him. "Drink it all. Take it in, girl, you cannot go without food. Don't do this to me again." On and on he encouraged her, but he doubted she was hearing him. She was too entranced with her meal.

A minute later he breathed a sigh of relief when the gray tint of her skin turned the familiar iridescent white. Finally she began moving, not using him so much to sit upright. She was moving into the beast, grabbing hold of its neck and downing giant gulps.

Her pale hair gleamed like gold in the brilliant rays of sunlight, and he was finally able to ease off her, let her alone so she could finish eating in privacy. Standing, he looked down at his pants, dusting them off when with a loud sigh she pulled away, groaning and holding on to her stomach.

"I don't feel good." Her eyes were wild, the irises shot through with pinpricks of fresh blood. Red covered her lips and chin, dribbled down her neck.

"It's because you starved yourself. You'll feel better soon. Just finish drinking."

She grimaced. "I don't think that's it. My stomach really hurts." She winced again, doubling over and kicking the deer away.

Mila looked like the drawings he'd always seen of wild women. The way her hair was standing up around her head, gnarled and knotted with grass and debris. Her clothes were torn and in desperate need of changing. Suffering a brief flare of remorse that he hadn't exactly been the best host, he shrugged it off; there was nothing he could do about it now.

She was moaning again, eyes squeezing tight, and bending over to rub her head back and forth on the dirt.

Starting to worry now, he took a step toward her, holding out his palm as if to rub her back, realizing just a second before he did it she might not thank him for it. "Maybe you're not a blood drinker, then. Maybe you need actual meat?"

"Oh gods, it hurts," she said in a breathless whisper, brogue thick on her tongue.

Deciding he didn't care if she thanked him or not, he placed his hand on her back and was shocked to discover she was burning up. "What the hell is going on with you?"

"Please." Her voice shook with tears. "Help me. I can't, I need…" She didn't finish her statement, because now she was crying.

Caught completely off guard, Frenzy found himself in panic mode. She was the first shampire he'd ever heard of. Was their physiology really so different from their makers? Forgetting all about trying to salvage his clothing, he shoved his hand deep into the deer's belly, searching around until he found the liver. Yanking it out, he offered it to her.

"Eat this."

"No." She moaned again, curling into her body.

"O'Fallen, I think that maybe you need meat more than you need blood. Try it and see. It's probably going to help you feel better."

"Oh gods, oh gods," she repeated over and over while holding out a trembling hand for the piece of liver.

He handed it to her, waiting on bated breath for her to take the first bite. Her nose wrinkled when she brought it to her lips.

"I think I'm going to be sick." She did a dry heave, clamping down on her lips before she could bring anything up.

Getting down on her level, he rubbed her back up and down trying to help ease the trembling running down her spine. "Do it. Don't think about it."

Normally he hated to see the way *others* ate their food. Death might take life, but they were cultured and infinitely more civilized compared to other species when it came to eating a meal.

But he was determined to stay with her, to give her whatever support he could to make sure she'd get it down, because he didn't like to see her suffer this way. He wanted the woman with fire in her tongue, the woman who sparred with him and made him feel, ache, and want. Mila was suffering and, for the first time in a long time, he was bothered by someone else's agony.

Bringing his hand beneath hers, he helped bring it to her lips. "Part your lips," he ordered softly.

She did it, with a whimper.

"Bite."

She bit.

It wasn't a large bite, just a small dainty one, but the effects were immediate. The shivering stopped, the trembling of her hands ceased. She took another, a bigger one this time.

"Oh gods," she moaned. "I can't believe I'm doing this." She didn't sound happy about it.

"You're feeling better, right?" he grunted, in no mood to deal with any sort of moral objections. She had to eat, period. It was essential to her health and well-being, and if he had to be the bad guy about this, then he would.

Taking two more bites, she swallowed them hard and then tossed the liver through the air so far it faded from sight into the distance.

"What was that for?" he growled.

"I…I…can't. It was…raw." And with those words, she gulped. Once, twice, three times, and then she was scrabbling forward on her knees and everything she'd eaten had come up.

"Mila, no!" It wasn't her that he was mad at; he was furious with himself. His heart was pounding, his breathing ragged. She had to eat. He wouldn't lose her, not because of something like this. Last night he'd decided to make things right, to work through this and be there for her. They were stuck with each other, and it was time to stop being enemies, and learn to work together.

"It's raw and warm," she hissed, smearing the blood across her lips. "I can't eat that way."

"You're going to have to. O'Fallen, it's a matter of sanity or insanity. This won't kill you, so please don't think to kill yourself that way. You're dead now and that's just how this goes. I'm sorry." And he really truly was; sorry to see her suffering so much, sorry that she'd never asked for any of this, sorry that he'd been so much of a problem for her.

"I haven't forgotten, you stupid bastard!" She stood to shaky feet.

"O'Fallen, you look like hell. You have to eat." He tried again, hoping to make her see reason.

"I *feel* like hell. What did you do to me last night?" She grabbed her head, stumbling forward in a drunken waltz.

"Me?" He stabbed his chest. "I was sleeping. I found you this morning, in a coma. A food coma. I'm trying here."

"Then feed me!" she hissed, before latching weak arms around the skinny trunk of a tree.

"What do you think I just did?"

And for a split second the old, closed-off Frenzy surged to fore. That she was ungrateful, undeserving...but then he stopped himself, because none of this was her fault. It was his, plain and simple. And maybe Lise's for not telling him how in the hell to properly care for a hybrid.

"Real food."

Grabbing both sides of his head, he glared. He'd taken down a deer; what else could he possibly do?

"I can't eat that, Frenzy. It makes me sick. You should have just let me die," she growled, still clinging to the tree as if for dear life. "This is too hard. If you can't help me, how in the hell am I going to survive any of this?"

"O'Fallen, giving up is not an option."

"Why does this even matter to you now? You sure as hell didn't care what happened to me last night."

His nostrils flared; he wasn't sure whether to share his epiphany. She was moody and food deprived, and she'd laugh at him. The thought of that galled him.

"You suck, death." She laughed weakly.

"Damn you, O'Fallen," he muttered, because they shouldn't have, but her words bothered him. The last thing he wanted was for her to believe that about him.

"It's Mila." She coughed weakly. Looking around, she finally seemed to become aware of where they were. "We're out in the open? Where are we?"

"George's place."

She coughed again and already he could see her strength weakening as she sank slowly to the ground. "We need to hide."

"I'm not going anywhere with you looking like a vampire's bride. You're covered in blood." He waved his hand at her.

Glancing down at herself, her nose curled, as if she was just now noticing how awful she looked.

"There's a small lake a few yards in the distance. You need to clean up. That blood will attract too many *things*."

She didn't ask what he meant by that, but he figured she understood he wasn't referring to forest creatures, but the possibility of *others* being drawn to the scent of death.

"Where we going after this?" Amber eyes stared at him, and there was no longer any fire or heat in them, just pure exhaustion.

He wanted to hate her; it would be so easy to give in to it, to wrap himself up in that sharp emotion and not let her get through, but it just wasn't in him anymore. All he really wanted now was to keep her safe.

"I haven't decided yet. Can you stand?"

Rocking forward on her butt, she made as if to get to her feet, but sighed and dropped back instead. "No."

"Here." Walking over to her, he held out his arm. She grabbed on and then he gently pulled her up.

Nodding her thanks, she clutched onto his back. Her body was no longer hot, or even warm—she was clammy and cool again. She still needed food.

"Frenzy," she whispered softly.

"What?" he asked as he scooped her into his arms. She was light as a feather compared to the deer.

"Did you catch that for me?"

He debated whether to lie or not, but finally just sighed. "Yes."

Laying her head on his shoulder, she nodded. "Thank you."

First she bit his head off for feeding it to her, and now she was thanking him. He'd never understand women. Surely Adrianna hadn't been this temperamental. Of course, she'd been cosseted and pampered her whole life; she'd never been thrust into an impossible situation like this.

"You still need to eat it." Turning, he walked toward the lake where he'd captured the deer. It wasn't that far of a distance.

"Not raw. Please." Her voice shook a little.

Why was she so bound and determined to hang on to conventional human strictures?

"Raw is the best and easiest way for your new body to metabolize food. But if you feel you can't eat it that way, then we'll figure something out. I still think raw is best, though."

"You just saw what happened with that."

He shook his head. "I think it's because you convinced yourself you couldn't eat it. You forget, I saw you moaning, inhaling it. You enjoyed the taste."

Mouth tipping down into a frown, she closed her eyes. "All my life, I've fought you guys. Seen the ugly and despicable things you're capable of doing. You tell me now I have no choice but to be this way, for who knows how long. Don't you understand, even a little?"

Those familiar amber eyes grew wide, pleading silently for him to get it. But he simply couldn't. Why would she want to hang on to a past that was so frail and weak that a mere vampire bite was lethal? The lifespan of a mortal was so impossibly short as to be laughable.

Dragging his nose along the length of her collarbone, he inhaled deeply. "Why would you want to change? You smell of fresh earth after a spring rain. Your skin gleams like you've been lit from within with candlelight. What is the appeal of returning to a form that sickens and decays? Withers from disease? Why would you want to hang on to any part of that past life?"

Her eyes were huge as she stared at him, her mouth lax, and he wondered at her strange transformation. Was she slipping back into a coma?

Trembling, she shook her head as if to clear it of cobwebs. "Don't smell me like that again. And to say that that's all the human experience is would be a lie."

"I'll smell you any time I want. And if that's not the human condition, then you tell me what is. Make me see the appeal."

"I'd need a lifetime to make you understand." She sighed.

He grinned. "Lucky for you, you now have one."

He'd expected at some point for her to tire of his holding her, but she must have been truly exhausted because she simply snuggled deeper into the shelter of his arms, looking around at the hilly green landscape. Stepping around a dense shrub, he jerked to the side when a pair of pheasants were startled into flight.

Frenzy liked her in his arms. He wondered if she was aware that his heart beat faster when she was near him.

"The beauty of our short lives is that we're grateful for every second of them. How can you truly feel gratitude at the beauty of a sunny day, or hearing that your grandmother beat breast cancer, or seeing a baby's first smile, first steps...unless you know that each and every one of those moments are gifts? Treasures to cherish? How can overcoming the odds bring any kind of jubilation when the possibility of tragedy isn't present?"

He frowned. "That does not make sense to me. I am not mortal. But I have enjoyed my life."

She shrugged. "Have you really? Or are you just saying that? Think about it, Frenzy, when was the last time you laughed? Cried? Showed any kind of emotion?"

Her look was pointed. Taking the challenge, he thought back on his long life. He'd laughed plenty. He'd even loved once. She had no clue of what she spoke, but when he tried to remember the situations, an unsavory truth began to dawn on him.

He'd laughed around *her*. Around Adrianna. He'd loved Adrianna. Adrianna had been a mortal. Mila, so newly turned that her mind still associated itself as human rather than *other*. When he tried to remember a time when he'd done those things without the presence of a mortal around, he came up empty.

Being around his queen was a study in court politics. The fae could be a chivalrous bunch; they laughed, made love and war...but every scenario was always tied to a human in some way.

Fae could not bear children unless they mated with mortals. There were many pairings among his kind, but all of them had human mates. They had to in order to survive. The Great Wars had even been fought over mortals. Fae may have planted the seeds that moved the wheels, but the wars had been fought primarily to control the mortal realm. To control humans, because while most fae kind turned their noses down at the lowly mortals, they also needed them around to thrive. Every type of monster did.

The vampires needed the mortals to feed upon. The shifters and fae bred with them. The power of the witch and sorcerer only manifested within human gene pools...

"I've laughed," he said with a frown, refusing to concede defeat.

Her brow lifted. "Hate to break it to you, reaper, but you're about as fun as an abscessed tooth."

"*Others* are infinitely superior to your kind. We are the evolved species." The words came out of him by rote; there'd been no thought behind it, just a lifetime of belief in that truth.

She sighed. "And that is why this argument is pointless. You'll never get it." Her fingers danced across the flesh of his neck. Just the slightest touch broke him out in a wash of goose bumps.

It was strange talking to her like this. He was used to the woman who screamed, pouted, stomped her foot. To see her calm and rational, it made him want to understand her even more.

She cleared her throat, and that's when he noticed they were finally at the lake.

"Can you walk?"

"I'm fine," she murmured.

Setting her down gently, he jerked his head back in the direction where they'd come from. "I'll be back. I'm going to bring some supplies to cook that deer with."

Looking up at the wide expanse of sky, she twisted her lips. "I don't like being this exposed. Especially if you leave."

His lips twitched, suspecting that was as close to begging him to stay as she'd ever get. "I'll mark the area with death. I shouldn't take long."

"Are we going back to your apartment?" she asked, leaning against a tree as she took several slow and deep breaths.

"Likely so."

She shook her head. "Frenzy, I know you really don't want to hear what I have to say, but I don't think we should stay in any one place too long. I've spent years hiding from the shadow. I blew my cover there. I don't think San Francisco is safe for me anymore."

Maybe she was right. But then again, his place was heavily warded. Not even the queen could get in if he didn't let her. "Give me time to think this through. In the meantime, bathe."

Nibbling on a corner of her lip, she eyed the water.

"There's nothing but fish in there. But if you want, I could kill them all." He held up a finger.

"What?" She frowned. "Kill a bunch of innocent creatures? Are you sick? Gods, no wonder you had no problem turning me into this freak." With quick, jerky movements she started to undo the buttons of her shirt, looking him dead in the eyes as she did so.

And the fact that he'd been thinking the same thing just a second ago made him feel ill. He wanted to apologize; it was on the tip of his tongue to say it, but the words were just too thick in his throat and wouldn't pass his lips.

He'd told Lise the truth when he'd said he was years out of practice on knowing how to properly socialize with humans.

Dropping her shirt to the ground, she notched her chin higher, and his lips twitched.

Last night the woman could barely glance at him without turning shy, and now here she was, stripping in front of him.

He smiled when she lifted a brow. "Blood looks good on you, O'Fallen."

Full breasts with tight pink buds jutted out invitingly; her ivory skin marred with crimson was a macabre but seductive look. With her wild blond hair framing her heart-shaped face, she looked like a sex-kitten Amazon ready to do battle.

Damned if he wasn't getting hard staring at her.

Her breathing inched a notch, as she was obviously aware of the way he studied her body. Eyes moving slowly down the length of her neck, across her slim shoulders, around firm, luscious mounds that made his mouth water for a taste.

The air was electric, charged and heady, making his skin prickle with heat.

"It's Mila," she whispered, then slipped her fingers to the top button of her jeans. "Like what you see?"

Letting the heat inching through his body burn inside his eyes, he said nothing.

She snorted. "I hate you."

Then, yanking the jeans off, revealing that she'd worn nothing beneath, she turned and leisurely strolled to the lake's edge, dipping her toe into the water. He was as confused now as he'd been before.

Her emotions ran hot and cold. She teased him, then turned

away. It pissed him off. Made him slightly crazy. And most definitely confused.

Running the perimeter of her area, he breathed a cloud of death like a barricade around her, then, cracking his knuckles, he swiped open a rift between the here and there, and stepped through into the tunnel.

The only things they had on them were the clothes on their backs, and hers were shredded. She'd need everything.

Entering his apartment, he immediately grabbed a duffel bag out of his closet and gathered as many toiletries as he could carry. Some girly smelling shampoo and conditioner, toothbrushes, toothpaste, dental floss, deodorant. He was sure he was missing some things, but he had to move quickly.

She'd not come to his place with bags of clothes. There was nothing in his house actually intended to be worn by a woman. Most of what he had was dress slacks and silk shirts. Marching to his dresser, he pulled out a pair of plaid boxers and a plain white tee. She only needed enough to get dressed in; they'd figure out some way to get her clothes later.

Not sure whether he should bring her a pair of socks or not, he paused, every muscle in his body freezing when the faint scrape of a chair moving back caught his attention. Straining to hear the minutest sound, he waited.

Normally such an innocent noise was just background in the music of his life, but knowing that she had a monster of the hunt tracking her—that every damn monster in all of the world was interested in possessing her—the innocuous made him feel like a meerkat guarding its mound.

He was ready to dismiss it as his mind playing tricks on him, when he heard the scraping sound again. But this time it was closer. It was coming down the hall. Snuffling softly, like a dog sniffing at scent.

Common sense said run, leave it all behind, and go back to her. But something didn't feel right. His house was warded; nothing could enter without his consent.

The sounds were closer still, and now they sounded more like a wet gurgle. Pushing as much glamour out of him as possible, he shielded himself within the magic inherent to his kind. Making himself nearly invisible. None could see him unless they knew exactly where to look and what they were looking for. He wasn't actually invisible, he'd simply distorted the perception of space and time, causing a ripple effect that made it appear he wasn't there.

Easing the drawer slowly closed, he gathered the duffel bag of items and made sure the room appeared as empty as it'd been this morning. The door opened.

And what he saw, he could not name. It did not appear like anything he'd ever seen. It was blackness—moving, rolling shadow with twin dots of red for eyes. A glowing-cinder kind of red, making it appear as if unholy fire burned behind it. There wasn't much of a face, just a distortion of one, a perception of it. If he looked dead-on, there was nothing, but when he tilted his face to the side, he could make out the blurry image of a nose, eyes, and mouth.

A mouthful of ragged, razor-sharp fangs. The creature, for it was definitely that, walked upright, but its long arms and webbed hands made him think it was more of a quadruped than humanoid.

Every step it took left a black streak of fog in its wake, and the rotten stench of sulfur made Frenzy curl his lip. Creatures of the hunt generally fell into two categories: gloriously beautiful, godlike in many ways, but it was a beauty so deadly it'd been known to cause any unwary, unlucky soul who glanced at it for too long to die of shock—then there were the monsters. The boogeymen. The bastards of the fae world.

This was one of those.

It sniffed again, and he wasn't nervous, but something didn't feel right. He was covered in glamour so thick not even his queen could find him, yet this creature was drawing slowly closer to where he stood.

A wet, slurping sound echoed through the nearly empty room. "You can come out."

The voice resonated angrily, rolling through the room like a windswept wave. His brows lowered, but he didn't move. There were still too many questions to reveal himself just yet.

"Can you see me, reaper?" it asked, and though the voice sounded like it'd been dragged from the depths of hell itself, it was also surprisingly cultured and refined. It smiled. "I've no quarrel with you. I only wish to find *her*."

The way it said "her," it was a like prayer and a curse. Heaven and hell, there was desire, lust, and hate all wrapped into it.

It came in closer, lifting its nose higher into the air, and the closer it got to him, the more it solidified, no longer moving like a shadow, but more like the sensual slink and curl of a snake, its head lolling from side to side as it followed Frenzy's scent trail closer and closer.

How the hell had this dark-court abomination found them? They'd never left the house, she'd not even peered out a window...

But last night, he'd left her alone. She'd gone comatose from lack of food; what had she done before that, though? But the moment he thought it, he shook his head. Mila had told him just seconds ago they needed to move on. The woman had survived this long by being smart. She would never have done something so stupid.

It continued its slow walk into his space. He hoped the thing was female. Not everything that looked male actually was, not within faedom. Frenzy had always been able to charm the fairer sex when he wanted to; it was how he'd been able to get in so close to the queen.

Studying its chest area, he tried to make out twin lumps, or anything else that would identify its sex. But though its form had definitely solidified, it was still indistinguishable as truly male or female.

"I smell her on you. All over you." It smirked. Something long and black poked out from where the mouth was. He could only assume it was a tongue, the way it ran slowly along its lips. "Tell me, reaper, how does she taste?"

Nose curling, he took a step back. The creature might know he was there, but it didn't know what he looked like. Keeping his identity secret might be the only thing that saved Mila in the end.

"What do you want?" he barked, throwing his voice to the opposite corner of the room hoping the creature would bite and turn around, but it didn't. It merely chuckled.

"You play a fool's game, death. As I said"—it stuck its face up in the air—"I smell my prey."

Light coalesced from the inside out, pouring through the shadow, but rather than obliterating the darkness wrapped like skin so tightly around it, it made it glow a deep, deep black. And from that blackness something else materialized: eyes. Dozens of them, painting themselves on its skin like living tattoos.

Green eyes filled with sorrow blinked. Blue ones burning with fury stared hard. Brown, black, and a vivid, vivid purple, every color of the spectrum, gazed back at him.

"What do I want?" it rasped, chuckling deep in the back of its throat. "I want her."

As it said it, the form of its body manifested more. Fine threads of hair sprouted on a balding, shiny head. Muscle demarcation became apparent across its flat abdominals. Fingers became claws with hooked, shockingly white nails.

The chest was obvious now; the nipples were too. The way the skin hung, it could have been a female, but it could just as easily be male. Taking a gamble, he made a call.

"Do you wish to rape my female?" he growled.

The thing hissed. "Rape your female?!" Glowing cinder eyes swirled with a hypnotic light.

The burst of anger made it obvious the thing was in fact female and affronted at the notion of raping one of its own sex. Human, fae, or otherwise.

Smiling, Frenzy released a little of his glamour. Not enough to reveal himself, but enough for her to feel him.

"Ahh, death." His moniker rolled off her forked tongue with satisfaction. "Where is she?"

"Patient, lady death."

Her entire form trembled and she sighed a breathy, moany sound.

"How did you find me?" That question would nag at him forever.

Lifting her hands, she touched the tip of his navel and drew a nail upward. Slow and easy. Women, no matter the breed, were easy. Always had been, he just rarely felt the need to put in the effort. Only once had he really wanted to, but the rules of seduction never really changed, no matter the century.

Setting his repulsion aside—he'd seen much worse than a shadow with eyeballs covering its body before—he traced the edge of her neck. The spot right above the collarbone, the one that seemed to drive all women manic. "Tell me, darkness. How?" He stepped in closer. "Did?" He leaned in. "You?" He blew a shivery tendril of breath along the shell of her ear. "Find?"

Tremors racked her shadowy form, her head tipped back, and her mouth parted just slightly.

"Me?"

Blowing out a heavy breath, she grinned. "You know your dance well. And though I am fond of you, death…" Her hands continued to run along his, but the shadow had more than just two hands. There were three, four, five sets of hands, running down his spine, his ass, the backs of his legs, cupping him.

He had no desire to look down and see whether the hands were manifesting bits of shadow or whether they were actually tentacles of some sort. He kept his eyes firmly on hers. Because though she shouldn't be able to see him, somehow she was. Maybe she couldn't see the true symmetry of his features, but she was seeing something; her touches were too accurate for her not to be.

To pull this off, she'd need to believe what he did wasn't a ploy to get her to talk.

"I am no fool."

"My lady." Palming what he hoped was her backside, he drew her tight to him, delighted to note the trembles still coursing through her. Painting too pretty a picture would make her see through the deception easily. Half-truths were what he would give; she was too smart for anything else. "You are correct. I know my dance well. And while I desperately wish an answer to that question—"

"Desperately?" Her face came more into focus. The fire in her eyes was still there, but it was no longer just fire. It was a floating flame in a moat of inky black. Her nose was sharp and angular, reminding him of a bird. Thin lips stretched across a face that bore not an ounce of unnecessary fat. Razor-sharp cheekbones and a high forehead that led to a thick mass of hair the same shade as her body. "I like the sound of that. And what would you give me in exchange? Hmm? The girl?"

He didn't answer, merely strummed his fingers along her spine.

She laughed, and the sound grated on his ears like the breaking of glass. "You ask for much, and give me nothing in return."

The best way to keep Mila safe was to keep this thing off of her trail. Strangely ready to get back to her, he released a little more of his glamour, enough to show lady shadow his eyes.

Frenzy had earned his name centuries ago, and not because of his fighting skills, but rather the way in which women fell for him. Shaking off the rust, he shoved his magic through his eyes, turning them a startling shade of liquid silver.

She gasped, panting like a dog in heat.

"A kiss," he murmured, feathering his lips along her dry slits. "Tell me, lovely creature, how did you learn where she was hiding?"

Biting her lower lip, she pulsed like the spark of electricity, beginning to glow a strange obsidian.

"So that you can deny me her?" Her voice was a heady whisper as her hands continued to play along his flesh. "You cannot kill me, death. I was born of the wild hunt."

"I know. But the woman is mine."

She hissed. "Did you bed her? Do not think to play me for a fool, reaper."

"Darkest beauty, as you say, I am death. What need have I of something so…mundane? Hmm?" He tipped her chin up.

She giggled.

"I have a taste for the more exotic."

Something long and thick wrapped around his hip. Goddess, it was all he could to do to continue on with this charade. The longer he stayed, the longer his woman was without supervision. Startled, he almost dropped out of character. Since when had he begun to think of Mila as his? But he no more thought that than he realized that's exactly what she was. His. And in order to keep this shadowy bitch off her trail, he needed that answer now.

Slamming his lips onto the hag's, he made love. Tasting and nipping, purring in the back of his throat, and his hands caressed the nearly flat bumps on her chest, but when she tried to shove her tongue down his throat he pulled away with a chuckle. "Wild minx." He flicked the tip of her nose. "You would make a fine female. But I need answers." He shoved angry urgency into his words.

"Then will you kiss me again, my love?" The leathery skin of her palm clamped onto his cheek.

"Tell me."

She sighed. "I am darkest shadow, wherever it gathers, there can I be also. As much as I my body desires yours, grim reaper, I will not stop until she is mine, and do not think to hie her off to faerie, for that land only makes me stronger."

Fury churned in the pit of his belly. Why had Lise not told him this? How could Mila hope to escape a creature whose sole purpose in this life was to consume her?

There had to be a weakness. There was always a weakness.

"My boon, then?" She smiled, so docile, so responsive to him.

His fingers curled, itching to trace the absurdly long length of her neck, wrap around it, and choke the very breath out of her. But she could not die. Doing that would serve no purpose.

"If it is a kiss you want"—he smirked—"then it is a kiss you shall receive."

This time when he took her, he breathed death into her throat. It would not hurt her—for a creature like her, death was nothing. But there was more to him than simply killing; when he looked into a soul, he *saw* the life. Saw every tear, every smile, the love, the hate, the need, the lust.

Visualizing death's kiss as a type of undulating frost-nipped fog, he forced it down her throat. She moaned, but not with pleasure. Her body jerked in his grasp and the hands suddenly stilled.

Pushing more of it through her, he shoved it deep into her belly, through her veins, into her pitch-black heart, and finally, into her brain, where he could access her memory banks.

A vision came to him then—indecipherable images of flashing light coalescing with shadow. *The woods. Famed fae hunters with bows. The Morrigan. Not as a woman, but in her other form—her raven form—she rode the air on powerful crimson wings. The darkness of night danced with golden flickers of sparkling color. This was the wild hunt. This was a vision of the shade's birth, how from the darkness she sprang. Fully formed. Living, breathing shadow. Neither child nor woman, she took her first breath, and then stepped out of the blackness, and there was only one purpose. One goal. Find a seer.*

It was an all-consuming hunger, a need to own. To possess.

The Morrigan dropped before the shadow, beady black eyes staring deep into her own, and a thought, a whisper passed between them. Then the crow was gone.

A loud thunk rang through the room. Pulled from the vision, Frenzy jerked his eyes open. She was cold, like living marble in his arms. She still breathed, but she'd gone rigor. He'd pumped so much death into her veins she wouldn't move for days, hopefully weeks.

Angry eyes stared at him as he gently laid her down.

Damn The Morrigan; it was no wonder the queen was so keen to learn of Mila's location. The magic of the wild hunt came not from nature, but from the queen herself. Nothing could be born of the hunt unless the queen willed it. She was the gatekeeper; she was the key to destroying the shadow.

Lise had known that—that was why she'd refused to allow the queen to listen in. Whatever the queen knew, Lise had to know as well. The Ancient One had helped Cian, surely she would help him also. After all, she was the one who'd forced him to guard the woman.

Grabbing the bag of toiletries that'd fallen at his feet earlier, he swiped open a rift in time and went to fetch his woman.

Chapter 9

W hat in the hell did he do to you?" the queen snapped at the beating pulse of shadow standing before her.

The Morrigan had been in her chambers when she'd heard the keening cry of the hunter in her head. Death's kiss had been forced down her throat. The shadow had relayed it all to the queen through visions.

Damn that insufferable Frenzy. She'd not thought to warn the darkness that the reaper was known to beguile even the most heartless of hearts. She'd assumed shadow had no heart to speak of. But Frenzy had proven his namesake true yet again.

The shadow's form pulsed like a throbbing heart. Death's kiss had knocked her silly and it was all she could do at the moment to retain any sort of form.

"He kissed me."

"Why did you let him?" She stalked to the creature shaking before her throne.

But she wasn't shaking in fear; the shadow shook in fury. She snarled when she looked up at the queen. "Because I want *HER*! And I would do anything to possess her."

The Morrigan narrowed her eyes. "The girl is mine. You are to track her only, *drochturach*. She is the last of her kind. Disobey me and it will be to your own peril."

With a shriek to rival a banshee, the shadow wrapped herself around the queen, her embrace like a python's grip. "I am not so weak that I cannot suck the soul out of you."

The Morrigan would rather die than admit how much the creature's grip hurt, or that it made her insides feel like they might liquefy from the pressure. Lifting her chin high, she growled, "I created you, creature. Release me. Now!"

The shadow laughed, slowly unwinding its body from around the queen. "I would never harm you. *Mother.*"

Taking a breath that hurt, the queen fought the tremor that threatened to give away her true anxiety. The shadow was stronger now than it'd ever been.

When she'd first created it, it was weak. Looking to her to be fed and cared for, and in return it had obeyed any and all commands. But she'd fed, gained too much power over the centuries. The Morrigan could not have seen how each time the shadow inhaled yet another seer's soul that she would strengthen, morph into a being even more powerful than the queen herself.

And this was when the creature was at less than full speed. Frenzy's kiss had weakened her. Casting Dagda a look from the corner of her eye, she knew her consort would not come to her defense.

Part of retaining the power and respect within fae was being able to control her own destiny. To control those around her. He would not come to her defense, nor she to his. That was not the way of things in faerie.

She'd already suffered a humiliating defeat when Lise had taken Cian from her care. She could not afford to appear any weaker than she already did.

"Follow them," she hissed out as an order to the shadow, pointing a finger at the black blob's chest. "Do not kill her, or I swear, I will end you."

The shadow chuckled a low, menacing sound. "I've scared death off; he will find her and they will run. How am I to track them now?"

Tracking death wasn't easy. Part of their abilities was that they couldn't be found unless they were harvesting. When their hands turned to bone, then and only then could The Morrigan get a lock on their location.

Frenzy was ten times smarter than any of her reapers. During his dark days (the period after his mortal's death) he'd secluded himself in outlying areas, terrorizing villages and mortals, always one step ahead of those who could catch him. The queen had finally found him when she'd discovered that she could trace him when he harvested a soul.

Knowing his pattern, he'd likely squire the woman off to some remote locale and, if the past repeated itself, there'd come a point where being constantly in her company would make the baser side of him come out. The side that would protect her no matter the cost.

The side that would kill to keep her safe. And when he did, she'd find him again, and by finding him, she'd finally find her seer.

She smiled. "You leave the tracking to me. I'll send for you in a few days. When I do, you will find her, and you will bring her to me."

The shadow didn't utter another word, simply turned and vanished within a plume of smoke.

It did not escape the queen that she had not agreed. The shadow could wind up being a problem. The Morrigan hadn't lied when she'd said she'd kill the shadow. The creature might think itself invincible, but no one truly was.

"Dagda." She turned to her consort. "Fetch me my black box."

Standing, the earth god bowed and walked toward their study.

The Morrigan smiled. It may not seem it, but everything was falling into place.

* * *

Mila turned at the sound of a twig snapping and then sucked in a sharp breath when she took in Frenzy's cold face and angry eyes. And though there was fury and fire burning through him, her body responded to his heat, to his nearness. Her nerves snapped and sizzled. He was gorgeous, dangerous, and she wanted him. Desperately.

Shielding her breasts from view with the curve of her arm,

she stepped backward into deeper water. She'd been invigorated to learn that her new unhuman skin didn't get cold the way her human skin would have. He'd been gone awhile, but she hadn't felt any fear thanks to the death kiss he'd let roll throughout her clearing. At one point she'd seen a deer, nose up in the air as it drew closer to the invisible barrier, and almost as if it'd sensed the wrongness of the place, it'd jumped as though startled and turned in the opposite direction.

Most animals seemed to know to stay away. One bird had flown too low, though, and, almost as if slamming up against a glass shield, it'd gone rigid and dropped with a thunk to the ground. It had hurt her to see the bird die in that way, but also given her a sense of peace. Even irritated at her as he was, Frenzy had protected her.

She'd tried to catch her bearings, get a rough estimate of where she was, but he'd dropped her off in the middle of nowhere. It was just one endless stretch of trees and rolling hills. Kind of peaceful, in an off-the-grid sort of way. In fact, she'd been floating on the lake's surface staring up at the sun without needing to blink or flinch, thinking that this was a type of eternity she could probably deal with. Smiling softly to herself, she lay there unmoving, until finally she got the sense that someone was definitely watching her. Prickles rushed over skin and made her stand up quickly.

"There will be no food cooked here, O'Fallen." His tone was brusque, his words gravelly, his stare intense. "We will do as you asked and move to another location."

She nodded, wondering what, if anything, he planned to do.

He was looking at her like he…needed something. Her sluggish heart thumped.

"Can I bathe?"

Her throat was so dry she could hardly speak. He was asking for permission to come in here with her, she knew it, felt it. There was an energy to him, something intense and primal and it called to every one of her new, baser instincts.

Deciding not to overthink it because she was actually glad to see him, she nodded, and could not have looked away even if told to when he began to undress. Except instead of being bashful as she had last night, she locked her gaze on his. There wasn't an ounce of shame on his countenance when he stripped.

Frenzy stood on the bank, his shirt off, pants gone as well. He was completely nude. But instead of it making her shy and anxious, she found she was quite the opposite.

There was a monster inside of her. Ever since turning she'd felt the slumbering beast unfurling sensuous claws deep inside, making her crave. Not only blood and meat, but sex. It was a lust-fueled haze that was slowly getting stronger, demanding its needs be met.

Fire and heat inched through her belly, making her hum whenever he was around. Making her aware of his scent of spicy male, a mix between spring rains and his own unique earthiness. The way he moved, like a graceful, sloping predator. How the softness of his shoulder-length hair could not distract from the rugged beauty of his face. How his abdominal muscles rippled like thick ropes with each step he took into the water.

His angry gaze never strayed from her own.

"What...happened?" she mumbled, shivering now, but not from cold, rather from a want so powerful it bordered on desperation.

Her legs trembled, her skin prickled with a wash of intense need, and it was all she could do to swallow and not jump on him, become a wild, ravenous beast.

Licking her lips, she stood her ground, curling her fingers into fists as she repeated slowly to herself that what she felt wasn't real. It was hormones. The mad passion of a vampire. They'd earned their reputation as lotharios honestly; there was none within the realm of *others* quite as depraved or desperate for sex as the vampires.

"We cannot go back," he finally said, stopping inches from her.

The world was electric, alive. Vibrant. She felt it move against her, felt the heat flowing between them. Biting down on her lip to prevent from moaning, she nodded. "The apartment? Why?"

"Because I met her."

She blinked. "Met who? Who's 'her'?"

His eyes narrowed to dangerous slits, and this time when he moved in to her, she didn't just feel the simmering crackle of pent-up energy; his thigh rubbed against her own and she sucked in sharp breath. Her entire being focused on the point of contact. Because being a vamp meant she was at the peak of perfection.

His thumb touched the tip of her jaw. "The shadow. It is a female."

Ears buzzing, blinking rapidly because her heart was suddenly fluttering in her throat, she started to back up, mud squishing between her toes from the slippery lake bed. "It…She found you? Us?" Glancing left and then right, she shook her head. "We have to go, I can't stay here. I can't. I have to—"

His arm wrapped around her waist, pulling her into his tight body. His gaze still menacing, threatening. "You know, don't you? How she tracks you?"

She shook her head, frazzled, finding it difficult to think clearly. "What are you talking about? I don't know how the bloody thing finds me."

His jaw working from side to side, hard fingers digging into the curve between her spine and the top of her rear, she couldn't pull her eyes away from his penetrating, soul-deep gaze. The silver swirled, reminding her of a mad spinning toy top. Her nostrils flared, fighting the instinct inside her telling her not to move.

Because she needed to get away from him. Away from the things he made her feel—not just lust, but protected. Safe. As crazy as that was, they were on the run, but when he was near, it was like nothing could hurt her. Being with Frenzy was madness, his world, her world now…It was scary and frightening, but she was okay as long as he was with her.

"So you don't know that there isn't a single ward that can keep that vile, black, soulless creature out? It can find you anywhere you go. Anywhere we run. It lives in the shadow it was born from; we cannot escape its hunt."

Shivering, feeling the cold in a way she hadn't before, she shoved him away. How could she ever have a hope of escaping it? If it lived in shadow, then it would always find her; whenever the sun set she'd be in danger. "That's how it finds me?" She squeezed her eyes shut. It made so much sense.

Why her mom and gran never stayed in one place long. Why they'd separated her from her father, from all those not part of the line. They'd never told her why, and maybe they weren't sure themselves, but they always said to never stay longer than two, three years in any one place. To not mingle much, to keep to yourself, trust only family. A few months back she'd reached out to her da, only to discover he'd died of a stroke ten years before. She was truly alone in this world, a thought that left her ready to weep if she dwelled on it for too long.

Living like this, it'd been a way of life for her. She'd seen so many different parts of the world and had grown used to the lifestyle. To the wanderlust she'd always thought her mother and gran possessed.

"You didn't know?" he asked softly, almost tenderly now, and she heard the bafflement in his voice, as if he was shocked to discover that she'd had no clue how the shadow had tracked her. She heard the pity behind his words too, and it made a fury blanket her mind.

She shoved him. Hard. Causing him to stumble backward and make her smile, if only briefly. "Why would you think I'd know that? And how the hell did you get that *thing* to talk?" Her words dripped poison, growing thick with the accent she tried so hard to keep penned up.

A cocky grin fixed firmly on his face, he said, "I seduced her. Of course."

Words could not do justice to the sudden hate and disgust she felt. Because it wasn't remotely similar to anything she could ever remember feeling as a human. This was a level of soul-sucking, mind-numbing fire that twisted her insides up, made her fingers itch to flex and claw and her throat burn to scream.

Not able to understand what was going on with the crazy surge of emotions, the up and down and hot lust mixed in with cold fury, she sank under the water. It was the only rational thing she could think to do. If she walked out of the lake, she'd run and he'd catch her; if she attacked his oh so disgustingly gorgeous face, he'd restrain her. She couldn't win either way.

Sucking in water through her nose and mouth, she was astonished to find it didn't hurt her. She didn't know why she'd done it—maybe to test the limitations of her new body. It didn't make her brain want to spasm with the need for breath. She couldn't drown, so she opened her mouth and screamed.

He'd touched it. Seduced it. And she hated him for it, hated that it bothered her, *hated* that it made her feel so damned jealous.

Her life was over. She couldn't die. Couldn't undo the wrong done to her. It all hurt so much and the worst of it was she had to entrust her life to a being she didn't understand at all. Frenzy didn't care for her, and it was ridiculous that that thought hurt.

Hard hands gripped her upper arms, dragging her up. It was all too much. She slapped him.

"Woman," he growled, not releasing her arm. "You've grown too accustomed to hitting me. No more. Do you understand?"

"Did you sleep with it?" She lashed out. And it so wasn't

what she'd meant to say. It really wasn't. She wanted to rant and rail and tell him to piss off. Tell him anything, anything but asking, *Did you sleep with it?*

He jerked, seeming astonished by her question. The firmness of his grasp didn't let up an inch. "What the hell are you talking about?"

"You seduced it. What else did that devil tell you, eh? What else does it know about me?"

Mila had grown up almost on her own. She'd lost her gran and her mom to the demon when she'd been fifteen. They'd never had a chance to tell her everything, to teach her how to survive. But she'd learned, she'd figured it out. Even thought she'd been somewhat successful at it. And she'd grown careless and cocky because of it. Sixteen years on her own, she'd thought working with HPA would be possible. Feasible. That for once in her life she could use her gifts to make a difference. Not to hide it from the world, but to make her life matter. She'd been stupid taking such a high-visibility job, but she'd only been a freelancer, working on the side when they needed help with a cold case or serial killers. If she hadn't helped that girl, if she hadn't stepped in, made a scene at a bar, maybe things would be different now. She'd still be living in the basement of that wonderful Ms. Henley, who'd baked her chocolate chip cookies every weekend and been one of the few people she knew who still made her lemonade the old-fashioned way.

She'd lost so much. Everything. And maybe it was stupid to have done it, but somehow, without her even realizing it, she'd begun to trust this man. The man whose eyes had been pumped full of terror when he'd found she'd stabbed herself in George's cave, the man who'd brought down that hideous deer just to make her eat something. It'd meant something, or at least she'd hoped so. Stupid her. Trusting was what always got her people killed. It was why they always scurried and hid like rats.

Mila had dared to live, and it had cost her everything.

Where there'd been coldness before, now his eyes seemed perplexed and at a complete loss.

"I did not have sex with the shadow," he finally answered, so low she had to strain to hear him.

She sniffed. "It doesn't matter."

He dropped his hands, his look growing earnest. "What is this about, O'Fallen?"

Squeezing her eyes shut, she bit the corner of her lip.

"O'Fallen?"

"Will you stop calling me that!" And that was all she could say, because her eyes were starting to tear up; there was heat building behind them, and if she didn't leave, he'd see it. He'd be witness to her misery, her fears, and she couldn't have that because it showed weakness. Gave him something else to exploit.

"Mila!" he barked at her back, but she was halfway to the bank and she wasn't stopping.

Jumping out of the water, landing gracefully onto a patch of grass, she ran. He might be faster than her, but she was plenty fast in her own right. Wind rushed through her ears as her legs chewed up the ground.

She'd barely contained her tears in front of him, but they were falling freely now. Trees passed in a blur. She knew it was only a matter of time till he caught her. This was never about running away, it was just about getting some time to herself.

Mila didn't hear the snapping of twigs, or the rustling of leaves behind her. He wasn't following.

Exhaustion claimed her. A settling in the bones type of weariness that made her finally stumble to her knees and drop to the soft grass beneath, crying. She released it. Everything. She had to, so she could move on.

One thing her gran had always told her: don't try to outrun the pain or the past, let it come, let the tears flow, and then let it go.

This was her way of finally letting it go. The impossible wish that somehow she could roll back time long enough for her not to die, not to be caught by those vampires, that none of this had ever happened, the pain of being a monster she never wanted to be, of being stuck with a man she didn't know, didn't really like. Of all the crazy emotions that made her feel things her brain didn't want. Pain, passion, lust, need, hate. That wasn't her. Before this, she'd been a good person. Quiet and shy, but good.

Now she barely recognized herself. Who was she? A vampire? A shifter? What?

"Woman." His voice was so low, so heartfelt, that the tears came harder.

Tucking her face into her knees, she shook her head, grateful for her long hair shielding her face. "Go away, Frenzy. I don't want to fight anymore."

"I did not have sex with that thing. You have to know that."

Wiping a tear with the back of her hand, she sniffed and noticed he'd taken the time to redress. "It doesn't matter. I don't care."

"Then what is this?" She felt his movement, felt his hot gaze boring into her skull. Knew that if she didn't look up he'd just continue to stay where he was.

Gritting her teeth, she peeked at him. "This is me having my first freak-out since this all went down. Do you think for a second any of what happened has been easy on me, Frenzy? Knowing you don't want the hassle of 'saving me'"—she finger quoted—"that one second I feel the very life slip out of my body, and the next I'm waking up and nothing makes sense anymore. The world I thought I knew, the one I'd lived in for thirty-two years, no longer makes sense."

His lips twitched, as if he were grappling with some sort of emotion, before finally huffing loudly and tucking a stray curl of hair behind her ear. "I'm as lost as you, woman. This isn't easy for me either. I don't know how to do this."

"Do what?"

"Keep you safe." His voice was whisper soft, the world felt suddenly pregnant with expectation. "All we do is quarrel, and it makes me..."

Rubbing her nose, she looked at him completely. "What?"

Running fingers through his hair, he shrugged. "I've been alone for years. I've not been around mortals for centuries."

"But I thought you were a grim reaper? Your job is to carry souls of mortals to the afterlife, right?" She cocked her head.

Folding his arms across his knees, he nodded. "It is." He sighed. "You want to know a truth, O'Fallen?"

It was on the tip of her tongue to remind him yet again that her name was Mila, not O'Fallen, but it really didn't matter. They were finally talking and she realized she needed to hear these things, because if she was going to trust herself to this man, she needed to know why.

Just then an image came to her. Odd, because since her death she hadn't had a vision. A part of her wondered if perhaps she'd lost her abilities since her monstrous ones had manifested themselves.

It was Frenzy. But he wasn't dressed as he was now. In fact, he was dressed as if from a completely different era.

Wearing a navy coat that came to his waist with long tails that dangled to the backs of his cream-trousered knees. There were gold chains dangling from his pockets and in his hand he held an elegant-looking top hat. His shock of red hair was caught back with a black silk hair bow.

She had no idea which decade he was in, but it looked old. Very historic.

One thing she immediately noted about him. There was no hardness in his eyes. He was smiling, laughing even. Bent over a mantel, reading by firelight to a woman dressed in a provocative red gown with white lace decorating the tops of her modest breasts.

Her face was plain. Her mouth was a little too thin, her nose a little too sharp, and she was covered in freckles. The most arresting feature on her was her eyes.

Eyes eerily similar to Mila's own.

Almond-shaped, with long fanning black lashes. Molten-amber colored. The way they stared at Frenzy, as if he was her world. Eyes were the window to the soul. You could read the truth of a person in their gaze. Whether they laughed often, or cried much. Whether they'd seen the worst of life, or were accustomed to the frivolity of wealth and good fortune.

The woman's eyes sparkled, danced as they snaked down Frenzy's fine masculine form. There was hunger, laughter, desire so sharp Mila inhaled a breath at the honesty of it.

Frenzy stared at her with the same level of need. While his beauty definitely outranked hers, he didn't see her that way. To him, they were equals.

But then the scene shifted and she was no longer viewing the world through Frenzy's eyes, she was in the woman's.

It wasn't often Mila could witness the thoughts of a ghost; generally she needed to be within the vicinity of the person to see their life. But it wasn't usual for her to witness the past either. Only on rare occasions.

But Frenzy was an immortal whose past was intricately entwined with his future.

The woman's name had been Adrianna. She was naked in a room with only a four-poster bed and white fluttering curtains. Moonlight sliced across her body. A dark shadow stood to the side.

Her porcelain skin gleamed as she writhed and moaned on the mattress, the masses of her dark hair the only coverings she wore draped across her breasts. She was waiting for her lover, playing with herself, getting ready for him. She'd convince him to marry her this time; she loved him. Soon her belly would be full of his child. He'd have no other option. He'd save her from being forced to marry the ancient Lord Abernathy.

Finally she spotted the shadow and jumped, springing to a sitting position, wrapping the sheet firmly around her body. "You scared me, lover." Then relaxing, she spread her arms, dropping the sheet and running a hand down the vee of her breasts.

But when the man stepped into moonlight and she got a good look at his face, she knew it was not Frenzy. The features were blurred and hard to make out, but the hair was blond, not the fiery red of her fallen angel.

Then he was upon her and there was blood. So much blood…

Jerking, Mila's eyes opened wide and she stared at Frenzy with her heart trapped in her throat. He was talking, saying things she could hardly understand. Hand trembling, she planted her palm against her breast, feeling the echoing beat of fear and Adrianna's adrenaline still pumping through her.

"…Do you understand now?"

Pinching the bridge of her nose, mouth tasting dry and parched, she shook her head. She'd not caught any of what he'd said. His hands were on her shoulders and he was looking at her strangely, eyes roaming all across her face.

"What's happened?"

Her eyes jerked to his. "What do you mean?"

"I was talking to you, but it was as if you weren't there. You were staring through me and now your pulse is beating out of control. Did you see something?"

Uncanny how he'd jump to that conclusion. He barely knew her. How much could she trust him?

"Tell me," he softly urged.

There were few times in her life when she'd shared a vision, and even when she did, she didn't give a complete accounting, only what needed to be known. This wasn't even a future she'd seen, but a past.

A past involving a woman with her eyes. A woman he'd obviously adored, a woman who'd maybe loved him back, but loved more what he could do for her. She bit the inside of her cheek.

Shrugging out of his grip, she took a step back, tucking a curl of hair behind her ear. Something about the two visions she'd seen made her think this woman had meant a lot to Frenzy. In all likelihood, she could be the very reason why he was now so hostile to mortals.

His lover had been brutally executed. Garroted. She squeezed her eyes shut.

"You can tell me." He said it again, so softly. So gently.

And it made her angry.

Furious.

Mila had always prided herself on containing her emotions, letting few see how she really felt. Because revealing too much made a person vulnerable. All her life she'd been running, forced to keep one step ahead. She'd screwed up so bad. Ruined it all because she'd allowed a moment of weakness in. But since dying, she'd lost her ability to remain neutral, to keep a lid on it. What she felt, she did, and she couldn't stop herself.

"Leave me alone," she hissed. "Just leave me alone." She didn't need his sympathy or understanding. Why was he trying to change the way they played this game now? She knew where she stood with him.

Whether he copped to it or not, he was her captor. Point. Blank. Period. He wouldn't help her die. All her life all she'd done was run and hide. And now death would be more of the same.

He looked as if she'd smacked him. Nose curling, upper lip pulling back, it was obvious she'd pissed him off.

Well, good.

So was she.

"I'm tired of all this shit!" she screamed. "Tired of running, tired of this life. Why keep me like this? You coming to me, trying to gain my sympathy; stop it!"

She tried to turn away from him. To run off again, it was fruitless and pointless, but it was all she knew.

"I'm not trying to gain anything!" he snapped. "You think I wanted this? I didn't. But we're stuck together."

"Why won't you just leave me to die? You don't have to stay here. You don't have to keep me safe. Just let me go, Frenzy. Let me go." Her eyes burned, but she'd be damned if she cried again.

She was done being weak, done feeling sorry for herself. Holding her head high, she challenged him, never blinking or swerving from his cold, hard gaze.

"You'd love that, wouldn't you?"

There was no point in answering; he obviously wasn't wanting one anyway.

"Grow up, O'Fallen. This is the real world." He gestured

around the empty field. "This is it. It doesn't get better. There is no white knight to rescue you. Death doesn't come for us all." His smile was pure malice, full of teeth and sarcasm. "Get one thing through your fool skull right now: you and me, we're in this together. I didn't get a choice in this matter either. You were the last person," he emphasized, "in the world I would *ever* have wanted to tie myself to. But I'm mature enough to understand there is no getting out. We either fix this, or we make our eternity a living hell."

His words shook her, brought the blasted tears out. Because he was freaking right. And she hated that he was. Hated that if she said otherwise it would just be her acting like an immature little baby. No matter how much she wanted to go back to what she once was, that night with the vampires had happened.

The vampires turned her.

A shifter had bitten her.

She craved food with an almost constant obsession.

A shadow wanted to suck out her soul.

And she was so sexually infatuated by a man she loathed, that it culminated in her slapping the hell out of him. His cheek flared red, and his eyes grew wide and filled with fury.

Grabbing her shoulders, he pulled her to him, hard. "Why'd you do that?"

"Because you make me…God!" she screamed, then grabbed the back of his skull and mashed her lips to his.

It wasn't gentle or exploratory. The kiss was about domination. She poured all her hate and loss of dreams, everything she'd ever clung to. Every illusion that so long as she did what she was told things would turn out okay for her, it all went into him.

Lifting her up, forcing her to wrap her legs around his waist, he shoved just as much of his passion back into her. She felt it in the way his teeth knocked with hers, the way his hands gripped so tight, bordering on the edge of pain. Their tongues dueled and she was so aware of it all.

Aware of the way her nipples puckered as they grazed the cool silk of his shirt. The kiss was potent and hard, lips and teeth nipping and grazing, sucking on the flesh of her neck, her jaw. Then he was back on her mouth, rolling her bottom lip between his, tasting and sucking on it.

Heat centered between her thighs, made her ache and need and want so damn bad. Because nothing made sense anymore, this life didn't make sense. Except this...the way he ground his erection into her, the way he growled in the back of his throat, how he consumed her...this was the only thing making sense.

Then he was slamming her against a tree, and her skin should have shredded the way he kept pressing her against the bark, but it didn't hurt. There was a sharp burst of pleasure at the almost-pain.

"Make me forget, Frenzy," she panted, clawing at his skull, running her fingers through his hair.

He tugged on her hair, causing her to inhale sharply at the burst of pain. "You're a crazy wench," he growled, and she nodded.

Because that's exactly what she felt like. Lost, confused, and scared.

"Take me now," she hissed, running her fingers frantically down the buttons of his shirt, popping them off one by one.

Pulling back just enough so that she could take the shirt off of him, Mila helped him tear it off. Then her hands were on his belt buckle.

"Nothing makes any kind of damn sense to me anymore. Make this go away, Frenzy. Make it go away," she said, then, frustrated that the belt wouldn't come off as easily as the buttons, she growled and snapped the buckle off.

He glanced down then back at her. His eyes were still angry, but they were also full of something else too.

Fire.

"O'Fallen," he growled, and then yanked the broken belt off, moving her hands away when she tried to unzip his pants. "I've got it."

Was it just her imagination or had his voice shook a little?

She bit her knuckle, panting heavily and completely unafraid that they were out in the wild, exposed to the sun and the wind. That anyone could see her if they wanted to. The sun was beating down all around them. The tree barely had enough branches to afford any kind of shade. There wasn't even a single cloud in the sky.

Everyone and everything wanted her, and her life just didn't make sense anymore. None of this did. She should be scared, but she wasn't. She was angry and horny and there was only one cure right now.

The moment his pants slipped down she grabbed hold of his hard length. He was enormous, bigger than any man she'd ever had, and for a second she could hardly breathe trying to imagine shoving that inside of her.

"Can you take me, O'Fallen?" He grunted, and the sound of it was almost painful to hear, like he was barely leashed. She had a feeling that if she said no, he'd freak. She'd pushed him too far. She knew that.

It was the Irish in her, too feisty for her own good. Her mum had always said that. Nostrils flaring, she turned to him and, staring deep into his eyes, she massaged his cock. "I'm not scared."

He licked his lips, and her stomach bottomed out because she now knew what those lips tasted like. How much fuller the bottom one was than the top one. How touching it was like taking a sip of fine brandy, drugging and intoxicating.

Framing her face with his hands, he forced her to keep his gaze. "Hold on to my neck," he ordered.

And for once she didn't fight him, because somehow this was bringing her back. All the fights and battle of wills they'd engaged in, it'd all been leading up to this moment. She'd known it, and deep down he must have known it too. They'd been a powder keg just waiting for a spark to set them off.

Wrapping her arms around his neck, she didn't have to wait long. Frenzy shoved into her, filling and stretching unused muscles.

She hissed and he trembled.

"You're so damn tight," he groaned, resting his forehead against hers as he waited for her to adjust to his girth.

Gritting her teeth, she used her feet to urge him deeper inside. He made a weird noise in the back of his throat, a mixture of a rasp and a moan. "You ready?"

The muscles in her thighs twitched as she rolled forward, getting him as deep as he could go in this position.

"Gods, woman," he hissed, and then took over the rhythm of their thrusts, shoving deeper and harder into her with each one, bruising her back against the rough tree.

But it didn't hurt, only heightened the pleasure. She was dead—this shouldn't feel so good. Shouldn't feel better than what she'd done when alive. It shouldn't make her body burn so bad, feel so full; it shouldn't make her want to weep and hiss because the pleasure was almost too much to bear.

With each thrust of his hips, darkness clouded her vision. A heart that she hardly felt beating anymore thumped painfully, chaotically in her chest.

She didn't hear the whistle of wind rushing through limbs, didn't see the flight of birds in the air, didn't notice the call of crickets or grasshoppers, because everything she had, all that she was, was completely focused on him.

On them.

On this.

"Woman," he growled again, and his thrusting became more intense. She knew he was reaching his peak.

Knew they were seconds away from falling over the cliff.

Frantic with the need for more, she scored her nails down his bare back. He hissed, bowing into her, pounding harder, going deeper.

And then they were there. A mere second away from the little death, and instinct kicked in, something primal and raw that demanded she take him, so she took him.

Mila grabbed a hold of the vein on the side of his neck and sank her teeth in. She didn't have fangs, the bite wasn't gentle, but he didn't seem to care.

Blood filled her mouth, and gods, it was amazing. Its sweetness coated the inside of her mouth, rained down her throat. Filled her belly with heat and fire. Rushed through her veins, bringing with it energy and life.

She screamed as he roared with their mutual release.

It took almost a minute before either one of them could move. He stirred first. There was wonder in his eyes and she could not deny that she felt that same wonder in her heart.

"What the hell just happened?" he mumbled, nostrils flaring from his heavy breaths.

She licked her lips, not wanting to waste a drop of the earthy red elixir. It should have made her ill with the realization that she'd just drunk some of his blood. Instead it only made her want more.

Which made her frown. She hardly knew herself anymore. The old her would never have done that. Not just the blood drinking, but letting a strange man touch her, taste her, make her crazed with a lust she could barely begin to comprehend.

"Stop it," he growled, stepping into her, framing her face with his hands, forcing her gaze up to his.

"Stop what?" she muttered, heart beating so much harder than it had in days. The blood inside of her body felt warm, alive and electrified. She was buzzing and snapping, her very pores tingling with life. Her skin felt flushed, her cheeks blazing. His blood had done something to her, made her feel alive and so aware.

"Stop overthinking this, stop wondering who you are. Stop comparing this life to the one you had before. Understand this, O'Fallen, what you had is gone. Forever. It won't come back. It is the one universal truth in immortality. We don't get second chances to right a wrong or redo a mistake. All we have is this second to see through the bullshit and decide."

"What are you blatherin' on about?" It was becoming harder to contain the lilt. For years she'd feared the lilt would give away who she really was. It was why she'd worked so hard to culti-vate a neutral accent, and in two days everything she'd worked decades for, everything that'd made her *her*, was unraveling. All shot to hell.

His hands were so warm, and she hated to admit this, even in the privacy of her own head, that it was nice. That in the topsy-turvy thing she now called life, it felt like an anchor. His touch helped her to focus, breathe easier, to panic less. Why? She hardly knew him and yet her very soul resonated vibrantly when he was around.

The way his hands had curved along the contours of her body, how he'd moved in her, tasted her, sipped at her lips like she was a fine wine, it'd all felt so…familiar. Like all her life had been a slow but inexorable progression to him. The dreams she'd had, the face of the red-haired stranger—he'd called to her on a level she couldn't understand.

"I'm going to keep you safe." Those molten silver eyes hooked her, blazed with truth. "Nothing will take you from me."

She wanted to believe that, so bad. Wanted to believe that after all the years of running and hiding alone, it was now in the past. That someone was finally around to help her shoulder this burden. Mila gripped his wrists.

"You want to know the truth?" she whispered, voice quivering because she didn't want to tell him this. Lightning quick, a million thoughts pinged through her mind. She was so used to bottling it all up inside. Keeping it all to herself. But she'd just opened herself up to him in a way she hadn't with anyone else before. Not that she'd been a virgin, but hookups had always been secret and brief. A way to relieve an itch. She'd never faced a partner while he'd entered, never let him see the truths in her eyes. Because truths were dangerous and bloody things that could kill as surely as stepping on a land mine.

Mila was tired of running, tired of being alone, tired of pretending that she didn't need anyone. Pulse hammering, throat so dry it felt like swallowing sandpaper, she considered a neverending life of either trying to figure out some way to commit immortal suicide, or running. Again. Alone and scared. Always just barely one step ahead of the shadow, one step ahead of a death that wasn't really a death. It was an eternal prison of torment; once sucked into the creature her conscience mind would remain trapped, like a fly in amber. Unable to ever stop being consumed by the creature who only wanted the secrets of the future and past revealed. She'd lived her mortal life that way with the knowledge that life wasn't long, that even if she lived to be seventy, it would one day end. But this—an eternity of running, always looking over her shoulder, always wondering where the enemy was, *who* it was—it was a dismal, deflating future. She was a freak even amongst monsters; there'd be no clan to offer protection, no one she could turn to.

Nothing.

She may not want to trust Frenzy—the instinct in her not to do so was overwhelmingly strong—but she didn't have a choice. It was either him or nothing.

"Me first." His thumb ran along the soft skin underneath her eye, slowly, back and forth. Hypnotic. She focused on that touch, casting out the fears that threatened to overwhelm, losing herself in sensation.

The way the sun kissed her pale flesh, the way the wind teased the locks of her hair, brushing against the swells of her breasts. How her body still tingled, still wanted him.

She nodded.

"I don't like people. Human or otherwise," he began, gritting his teeth as he said it, as if forcing the words out was hard for him.

She snorted. "Not much of a surprise. And not much of a secret."

He grinned and it stole her breath. Because this wasn't a lascivious smirk meant to throw her off-balance, or a hot and smoldering smile meant to make her lose her head. His touch was an unguarded moment of tenderness, something she wasn't quite sure whether he'd done on purpose or not. But his eyes danced, they sparkled the way they had in her vision when he'd gazed upon his Adrianna. It made him seem more approachable, much less like a monster.

He laughed and, by the gods, it was like being sucker punched. That smile moved through her body like a fiery bolt, making her scalp and toes tingle. Who was this man? Not the same one who made her manic to either claw out his eyes or rip off his clothing.

"I'm not sure I even like you much."

The way he said it, she could tell it was a joke. Not meant to insult. Honestly, it was easier and more believable hearing that than hearing a lie. That he loved her, needed her, cared for her—none of which would be true; they hardly knew each other. For the first time since the panic attack gripped her, she felt herself relax. The anxiety began to slither away, slink back into the darkest recesses of her mind.

And for the first time in years, she felt her lips tip up, felt them stretch and pull, felt muscles work that she'd thought had atrophied after her mum and gran died.

He sucked in a sharp breath, brushing his knuckles along the curve of her cheek. "You should smile more, O'Fallen."

"There hasn't been much in my life worth smiling about," she admitted reluctantly.

Frenzy gazed up at the sky, squinting into the brightness of the sunlight, then he sighed. She was amazed to note the savaging bite she'd given him was already healed up; to look at him you'd never think she'd just fed off him. There wasn't even a trace of blood on his gold-kissed skin. He was perfect and without flaws, as all fae were.

And it suddenly dawned on her: she was still as naked as a jaybird and he was wearing nothing but his slacks around his ankles.

She giggled.

His brews drew down. "A laugh? I did not think the shrew had it in her."

That made her laugh harder. Life was absurd. After all the years of seeing futures, of gleaning the darkest truths of someone, she finally understood what she never had before. "All my life I hid, I fought to survive, to eke out an existence because it's what my mum and gran taught me to do. To hide, to run away, to never let others in, and now I see…how pointless it all was. They died protecting me, both sucked into the void that is the black-hearted shadow. I did everything they taught me, Frenzy, and in the end none of it mattered because I died too."

Tugging her face in, he planted a hard kiss on her forehead. "But you're not dead. You've been reborn and this is your chance to get it right. Do it right."

She wanted that so bad it was almost painful. It was a sick churning in the pit of her stomach. A lease on a new life. "But we're still running. And you shouldn't be forced into this with me. Why are you here, Frenzy? Tell me the truth."

"Okay. But not here. We're going to talk some things out. But we're too exposed. I should have thought of that earlier—"

"What? You mean instead of groping me arse?"

His lips twitched as his hands curved around the base of her spine, feathering along the top of her bottom. It made her hot and cold and achy in places that shouldn't feel achy anymore.

He'd filled her, given her the best orgasm of her life. It should have been enough, but it wasn't.

"It's your fault for having such a nice one." Serious again, he threaded his fingers through hers. "We have to move away from here. I know a place. But first let's get you dressed."

Chapter 10

Since reapers traveled the globe harvesting souls, there was never a guarantee of making it back to faerie. Sithens—entrances into the fae realm—were only in a few spots around the world. Unlike most of his brothers and sisters, Frenzy had always planned ahead for the nights when he couldn't make it back home. He had homes scattered all over, cabins that he hadn't visited in decades, sometimes centuries, keeping them guarded from rust or decay with wards and spells.

Gathering up what few supplies they had, he wrapped Mila in his arms and transported them to a small cabin lost in the middle of the redwood forest. She didn't speak, just clung to his back, still practically naked except for a pair of his boxers and a T-shirt.

That he didn't mind at all.

He smirked, but quickly turned serious again.

Something had happened to him, to them, back there in George's woods. The sex had been incredible, but that wasn't the difference. Perhaps he hadn't been fair to her, expecting her to adapt to this new lifestyle without incident. Because in his head, things were as they were. There were no grays in his world; it was all black and white, yes and no. Life was what it was, and he accepted it and moved on.

Adrianna's death had taught him that. There were things he could not change, no matter how badly he might want to. But maybe he was wrong.

It irked him to think so. Old as he was, he'd prided himself on seeing truth for what it is. Inevitable. Unyielding.

And yet staring into Mila's eyes, he'd felt like he'd glimpsed a vision of her soul. Of the ugliness that she'd battled through the years. It'd been humbling and disconcerting because there was so much pain inside her it'd stolen the breath from his body. He understood that pain, understood the need to guard and keep others at bay. Far from your heart, from your soul…to not let others in because it hurt too damn much.

He'd closed himself off after Adrianna. Become a monster, become vicious and so cold that eventually it'd been second nature. Eventually he'd turned all emotion off; any need he'd ever desired to know and be known had died with her.

But this little *other*, this baby…she understood that need. He'd read the truth of it in her eyes and he couldn't help but respond in kind.

The sun was just beginning to set, casting the world in long shadows. The woods were eerily quiet, a rolling white fog curling slowly along jewel green moss. This land did not belong to faerie, but it filled him with peace all the same. Made the angry hornet's nest of too many thoughts quiet down, helped him to take an easier breath. A fae was tied to nature, to the balance and harmony of colors and the purity of a land undisturbed by the poison of those who only sought to control and possess it.

Trees with clay-red-colored bark towered above them, standing like sentinels, guarding them from prying eyes.

The cabin was nothing more than a solid A-frame of logs, with two small windows and a small stone chimney on top. He'd built this place back in the early nineteenth century; nothing fancy, just a place to rest his head during the long winter nights.

It was dark and slightly foreboding, but that was simply part of the ward he'd placed on it. A repellent to make any unwary passersby continue on.

Adjusting the strap of their shared duffel bag, he gestured toward the door. She stood a little to the side and behind him, her liquid amber eyes huge in her pale face. The way the sun shone through the leaves highlighted the prominent scars on her cheeks. She looked like some wild thing with twigs and bark poking up from the strands of her blond hair. There was blood streaked across her neck and jaw, and peach-tipped nipples jutted proudly from her smooth, alabaster breasts. He swallowed hard. She was a nightmarish vision and his mouth watered because what they'd done back there had only fed his beast.

The way she moved, stealthily, easily through the trees, how she no longer blushed about her nudity or his...the transformation from human to other was fully beginning to grip her. But he couldn't help but wonder which side would manifest strongest.

Vampires were sensual creatures, consumed with their need for violence, sex, and blood. Shifters merely for the feed. It'd taken George a millennium to break the hunger's hold on his sanity.

Her eyes roamed his body, languishing, reveling in every dip and curve of his flesh. Making him hot and aware that they were alone, that for now, the shadow couldn't find them.

"What?" he asked finally, sensing her need to talk.

At first it appeared like she might not say anything. "This." She gestured at the open space. "Even out here, in the middle of nowhere. I'm not safe, am I?"

The melancholy was back in her eyes, but not the anger this time. "Did you enjoy my blood?" he finally asked, not sure why. He knew she had; he'd felt it in the way her body had trembled, her touch had turned frantic.

Her lashes fluttered, but her stare did not waver.

Stepping toward her, he nodded. "Because I did."

She licked her lips. "Really? It didn't turn you off?" The last was a mere thread of sound.

Lips twitching, he shook his head. "Come inside, woman. We have to finish this discussion, but I don't want you out here another second."

Glancing over her shoulder, she reached his side, taking the hand he offered. In less than a minute he was opening the door.

The cabin had the old musty odor closed homes usually did.

"Where are the lights?" She traced the wall with her hand, gazing at him, perplexed.

He smiled. "I built this home in 1901."

Her nostrils flared. "You *built*?"

"I did. Try not to sound so disbelieving."

She laughed and the sound was nice. Shivery and dulcet all at once. She seemed different now. Not quite so tense or ready to do battle.

"That's very domestic for a faerie."

Frenzy snorted. "I like to work with my hands, it helps me think."

"Think?" she inquired, and he had to admit, he liked this more open side of her. For so long he'd been closed off, not willing to share any part of himself with another soul, but he sensed she needed this. They were walking a tightrope right now: one wrong word or move and they'd be back to arguing, hissing and spitting at one another. He didn't want that and, he sensed, neither did she.

Rubbing at a speck of dust on the counter, he shrugged. "After Adrianna's death, I was lost. I became the monster of nightmare." He shuddered remembering the countless times he'd wake up and realize he was coated in blood, a snarling, raving lunatic hell-bent on revenge. It was like he'd been two different people: one who was void of emotion, so numb that even a child's laughter couldn't have pulled a smile onto his face, and then there'd been the creature walking through the night, wreaking chaos and mayhem wherever he went. Using his hand to fell anything that dared to walk in his way.

She smiled softly, as if unsure. "I'm sorry. I probably shouldn't have asked."

Waving off her concern, he walked over to a drawer in the kitchen. Opening it, he pulled out a thick, cream-colored beeswax candle and a book of matches that he'd left sometime in the late seventies. Pointing at a small cabinet inset within a pantry, he jerked his chin. "There are a few more in there. Grab what you can."

He probably should say more, try to calm her worries that she'd insulted him somehow, but he didn't want to dredge up any memories of Adrianna's ghost. Not now. She didn't belong in this moment.

Turning, she did as he asked, pulling out another five. "Where do I put them?"

Her voice was calm, taking her cue from him, and he felt an inexplicable urge to hug her, which he promptly ignored.

His cabin was as sparsely furnished as his apartment in San Francisco had been. This was a one-room home: kitchen, bedroom, bathroom all shared the same space. There was a bronze horse trough he'd used to wash in resting against a corner, a small frame bed big enough to sleep two with a feather-down mattress he'd stuffed himself. A kitchen table that would seat four. An armoire to fit his clothes in, an icebox to store perishables, and a farmhouse sink he'd installed. Water ran in from the natural spring well out back.

"Put them on the table."

Licking her lips, she set down the fat candles, which he proceeded to light one by one. "I hate to break it to you, but this place needs some serious updating." She chuckled, and the sound of it washed against his flesh, brought color to her snow white cheeks.

"Part of its charm."

"Charm?" Turning in a slow circle with her hands planted on her hips, she shook her head. "Is that what we're calling it nowadays?"

Setting the matchbook aside, he leaned against the kitchen counter. He really needed to get her more clothes, something not quite so revealing—it was distracting to look upon so much female beauty and not want to return to what they'd been doing not even an hour ago.

"What would you call it?"

Picking up a crocheted yarn blanket off the foot of his bed, she sniffed it. "Antiquated. Old. Ancient—"

He snorted and crossed his feet. "I think the word you're searching for is 'charming.'"

"Pft. You wish. It stinks like my aunt Telly's rubbing ointment for her bad knees. It smells like old people and"—she laughed again—"I thought the other place was minimal, this is positively medieval."

He shrugged. "It suits me. Does what I require." His eyes drew down her form. "You need clothes. And another bath."

She rubbed her chest, smearing the caking blood. "What? Red doesn't suit me?"

"Suits you too well." He shoved off the counter. "I'm going into town to get some supplies. The shadow arrived too soon for me to grab much other than some soaps and toothbrushes."

At the mention of the shadow she visibly pulled into herself. The verve and vitality so present just seconds ago vanished as her eyes roamed around their place, out the windows into the woods beyond.

He shook his head. "You are safe from her tonight."

"How do you know that?" She crossed her arms over her breasts in a defensive posture.

"Because I injected enough death into her to sink her into a coma for at least a couple weeks. Go out back, there's a lake. Take some of the supplies in the bag, whatever you need. Don't stay out too long; this cabin is very isolated, but I don't want to take any chances. I'll be back in about thirty minutes with food and clothes."

Her jaw jutted out and she merely nodded an okay where before his ordering her about would have turned into a battle of wills.

Zipping open the bag, she knelt and began rummaging through it. The flickering flame played off her body, highlighting the sweet curves of her ass, the graceful line of her back and supple thighs. His body responded and it shocked him that it could. He hadn't felt a need to be with a woman for too long, so long he didn't know how to act or think.

She must have felt his look because she turned to look at him, cocking her head in question.

"Nothing." He turned on his heels and headed back out the door.

* * *

Mila watched him go with questions pounding through her skull. After the sex in the glen, they'd been doing a weird sort of dance around each other. The stupid cry fest had been good for her, gotten rid of the festering poison inside, but now she felt exposed. Like he'd seen a side of her few ever did; it made her anxious and aware in a way she hadn't been before—that this was it.

This was her life now. She could rant and rave and piss and moan about it, but it changed nothing. The thought of offing herself felt wrong, not because she was suddenly in love, but because when he'd kissed her, moved inside her body for the first time in so long, she knew she wasn't alone.

It wasn't a fight she'd have to shoulder full responsibility for again. And it was strange thinking that, because she wasn't sure where they stood. She hadn't exactly made a habit of one-night stands in life, so she was socially inept at navigating these waters.

You'd think in afterlife, things like embarrassment and humiliation would cease to exist. They really didn't; in fact, they intensified by about tenfold.

Riffling through the bag, she yanked out a bottle of shampoo and conditioner, a hairbrush, toothbrush and paste, and a towel. There were some clothes in the bag, but mostly his stuff.

It was surprising to her that she really didn't care about wearing so little clothing, being practically naked in front of him constantly. Just yesterday it'd been hard to watch him sleep in the buff. Now today she was walking around with her breasts hanging out and her hoo-ha on display and barely thought about it. Just didn't seem all that important anymore.

But the way he'd been eyeing her, maybe it was best if she at least attempted to cover up. Feel more human. Grabbing a plain gray T-shirt from the bottom of the bag, she exited the depressingly small cabin and made her way to the back.

The woods were electric.

It was amazing how different the world smelled, tasted, looked, now that she was immortal. The setting sun was a deeper shade of yellow. The orange and pink streaks across the sky more jewel-toned, and the green of the leaves was an intense shade of color.

The water was also different. She could smell it in a way she never had before. There was the obvious, fish and muck and brine, but there was more. Each molecule within each individual drop had its own distinctive scent. All her life she'd been taught hydrogen and oxygen had no odor, but that wasn't true. Even the most sensitive machine couldn't pick up on it, but there was a smell.

It was salt and mineral, earth and clay all rolled into one. She inhaled again, letting it coat her lungs.

Nesting owls in the trees above smelled of rodent and berries. The soil was rich and pungent. A blackberry bush beckoned her with its sweetness.

This was it.

The vibrancy of life she'd never known existed before manifested itself in a new way—it was more than the colors or the scents, it was tangible. Awed, she held her arms out, watching as the sun played off her skin, and smiled, because it didn't burn. She wasn't sure what it meant to be a hybrid exactly, but maybe being part shifter and vampire had its perks, because she didn't have to fear the sun or the night.

She inhaled deeply, calmer than she'd been in ages.

A hand clamped onto her shoulder and she screamed, tossing everything she held as she jumped onto the nearest tree branch.

Frenzy gazed at her with a perplexed question in his silver eyes. "It's only me." He held up his hands.

She frowned, heart still thundering a violent cadence in her chest. It was strange how she felt her heart's movement since drinking from his vein. Before that it'd been a hollow, empty feeling inside of her. Drinking his blood had made her feel human again.

"Why'd you come back?" She grabbed her chest, flattening her palm against her breast, scanning the woods. "Did you see something?"

Greasy fear twisted her stomach in knots.

He frowned. "I've been gone nearly forty minutes. I worried that you might wonder where I'd been off to."

"Forty minutes?" She shook her head, finally prying her fingers from the branch, jumping back to where he stood. "I've only been out here for like two minutes."

His smile was tight. "You became entranced." He touched her brow with the back of his hand.

She closed her eyes because it felt good.

"You're hot." He sounded worried.

Shrugging him off, she shook her head. "I don't feel it."

"You need to eat."

"I did. I drank your blood." Just saying it made her want to lick her lips. The taste of his blood had been…ah gods, amazing. Sweeter than grape juice, more addicting than a fine wine. It'd heated her veins, slid warm and hot down her throat, and she swallowed hard because just thinking about it made the hunger return.

She grabbed her stomach.

"No, O'Fallen. You're part shifter too. You need food, I suspect."

Wrinkling her nose, she took a step back. "I'm not going to swallow anything raw, livers, or…" Mila thinned her lips. "I can't do it."

"We need to talk. Go bathe quickly, and dress." He shoved a pile of clothes into her arms.

There was a pink shirt with a picture of a fish on the front surrounded by hearts and the words I HEART BASS LAKE. There was also a pair of size-five blue-jean shorts.

"How'd you know what size I am?"

He smirked. "I may not like many people, but I watch."

"Women." She stuck out her tongue.

Frenzy shrugged.

"Whatever. Thanks." She gestured.

Crossing his arms across his chest, it finally dawned on her that he'd changed too. Instead of the slacks and silk shirt she was accustomed to seeing on him, he was in denim jeans and a ribbed black shirt. It highlighted the thick strands of his crimson-colored hair and made her body suddenly ache.

"You look good in that," she admitted without stuttering.

There was one thing she liked about this new vampiric body of hers: it was owning up to her sexuality, being free and unashamed to admit what was on her mind.

His lips curved into a wicked but sensual smile that stole her breath. "Thought you might."

"Gods." She rolled her eyes. "Vain much?"

"How is it vain when I'm only telling the truth?" He winked. Winked!

And why that should bring her such joy, make her feel suddenly so alive, so hot and bothered—it didn't make sense. Then again, none of this did. She smiled. "Aye, whatever."

He moved into her space, so close their bodies grazed, shared heat and air. She shivered, swallowing hard.

Then he was trailing his thumb along her jawline, pressing it into the tip of her chin. "The accent," he said.

She sighed, letting go of the pent-up breath. Her voice was breathy and soft when she said, "I can't seem to stop it from escaping anymore. All my life I kept myself closed off, alone, and I canna…" She licked her lips, not sure what to say.

"Do it anymore?" he supplied.

Looking at him, she nodded. "I suppose."

"Bathe. There's a conversation to be had that's been long overdue."

She nodded and bit her lower lip. "I'm sorry about that. I really should have finished by now. Did I really hypnotize myself?"

It seemed hard to believe that she'd stood standing in the middle of the woods stark-assed naked for close to forty minutes, but she also couldn't deny that she now had clothes and he'd changed.

"Go." He nudged her. "I'll wait and watch and make sure it doesn't happen to you again."

Mortified about her slip, she turned on her heel, grabbed her toiletries, and headed to the bank. Setting her items aside, she jumped into the water, which was, again, nice and temperate.

It wasn't even spring yet. The water had to be at least in the sixties, if not lower.

Making quick work of washing, not wanting to get lost in the lull and movement of the life pulsing all around her, she moved briskly from task to task. How stupid had she been just standing there that way? What if something had come upon her unawares? She'd dropped her guard; she never did that. Ever. Her life had always been about staying one step ahead. But too often she was losing focus on what mattered, too busy squabbling with Frenzy over asinine stuff. Wanting to change what obviously couldn't be changed.

Scrubbing her nails across her scalp one last time, she dipped her head under the water. Grabbing some sand, she rubbed it over her flesh, particularly where his blood had been, trying to strip as much scent off of her as possible.

Once she felt seminormal again, she swam back to shore.

He was still where she'd seen him last.

"Have you even blinked?" she teased.

"Not often. Didn't want to miss the show." He grinned, revealing even and strong white teeth.

Handing her the towel, he bent and retrieved a bottle of

water. Quickly drying, she took the bottle from him with a question in her eyes.

"To brush your teeth. I noticed you brought out the stuff."

"Thanks." Taking it, she dipped her head. Then proceeded to brush her teeth. It was weird because she didn't feel at all like she smelled or even had morning breath. Her body was different, but this was just a way for her to hang on to some sort of humanity.

Brushing the tangles out of her hair with her fingers, she glanced up to note he was still looking at her. But this wasn't just a look, it was a scorching brand. Primal and raw and full of need.

"How do I look?" she whispered.

"Like dinner." The sound of his deep voice mixed with the way he was mentally undressing her made her weak in the knees. Made her stomach tickle and heat pool between her legs.

"Come." He held out his hands. "We've been out here long enough and before we give in to this hunger"—he let that word dangle and she knew exactly what he was talking about. She should be offended, but she wasn't, she so wasn't—"we need to figure out our strategy."

Mila licked her lips.

She followed him back to the cabin in a sort of daze, eyeing his ass as he walked. The way the jeans hugged his hips.

Back inside, she noticed that he'd done stuff while she'd been hypnotized outside. The smell of cooked steak teased her senses, and suddenly she wasn't hungry for sex. Her stomach didn't just growl, it roared.

"I figured you'd need to eat too. And since you seem inclined to deny yourself meat that's raw, I bought rib eye, barely seared on both sides."

It touched her that he'd notice something like that. And that he was also giving her a way around the whole bloody-meat thing. Eating raw steaks wasn't abnormal or gross, it was the way her nan used to prefer her meat. It felt safe and right now; she needed that.

"Thank you." She dipped her head as he led her to the table that bore two plates. Both had steaks on them, but one of the plates also had a potato dripping in butter and a mound of broccoli.

Neither of those two items did anything for her, but she couldn't stop eyeing the steak like it was her newfound lover. Her fingers curled.

"George mentioned that so long as you keep up eating a steady supply of mostly raw meat, the type of meat doesn't matter."

She smiled. "Poor lone wolf. He's gotten a bad rap, hasn't he?"

"Considering that the zombie he slept with was his wife of forty years, who he had no clue had gotten infected earlier in the day, yes, I'd say he's gotten a very bad rap."

That actually was kind of sad and made her feel horrible for how she'd treated him before. She'd heard rumors of the lone wolf who'd been kicked out for sleeping with a dead body, but she'd had no idea the dead body was actually the reanimated corpse of his beloved wife.

He pulled out the chair for her. This all felt so domestic, so comfortable. It was still hard to believe that she didn't want to gouge his eyes and rip his heart out of his chest every other second. It dawned on her as she sat that most of the battles they'd had, she'd instigated. Maybe if she hadn't been so determined to be a bitch from the beginning, things might have been different between them from the get-go.

"Would seem so."

Staring at the hunk of cow meat, mouth salivating with want, it was all she could do not to snatch it up and rip chunks out of it. It felt like forever since she'd eaten a thing. The burned squirrel in George's lair had nearly made her vomit.

"Dig in." He gestured, picking up his fork and knife. "I'm sure you're starved."

Licking her lips, she grabbed the utensils and sliced off a chunk both big enough to satisfy and small enough not to look like she had no manners. The first bite was succulent and sweet and she couldn't help but moan in appreciation.

"I didn't sleep with the shadow, I know I already told you this, but it's important you really believe me," he said quietly just before slipping a forkful of meat and potato into his mouth.

She glanced up, chewing. It'd been gnawing at her whether he was being honest then, she wouldn't deny it. Not that it should matter, because they weren't much of anything. Sleeping buddies, if that. There was nothing between them.

"You said you kissed her." She finally admitted the one thing that'd been bothering her most. "Why?"

Spearing broccoli into his mouth, he swallowed before saying, "To learn the truth. How much about me do you know?"

She knew he wasn't asking about him specifically so much as his kind. Deciding that it was time to be fully honest with him, she nodded. "Not much, truthfully."

"Tell me what you do know so we can go from there. And don't stop eating." He pointed to her plate with his knife.

She snorted. "Aye, death." Sawing off another large chunk, she chewed and then swallowed. The blood had made her feel powerful, invincible, but the meat helped clear the cobwebs, made the pounding and incessant need for sex not so manic. "Most of what I've learned about the *others* I was taught by gran and mum."

"And HPA?"

Mila shook her head. "I only freelanced. Enough to get me by, to help me survive. That was it."

"Who were the vampires following you? Did you know them?" he asked, taking a sip of red wine.

Holding out her glass for some, she waited until he'd poured to answer, curious to see if she could handle drinking wine, or if it would be blood only for the rest of her life.

"I didn't know them. But I saw them."

"In a vision?" He lifted his brow and she nodded.

Amazed again at how he seemed to anticipate her answers. "Yes."

"Why did they want you?"

She laughed, but it lacked mirth. "Same reason I'd imagine everyone else does. My eyes." Mila pointed to them. "The power to read the future rests in them."

Studying her, he took another sip of his drink and she did the same, a relieved *ahh* coming out of her when it went down with no problems. It was sweet and spicy, cool, and filled her mouth with the essence of blackberries and smoked cherries. Best meal of her life.

"I thought the shadow sucked out your soul."

"Because it's a gluttonous bitch," she bit out. "The power rests only in our eyes, but I think it enjoys our suffering as well."

He nodded. "The thing was"—his look was thoughtful—"intense."

She snorted. "That's one way of putting it. It's got a ravenous appetite and will not stop until it hunts me and my kind to extinction. We're very nearly there. Last I'd heard, there were less than a handful."

"How did the vampires find you?" When she didn't answer immediately, he wiped his mouth off with a napkin and sighed. "A reaper has many talents. Not all of us share the same. One of mine is called death's kiss. If I concentrate, I can shove a part of my essence into another, killing them instantly if it's a mortal. She was not. So rather than stop her heart, death spoke to me. It crawled inside her and drew out a part of her consciousness."

She blinked. The power he claimed to possess was almost frightening, but also exciting. "Did it affect it at all?"

"Yes. It stunned her. She's probably still lying on my bedroom floor in full rigor."

Excited, buzzing with a sudden rush of adrenaline, she leaned forward, ignoring her half-eaten steak for the moment. "What did you learn?"

"I learned that once a seer's scent gets into her she's like a bloodhound. She never forgets and becomes obsessed with finding that particular seer. She's so obsessed that she will not move on to another subject until she's trapped the first one."

Bringing her fingers to her nose, she sniffed, smelling only the roses from the shampoo she'd used earlier.

"But you've been porting us around; how can she still find me? Shouldn't that kill off the scent so that she can't trace me?" Fear gripped her heart in a vice.

He bit his bottom lip. "I'm not sure. When a creature is born of the wild hunt, they aren't stable. Or normal."

"Normal's relative." She snorted. "I doubt I'm normal. Half-shifter, half-vampire."

"Yeah." He grinned, swallowing another sip of wine. "I guess you're right."

Making a joke about it was easier than giving into the pounding fear sinking its twisted tentacles into her.

His face was serious again, as were his eyes, and she knew it was worry.

"What is it?"

He looked at her. "She can slip through protection wards. I don't know how, but she's very powerful."

That was the death knell to her. "So in essence you're saying you can't kill her, you can't keep her out, and she'll follow me until the day I die, which now isn't likely to happen any time soon."

She shouldn't be pissed at him, but she was. It was irrational and she wasn't going to flip out the way she had earlier, but why in the hell had he saved her when her fate remained unchanged?

"I see where you're going with this."

Mila shook her head. "Where?"

"You're transparent. Listen, I didn't say she wouldn't be stopped. Everything has a weakness. You should know that by now."

His words were gentle. She set down her utensils, then steepled her fingers. "I've been running all my life. So did my ancestors. In all that time not one of us learned how to slow the shadow down, not wind up either dying by our own hand or having the very soul ripped from us."

Frenzy scratched his cheek. "The wild hunt is a time of chaos and madness; more than just the shadow was birthed from it. But anything that comes to life during that time is the manifestation of The Morrigan's will. When I kissed it, I saw a vision of darkness floating before my queen."

Her nostrils flared. "I don't understand."

"It means that the knowledge of how to destroy that creature lies with her."

She laughed, but it was more ironic than happy. "The queen of darkness? Are you seriously suggesting we go and beg her to tell us the secret? She never will. I'm no fae, but even I know the queen would never help anyone without benefiting from it in some way."

"Exactly."

His eyes danced and she felt like she was missing something, like the obvious was right under her nose but she couldn't make heads or tails of it.

Tapping the table for emphasis, he said, "We make it worth her while. Only there's a problem."

"Isn't there always?" Mila rolled her eyes.

He ignored her comment. "The queen rarely leaves faerie. Which means we'd have to go there."

"Ah," she said, understanding finally dawning. "I'd have to walk into the lion's den." Much as she wanted to end this thing, there was no way she could do that. Out here she wasn't all that safe, but knowingly walking into faerie, into a place where everyone and anyone was gunning for her, it was suicide. "You know I can't do that."

"I've tasted the powers of that creature. I cannot stop it. My kiss only stunned her, and for how long, I have no idea. A day, a week, month? Who knows." He shrugged. "Then we're back to running again and starting all over from square one."

"Can't you kiss her again?" she asked in vain hope.

"No." He leaned back in his chair. "To kiss her I'd need to get in close and have her unawares; the element of surprise is gone. The only way to stop her is to take this to the queen."

Her heart quickened as a terrible sort of feeling rolled through her gut. "I'm not safe, not even with the queen. You don't understand, she'll use me, just like everyone else. She'll—"

Getting up quickly, he walked around to her side of the table and latched on to her wrists, dragging them into his chest. "I won't let her do that to you. I won't let that happen."

His gaze was so sincere, his silver eyes hypnotic, helping to ease a little of the anxiety flowing hot and hard through her.

"Why are you doing this? Why are you being so nice to me all of a sudden?" Her voice was a small thread of sound.

Brushing his knuckles along her cheekbone, he tucked a strand of hair behind her ear. "Because I was tasked with this duty…"

Heart sinking to the region of her knees, she whispered a small "Oh." Having sex didn't automatically mean he'd have to confess undying love to her; she was a vampire now, with vampire's needs. She'd wanted the satisfaction of his body as much as he'd wanted hers. But there was still that part of her, would likely always be that part of her, that needed to be wanted. Needed to hear that she wasn't alone because they *wanted* to be with her and not because of being tasked with a duty.

Lifting her chin with the tip of his finger, he shook his head. "And because no one should have to be alone. I didn't give you a fair shake when I first met you, O'Fallen. I was angry and jaded." He shrugged, lips quirking self-consciously. "None of which was your fault." Chewing on a corner of his lip he turned his face to the side, eyes staring off into the distance, as if in thought.

She sighed. "I saw a vision of you. And a woman in red."

He jerked his gaze up.

"A woman with eyes a lot like mine."

Releasing her, he stood back. "What did you see?"

She shook her head. "You loved her. And she was mortal. Once upon a time you didn't hate humans."

He didn't speak.

"Is she the reason why you do?"

Gathering up their dishes, he took them to the sink. She

hadn't been done with the steak, but she was satisfied at least. Felt better than she had in days.

"How much did you see?" He asked with his back to her, turning on a faucet as he set about to clean their dishes.

Seeing wasn't something she could control. She couldn't look at a person and decide she wanted to know all their dirty little secrets. It was something that in the past she didn't get concerned about, so why did she suddenly feel as if she'd peeked into something personal and private?

"You have to understand, Frenzy, I can't control when—"

"What!" he snapped, spine rigid and still not looking at her. "Did you see?"

Jerking at the boom of his sonorous voice, she shook her head. "Not much." Which wasn't really true; she'd seen enough. Her life and love, her grisly murder. She nibbled her lip.

The silence was thick and so loud she heard the echo of her heart beating through her ears.

"Talk to me," she whispered, raising a hand as if to touch his shoulder.

He was gripping on to the edge of the sink and counter and shifted out of her reach the moment she got to him, as if he'd sensed her nearness. But then she caught sight of his eyes watching her from the reflection in the glass window. They were dark and stormy, angry as they'd been when the two had first met. She had a decision to make: lash out and be vindictive, or breathe and realize that this was genuine hurt he was feeling, and try, for once, to empathize with another.

Swallowing, she grabbed on to his hand. His fingers were

strong and so deliciously warm, and she felt the heat spread through her limbs from the point of contact. "I'm sorry, Frenzy. I shouldn't have told you that."

Rather than let go, he squeezed, and though she still felt the anger vibrating through him, he moved in closer to her instead of away.

Relieved, she began to prattle. "My mouth has always gotten me into too much trouble. It's why the vampires found me."

"What'd you do?" he asked after a second's pause.

"I saw something."

His brows lowered. He looked so breathtakingly gorgeous in the faint flickering of candlelight. It was still astonishing to her that she could see so much better in death than she had in life. It was dark as pitch out and there was very little light in the cabin, and yet she had no problem making out the deep red of his hair, the bearded shadow along his chiseled jawline. The smoky gray tint of his black, fitted shirt, which helped highlight muscle rather than hide it.

She'd touched him today and he her. Everything was different now. And like a junkie craving his fix, she needed to touch him again. Moving into him, knowing full well he could reject her if he wanted to, she planted her hands on his powerful chest, liking the feel of his heart beating beneath her palm.

"What did you see?" His low voice shivered across her flesh, made her hot and cold, and now that the craving for sustenance had been satisfied a different craving took hold of her again.

They held gazes, the air expectant and pregnant with desire and need so sharp it was a visceral yearning. Her fingers twitched in the soft cotton of his shirt, and her breath came out quivery and airy.

"I saw a little girl. A beautiful little blond girl. She was playing outside the doors of the pub I'd been drinking at for the past hour."

"Who was the girl?" His minty breath feathered across her lips, making her pulse thunder and her loins tighten with heat. Damning her wildly inappropriate responses to his innocent questions, she closed her eyes and tried to concentrate.

The best thing, of course, would have been to step away from him, put some distance between them. Maybe then she could think, reason, and not act like such a sex-deprived fiend, but her brain and her body were two opposing forces.

Swallowing hard, she turned her face to the side. Breaking eye contact helped clear some of the fuzz.

Thinking about that day, she could see the scenario so clearly. Like a picture in her head. The little girl dressed all in pink.

Mila had been feeling low that day, having another one of her "woe-is-me" pity parties. Wondering what the meaning and purpose to her life was. That day she'd been on scene with HPA at a downtown park. They'd found the Candyman's latest victim on display. The vibrant redhead had been posed as a lounge singer. Wearing a glittering green cocktail dress with red pumps. Her hair had been styled in a fifties poodle haircut, tight sleek curls around her elfin face with a smooth part down the middle. She'd been gripping one of those big silver RKO mics, and on her middle finger was a large red candy ring.

The scene had been no different from the countless others

she'd seen. The eyeballs had been taken out and lids sewn shut. The mouth twisted up into a macabre version of a smile.

But this time the killer had made one mistake. A mistake she'd instantly recognized. One that made Mila break out in a wash of cold sweat, made her realize it was time to pack up and go.

They'd found it on the cadaver's fingertips: a faint blue smudge that'd smelled sweet. The techs had been baffled, murmuring whether the killer had somehow gotten a little clumsy this time, as he'd never left a mark or mar on the bodies before.

Mila had known the truth immediately.

The killer was the shadow. Whoever had been creating the macabre puppets was simply the shadow's lackey. A way for the shadow to hide what it'd been doing.

The shadow was looking for her.

And now that she knew it, she knew she couldn't go back home. Couldn't stay in San Francisco any longer. It was too dangerous. When the techs had asked her if she'd gotten any feel or vision for the woman, whom she may have been, she'd simply shrugged and smiled, feigning exhaustion.

It hadn't been true.

The moment she'd touched the woman's hand she'd seen who she was. The first of the four victims she'd gotten a lock on. A Cal-Berkley coed visiting her boyfriend on holiday. Her name had been Sara Thorne and she would be greatly missed.

It was why she'd gone home, packed, and asked her boss's mother if she could rent out one of her bed-and-breakfast rooms for the night. Mila had wanted to fly out of San Francisco, but the shadow was too smart. It was likely keeping tabs on flights, so she'd planned to leave by boat, but by that time of day, all boats were docked and wouldn't set sail until the following morning. She'd had no choice but to stay one more day.

All the questions and the anxiety had been too much for her. She'd done something stupid, something her gran would have killed her for. Mila had gone out. She'd worn a disguise of a baggy sweater and pants, a ball cap on her head, and shades. Gone into a dump of a pub to drink some scotch just so that she could settle her nerves.

"O'Fallen?" he said, voice low and gently drawing her away from the memories.

She blinked and swallowed, coming back to the present.

"I was so stupid." She snorted. "I was sitting in that filthy pub, tucked away in the deepest part of it, where there were hardly any lights, so that no one could really see me. Then a man sat about three seats over from me. You have to understand, I cannot control the visions. They simply come, or don't; I cannot bring them forth no matter how much I want to," she said, but she was hoping he understood that she was speaking of more than just that night.

His jaw clenched, an infinitesimal movement, before he nodded and moved deeper into her space. She sighed, gave him a crooked smile.

"Go on," he gently urged.

She shrugged. "I saw a little girl, like I said. He was a drunkard; the call of whiskey was no match for that child. He'd hidden her in an alley behind the pub, given her some chalk to draw on the street with. I saw three men coming for her."

"How do your visions work? Are they past or future?"

"Both. Sometimes the past, sometimes the future. I canna control what it is I see, as I said. It simply seems to depend on the individual and their circumstances. But you have to understand"—her voice drifted off—"I've seen visions like these before."

"Of death?"

"Aye." She nodded, heart trapped in her throat as she remembered what that little innocent would have gone through.

He tipped her chin up, then wrapped his arms around her waist and drew her close. "So why didn't you let it happen with her? They all die in the end."

The way he said it, not with scorn or malice, but a deep and honest sincerity, it touched her to her very soul. "We all do die, it's true."

Frenzy sighed. "But her death was different. It touched you. Made you reckless?"

Feeling safe and secure in his arms, she rested her head against his chest, taking another step into him, before nodding. His hands rubbed along her back, up and down, soothing her in a way very little else could. In some strange way, letting him hold her, opening herself up this way and being completely exposed, it made her feel stronger, not weaker. It was weird for her, this feeling of safety she felt whenever he was around. Like nothing bad could happen to her while he was here. Which was nuts because they'd been on the run the entire time. Nothing had really changed and yet, in some ways, it felt like everything had.

It was scary to feel like this, but it was even scarier to think it could all go away and she'd be alone all over again.

"She was innocent. If her da hadn't taken her there, if he'd left her at home as he should have, that future would never have happened. I had a choice to make. I'd seen so much death in my life, I was tired of it. Something just snapped in me. I walked over to him, punched him in the head, and told him his daughter was in terrible danger and to go get her right away."

He chuckled. "You punched him?"

"Yes. Rather stupid of me to punch a drunk, but I was drunk myself. The man went off, called me all sorts of stupid, flipped over a chair. His breath reeked of liquor."

"And the girl?"

She sighed. "Still in danger. But now I had the bartender threatening to throw me and the father out, and no one was listening. So I ran to the back. All the while the father was screaming at me that I was crazy, that he had no children. A few of the patrons must have followed, because someone filmed the entire episode on their phone. I found the girl, who was already set upon by attackers. I went nuts, screaming and raving like a lunatic. I was piss drunk and remember little of what I said until I saw it on the news that night. 'Drunk woman recues child from gang rape,' or some such crap. I knew the moment I saw my face on that screen I was in trouble."

He frowned. "In a city the size of San Francisco, how did the vampires learn you were a seer?"

"Because of what I was screaming, I suppose." She shrugged. "It's all still very fuzzy. I didn't even finish watching the show.

The cops were looking for me, HPA was ringing constantly trying to figure out what in the hell I'd done, and I knew it was
only a matter of time before all the dots were connected. I'd had
a sick feeling in the pit of my stomach that night, but I had only
forty dollars to my name. I'd spent the rest of what I'd had on
that ferry. I was stuck and could no longer stay at the bed-and-
breakfast. So I snuck into a neighbor's home in the middle of
the night, intending to only get a few hours of sleep before the
sun came up. I knew if I made it to sunrise I'd make it out of
there. But obviously, the vampires found me. And that is my
story."

Leaning back so that he could look her in the face again, he
brushed a tendril of hair out of her eyes, rubbing her cheek with
his knuckles. "That was a very stupid thing to do," he gently
chided, and she winced.

"I know. And yet"—she searched his gaze to see if maybe
somewhere deep down he understood why she hadn't had a
choice—"I'd do it again. I could not imagine a worse fate for
a child. I'd maybe handle it differently. I wish I could read
my own future. That would make my life so much easier." She
laughed, but it lacked humor. Scratching the back of her head,
she studied him. "So now you know my secrets. I've got to
know, why did you let George bite me? Why couldn't I have
remained a vampire? These cravings I get"—she swallowed
hard—"they drive me close to mad."

The pads of his fingers brushed along the scars lining her
cheeks. "When I found you, you were less than a second from
death. Lise came to me."

"The Ancient One?" What would Lise want with her?

"Yes. I didn't understand it then, but having been with you these past few days I understand why she ordered George to bite you. What do you know of vampires?"

She chuckled. "Firsthand knowledge or what I learned post-death?"

His lips quirked. "Both."

"That they're sexually depraved monsters who obsess about blood." She wiggled her body into his, because just talking about it made her breasts tingle, her thighs tremble, and her center feel heavy and wet. She was so ready it was almost embarrassing.

Snorting, Frenzy said, "All that is true. It is also true that when they bite you and turn you, you become slave to their whims and fancy. They own you."

She frowned. It was true. Vampires were sired creatures who formed strong, dysfunctional family units. "I haven't felt—"

Slowly he nodded, as if waiting for her to fit the pieces together, and it was stupid that she hadn't already. She knew much more than the average human about the *others*; in hindsight it was obvious. "Shifters do not sire. His bite interfered with that."

"Contrary to popular belief vampires rarely turn a mortal, and when they do it's because they desire something. In your case it was your abilities. They would never have killed you—mutilated you, yes, but not true death—because they wanted what you had and I think were smart enough to realize that without you to interpret the visions, the eyes were useless.

Had George not bitten you, you would have been slave to your sire's whims."

Mila shook her head.

"Lise didn't stick around long enough to explain herself to me, but I theorize that George's bite killed off the bits of the vampire's poison that would have made you loyal to them. You are your own person."

"But George cannot regenerate. I've seen him. He looks worse than a zombie." She touched the scars on her cheeks, wondering if maybe that was why these ghastly things still remained.

He chuckled, stepping into her. "I shoved you up against a tree when I pounded into you earlier. Shifters can regenerate. The reason why George can't is because he lacks pack magic. A lone wolf, while still strong, is also weak in the sense that he doesn't gain the added strength and healing abilities a packed shifter would. But his bite is still a true shifter bite. You seem to have gotten the best genes of both. Stronger than either one of them."

"But my scars." She cupped them in her hands.

He gently pushed them away. "I saw you. You were battered and bruised, with bites all over your body. It was a horrific sight."

Shuddering, she said, "Sure seems like they planned to kill me."

"No." He shook his head. "You'd incited them to a fury. They were angry. If they'd wanted to kill you, they would never have toyed with you as they did. They were trying to teach you a lesson." He feathered his fingers along the tops of her eyes. "You healed. The scars, they came from a spelled blade. There is no regeneration from something like that, not unless you go to the witch who created the spell in the first place and ask them to reverse it."

The odds of ever finding the witch who'd spelled the blade seemed slim to none. At least Frenzy didn't seem fazed by her deformity.

"Do we really have to go to faerie, Frenzy?" she asked softly, afraid to say it too loud, afraid of who was out there, of what they might hear.

"I wish I could think of another way. The thought of going to faerie doesn't sit well with me, but it's the only lead I've found. If not there, where do you think?"

She sighed. "Gods, I don't know. I wish I did."

He hugged her tight, rubbing her shoulder blades in his strong warm hands. "Let us sleep on it tonight, see if we can come up with something else in the morning."

"Yeah." But in her heart she knew there wasn't anything else. If there had been, they would have thought of it already. Going to faerie was suicide. But so was staying put in any one place for too long. She was screwed either way.

Chapter 11

They walked toward the bed, Frenzy leading her. Today had been long and strange and he wasn't ready to call it a night, doubted she was either, but they needed to rest, to at least try and sort out what to do tomorrow.

"I'm not tired," she said, echoing his thoughts. "My teeth are hurting." She grimaced and rubbed at her gums with her fingertips.

Sitting her down, he walked back to the kitchen sink and grabbed a bowl from one of the pantry shelves. Filling it quickly with water, he poured some salt in it and stirred it with a wooden spoon. "It's normal. Vampires like to bite."

She licked her canines. "But I don't even have fangs."

Moving her hands, he dipped his finger in the water and then lifted it to her mouth. She wrinkled her nose, jerking her head away.

"Please tell me you're not trying to stick your finger in my mouth."

Realizing that was what he'd just been about to do, he sat the bowl down on her lap and shook his head. "A moment of insanity. Dip your finger in the water and rub it along the gums that hurt. It'll help ease some of the throbbing."

Sniffing the water, her brows screwed into a question mark. "It's only salt water."

Sitting down on the other end of the bed, he rubbed his brow. "Salt has many curative properties, especially for an immortal. Just try it."

Looking unsure, she did as he instructed and dipped her finger in then rubbed, sighing a moment later as the tension drained from her shoulder blades.

"My gods, that's amazing."

Frenzy got up to walk toward the kitchen table, pulling out one of the chairs.

"What are you doing?" she asked, staring at him with those haunting amber eyes he'd come to love and hate. Hate because they did not belong to Adrianna, love…because they did not belong to Adrianna.

He was such a walking contradiction.

"I'm going to take a nap, and you should too."

Her brows dipped as she set the bowl on the floor. "I thought vampires slept during the day, grim reapers not at all."

Growling under his breath, he rolled his eyes. "True enough, but I've developed a fondness for it. And you're not just a vampire, you're a shifter too, so you can and should try to rest."

Scooting back on the bed until her back pressed against the wall, she crossed her arms, appearing almost delicate in the candlelight. "Do you dream?" she asked, clearly intending to ignore his last statement.

He shrugged, taking a seat as he rubbed his hand back and forth along the wood grain. "Not really, no. I just quiet my mind."

"Sounds sort of like dreaming."

"I guess." He brushed some imaginary crumbs off the table.

Silence stretched between them, but it wasn't uncomfortable. Finally she broke it by saying, "Frenzy?"

Turning his gaze aside from the window, he nodded. "Hmm?"

"You don't have to sleep at the table." She patted the empty side of the bed.

Things were suddenly so different between them. Before today he would have sworn she hated him, and he definitely hadn't felt much favor toward her.

"Are you sure?"

Biting her lower lip, she nodded. The moment he sat next to her, things got awkward again. She covered her bottom foot with her top one and scooted a little off to the side.

"You know we've already slept together." He lifted a brow at her.

Blowing out a raspberry, she chuckled. "Yeah, we have." Immediately the tension in her body fled. Turning to look at him, she nodded. "Look, I'm sorry for acting an arse with you from the get-go. It's hard for me to let others in, to let my guard down. It doesn't come easily. I'm trying, though."

Feeling an odd need to reassure her, he draped his arm across her shoulder, dragging her into him. Again a spark, like a bolt of electricity, traveled through him at the point of contact. He'd felt it earlier, in the glen, when they'd torn at each other to get closer.

Being with her, it felt electric, dangerous. Her breathing inched up a notch as she turned to stare at him.

"Your eyes are such a perfect shade of liquid amber." His voice was rough and unsure. He wasn't sure why he'd said it, but looking at her, staring into eyes that'd haunted his dreams for years…it felt right.

And maybe it was because of those eyes that he was letting his own guard down. Letting this woman wiggle her way in where none had before.

Breasts rising and falling with her heavy breaths, she swallowed.

"I dreamt about you for years," she whispered, then grabbed his hand and brought it up to cup her cheek. "I can't see my future. Never have, and yet I've always seen the mysterious man in red. Who are you, Frenzy? What are you going to do to me?"

The point where his body touched hers flared to life. "I'm going to save you."

Her look was incredulous, but she didn't speak on it. What more was there to say? He knew the odds were slim, so did she, but for one night at least, they could pretend.

Words were pointless and sleep elusive. Gripping the back of her neck, he watched her, waiting for a flicker of disapproval as he dragged her lips to within inches of his own. Their shared breaths mingled and he inhaled greedily, taking her unique scent of fresh earth and frosty winds deep into his lungs.

"I've never smelled anything quite like you," he murmured.

Her lips twitched. "Good or bad?"

"Different." Not giving either one of them a chance to think about anything else, he took her lips.

She still tasted of wine, sweet and spicy, delicious. Running his tongue along her lower lip, teasing her to open up for him, he smirked when she trembled, latching her daggerlike nails into his shoulders.

It'd never been so raw or wild with Adrianna. She'd been human, unable to handle anything other than soft, tender strokes. Mila crawled onto his lap, still devouring his mouth with her own as her hands frantically tore at his T-shirt. It took some skillful maneuvering on his part to lift his arms and still remain kissing her. She laughed, a deep and throaty burr of sound that brushed his skin with pinpricks of excitement.

They pulled apart only long enough to lift their shirts over their heads. Pushing hair out of her eyes, she grabbed on to his zipper next and quickly pulled it down. The sound vibrated like thunder through the room, made his pulse stir and quicken.

Her hands were on his face, dragging him back to her as she pressed her full, naked breasts into his chest. He hissed when her nipples rubbed against his, making him bow with the pleasure. Bending her over, he held on to her back as he tenderly laid her down on the bed.

They were both panting for breath as they stared deep into each other's eyes.

"I can't get enough," she moaned in reluctant admission. "I tasted you out there; it should be enough. It should."

"And yet it's not," he finished her sentence, shushing her with a growl as he once again reclaimed her lips, taking her tongue into his mouth, sucking gently on it over and over.

The frantic beat of her pulse mixed with the way her nails kept gouging into him, it made him mad with desire. Made his vision almost hazy, because all he could see, all he wanted, was her.

"Take the shorts off," he ordered, undoing her zipper.

Grabbing on to the tops of her jean shorts, she shimmied her way out of them, pulling them down her long, lean legs. The satiny feel of naked thigh rubbing against his waist pulled a groan from his lips.

"You're so bonny," he breathed, using her Irish word for "beauty."

Her eyes widened at that term of endearment and then she snorted. "I'm already gonna sleep with you, death; no need to flatter me."

Shaking his head, fighting his own smile, he paused, enjoying the feel of her legs wrapped around his middle, the scent of her desire tickling his nose. "It's not flattery, O'Fallen, it's a simple fact."

Blinking, as if not sure how to take the compliment, she jerked her chin in the direction of his legs. "Not fair that you're still wearing your clothes and I'm pretty much naked."

"Did you know I could do this?" Arching a brow, he pulled on his own inherent magic, willing his clothes, and the scant remains of her own, off their bodies. They were now completely nude and what he hadn't been able to do back at the tree, he did now. Tracing the contours of her body, not only with his eyes, but his hand. Trailing his finger across the tight rosebud of her nipple, moving to the other one, before gently drawing a line down the center of her flat stomach.

Her thighs clenched, hard. If he'd not been immortal himself, the strength of it would have likely bruised muscle. She sighed, arching into him like a cat in heat.

"Bloody hell," she moaned.

Replacing his finger with his mouth, he sucked on her nipple, pulling and rolling it between his teeth. "Good?" he asked as she tugged on the ends of his long hair.

"Different," she said, tossing his words of earlier back at him. He snorted. "So very, very different."

In this case he took "different" to be code for "amazing." Or at least that's what he'd tell himself. With one final flick of his tongue over her breast, he moved down her body.

"Oh my gods," she breathed, "where are you going?"

Planting a wet kiss on her navel, he peered at her from between her thighs. The way her skin was flushed so rosy, darkened at her cheeks, it was a sight he'd thought never to see again.

Mila had awakened a hunger in him, one he hadn't felt in far too long. It could be a side effect of her vampiric hormones run rampant, the way her body signaled to his constantly that she was on a painful stage of arousal, bringing forth his own desire to meet her needs, but it was more too. Her eyes, so beautiful, so perfect. Not because they looked identical to Adrianna's either, not entirely. Talking with her today, sharing her body, he hadn't been this close to another soul in so long, hadn't allowed anyone too deep into his life. He hadn't realized how lonely he'd been until she showed up, until Lise had given him no choice but to keep her, to guard her life with his own.

"What?" She smiled a lazy, graceful smile.

His mouth watered as her scent, the essence of woman, filled his head with a longing so profound it twisted his insides into knots. "I want to taste you. I want all of you, tonight."

He left it unsaid that tonight could be it for them; they both knew it. Heading into faerie tomorrow, it could very well be the suicide mission she feared.

Nibbling on her bottom lip, blond hair splayed out around her head like a golden halo, she nodded. "I've never had anyone do that before," she admitted shyly.

Kissing along the soft flesh of her inner thigh, he worked his way down to her hot center.

"Frenzy?" His name was a question, but he didn't think she was really looking for a response, more excitement and the fear of the unknown trembling on her tongue.

"It's okay," he murmured, trailing just along the juncture of where her thigh and her center met.

She hissed, curling her fingers into his scalp, digging in hard enough to make him groan in response. Unable to resist the temptation anymore, he flicked his tongue over her bright peach nub.

Her head moved violently back and forth as he took her

sensitive clit into his mouth, sucking and rolling it around his tongue.

"Oh my god," she moaned, panting harder. Her knees pressed into the sides of his head.

Chuckling, he gently patted her kneecap. "You're stronger than you know."

Biting onto her knuckle, she laughed. "That feels...oh my god," she said it again, this time pushing off her feet, lifting her lower half, and giving him a better angle. "I'm close."

He lapped at her like a cat with cream, sucking and licking, then using his thumb right on the hood to help her come in an earth-shattering spasm in his mouth.

It took a minute for her to regain herself. He leaned back on his knees, watching her with pride, knowing he'd been the one to bring her to this level of ecstasy. Her fingers played along her stomach as she threw her other arm over her eyes and laughed.

"Wow," she breathed.

And in that moment he saw her, a sexy, beautiful, passionate woman, and the empty place in his heart felt suddenly not so empty. Blinking from between her fingers at him, she smirked, looking down at his raging hard-on.

"Somehow I don't think you're nearly as satisfied as I am."

He didn't want to talk. Didn't want to make chitchat, because something was happening in his chest. Something he'd never thought could happen again. She was coming to mean something to him.

Her shrewish tongue and temper, the way she felt fearless in trading barbs with him. Her bravery in life, being willing to expose her secret to save the life of a little girl. He wasn't sure he liked what he was feeling; it was too overwhelming. He'd lost a lover before, and it'd nearly wrecked him.

She must have noticed something was off with him because, frowning, she sat up and grabbed on to his shoulders. "Frenzy? What's wrong? Did I do something wrong?"

Big, luminous amber eyes stared back at him and he had to swallow to push the stupid lump back down his throat, where it belonged. What in the hell was going on with him?

But he didn't want her thinking his sudden epiphany had anything to do with her lacking in the sexual department. He shook his head.

And he didn't know how she did it, but suddenly light dawned in her eyes and her rosebud lips parted into a tiny *O*. She nodded. "You're remembering her, aren't you?"

Physically they didn't look that much alike. Adrianna had been an English beauty, pale and freckle-faced. He brushed Mila's cheek. "Sometimes your eyes…" he admitted in a scratchy voice.

Hanging on to his hand, she laid a tender kiss on his knuckles. Again the fire was back. That simmering heat he felt any time she touched him. It was a slow burn that would rage out of control the longer he was with her. He knew that, felt it happening all over again.

"Don't worry, Frenzy," she whispered, "I will never try to take her place. You must understand that. Don't panic." She pressed a heated kiss to the side of his neck, right over the throbbing vein, causing his pulse to leap and his cock to grow even more painfully hard. "This is just two grown adults scratching an itch. That's all."

The panic laying siege to his soul slowly began to fade the more she touched and petted and cosseted him. Her clean, beautiful scent filled his head like a drug, making him dizzy with want and need.

Pulling his head against her breast, she patted his hair over and over until finally all that remained was a razor's edge of desperate wanting.

This time she was the aggressor. Crawling onto his lap, she spread her legs, allowing just the tip of his swollen cock to rub against the warm wetness of her. He hissed, digging his fingers into her hips, trying to pull her even closer, while also dragging out the moment as long as possible because he wasn't ready to end it yet and he knew if he entered her, it would be over in a matter of minutes.

"Look at me," she said, framing his hands with her delicate fingers. She bit her bottom lip before running her bright pink tongue along the seam of it. "Do you see me?" she asked.

Shadow and moonlight kissed the planes of her face, revealed the faint freckles scattered along the bridge of her nose. Her wild mane of blond hair framed her delicate heart-shaped face, and he wondered how he could have been so blind in the beginning.

He nodded, hypnotized as her finger grazed his jawline over and over. "I see you."

Her smile was radiant and then there were no more words

as she lowered herself, slowly, inch by torturous inch, down the length of his cock.

Death. A stigma. A blight on the world. That's what his kind was, even within faerie. They did the job no one else wanted to do, but once the job was done, once the kill was over and they were no longer needed, none wanted to be around them.

Adrianna hadn't known what he really was. She'd loved the titled man she'd thought him to be. She'd loved him, he had no doubt, but she'd loved the position in society a marriage with him would have brought too.

Mila stood to gain nothing with him. There was no guarantee he would save her. She'd been a fighter and loner most of her life.

He flexed into her body, seeking and receiving absolution. She was so clean. So pure. Burying his face in her neck, he pumped in and out, hissing at how tight she was, how her inner muscles clenched him like a wet fist. The sensation was incredible and he hissed again, gritting his teeth as his stomach tightened with the first stirrings of climax.

Lifting his face to her lips, she breathed against his mouth. "Give me all of you, death. I can take it."

It was more than he could bear. A rushing tidal wave of energy filled his cock and he squeezed his eyes shut as the very soul of him seemed to drain from his body into hers. She howled, giving in to her animal nature, tossing her head back and looking like some wild Valkyrie of legend as she came, before finally passing out on top of him and breathing heavily.

Breathing easier than he had in decades, he held on to her,

still joined to her body, reluctant to release her just yet. Pushing the hair out of her sparkling eyes, she laughed. "I think I just woke the neighbors."

His lips twitched. "Nearest neighbor is more than twenty miles down the road."

"Did I really just howl? My god, that was"—she snorted adorably and shook her head—"insane. I don't think I've ever howled before."

"You haven't been shifter long. In fact"—he circled the base of her breast with the pad of his thumb—"I think you've definitely got more shifter than vampire in you."

"Oh yeah?" She arched a delicate brow. "What makes you think so?" She kissed his nose before finally standing up from him.

Arms feeling strangely bereft without her in them, he leaned back against the headboard and tucked his hand behind his neck. "You kept sniffing me."

"Sniffing you!" She twirled at the kitchen sink, a look of delight mixed with mortification scrawled tiny laugh lines around her eyes. "I didn't even."

Ready to continue their playful banter, he was silenced when the familiar fire rushed down his left arm, turning his hand to bone. Scowling, he shot up from the bed.

Mila pushed off the counter, looking around. "What's the matter?"

Realizing something had just died, but not sensing the presence of a mortal, Frenzy shook his head.

"What's going on, Frenzy?" she asked in a hushed tone as she walked to him and moved onto a corner of the bed, sitting on her knees as a visible shiver rippled down her spine.

Holding up a finger to his lips, he strode to the front door. This cabin was so isolated it may as well have been on another planet. "Something has died. Stay where you are, I'm going to investigate."

Opening the door, he psyched himself up for whatever might greet him. A full moon cast its luminous light around the front porch, giving everything a hazy lavender appearance. The death was so recent there wasn't an odor of decomposition; the only thing he smelled was rodent.

Frowning, he glanced down on the porch itself and finally chuckled as he stooped over to retrieve the furry body of a squirrel. Lifting it by its tail, he turned to show it to Mila. "Just a squirrel."

Nodding, she smiled back at him, relief evident in her gaze. It took him only a moment to walk the squirrel far enough from his cabin that his hand could then return to flesh.

Coming back inside, he washed up.

"I didn't know your hand turned when there was no human soul to harvest," she said casually.

"Our hands turn whenever we're around death. But it's gone now. I saved the day." He grinned and she laughed.

A second later, eyes twinkling merrily, she said, "Now, about that sniffing thing…I think you're lying."

He snorted, crawling back onto the bed with her. "You did. I think you like my scent, little shifter."

"I think you stink, faerie; you smell like squirrel."

"Stink!" He feigned indignation, then, taking her shoulder, he maneuvered them until she was once again tucked beneath his body, and he was already hard for her again.

He enjoyed this side of her, this laughing, smiling side. It was as if they'd mutually decided to get along. It was refreshing and made him see her in a whole new light.

"Umm. Is that normal?" She peeked down between them, where his cock brushed against her center. Biting her lip (he was recognizing it as a habit of hers when sexually aroused), she wiggled deeper, eliciting a moan from him. "Didn't we just?"

"We did." A wicked grin stole across his lips. "But I'm not human, O'Fallen. Faerie sex is the best sex out there, or hadn't you heard?"

Groaning, she wrapped her arms around his neck. "Good, because I'm still so freaking horny. I thought it was just me."

With a growl, he latched on to the side of her neck with his teeth in a gentle (by immortal standards) bite. "Then let me scratch that itch, shall I?" He swirled his tongue around her fluttering vein.

"Oh gods, yes," she sighed and he slipped inside her, feeling as if the world had finally righted itself.

She was perfection. Her scent, her body, her smiles, her moods, even her sass…He found he liked it all.

They made love into the wee hours of the dawn.

* * *

The Morrigan stared at the shadow as it danced and swayed before her throne. "You killed the butcher. Why?"

The creature hadn't taken on form yet; she was still just an inkblot of shadow. "Because he was useless. The seer is no longer in San Francisco. I did not need him for cover," she hissed. "Where is my morsel, Queen?"

The seething mass of darkness expanded and The Morrigan lifted her head, realizing there was a problem: the creature was growing stronger by the day. Death's kiss hadn't drained her nearly enough; in no time she'd be back to hunting the seer, and The Morrigan couldn't have that.

Knowing her options were limited, the queen knew there was only one way to regain firm control over her creation. As much as the thought rankled.

"Do you even know?" the shadow taunted, her voice like a blast of arctic spray.

Hissing, the queen gripped the rails of her throne and sat forward. "I know where she is. Be prepared."

Standing, The Morrigan strode for the door of her chamber.

"Where are you going?" the shadow demanded.

And then a bolt of raw, sizzling power blasted The Morrigan from behind, a darkness that tried to leech its way inside her. Eyes going wide, The Morrigan wrapped her fists around the darkness trying to worm its way inside and tossed it to the ground.

Twirling, she glared haughtily at her creation. The shadow swayed, giving her a mocking, menacing glare. It'd tried to taste the queen's soul. Had she been stronger, who knew what could have happened then.

"Do not ever think to defy me, shadow; you'll find me to be a much more formidable foe than your puny seers."

"Then get me the girl."

Spine ramrod straight, the queen bit down on her cheek hard enough to draw blood. Revealing her hand too soon would ruin any chance of success for her plan to come to fruition. She gave the shadow a smile of teeth and menace. "Just be prepared for my call."

With that, she walked out to see a woman about a box.

* * *

The woods around the cabin were the murky twilight of predawn when Mila finally emerged from their sex nest. She smirked, her body finally sated after four hours of petting, touching, and moans.

Sometimes it felt like she'd known Frenzy for an eternity. The days of constant bickering and squabbling seemed miles away.

He was lying in the bed still; he'd not wanted her to leave his side, but unlike him she wasn't ready to lie down and close her eyes. The world was too alive, too full of noise to let her rest. There was now no denying that things were definitely changed between them. Good or bad, she wasn't exactly sure. It was odd to her to think where her life was now.

Here she was standing in the center of a crowded redwood forest, staring up at the tree line and waiting for the sun. Vampires couldn't greet the morning, but she wasn't a typical vampire. There was shifter in her too, courtesy of George. At first she'd hated what she'd turned into.

But barefoot and naked, she felt free. The cool air caressed her skin, the gentle berry-laden breeze curled through her hair. Taking a running leap, she jumped into the branch nearest her, at least thirty feet up, and did it with ease. Grabbing on to the corrugated bark, she drew her hand down it over and over, touching it as if for the first time.

Noting that the bark wasn't just rough darkened wood as she'd once viewed it when a human, but that it was also full of life. It was nourishment for the colony of ants that made the tree its home.

She played with the rough texture of the bark, watching as the ants milled in uniform from one knot to the next. A low droning rang in her ears and when she sniffed she smelled the wet mulch of a burrowing grub deep inside.

The velvety navy sky began to gradually turn a light lavender. While she would never have chosen this life for herself, it wasn't altogether terrible either. Now that she finally let it sink in that there'd be no going back, she was determined to make the most of this life. For however long she had it.

Her thoughts drifted to the shadow. This quiet interlude couldn't last, it wouldn't. She knew that. Mila closed her eyes, trying in vain to think of any alternate plan to heading into faerie. But if Frenzy was right, and The Morrigan was the one who'd created the shadow, there really was no choice but to beg her help.

Instantly the feeling of hard eyes on her made her whirl

around in a crouching stance, fingers curved downward with suddenly elongated claws. But what was staring back at her wasn't at all what she'd expected to find.

It took her brain a moment to process that it wasn't the shadow she was staring at, but a woman so breathtakingly beautiful that it was almost unbearable to gaze upon her for long.

Dressed in a robe of midnight silk with thousands of small diamonds inset within it, winking and sparkling as she neared, the woman was hovering in air, not standing on a branch as Mila was, and looking around at the canopy of trees with curious, bright ruby-red eyes.

Her hair was thick, interspersed with threads of red and black. The red gleaming like fire, the black like rich oil. It curled around her oval face becomingly. A patrician nose and full, red lips had Mila realizing this could be none other than The Morrigan herself.

She gasped, opening her mouth and ready to cry out to Frenzy.

"I wouldn't, dear." The Morrigan smiled. But it wasn't a pretty one: it was full of sharp teeth, and the way her lips curled up at the ends made Mila think of the devil incarnate.

The Morrigan could kill her with a whisper of breath. There was none in faerie as awe-inspiring or frightening as the queen of darkness and shadow.

"What…do you want with me?" Mila grabbed her chest, wishing like hell for the millionth time that she could read her future as easily as she could others'. That somehow she could have known the queen was headed her way, that she and Frenzy could have prepared themselves for this.

She blinked, a befuddled look on her face. But Mila wasn't fooled in the slightest; The Morrigan was never confused.

"What I've always wanted with you. Your talents, of course."

"How did you know where to find us?"

"Us?" She quirked a brow. "Quite a proprietary statement. You do realize"—she took another step closer, causing her robe to flare out around her knees—"that Frenzy belongs to me." She tapped her chest with a red-painted nail. "They all belong to me."

Again she gave her a vicious grin of sharp teeth.

There wasn't much Mila would ever back down from; her hot Irish temper rarely allowed it. But even she wasn't stupid enough to tangle with the goddess of strife and war.

"Frenzy is my guardian; it's all I meant by that."

A look of annoyance flashed so quickly across the queen's face that Mila doubted whether she'd seen it at all. Because now the queen looked smug and self-righteous. "I allow him to stay with you out of the kindness of my heart, you see."

Quicker than Mila could track, the queen was no longer standing in front of her, but now she was beside her, and latching on to Mila's shoulders, dragging her nose through her hair and down her neck before setting her quickly aside with a powerful shudder.

"You stink of dog," she hissed. "That stupid cow Lise."

The queen didn't seem to be talking to Mila anymore. Feeling all sorts of violated, even though the woman had only sniffed her, she hugged her arms to her chest and scooted a little bit away, just to put some space between them.

Obviously noticing, she laughed. "Do I scare you, little neophyte?"

She shook her head, tongue glued to the roof of her mouth as she tried to figure out what the queen was doing here.

Frenzy had told her the queen rarely traveled to the human realm. Even she knew if the queen had a message to send she did it through her crows Badb and Nemain. Whatever The Morrigan wanted, she wanted it badly enough to come herself.

She waved her hand as if it was no matter to her one way or another. "Time for truths," the queen said in a sonorous voice that at once boomed and whispered.

The trees, the very world around them, grew heavy and silent. Almost still. Like the world was frozen, except for them. Mila kept casting glances at the cabin, expecting Frenzy to realize his queen stood mere yards from him.

Shouldn't he have some sort of internal beacon when it came to his monarch? Not that she needed him to rescue her; as much as The Morrigan unnerved Mila, she didn't actually feel she was in any sort of danger.

Taking a deep, cleansing breath, she forced herself to think through the panic of having the one immortal she would have rather died a ghastly, brutal death by poisoning than to *ever* see in person standing before her in all her regal glory.

"What truth?"

Doing that snobbish, prim sniff, The Morrigan turned jeweled eyes on Mila. "The Candyman. The vampires that attacked you. Which would you prefer I touch on first?"

"How in the hell do you know all that?" she snapped, not stopping to censor her thoughts.

Waving her fingers with a bored expression, The Morrigan simply rolled her eyes. "Because, my dear, I set the whole damn thing into motion, of course. How could you have not figured that out by now?"

It took a second for the shock to wear off. Well, more like a minute. Because she was pretty sure she'd just heard the queen of faerie admit to siccing the vampires on her, ruining her life with the HPA, and, if she was to be believed, doing something with the Candyman?

Brain a complete muddle, she shook her head. "I don't understand—"

"Of that I am perfectly sure."

It was annoying how beautiful the woman was. How the wind teased through her hair, making it billow behind her like a soft cloud of deepest shadow. How the robe fitted around her amazing body like a glove, showcasing a long, elegant thigh and supple calf. Mila, on the other hand, was very conscious of her disheveled appearance, the scars running along her cheeks, making her look like she wore a permanent and macabre jack-o'-lantern grin.

"I want you, Mila O'Fallen. Is that clear enough for you?"

She shook her head.

"Pay attention," the queen snapped. "Since your dim-witted brain has a difficult time keeping up, listen and don't ask questions."

It took everything she possessed not to snap and at least try to rip the woman's smug head off her milky white shoulders. Breathing deeply, she indicated that the queen should proceed.

"Seventeen years ago I met your gran—"

Mila's eyes nearly bugged out of her head. Her gran had never spoken to either her or her mum about a meeting with the great fae queen.

The queen smiled. This one was pure joy; it made her eyes sparkle with verve. "She had such power. It simply radiated out of her pores. I knew then I must possess her. Possess all of you. I would have cosseted and pampered you; I simply wished to use your powers, not kill you to own them myself."

Mila snorted. "Aye. I'm sure, that's all it was. You'd be the first. You'd have enslaved us."

"Enslavement," she scoffed. "I would have treated you as the queens that you were. All would have groveled and bowed down to you. With the exception of myself, of course. But your gran refused to hear me."

"Bowed and groveled. Forgive me, Queen, but that sounds like a fate worse than death."

"Funny." Her smile said she thought it was anything but. "Those are the exact words your gran used. I couldn't convince her. I tried to go the friendly route, but she refused to hear me."

A cold shiver washed down Mila's spine, and her lips tingled and felt numb as she said, "What do you mean, you tried?"

"Well, dear, when she refused to hear me out, I simply had no choice. I always get what I want. And what I want is a seer in my retinue."

It was hard to swallow—Mila's throat felt suddenly swollen and her tongue too thick for her mouth. Adrenaline flooded her nerves, made her hands jittery. "You created the shadow because of her?"

"No. Because I wanted a seer. It didn't matter who, so long as I got one."

A seer had been born to help humanity, to be the voice of reason and hope within a community. Eons ago, that's the way it'd been. A seer had been as vaunted and respected as any chieftain in any clan. But greed could make even the kindest corrupt. Eventually the monsters that'd sought out their help had suddenly decided that they no longer wanted to pay tithe for the privilege: instead they wanted to enslave and dominate a seer. A seer became a prized possession and commodity, and many a war had been fought over them.

So much so that the women had decided the only way to stop the bloodshed, to stop the fighting, was to slowly allow their bloodlines to die out. At least three of the five lines were already extinct.

"She would not listen to reason. I simply wished to scare her." The Morrigan shrugged as if it was just a minor oops.

But it wasn't. Because if the queen controlled the shadow, then it meant she'd sent that vile creature to kill them.

Mila had been haunted by her family's death, haunted by their screams as first their buttery, golden souls had slipped from their bodies into the demon before it consumed their eyes. The only reason the shadow hadn't found Mila was because gran and mum had used themselves as decoys.

They'd been trapped by the beast in a darkened alley. They'd all been running toward the cathedral, hoping perhaps the sacred soil of the church would prevent the nightmare from stepping foot inside.

Then the screams had come and when she'd turned, she realized they'd turned around and surrendered. Gran's eyes had been huge in her softly lined face. Pleading with her not to come back for them, to keep going, to survive. And she had, at a price.

"You lost control of the beast, didn't you?" She hurled the accusation like a stone.

Hissing, exposing sharp fangs, The Morrigan shoved her face into Mila's. "I lose control of nothing!"

However, the way she said it, Mila didn't really believe it. She shook her head. "You did, Queen. You've lost control."

The queen vibrated, the stench of her anger a palpable offense to Mila's nostrils. Then she was calm and closing her eyes, she shook her head. "I did not lose control. But if the beast sees me coming, she'll know what I'm doing. So it cannot be me."

"Why are you telling me this?"

"Because I still wish to retain a seer and because, whether you believe me or not, I developed a strange sort of respect for your idiotic gran."

Gnashing her teeth seemed the wisest course of action. Because what she really wanted to do right now was wipe that haughty visage off the queen's face and tell her to go straight to hell. The only thing stopping her was the thought that if gran were still alive, she would have beaten Mila to within an inch of her life for even thinking it.

"What about the Candyman? HPA?"

She sighed. "I used them to draw you out."

Rubbing the bridge of her nose, because none of this was adding up, Mila tried to think through this. "But you said you know everything. You should have known where I was?"

It was now the queen's turn to look like she'd been asked to swallow a lemon. Reluctant words came out of her. "I cannot track a seer the way I do others. The patterns of your brain move too randomly and fluidly for me to pinpoint you down to a specific spot."

"Then how did you know I was in San Francisco?"

Staring at her nails, she said, "I can get a feel for a certain location. But you were so clever, so quiet, that it took me forever to figure out where you worked. Once I did, I knew I'd have to create a case in which HPA would be required to use your services more frequently than normal."

"Who is the Candyman?"

"Just some pervert I extracted from the loony bin."

This still wasn't adding up. "How does the shadow fit into all this?" Mila knew from working the case that the Candyman and the shadow were working together, but she could never figure out why.

"The shadow is a clever little wench," the queen hissed. "If she'd seen me at all she would have known what my ultimate endgame really was."

"To find me for yourself."

"Aye," she said without an ounce of remorse. Not that Mila had expected her to show any—the queen wasn't exactly known for her graciousness.

"So you did what? Fed intel to the Candyman?"

"You make it sound as if that was a bad thing." She lifted a brow. "I needed to find you."

How in the name of all that was holy could The Morrigan not recognize that what she'd done had been an abominable thing? "Do you realize how many lives you ruined? How many women died for the perversions of that twisted freak?"

Tucking her hands behind her back before she throttled a queen, Mila mentally counted to ten. The Morrigan looked perplexed by her outburst, which only pissed her off more.

"They would have died anyway. They were mortals," she finally said, as if it made all the sense in the world and Mila was too dense to figure it out herself.

"Oh my god!" She slapped her forehead. "Do you honestly think you're endearing yourself to me with this load of shite? You let loose not only one, but two monsters. If you can't see that as heinous, then—"

The queen laughed, but it wasn't pleasant. It was an angry, scornful sound. "I'm not here to make friends with you, neophyte. Do you honestly think I care at all what you think of me?" she scoffed, tossing her hair over her shoulders. "I'm here because that damn meddlesome Lise ruined my plans and now I must rectify it."

Gods, the woman was amazing. How could she sit here and laugh and act as if Mila were the one in the wrong? Had she lost all her humanity, all her…and then it dawned on Mila: the queen had never possessed any.

She was a faerie. An immortal, one used to viewing humanity as little more than a nuisance. The same way Frenzy had viewed her when they'd first met. Just when she'd begun to find the positives in this life, she was once again faced with the brutal, stark ugliness of it as well. Would this be her someday? Did Frenzy even care for her? If this was how he really thought, then just what had they been doing all day yesterday? Was it all just a game to him?

That the queen was able to toss away a few lives for the sake of her endgame because humans meant nothing? It made her sick.

"I will not help you."

"Oh, but you will." She nodded and the air rushed with the shiver of a thousand sparks. It rippled along her flesh like a low, burning fire. "I'm not asking, I'm telling you."

"How did you find me?"

"What?" The queen's brows gathered, as if she was confused by Mila's sudden change of subject.

"You said you couldn't find me; how did you this time?"

"Frenzy belongs to me, darling. How else do you think I found you? Any time a reaper's hand turns to bone I can find them. It happened to him last night, did it not?" Her look was so knowing and damn smug it made Mila want to vomit.

"But Lise—"

The Morrigan's face contorted into a frightening mask. "Lise, that bitch," she spat. "The woman oversteps her bounds. Death is mine and always shall be. You have one way out of this mess,

Mila. I will give you the same choice I gave your gran."

"Work for you or have my soul ripped out of me? That it?" she snapped, at her wits' end with the haughty beauty.

"In a word, yes."

Mila opened her mouth, ready to rip the queen a bloody new one, when she held up a finger.

"And before you tell me to go to hell, remember that I can make Frenzy's life a torment."

It was on the tip of her tongue to deny that there was anything between her and Frenzy, that The Morrigan had anything on her. But after what they'd shared last night, the truths that'd passed between them, it would be a horrible lie.

"If you want your freedom from that devil, then take this." The queen shoved a black box that'd materialized from thin air into Mila's chest.

Grabbing it, she looked down at the heavily lacquered box. It was cool to the touch and gleamed with a strange luminescence when sunlight hit it a certain way.

"And what am I to do with this?" She held up the palm-sized box. "Toss it at its head?"

Covering the box with her hand, the queen glared at Mila. "It is simple. Get close enough with the lid open, the rest will take care of itself. There is more power inside that box than in an ounce of plutonium. Don't make me regret helping you. Wait for the shadow; I will send her soon."

And with that, the queen of air and darkness was gone.

Chapter 12

Frenzy stared at the box sitting on the kitchen table. "The queen was here? She gave you this?"

His mouth tasted of sawdust. Death had no need of sleep. And yet, he could remember nothing in the hours that Mila said she'd been outside speaking with his queen.

He felt her eyes on him, burning like questioning embers. Frenzy looked up. "What did she want?"

Yanking the pale pink shirt he'd bought her yesterday over her head, she brushed back her hair with her fingers as best she could before shrugging. "As best as I can tell, she wants me to somehow stop the shadow with that." She pointed at the innocuous-looking piece of wood.

But he knew better than most that power wasn't measured by the beauty or worth of an object; the most powerful usually rested within an object easily overlooked. Picking up the minia-ture jewelry box, he cracked open the lid. The inside was cov-ered in dark velvet. On the surface there was nothing extraordinary, but there was a definite tingle of power emanating from within the object. It hummed along his skin like electrical static.

"What is it?" she asked in a hushed tone.

"If I had to guess, this is a containment device."

Nibbling on her thumbnail, she eyed it speculatively.

Setting the box down precisely where it'd been, he gripped onto the kitchen chair. "The queen does nothing without an interest being met. What did you offer her?"

It didn't seem in keeping with what he knew of Mila to think she'd ever knowingly work alongside the queen. It made him sick to his stomach that he'd been unaware of her presence. Yes, they'd been considering heading into faerie today, but that was with him to guard her. To keep her presence hidden from the masses, to protect her. She'd been alone with the queen of darkness. The thought of it made his blood run cold.

Rubbing the back of her mouth with her hand, she shook her head. She looked tired. Not so much in her actual appearance, but the vitality of her flesh now looked muted, the whites of her eyes were bloodshot, and she kept pinching the bridge of her nose.

"I didn't offer her anything. But she definitely wants something."

She didn't even have to say it—Frenzy already knew what the queen wanted. The same thing she'd always wanted.

Power.

And this seer was that.

Tunneling blunt fingers through his bed head, he growled, "Did she say anything else?"

She nodded. "Aye. She said she'll be sending the shadow our way."

Pushing away from the chair so hard he caused it to rock back and forth on its legs, he strode to the bed and began hastily dressing. "We're leaving."

She looked around. "Where?"

"We're going to the X."

Her eyes widened. "To Lise's club? That's in the heart of San Francisco. Now that my cover's been blown—"

"Your image isn't plastered all over the city. If we go in under the cover of darkness you shouldn't have anything to worry about. And I'll be there." Walking up to her, he grazed her cheek with the pad of his thumb. "I'll keep you safe. I vow it."

Clutching onto his wrist with both of her hands, she took a deep breath.

"It's the only way. We cannot stay here until The Morrigan sets the shadow on us. The queen does nothing out of the kindness of her heart. We have to discover her true motivation. Only then can we formulate any kind of plan."

Nibbling on her bottom lip, she made his heart clench in his chest because she looked so innocent, almost fragile. Bringing out a masculine need to guard and protect, he clipped his head. "We'll be fine," he said with determination, but he wasn't sure whether he was saying it more for her benefit or his own.

"I trust you, death," she finally said. "Do I have time to at least brush my teeth?"

Brushing his lips gently over hers, he nodded. "Go ahead. It'll take me a quick second to pack up our stuff and ward the cabin again."

In no time he had what few clothes and personal items they'd collected gathered up and was walking outside to reactivate the wards built into the frame of the house.

He pressed his palm against the heated section of wood, his touch activating the magic, his power radiating like a spider's web from the center of the ward, branching outward and encasing the cabin. Quickly he moved around the last three sections, ensuring that the individual threads twined, forming a net over the entire structure.

Done with his task, he leaned against the wall, staring out at the woods. They'd been on the run from the moment he'd met her. It seemed like a lifetime ago. They hadn't known many seconds of peace, except here. Deep in the redwood forest, where their only neighbors were squirrels and the occasional black bear.

His mouth turned down into a frown. This had been her whole life, running from one safe spot to the next until her cover was blown and she was forced to start fresh all over again.

She'd blossomed out here, laughed, and touched something cold and hollow in his heart. Made him feel again. He wanted better for her than this, wanted to make things right.

It was too early in the day to head to Lise's yet, but they couldn't stay here either. Not with The Morrigan planning on sending the shadow here.

"You ready?" she asked in the throaty, sultry morning voice he was coming to crave hearing.

She'd pulled back her hair, exposing the sharp slashes of cheekbone and dark hollows beneath her bloodshot eyes. She needed to eat again. Even the shirt and shorts she'd filled out nicely just yesterday now seemed to hang on her frame. It frustrated him how little he knew how to take care of her. Lise and George had been correct when they'd accused him of losing touch with the world he now lived in.

She shivered, staring over her shoulder at the cabin. "I don't know what just happened, but all of sudden I want to get away from this place. Feels creepy as hell."

"It's the wards," he said distractedly.

She must have noticed his tone, because she turned to him sharply. "What's the matter? Did you see something?" Her eyes scanned the perimeter.

The thundering pitch of her sluggish heartbeat vibrated through his ears. "You need to eat."

She curled her nose. "I'm not hungry."

"Then if you're not hungry, you need to drink, don't you?"

Grimacing, she wrapped her arms tight around her chest as her tongue poked out, touching her gum line. Closing her eyes, she didn't answer.

"Should I find an animal?"

"No," she said in loudly accented Irish. "I don't want to drink from an animal." Her eyes were bright, almost fevered looking.

"A human?" He raised a brow. What little he knew of the vampires, he understood that the best source of food came straight from their preferred marks. Mortals.

Her nose curled. "I won't do that either."

She'd enjoyed drinking from him the other day. Perhaps he could convince her to take from him again. Stepping into her space, wrapping his hands around her waist, he tilted his neck to the side. "Then take from me."

Hunger scrawled across her face, and her irises bled through and slitted like a cat's. The smell of her desire was a heady musk in his nostrils and it increased his own desire for her to tap into him. Planting a quick kiss against the hollow of her neck, he whispered, "I can smell your desire."

She was trembling in his arms, he could feel her latent power roiling throughout her frame, like holding on to a live wire that was seconds from exploding. She lowered her head, and her heated breaths licked his flesh, made him shiver in anticipation of the pain and pleasure.

"No." She shoved him back, shaking her head several times. "No," she said again, more powerfully. "Biting into your flesh"—she swallowed hard—"my teeth are blunt. I'm just chewing at your throat...It's"—her upper lip curled back—"repulsive."

Mila said that, but he sensed that she enjoyed it more than she felt she should.

"You have to eat." Calling forth his change, he turned his hand bony then touched the tip of it to his carotid. If she wouldn't bite him, he'd open the vein himself.

"Stop it, Frenzy." She slapped his hand away. "I'm not going to feed off you. No more."

"Why not?" he growled, glaring at her.

"Because when I do I want it more. I want so much more. And I don't want to lose myself. Don't you understand? I don't want to become a monster with no conscience. I accept what I am, but I don't want to lose my ability to view people as people rather than food." Her words were pleading and so heartfelt he couldn't help but understand.

Even if he didn't agree.

"There are vampires who can make the feeding something to be desired by a mortal. You do not have to drain them. And I do not care if you feed on me; I enjoyed it."

"Well, you shouldn't. I ripped into you with my blunt stupid teeth. I can't even pierce, Frenzy. What is to enjoy about that experience?"

"You have to eat," he said again, stubbornly.

"Fine!" She tossed up her hands. "I'll go find a squirrel." So saying, she took off.

She wasn't as fast as she typically was when in full strength, but they were putting miles between themselves and the cabin at the very least. They ran for hours and, sensing that she was trying to put distance between them, he paced her, but far enough back that while she'd know he was around, she wouldn't have to see him.

Eventually, after five hours of running, she finally stopped, panting heavily against the trunk of a tree. "I'm sorry," she admitted.

Realizing it was now safe for him to show himself, he stopped just to the side of her. He'd had hours to think about what this might be. More than just the food, or the feeding methods she'd have to employ, this was about the queen and how shaken she'd been.

"You're spooked, Mila."

Her gaze shot to his, and though her face looked haggard and worn, there was a sparkle of surprise in their depths as well. "You called me Mila," she whispered.

Only because he'd wanted her full attention, and now he'd gotten it. Unable to resist touching her, he caressed her jawline. Her skin was hot to the touch and paper dry. He nodded. "Understand that going without eating will not kill you. It will only make you crazed."

She squeezed the trunk of the tree, splintering sections of bark off in her hands. "I know. I ate the steak last night. I loved it, so why do I crave blood? Why is it when I blink all I see is red?" Her breathing stuttered. "The queen found me through you," she finally whispered.

Grabbing her by the shoulders, he pulled her into his chest, patting her spine up and down, soothing her as best he could. "Was that why you were angry with me?"

"I wasn't…" She sighed. "I'm not angry with you, Frenzy. It's just…" She sniffed, shaking her head against his shirt. "I don't want to run anymore."

His brows dipped. "Are you considering doing the queen's bidding?"

It took a minute for her to answer. "I don't know what I'm thinking."

Just then a chirping sound caught his attention. Looking up, he spotted a bushy red tail disappearing around a branch. "I'm going to get you food. You're weak and you need to drink."

Disengaging herself, she leaned heavily against the trunk of the tree. "I'm always apologizing to you. I'm sorry, Frenzy. None of this is your fault; sometimes it's just easier to let my temper get the best of me than to cry."

Tipping her chin up, he gazed into her eyes, eyes that he no longer compared to Adrianna's. She was Mila; he saw her. He finally saw her and now that he did, he wasn't going to let her go, not without a fight.

"No more. You hear me?" He lifted a brow. "You have a problem, you talk to me. You do not run away."

She nodded, and then sealed that with a kiss. Taking his lips in a short but sweet exploration, knocking the breath from his body.

When they pulled back he was at a loss for words, and with one final look of adoration he jumped, landing gracefully on a thick branch. Closing his eyes, he listened. It would be so much simpler to breathe death into the tree, but it would kill the squirrel, and it was vital Mila was able to tap into a living source.

The faint chatter of not one, but two squirrels pricked his senses. It would be easier to come from behind the animals than to pursue them like a stalking predator. Opening a rift in time, he stepped inside, quickly triangulating their position in relation to where his had been. Something he'd done all his life.

Stepping out, he snatched up the rodents by their tails, careful to not allow any part of death to leak into their bodies. They went wild, nipping and clawing at him, making him wish for a second they weren't much-needed food, because he was sorely tempted to wring their necks.

When he returned to Mila, she looked even worse. She was sitting with her arms draped over her knees and her head hanging down.

"Here." He handed her the nearly rabid creatures.

Even the way she turned to look at him made it seem like she'd expended a lot of effort. "I…can't," she croaked.

"Damn it, O'Fallen!" he barked. "You will eat." Setting one of the squirrels down, he planted his foot on its tail to keep it from running, then, calling forth his own glamour—the magic inborn—he turned his own teeth to fangs and pierced the furry animal's neck.

It whimpered and spun in his hands pitifully as it fought in vain to get away. Tipping Mila's head up, he shoved the squirrel into her mouth, letting gravity work as it forced the blood down her throat.

At first she was pliant, but after three seconds she grabbed on to the squirrel herself and sucked deeply. Color returned to her cheeks. Not a lot, but she no longer looked mummified.

When she pulled it out, the creature was obviously dead. "More." Her lashes fluttered.

Deciding she could probably handle the next one, he passed it along to her. But just as she had with him, Mila's frenzied bite ripped out of the poor animal's neck. Groaning, she lapped at the mess she'd made. Blood was all over her previously pink shirt. But even as she sucked up the blood, shame spread across her face. Her mouth turned downward and she shifted on her bottom, trying to turn away from him.

Deciding he didn't want to humiliate her, he turned on his

heel, giving his back to her and hopefully giving her enough time to try and right the mess she'd made.

"You…you can turn." She whispered after a few minutes.

When he did, his jaw dropped. She'd stripped the shirt off and was now only in a sexy red bra. His nostrils flared, heat pooled thick into his gaze, and he wanted her to see it. Wanted her to know that he didn't view her as a monster or as something vile.

She wiped the back of her mouth with fingers. Holding up the bloody shirt, she twisted her lips. "It was dirty."

"It's okay." He grabbed it from her and tossed it to the ground. "We'll get another."

She merely chuckled, but didn't respond back. "Can we head to Lise's now?"

Glancing up at the darkening sky, he nodded. "It'll be night soon. We're safe to head into the city. Are you okay, though? Do you need more?"

"No." She shook her head quickly, tucking a loosened strand of hair behind her ear. "I'm satisfied."

She was too quick with her words, which made him wonder whether she was lying.

"Really." She smiled and it was dazzling. Her skin looked flushed and pearly again.

Holding out his hand, he said, "Then are you ready?"

Looking down at her half-nude self, she laughed ruefully. "Since I can't go back for a shirt, I suppose I'm as ready as I'll ever be."

* * *

She hadn't wanted to tell him the truth. The animal's blood, while it'd been warm and delicious going down, was settling wrong in her stomach. It called to mind the deer she'd taken from and what had happened afterward. Was she allergic to animal blood? As much as it'd disgusted her to feed from the animal, she knew Frenzy was right. She had to feed. But her stomach was not adjusting well to her most recent meal.

She didn't have this reaction when she drank from Frenzy.

He was like a god among men, and his blood had been ambrosia. She had a feeling drinking from him would never be the same as drinking from anything else, even a human. And as much as she'd craved more, yearned for it to the point that she'd nearly attacked during sex last night, she'd refrained.

She hadn't lied when she'd told him that it'd been too good. The only comparison she had for it was like someone taking a hit of heroin for the first time. Her senses had flooded, her mind had been clearer, sharper; and the taste of him, like champagne.

Gods.

It'd been so overwhelming, made her feel ravenous, and for a split second the thought had crossed her mind that being an immortal, she could drink and drink and drink her fill of him, knowing he'd never die.

But she knew something about vampires, something he didn't seem to be aware of. The more they took from the same source, the weaker that source would eventually become—*even* if they drank from immortals. She could literally suck all vitality out of him to the point that he would live only to be her food.

Faerie were strong, and there was a lot yet she didn't know about him. It was entirely possible that she couldn't trance him that way. But she had no real way of knowing since she'd never heard of a fae offering himself up to the avarice of the vampire. It just wasn't worth the risk.

His thumb rubbed circles at the base of her back. She shivered, clutching him tight. The trip through space and time wasn't as scary this time around as it'd been the first, but it was long, only helping to increase her dread of stepping foot back in that city.

"Are you okay?" he asked, his lips close to the shell of her ear, which made her stomach curl with sexual longing so fierce she had to shut her eyes and count to ten before trusting herself to speak.

"I'm fine."

Silver eyes stared at her, as if knowing she was lying. He knew; he wasn't a fool. But he also didn't push it, and for that she was grateful. In fact, there was a lot about Frenzy that she liked.

He wasn't at all what she'd expected when she'd first met him. It made her ashamed of how she'd treated him in the beginning. Cuddling into his warmth as much as possible, she leaned her head against his shoulder.

The starry tunnel they'd been traveling through suddenly turned opaque and, like a mirage in a dessert, it looked like they were staring through a sheet of shimmering heat. Objects on the other side manifested. A green Dumpster, potholes full of brackish water, brownstone apartments with fire escapes.

Frenzy hissed. "What the hell is this?"

After that, everything happened so quickly. Like an invisible giant grabbed hold of her and snatched her out of his arms, dumping her into the alleyway head over feet. Realizing instantly that they'd likely been ambushed, she swallowed the scream in her throat, landing like a cat on all fours, sniffing and scouting her surroundings.

When they'd left the woods dusk had just been starting. But the way the streetlamps hit the paved sidewalks and the absolute stillness and quiet of the usually teeming streets meant it was well past midnight.

Licking her lips, she scuttled behind the Dumpster and scented the air. There was nothing, literally no one. Where was she? This was San Francisco, but something felt very wrong, off.

"Frenzy?" she squeaked. So quiet it was more of a whisper, every flight or fight instinct inside of her was going off like the sound of a raging klaxon horn.

After five minutes, some of the panic began to wear off, helping her to think more clearly. When it did, it dawned on her that the ache in her stomach as they'd been traveling through the tunnel was definitely more intense, squeezing her intestines in a tight fist. Swallowing the bile trying to work its way back up her throat, she squeezed her eyes shut and tried to breathe through the churning nausea.

Grabbing on to her stomach, she inhaled and told herself that now was not the time to be sick. But as much as she damned herself to hell and back, her brain refused to believe that what she was feeling was all in her head. Her body suddenly broke out in a wash of sweat. Her limbs shook, a malaise unlike any she'd ever known took hold of her, and, dropping her to her knees, she threw up everything she'd just drunk.

When it was over, all she wanted to do was sleep. For an eternity. Close her eyes and never open them again. Her head was full of fuzz, her mouth tasted terrible, and her ears were ringing.

She rolled onto her side, and her breathing slowed to a crawl. It was so hard to think about anything other than the exhaustion lancing through her bones, piercing her skull. Closing her eyes, ready to give in to the sleep that beckoned, she finally heard something.

A heated whisper of conversation. "Are you sure this is where she was going to be dropped?" a deep voice rumbled.

Frowning, she tried to focus.

"Aye," an obviously female voice snapped, "the reaper's route was redirected. She'll be here."

"Nailia, you know what Frenzy will do. You've seen his—" The male sounded anxious.

"If you're going to act like a whiny little bitch about this, Tronos," Nailia hissed, "then you can return to the queen and tell her why you failed." Her words dripped venom and spite.

Bloody hell, the queen had done this?

Mila blinked, trying to force her body into action. Slowly, inch by painful inch, she crawled backward on her hands until she was kneeling, panting heavily from the exertion used.

Somehow they hadn't sensed her, but neither could she sense them. If she hadn't heard them speaking she would never have known they waited just beyond the alley for her. As she took the wind into her lungs, the only things she smelled were rotten garbage and a hint of roses...

Then she frowned. Realizing what an idiot she'd been. Frenzy smelled of summer, of trees and flowers in bloom. Here in the middle of this dump she smelled roses.

The fae, they smelled of nature.

Looking up the walls of the apartments blocking her in on three sides, she knew she could jump to the rooftop. But what if there were more up there?

Why had the queen done this? She worried her bottom lip. How had she known that Frenzy and Mila would come back here?

Had everything the queen said been a lie? What was the box? Was it even anything? When they'd spoken this morning the queen had made her believe that she'd regretted the creation of the shadow almost as much as Mila did. But what if that wasn't true? What if the queen actually did control that beast and was even now letting it stalk closer and closer to her?

Squeezing her eyes shut, wishing like hell Frenzy was close—she realized just how much she actually did need him. She'd always prided herself on being able to handle anything.

"We can't just hang around here all night; the queen expects results," Tronos whined.

"Gods, brother," Nailia scoffed, "you are such a disappointment. The chit is going to be weak from no food."

Mila could literally hear the vicious smile curl through her words. It made an icy shiver rush down her spine.

How did they know she hadn't eaten?

"We bring her bait?" Tronos said in an "aha" tone.

"Exactly. Bring her bait," Nailia crooned.

The way she said it, with that lilt in her tone, it made Mila's skin crawl. She needed to find some way of escape; this couldn't be it. She wouldn't let it. Making her way painfully slowly to her feet, she gripped onto the edge of the green Dumpster, curling her fingers in so hard the metal began to dent. She wasn't nearly as strong as she'd been, but she still had some strength. Not much, but maybe there was enough to get out of this mess.

Scanning the buildings one more time, she noted the nearest fire escape was at least twenty feet up. All her life her gran and mum had taught her that the way to winning was to holding on to the one thing she didn't want to live without. To fight for something.

When she'd been alive, she'd fought for pride. Fought to prove that her gran's and mum's deaths hadn't been in vain.

Then she'd met Frenzy, seen his fire and passion, the way he touched her, looked at her. How he'd tell her over and over that she wasn't alone…He'd given her something she hadn't had ever.

Hope.

Crouching low, she clung to that like a lifeline and willed her exhausted limbs to work one last time. Even if there were other fae waiting for her atop the roofs, at least she'd fought, at least she hadn't stood here and waited to die.

But just as she was set to make that leap, she smelled something that sent shards of ice through her soul. Fresh, sweet, and tangy. The smell of blood. And, gods, it was heavenly. The scent of it crawled up her nose, infiltrated every thought or reason, made her unable to think about the fact that even now the fae were closing in.

That the thudding, beating heartbeat exciting her nerves to a fever pitch was most definitely the bait set out for her. That not only could she smell the blood, she could smell the fear of the human. The panting and sweating musk sliding out of his pores. It was primal, elemental. This was what she'd been created for.

What she was destined to be. A monster. The hunger grew and stretched malignant fingers deep inside her emaciated gut, whispering over and over that this was right, good, that she could not deny her nature any longer.

Eyes rolling in her skull, she took a tentative step out from behind the Dumpster. The fluttering beat of that heart was like a siren's call, and where she'd been weak just seconds ago, a new surge of power filled her limbs.

The last dregs of her energy she'd saved to jump to freedom were now being used for one thing. Finding food.

A hunter's instinct took over. Jumping against the wall, she dug her fingers into the brick, ripping into it like a hot knife sliding through butter. She was suddenly strong, sure. She was power; the mortal would die.

"Die," she hissed, surveying the empty alley, stealthily moving, making sure to keep to the shadows so as not to alert her prey.

Mouth watering, she walked to the very edge of the alley and peeked her head around the building.

The two fae were standing upon a stoop. She recognized them immediately by the blast of roses in her nostrils. The man had long hair, falling down to his ankles. It was a blond that looked spun from moonlight. The female also had the same kind of hair. He was dressed in long black trench coat; she was in black leather and boots. Their faces were the same haughty, gorgeous ones she'd come to associate with the fae. Long, patrician noses, perfectly sculpted lips, and both with glowing blue eyes. The same kind of eyes she'd seen on the vampire who'd turned her.

Obviously they were twins, and it quickly crossed her mind that here was the proof the queen had indeed been in on it from the very beginning. When she'd first seen the vampire she'd had a fleeting memory of something odd about his eyes, but had quickly dismissed it since she was fighting for her life. Now she remembered mum had shown her a book once. A very old book that spoke of pledging one's soul and honor to the queen of fae and how that pledge was sealed within the eyes, turning them an electric, shocking blue.

The queen had confessed to that this morning, but in hindsight Mila felt stupid that she hadn't recognized it immediately.

The fae struggled with the woman in his arms.

A terrified human woman. Her brunette hair was caught up in a stylish chignon. She wore a polished plum business skirt suit with nude pumps. She obviously worked out. Her body was trim, lithe, and sleek.

Mila licked her lips, already tasting the salty sweetness, already feeling the glorious thickness of that crimson tide rush down her throat. She licked aching gums as her stomach groaned painfully, making her dizzy and breathless with hunger.

Studying the layout, she realized quickly that there were only the two fae. There were none on the rooftops, but it no longer mattered, because running away was not her priority. Getting to her food first was now the obsession.

However there was no way to snatch the woman and run. She'd be caught, likely taken by the queen's bitches.

She snarled.

Famished as she was, going down that way pissed her off. The queen had set her up. But the hunger was making it hard to care.

Just then an image of gran's face popped into her head. Her big, beautiful brown eyes pleading with Mila to make their sacrifice worth it. She'd be so ashamed of her now.

Breathing heavily through her nose and mouth, she tried to beat back the beast demanding the kill.

Dragging her head back and forth against the rough brick surface, she prayed for clarity. Prayed for a miracle. Her resolve was weakening by the second.

Frenzy was right: she should have fed. Should have taken from him, just once more.

She jerked to the right as the soft scratching sound of shuffling footsteps pounded through the window to the right of her. Sliding away from the edge of the building, she crawled over to the window, peeking inside.

There was a man inside.

And he was staring right back at her, terror wide in the stark whites of his eyes.

Everything went blank. She stopped thinking, stopped empathizing, because he was close and he smelled like food. A switch had flipped inside her soul, shutting off who she was, who she'd been trying to be. She wasn't Mila, she was a monster, a vampire shifter, and she was ravenous.

Smiling, she tapped on the window. "Hello, mortal," she breathed, and he turned on his heel to run just as she punched her fist through the glass.

With a loud cry, she chased after him, tackling him to the ground just a few feet away.

Wrapping him up, she rolled him over and then proceeded to coo in his ear, "Hush, hush, it will only hurt but a minute. Hush now..."

Then she bit.

Chapter 13

Frantic with worry, it'd taken Frenzy a minute to catch his bearings. To realize he'd been dumped at the far end of Fisherman's Wharf, the opposite direction from Club X. The moment he'd seen the chimera (the spelled, wavering illusion) netted across the exit from their time jump, he'd known it was The Morrigan.

He'd been an idiot to believe she wouldn't have covered her bases, wouldn't have set up traps in case they attempted to contact the Ancient One. Mila had been ripped from his arms, but not before he'd used his glamour to keep her scent hidden from the *others*.

He would have cloaked her in invisibility as well, if he'd only had enough time. But it had been all he could manage before she was gone and he was roaring into the night. When he'd obscured her scent, he'd also left a marker on her, one he could track. It would be so much easier to get to her by time jumping, but likely anywhere he tried to jump in San Francisco would result in the same scenario: him being dumped out at precisely the opposite spot of where he wanted to be, so he had to track her trail the old-fashioned way.

There was the equivalent of a beacon on her, one only he could hear. The fainter it got, the farther he was, the louder, the closer.

The noise was earsplitting now.

Gaze wandering all along the rows of houses, Frenzy ran. But some instinct, some knowledge of her, made him stop. Her sweet scent of frost and rich earth tickled his nose.

She was in one of the buildings.

He was just getting ready to ascend a set of stairs to his left when a scream, so steeped in terror, set his teeth on edge.

It was a male voice. Turning, he practically flew to the door and yanked it open.

That's when he saw the pale-haired twins Tronos and Nailia. They were a flight above him and headed directly for the source of the screams.

He knew immediately they were after Mila. A frenzy like he hadn't felt in centuries overcame him. A blinding, black rage that took hold of all his senses. There was only one thought consuming him, and that was getting to her first.

Bounding up the steps, he leaped like a jungle cat.

Nailia glanced down first. She hissed. "Tronos, death is upon us! You must stop him. I will get to her."

She might as well have called for his head, because Frenzy's focus shifted entirely to her. It didn't faze him when Tronos landed on his back, when his hands wrapped around his neck, or when the fae squeezed so hard that it made spots appear.

Because that was secondary to stopping Nailia. To saving his woman.

Heart thundering like the galloping hooves of a stallion in his chest, he shoved his bony hand into the side of Tronos's neck.

The scent of crisp autumn apples flooded the stairwell as the fae's blood spilled. But a fae was much harder to kill than that; merely cutting an artery wouldn't do it. Suddenly a dagger appeared in his line of vision, and then a pricking in his side as Tronos stabbed him.

Adrenaline buzzed through his body like an angry hornet's nest as he forced his feet to take two steps at a time, breathing heavily because of the burden of carrying another body.

Nailia was so close to the door.

To his woman, his world.

"Mila!" he roared, when for a split second Nailia turned, big blue eyes darting quickly at him before turning the knob.

Fury gripped him. Swatting at the hand that continued to stab into his side, Frenzy grabbed Tronos by the neck, sliding him off his back and in front of him.

"If anything happens to my woman," he growled, "I swear by all that is holy that I will haunt you even after death."

"The Morrigan made us, Frenzy. You must believe me—"

But Frenzy did not give him time to finish his statement: with a flick of his wrist he'd twisted the fae's head off, and to ensure that there would be no reviving it, he pressed the soundless lips to his own, breathing death's dark kiss into Tronos's brain.

Dropping the head like a sack of stone down the stairwell, he ran for Mila, gasping when he reached the door. Inside there was chaos and madness. Blood was everywhere. Mila stood before a male's body, crouching on the balls of her heels and her hand as she walked spiderlike around Nailia, who was desperately trying to grab ahold of her wrist and yank her through the portal between the here and there.

Fear beat desperate wings in his chest. All he knew was that if Nailia grabbed Mila, he'd never see her again. The queen had overstepped her bounds this time. She'd lied to Mila, lied to him—any fledging love he'd once held for her died an insidious death.

"Frenzy," Mila cried, eyes lighting up with a fever-pitched excitement, enough to help ease some of the darkness creeping through his soul.

To help him remember that he wasn't the beast of legend anymore, that his woman was alive and well and waiting for him, it brought him back from the brink of no return.

That's when Nailia turned, eyes gone wide. "What did you do to Tronos? You've overstepped yourself, Frenzy. The queen will have your head, she will—"

With a snarl, he had his hands around her neck. "Mila, you might wish to look away," he thundered, barely able to restrain his need for violence. To hurt every last thing that'd ever tried to hurt her.

His blond priestess shook her head. Taking that to mean that she wouldn't try to hinder him, he torqued on Nailia's head and, just like her brother's, ripped it from her shoulders.

Faerie did not bleed out, because unlike most other creatures, the only true way to end a fae was to either have it be done by the queen's hand, or feel death's kiss.

It was why even amongst the fae a grim reaper was so hated.

Bringing cold lips to his own, he shoved the kiss inside her brain, dropping her like stone to the floor.

A second later Mila was in his arms, trembling and acting like she wanted to crawl into him.

"Shh, shh." He rubbed her hair, peppering her forehead with kisses. "I'm here. You're fine. We're fine. We're fine."

The last was definitely said more for his benefit than hers, as right now he felt anything but fine. He'd almost lost her. Adrianna's death had nearly ruined him; Mila's would kill him.

He'd learned one unsettling truth today: he loved her. Somehow, someway, she'd slithered her way into his cold, dark heart and he could never be without her. Adrianna had loved him in her way, as much as a woman of her day set on making a quality love match could. Mila accepted him for the being that he was.

Adrianna had never known his true identity. The reason why the lord of the manor was always away on business trips—not because he was out in gaming hells, but because at night he'd be cleaning up the city. Carrying souls into the afterlife.

At the time he thought he could deal with an arrangement like that. Could be happy to just spend his days with a woman in his arms, but now he knew better. What he'd felt for Adrianna had been absolutely nothing compared to what he would do to keep Mila by his side.

"I'm sorry…I…I…" she stuttered.

Realizing she was going into shock over the violence she'd perpetrated, Frenzy tipped her jaw up to his. They had to get out of here. There was the very definite possibility that the queen could be making an unplanned visit any second now. Especially since her latest plan had failed.

But he'd almost lost her; he needed her touch as much as she needed his.

Taking her lips in a swift but almost violent kiss, he tasted and loved on her. Just the touch of her set his body on fire, made his blood roar in his ears.

"It's okay," he whispered again, pressing a much gentler kiss on her forehead. "We're together and I'll tell you everything, but we have to get out of here. We don't have much time to get to Lise's."

She nodded, and as much as he didn't want her to, he helped her disentangle herself from him, setting her on her feet.

Amber eyes studied him. "You're hurt?" she said in a neutral tone, as if she were still in shock.

Worried more for her than himself, he shook his head. "I'm fine, Mila. I'll heal."

Gingerly she touched the wound in his side. He swallowed the hiss he wanted to expel and smiled instead. He was healing; another few minutes and the wound would be closed. Only a beating by his queen could leave lasting damage—reapers could heal from almost anything.

Brushing a stray hair off her shoulder, he took one last look at the nearly expired body of the mortal on the ground, almost certain she had caused that to happen because of her lack of feeding earlier. If he stayed too much longer he'd be forced to harvest the soul, thus taking him away from her once again.

She'd hidden her face behind her hair; her shame was obvious. For a woman so proud and so unyielding in her beliefs, to have been overcome by her baser desires could kill the light inside of her.

He couldn't let that happen.

"Lise!" he cried, tipping his head skyward. "We need you."

No sooner had he called then he smelled the unmistakable scent of more fae. They were just outside the door and there were too many of them for him to brave on his own. He couldn't swipe a portal open. He didn't trust that method of travel at the moment. If he tried to jump out the window with her, there was likely an ambush already waiting for them.

The queen was never stupid.

Just as the first head peeked around the corner, time stilled. A hint of frost crawled through the window and then there was a brilliant flash of white.

"My word." Lise's voice had Frenzy taking a violent breath, realizing just how close he and Mila had come to being prey.

Mila had her head tucked into Frenzy's neck, and she was still trembling violently. It was the quietest he'd ever known her to be, and it had him worried.

"Darling." He rubbed her back gently. "This is Lise."

She looked up then, blinking her eyes slowly at the woman standing before them. This time Lise had shown up not as the crone, but as the mother. Her skin was firmer, her hair not white but a rich chestnut with a loose sprinkling of silver throughout. Around her head she wore a wreath of laurels.

"My dear," she said in a clear, dulcet voice that had him shivering. "What have they done to you?"

Lise took Mila's hand, patting it gently. It was hard for him to see Mila so shaken up.

"I…I killed him," she said, ending her words with a whimper that tore his heart in two.

Lise glanced down at the body of the man. He was youngish, maybe early thirties in human years, dressed only in boxers. It was obvious by the light of Lise's warmth that Mila had savaged the poor man.

"Well, you haven't killed him," Lise said, "yet." She smiled to lessen the blow.

Grabbing ahold of Mila's chin, Lise turned her face from side to side. And then, lifting up first one arm, she walked in front of Mila—back and forth—before lifting up the other. "You are a miracle, girl."

Frenzy smiled, feeling oddly as if the compliment was for his benefit as well.

"How can you say that?" Mila's voice lowered in pitch and Frenzy knew she was close to breaking.

Hugging her, he kissed her forehead.

Lise looked between the two of them, a knowing glint in her milky white eyes. "It is as I expected."

He tipped his head in acknowledgement, her lips merely twitching in response.

"Little one"—she smoothed a hand over Mila's brow—"I will

protect you as I could not the night the vampires found you. All of this had to be set into motion, can't you see? A seer, you must understand, right?"

Still clinging to Frenzy's shirt, Mila nodded. "Why did The Morrigan betray us?"

"She didn't, dear. As she views it, the betrayal was on your end. Had you stayed at the cabin, she would have sent the shadow as she'd mentioned. But one thing I can say for the queen of war is that she's always prepared for any eventuality. If you fled, she'd catch you. You see, the queen always gets what she wants."

"But you said—" Frenzy cut in.

"Ah"—Lise raised a quieting hand—"I said not to go to the queen until it was time."

It hadn't made sense to him then; he remembered thinking how odd the wording was, but with everything that'd happened since, he hadn't given her words much thought. "Meaning?"

"Meaning, death, that the queen had to see she was out of options. For so long the queen has expected to control everyone and anything." Her smile was smug. "I alone am her Achilles heel, and she hates me for it. What she did tonight, it wasn't for you. It was for me."

His brows dropped.

"It was to see whether I'd fight for you." She jerked her chin toward Mila, who was starting to finally relax in his arms. "She was drawing me out. I'm out." She shrugged with her arms outstretched.

He grinned. "So now the field is level."

She touched the tip of her nose with a "now you've got it" expression.

"What do we do now?" Mila asked.

"You're not going to like what I say." Lise cocked her head, tightening her lips.

The truth was so obvious it was almost as if it'd been written on the wall in front of him. "Do as she initially intended."

Nodding slowly, Lise sighed. "Aye. The queen would never admit it, but she does actually need your help. When she created the shadow it was with the express purpose of using it as a scent hound, if you will. To help the queen draw out a seer. As you know, you're all quite valuable."

"Anyone that controls the future, controls the war," he mumbled.

"Exactly."

Mila shook her head. "She's whittled us down to near extinction. I'm the last of my line."

"Yes." Lise toed the shoulder of the fallen man, frowning slightly at the body. "As I said, her intention was merely to track you down. To compel you to fight for the light court. But the shadow evolved over time…"

"And desired that which she was created to find," Frenzy finished for her. "It is a case of absolute power corrupting absolutely; the shadow grew too strong and wanted more than she should."

"Indeed." Lise twirled, smiling benevolently at them. "Ergo, the queen now finds herself in an unenviable position."

Mila snorted. "So she does need me? Then why did she send her goon squad to kill me?"

Lise's laughter rippled like a gentle wave around them. "They weren't sent to kill you, dear, merely to take you forcibly away from your protector. Though if you ask me, the queen forgot just who Frenzy is, what he is capable of when fighting for a thing he loves."

Uncomfortable, and not sure he was ready to talk about things like feelings with Mila, he cleared his throat, quickly switching the subject.

"Taking Mila onto fae soil is too dangerous. She knows that. She'd have every breed of fae banging down her gates to get at her."

"Again, true." Lise twirled the tasseled end of her belt. "But she is desperate, and desperation makes one do strange things. However"—her smile was full of sharp teeth—"we now have the upper hand, as well she knows it."

"Then what do we do about it?" Mila wrapped her arms around his waist again, and Frenzy could no longer deny that the feel of her in his arms felt right in a way that nothing had before.

"We call her to us."

He scoffed. "We can't just call the queen of darkness. She is not one to be commanded."

A mischievous twinkle sparkled in the depths of Lise's shimmering white eyes. "Ah, you just leave that part up to me, death."

Staring at the faces peering around the edge of the doorway, the hungry, lecherous looks on their hauntingly beautiful fae faces, Frenzy realized just how close Mila had come. If The Morrigan had gotten her hands on his woman, he would never have seen her again. The queen would have taken her to a hidden realm that only she knew how to find. He'd have lost her forever.

It was like a fist to the gut thinking it. Made him furious. She'd double-crossed them, it didn't matter what Lise said. The Morrigan was petty to resort to such trickery, regardless if she thought they weren't planning to keep to their end of *her* deal. He gripped Mila's waist tighter, clinging to her as if by will alone he could make it so that the queen never attempted to take her from him.

In the time they'd spent together he'd learned one ridiculously simple truth. She was his and he'd be damned if he lost her again.

As if sensing his disquiet, Mila ran her fingers along the scruff of his jaw. "I'm right here, Frenzy. I'm right here."

In that moment he didn't think about Lise being in the room, or the nearly dead body frozen in stasis beside them, or even the suspended bodies attempting to rush through the door to get their hands on her, because there were truths that needed to be spoken.

Brushing his knuckles along her cheekbones, he gazed into her eyes and smiled.

"You make my life better, woman," he said, voice gruffer than he'd intended.

Her nostrils flared, but she didn't turn aside or blink.

"I could not stand to lose you. Do you understand?"

"I think I do," she admitted in a near whisper.

Lise sighed. "Isn't love grand?"

When they looked up, startled, Lise winked and then clapped her hands. The land, which was still very much suspended in time, rumbled, shook so violently for a second, Frenzy feared Dagda might be making an appearance.

Outside the rattling windows, twin forks of lightning struck the ground, filling the room with the electric stench of ozone. Then his skin was crawling with the sensation of eyes watching. A second later Mila gasped, but rather than cower, she walked out from Frenzy's arms and lifted her chin high.

"You tried to kidnap me!" she accused the queen.

The Morrigan wasn't standing; she floated several inches off the ground, causing her silken dress of shadow and moonbeams to undulate like a wave beneath her feet. She'd left her inky black hair down to swirl around her head like a charmed cobra. Coming in all her pomp and glory, it was all a show. Glorious and beautiful, but this time Frenzy saw right through it and sneered in her direction.

Her eyes immediately latched on to his, ignoring Mila as she said to him, "And yet another death defies me." The husky quality of her voice shivered with contempt and the faint strains of fury.

"I did not defy you. You came to my woman, glamoured me so that I'd remain in the cabin, unaware of your true intentions."

Her aquiline nose curled. "True intentions? You speak to me so. How dare you!"

The lifting of her voice caused the rafters above their heads to tremor.

Rolling her eyes, Lise clapped her hands. "Queen, I've told you time and again that death belongs to me."

The way the queen's hair waved and the hissing sound that emanated from between her lips, she was Medusa incarnate. "Death is mine." She lifted her fist. "Since the moment of its creation—"

"Goddess sakes." Lise held her hand up. Frenzy saw no magic but he felt it quicken raw and powerful around them, making the air feel ten times denser. "Enough with the theatrics."

Like a powerful hand had shoved the queen to the ground, she fell to the floor, eyes bugging in her head as she stared at the Ancient One with undisguised venom.

Lise shook her head. "I did not want to believe that we'd been forgotten, did not want to step in, be forced to flex my will against my own creation, but you've left me no choice."

"What the hell are you talking about?" The Morrigan's upper lip curled back.

"You've grown too old, too full of yourself, Queen." The last came out as a sarcastic inflection. "Have you forgotten fate so easily?"

Fate.

Lise *was* one of the fates. Frenzy had already suspected it, but hadn't been sure.

"We create the strands of time, creation, destruction; it is all ours, Your Highness." She paused, walking a tight circle around the suddenly still queen.

"Ah yes." Lise smiled, tucking a strand of hair behind her ear, each step causing the bells tied to her sash to toll. "Have you begun to remember now?"

Mila's hand gripped onto his, but Frenzy couldn't turn his eyes away from the petite woman circling his queen like a predator coming in for the kill.

The Morrigan bristled, and it was obvious by the strain in her neck and shoulders that what she really wanted to do was not stand still under the fate's scrutiny, but rather rip the vocal box out of Lise's throat.

Tapping an elegant finger against the corner of her mouth, Lise laughed. "This just kills you, doesn't it?"

"You bi—"

"Uh-uh." Lise waved her finger, tsking. "Not in front of the baby hybrid."

Frenzy had never seen Lise so viscous, nor his queen so helpless. It was a disturbing, but still somewhat fascinating, experience.

He wasn't fooled into thinking his queen weak, though. He'd not laugh at her predicament, because while she may not be able to hurt Lise, she was still more than powerful enough to hurt him, or worse, Mila.

She hissed, turning her eyes on Frenzy. Her gaze was full of hate and contempt and he knew if he ever found himself alone with the queen he'd live to regret it. Her capacity to bear a grudge was legendary.

He stroked Mila's back, not sure if it was more for her or him.

"So this is what we're gonna do." Lise smiled sharply. "We will help rid you of the shadow problem."

Narrowing flinty, dark eyes, the queen quirked her left brow. "I do not need your assistance, Lise. I'm fully capable—"

The Ancient One made a sound between a scoff and a chuckle, then ran her palm down the queen's bare arm.

For a moment Frenzy held his breath, expecting an all-out war to brew between the two of them. But she merely glanced down at the hand resting on hers and sighed.

"Nothing that gets spoken of in this room will *ever* leave this room," Lise said, but Frenzy knew the words were for more his and Mila's benefit; the Ancient One was telling *them* to never speak of this.

He nodded his head, as did Mila. "You have our word," Mila replied solemnly.

The heart in his chest beat a little faster, a little harder. She was amazing in so many ways. He ran his fingers along the base of her spine, just to touch her, just to let her somehow know what he felt. Words were sometimes hard, but the truth of a person, he was convinced, could be seen in the actions they took.

She leaned into his touch, turning a sweet but tempting smile on him.

Lifting her chin, looking as regal as any queen should, The Morrigan spoke. "When I created the shadow, it was with the hope of acquiring a seer. I knew the lines were rare and delicate thanks to all the wars and skirmishes fought. She was simply supposed to find you. But she became greedy, and at first, it was of no concern to me."

Mila tensed beneath his hand. "So you say the shadow became greedy, which can only lead me to believe she was killing us off. How was that an effective method of tracking us?"

"Because, little hybrid," The Morrigan sneered, "the shadow developed your powers. For each soul she took, she became a little stronger. A little better at deciphering the secrets of the universe."

Figuring that Mila was seconds away from throwing a punch at her face, Frenzy wrapped his arm around her trembling shoulder, hauling her tight to his side. "So why hadn't she seen the kiss I'd given her?" he asked.

Clenching her fists and jaw tight, it seemed the queen wouldn't answer.

"Morrigan." Lise licked her lips. "Tell them."

As if she'd been asked to choke down her own bile, the queen turned her face to the side with a furious grimace. "Because the powers do not last."

"So you didn't care how you gained the power, then—all those things you'd told me in the woods, all lies?" Mila spat. "My gran and mum must have seen right through you." She crossed her arms over her chest. "Is that why you had them killed?"

"No," the dark-haired queen snapped, then, taking a deep breath, said in a softer tone, "I did not want either one killed. To get my hands on all three of you, there was much I would have given up to acquire you. I wanted you whole. The shadow could not retain the skill for long, which is why her cravings are so fierce. It's like a drug for her. She will always need more and when she's finished you off, there will be none left."

At that statement, Mila seemed honestly shocked. Her mouth parted and she inhaled a sharp breath. "What... there's...it cannot be..."

Lise nodded slowly. "Aye, dear. In this the queen speaks truth. You are the last of the seers and what the queen won't say is that once the shadow takes you, she will then turn her dark power against the queen herself."

The tendons in The Morrigan's neck were strained and taut. "It is not just me she'll come after, but all of faedom. Her thirst for power will not stop."

Mila's smile was anything but kind. "So that's the real reason why you came to me, and yet you still tried to blackmail me, even knowing your back was against the wall."

A dark glint glowed in the queen's eyes. "My back is never against the wall."

"Then why don't you take the shadow out yourself?" Frenzy growled, forcing the queen's ire to shift from Mila to himself. "Open the box and destroy it."

"Because she can't. She is not strong enough." Lise's words were soft, but running with an undercurrent of irony.

Curling her lip, The Morrigan jerked her chin in the direction of the Ancient One. "Then why don't you do it?"

"Because a fate's duty is to make the strands of time align as they should have always been. It is not my destiny to destroy the shadow." She turned to Mila. "It is yours."

"And when we kill the shadow, what happens to the souls trapped within?" he asked. Hadn't Mila told him her mother and grandmother had been devoured by the creature?

A beatific expression crossed Lise's face. "They are to be harvested."

Mila sucked in a sharp breath, because to her it must have felt like watching them die all over again.

"If I do this," she spoke slowly, but surely, "will it end?"

The queen shrugged. "For you." She clenched her jaw, and a hot feeling spread through Frenzy's gut.

"What does that mean?" Mila asked quickly, glancing first at the queen then at Lise.

"It means," The Morrigan sniffed, "that *he* is still mine."

"Lise?" Mila pleaded with the Ancient One, who was now strangely silent, looking at none of them.

Heart sinking to his knees, he knew what he had to do. "It's okay, O'Fallen. At least you'll be safe." He petted her shoulder, biting down on his tongue because the thought of never seeing her again made his head reel.

The queen would never allow him within her presence again. It would be her form of punishment to him, taking away that which he most wanted. It would be the only way for her to feel like she'd regained her power.

Wringing her hands, Mila stepped forward. "Give him to me," she spoke directly to The Morrigan, and it made his chest warm.

He was crazy about this fierce, tiny, shrewish woman. Proud to have known her, proud to realize he'd been so very wrong. Because if she was the face of humanity, then humanity was well worth saving. Mila may never know it, but she'd healed his soul and restored his faith. He wanted to hug her, to whisper his adoration in her ear as he slipped within the slick folds of her luscious body. Just one more time.

"And in return, I'll give you ten years of service."

Realizing what she was doing, Frenzy shook his head. "Don't do this, Mila. You do not have to do this. You're free; stay away from civilization and you'll never be found again. You're strong, you won't have to run again. I'm not worth this."

Turning, she pulled his hands to her chest, laying them against her heart. "You're so worth this, reaper. You're worth every sacrifice."

"Fifteen and you live in my court." The queen's excitement was palpable, like the flutters of a moth's wings.

Wrapping his arm around her waist, she turned back to the queen. "Fifteen, I do not live in your court, and he remains with me in a place of my choosing."

Nostrils flaring, The Morrigan looked from death to his madcap woman. Heart pounding, Frenzy couldn't even speak.

Why was she fighting so hard to keep him? He'd been cruel to her, called her names, mocked and laughed at her. It was humbling and made him feel the full weight of his shame for treating her so cruelly in the beginning.

Mila cocked her head. "Do we have a deal, Queen? Fifteen, my choice, you can reach me at any time?" She held out her hand.

They waited for what seemed an eternity, but was probably only a few minutes before she shook Mila's hand. A rush of power rolled like a tidal wave through the room, as a blinding light emanated from their clasped hands.

Lise clapped her own. "It is binding. Neither of you may break this oath. We will be in touch, Morrigan."

The moment she'd finished speaking, the queen disappeared, sucked back into the darkness from which she'd come.

"Now, about this body." Lise looked down at the man lying on the ground. "Keep a better eye on her next time, Frenzy; the girl does not need the strain of being a mass murderer on top of everything else. Do not fear, little hybrid, I will bring him back, none the wiser for the experience he went through. And, reaper"—she looked Frenzy dead in the eye—"it must be her. Do you understand? I've undone the damage the queen did to time. Now go."

With a nod she waved them off, and before they knew it, they were hurtling through space and time. He wondered what she meant by "it must be her," but it wasn't as pressing as holding Mila in his arms was right now. Regardless of where this tunnel of time led, they were together and Frenzy would never leave her side again.

Chapter 14

They were back where they'd started, at his cabin in the woods. The faint rays of sunlight were beginning to filter through the trees. Mila stretched out her arms, tipping her face toward the light.

Early morning and dusk she had no problem with. During the heat of the day her skin started to feel uncomfortable on her body, but she wasn't frying to a crisp. Yet another adaptation her hybrid status had given her that made her almost happy to be who she was.

Frenzy's scent of clover and moss surrounded her, seconds before his arms wrapped around her waist. "What are you thinking?"

Inhaling deeply, she turned in his arms, framing the handsome face of the man who'd come to mean so much to her in such a short time. "What if I can't defeat the shadow? What if she's fooled me again and I…lose you?" The last was barely a whisper.

Brushing his knuckles along her cheekbones, he bent and

lightly took her lips into his. Her body responded as it always did. Heat and fire traveled through her veins, lighting her up and making her ache.

She always wanted Frenzy. *Would* always want him. He released her with a sigh.

"She can't break her vow; Lise sealed it. To break the vow would mean her death. The queen is not so stupid. She will do as she said." With a flick of his wrist the black box the queen had given her yesterday morning materialized from out of nowhere.

Tracing her finger along the smooth, cold surface, she shook her head. "Is it really possible that a stupid black box can take the shadow down?"

Grabbing her fingers, he brought them to his lips, placing one kiss along each pad before smiling. "This will work."

He sounded so sure, but she wasn't. Not about this, not about anything. Because her life had never been this easy. She just wished she could *see* more, know more. The nerves were threatening to eat her alive.

"Come on." He pulled her toward the cabin, walking to each corner of it and laying his hand upon a particular piece of wood that'd been smoothed out over the years. Lifting the repelling ward, he walked her to the door and opened it.

She was silent, allowing him to meekly guide her in, trying to take as much strength from him as she could.

Lise had made it pretty clear that it would be she and she alone who had to fight the shadow. Problem was she didn't have the first clue how to do it. Holding up the box and saying *Get inside if you please* seemed rather asinine. And there would be no fighting it. The power rolling off the creature was immense.

"Sweetheart"—his voice shot like sun-warmed honey through her body, made her shiver—"look at me."

It was the first time he'd ever referenced her in such a way. Nibbling on the corner of her lip, she turned her eyes to his. They were such beautiful eyes. Mercurial silver with flecks of stardust swirling throughout. Heartbeat stuttering in her chest, she stood still as he placed his large hand against the nape of her neck, gently guiding her mouth toward his.

"We can do this. I really believe that."

"Why did you call me your sweetheart?" She hadn't meant to ask it, but the moment the words escaped her she realized she desperately wanted to know the answer. What were they doing? She'd all but bartered his freedom away, tied him to her forever, without even asking his permission first.

In hindsight it seemed stupid. Why had she done it? What if he resented her for it over time? They'd made no vows to each other; he'd never told her anything to make her think that he'd appreciate the idea of remaining with her eternally. And she could not deny that the specter of Adrianna worried her. Was he still pining for a woman so far in the past Mila never had a chance at overcoming?

But when she thought of her life without him by her side, it was dark and empty and pointless. She couldn't be a George, she wasn't built that way. She'd had enough of it as a mortal. She needed a lover, a friend, a confidant. She needed Frenzy.

His smile was perfect. Everything about him was so perfect it made her stomach ache, her heart hurt. The possibility of eeking out an eternal existence without him made her want to do horrible, violent things. Made the darkness crave violence, to herself, others…it was wrong to hang her happiness on another this way, but being with Frenzy felt…vital.

"Don't you understand, little shrew?" His words feathered across her lips, the air between them was charged, frenetic. It popped and crackled and made her body hum with need and anticipation.

The world was falling down around them, but all she could see, all she wanted, was him.

"Before you, I was surviving. You asked me once when was the last time I'd laughed, loved…" His hands trailed warm down the sides of her body, leaving heat in its wake; silver eyes held her thralled. "You, Mila O'Fallen. You make me feel again. I'm alive, and not because I'm forced to be, I'm alive because I want to be. I'll do anything for you. Anything." Then his hands were gripping her ass and she was helpless to prevent the hard moan from spilling out.

"I love you, Frenzy." The words burst from her mouth and she wasn't ashamed. She didn't want to take them back, because they were real and true and if she didn't survive, then he'd know. "I'm sorry for acting like such an arse in the beginning. For being hotheaded and stubborn, for failing to see what a wonderful, amazing, and—"

"Sexy. You were going to say sexy, right?" he growled, nipping at her lower lip, and she laughed, because now she wasn't anxious.

She wanted him with a fire that consumed, that obliterated

any sense she had. Shoving her hands down his jeans, she felt him hard and full. His thick cock twitched in her hand as he groaned, and a feeling of supreme satisfaction took over because it was amazing that just her touch could make this powerful man weak in the knees.

"O'Fallen, from the moment you first opened your mouth and spoke to me with that sharp tongue of yours, I fell hard and fast. There is no other for me." The timbre of his words deepened, shivered across her skin like dark chocolate, molten and decadent.

He hadn't said the words, but it was still a proclamation of love, and it was enough for now.

Purring in the back of her throat, heart so full it felt like it might burst from her chest, she raked her claws down his shirt, ripping it in two. Grunting, he shrugged out of it. But his hands were just as frantic. Between sharp, biting kisses, they were undressing each other.

Both aware of the time, aware that at any moment the shadow might return, might rip them apart. It was now or never, and they weren't going to waste a single moment of it.

"Mila," he grunted, sucking in air sharply and causing his stomach to go concave when she'd feathered her fingers across the tight skin of his muscle.

It was still a wonder to her that she could touch him this way. They'd come so far since meeting. She was glad she hadn't seen her future, hadn't seen them as they were now because it made the discovery of it new and fresh and endlessly thrilling because it was all so unknown.

At any moment the shadow could bust through the door; at any moment the battle for their lives could commence. It lent then a frenzied urgency to touch and taste and mark themselves on one another.

With a growl, he'd torn her bra off and tossed it only goddess knew where. Her shorts were the next to follow. In no time they were both nude. There were no pleasantries, no witty exchanges. This was pure and primal, lust at its most basic form. Shoving her back until her knees collapsed against the edge of the bed, he crawled on top of her, reminding Mila of an advancing, sleek panther the way his body moved and muscles rippled.

The dappling of sunlight brushing against his burnished skin made her body shiver and her breathing quicken.

"Are you ready for me, little hybrid?" he whispered between heated kisses right at the swell of her breasts.

Burying her fingers through his thick, red hair, she nodded. She didn't have to touch herself to feel how wet she was for him. "I'm always ready for you, reaper."

His large hand traced a sensuous trail down her waist, molding around her thigh before sliding downward and swirling his fingers through her slick folds.

Gasping, her back arched as she opened wider. "Frenzy," she moaned as the bliss zipped through her veins like a shot of heroin.

Working his magic fingers like a piston, he brought her to the edge of the spiraling pinnacle. Drunk on him, she dropped her knees wide on the bed and, being brazen, she twined her fingers through his, joining him as he brought her to the peak of pleasure.

"Mila." His voice was gruff and thick as he stared at their twined hands.

Giving him a wicked smile, she felt her eyes shut as the powerful orgasm ripped like a gunshot through her. Screaming with release, she frantically clawed at his back, causing him to hiss and then grunt with laughter.

It felt like forever before she could actually breathe again, and the moment she could she realized he was still hard as a rock and the head of his cock rested heavy at her entrance.

Dazed and deliriously happy, she nodded at him to go all the way.

With a jubilant howl he buried himself so deep she felt his thickness move through her womb. Wrapping her long legs around his slim waist, she joined him, moving at his rhythm.

At first their pace was fast, almost angry, as if they sensed their time was quickly running out. But after a moment, things started to slow down. Rather than meeting their lustful demands, they began to whisper and tenderly caress. His lips hovered inches above her nipples, heating them with his moist breath.

"Mila," he said again, and this time he sounded confused, almost enraptured by her.

Pausing, she stilled as she took the time to look deep into his eyes. They were full of questions, full of hope, but mostly they were full of love. And then she felt something she hadn't felt in all the times they'd bedded each other.

Warmth.

Not from his sweat-slickened body pressed to hers, or because the morning was less cool than normal. This warmth lit her up from within, rolled through her blood like a low, creeping fog, saturated her limbs, filled her head.

"Frenzy?" she gasped, looking to him to see if by some miracle he was experiencing what she was.

Licking his lips, he nodded, and then they glowed.

Light poured from them, from inside them. She glowed purest white like the light she'd witnessed surrounding Lise. From Frenzy came black. But not the hateful black of the shadow or the queen. This was a luminous black flecked with silver starlight.

Moving within her slowly, he kissed her neck. "We're joining, love," he murmured, before licking the hollow of her throat.

Hissing at the delicious friction burning through them, she licked her teeth as another desire began to manifest within her.

The rushing of his blood was a melody in the night, a beautiful toll of bells that entranced and delighted her.

"What is this, Frenzy?" she asked, more to distract herself from the crushing desire to take his blood by force.

Still embedded deep inside her, he leaned onto his elbow, tracing a pattern between the black and the white. The quicksilver of his eyes seemed richer, like a thundercloud rolling in from the horizon. "The bonding of our souls."

It seemed like he wanted to say more, but he must have noticed something in her face that told him she was waging an internal battle.

Grabbing her chin, he nodded. "Take my blood."

His face was so serious, and she squeezed her eyes shut, wanting to more than anything, but knowing she needed to tell him of the possible consequences. "Frenzy, if a vampire feeds too often on one person, there is the chance that their will, their desires will become nothing more than to be our food. Fed upon. You'll be my slave."

His brows twitched. "Are you telling me this is why you've been refusing to feed on me?"

Gums aching, but body still throbbing for release, she nodded miserably. "I couldn't do that to you."

Smacking her lips with a laugh, he ruffled her hair. It shocked her so much she momentarily forgot about her aching gums.

"A fae cannot be enthralled, woman. Next time, just ask. Now…" He took her face gently between his large palms and placed her at the juncture of his neck.

His heady scent washed over her, made her stomach growl and her nails lengthen. "It doesn't hurt?" Her voice was a whisper of sound, the temptation to take him almost obliterating all common sense.

"I vow it," he said, and then shoved deep inside her again.

Wrapped up in their light, with his cock so thick and hitting all the most private places in her, she gave in to her desires with a joyful cry and bit.

She drank deep of the ambrosia; it filled her mouth with the taste of sunshine, moved through her veins, and again she felt the gathering pressure of a pending orgasm. It rushed through her. His moans of satisfaction only fueled and fed the beast coiling tighter and tighter.

"Look at me," he hissed after a while, forcing her to release her hold. With one final flick of her tongue, she turned to his eyes.

They were full of joy and passion and desire.

It was her undoing; tossing her head, she fell into the black abyss.

"Keep your eyes on me," he gritted out. His thumbs rested on her chin and she couldn't have looked away even if she wanted to.

Because his eyes were no longer the silver of liquid mercury, but they were rolling with stars. Birth and death. A seedling shooting from the green earth, budding, then blooming into a lovely red rose before petals slowly floated down around it. The cycle of death and life repeated in the hypnotic gaze and she howled as his hot seed flooded her insides.

Then they were panting, collapsing on top of each other, and she could only lie there as his hand rubbed along the column of her throat, back and forth, back and forth. The lights that'd flooded from their pores gradually receded until they were no more than flesh and blood again.

After what felt like an eternity, Mila laughed, turning her head into Frenzy's shoulder to give him a playful nip, the taste of his sweet blood still coating her tongue. "What in the hell was that?" she asked, and she knew he wouldn't require her to clarify what she was talking about.

"The lights?" he asked with a smug grin.

She lifted her brows.

"Means you belong to me forever, little hybrid." He nipped the corner of her lips. "You're mine woman, all mine."

With a growl, she smacked the hand that he'd wrapped around her breast playfully. "You better believe that goes both ways, you bloody, awful man."

"Awful," he snickered and squeezed her breast, not so much that it hurt, but enough to make her suck in a sharp breath. "Those lights were our souls becoming one. You've taken a piece of me and I a piece of you. What we've done can never be un-done." His voice was deep and throaty and it filled her with a sense of empowerment, but also made her want to cry, though she wasn't sure why.

"You sure you want that, death?" she teased, because if she tried to be serious, to let him know what she actually thought about it, she'd definitely cry. "I've been known to be a bit of a shrew."

"You?" He grinned. "Surely you've been misunderstood."

She laughed. "That's what I've always said." Then, unable to resist touching him a second longer, she traced the area where she'd bitten him. It was amazing to her how fast he healed. Of course, she was able to heal herself, but so much of this was still new to her. To know that she could have him whenever she pleased, it made her stomach swirl with a band of butterflies. "I can't believe you asked me to do that to you."

Kissing the now-smooth section of his neck, she continued to strum her fingers gently across the strong, corded muscles.

Rolling over so that she was now on top of him, he framed her arse with his large hand, and though he was already getting softer, they were still joined. Mainly because she didn't want to leave this bed. Every memory she had of this cabin was happy, and that's how she wanted it to stay. She didn't want ugly memories to taint what they'd done here. Who'd she finally become. A woman willing to bend and yield, a woman willing to admit that it wasn't a weakness to love.

"And why not?" His deep voice tore her from her lovesick thoughts. "I told you before, I like it."

"You're crazy." She licked the spot on his neck, which had already healed, her body satisfied, but that never really took the hunger away. She always wanted more of him.

"About you, Mila O'Fallen." He turned so that they were forced to stare into one another's eyes.

She couldn't stop her smile. "You know, the thought of feeding off of anyone else, it disgusts me." She grimaced. Mila couldn't hide the shudder that rippled down her spine. "But not with you."

Frenzy was so relaxed beside her, his hot hands gently stroking her body. She shouldn't be ready so soon. Shouldn't feel the need start a slow but inexorable crawl up and down her limbs, making her tingle and her stomach knot up with nerves. Seeing his smile, how the perpetual scowl he'd always worn around her when they'd first met was now nothing but a memory, it made her realize that he was it for her.

"I'll let you in on a secret, woman." The deep timbre of his words boomed like an echo through her chest. "I hate the thought of you experiencing that with anyone else. I, and I alone, will feed you."

He wasn't asking, and it was on the tip of her tongue to scoff or laugh, but the truth was, what she'd done with him, it was so intimate. The feeding of blood was almost as good as orgasm, taking another's essence into her body was too personal for her to want to do that with anyone else.

She smiled. "Better watch out, reaper, I'm pretty ravenous. In fact…" She crawled up his body, pushing her hands against his chest to get into a sitting position, aware of the fact that his cock was definitely beginning to stir deep inside her. "I think I could—"

Cold unlike anything Mila had ever felt before engulfed them, making her teeth clack and her head hurt. She'd not experienced any type of cold since turning, and it sent her body into chaos. Heart pumping like a fist in her rib cage, she jumped off of Frenzy's body, twirling on her heels, knowing immediately that they were no longer alone.

* * *

Frenzy's need to protect his woman was an all-consuming obsession. The skin of his arms prickled as fire shot down his left arm, turning his hand to bone.

The shadow hovered just in front of the door frame, nothing more than a thin band of darkness.

"Get behind me, Mila," he growled.

They'd been prepared for this ever since Lise instructed them that this was how it was supposed to be. The black box rested on the floorboard just beneath their bed. All they had to do was get to it without alerting the shadow to what they were doing.

Mila didn't take her eyes off the creature as she backpedaled very slowly, like one would when trying to escape a rabid beast.

"And so we meet again, death." The shadow's voice was reed thin, nothing at all like the nasally scratch he remembered from his apartment. She was still little more than a streak of darkness; perhaps death's kiss had weakened her more than he'd anticipated.

Experiencing a short but quick thrill that this might be easier than they'd thought, he yanked on Mila's arm, dragging her fully behind him. Kicking his foot backward into her shin, he hoped she understood that he was silently urging her to get her hands on the box.

"Why are you here, creature?" he hissed, playing dumb and acting as if he didn't know the queen had set the shadow up.

The faint scratching of Mila's toes dragging along the hardwood floor told him she was slowly bringing the box toward her. And if the shadow heard, she'd never be able to suspect it was anything other than the tiny scampering of a rodent. All they had to do was get in close, open the box, and it was all over.

His woman would be safe.

Satisfaction flowed hot through his veins.

"You bastard," the shadow hissed. "You lied to me. Her stench clings to you."

All he had to do was distract her for a second longer. Just to give Mila enough time to secure the object.

Taking a tentative step toward the band, which was now beginning to lengthen and swell, take on the appearance of what it'd been back at his apartment, he beckoned her closer with the bone of his hand.

"None can resist death's lure, apparently not even you, creature." He toyed with the bony edge of his pinky finger. "Did you really think I would want you?"

The shadow quivered as the appendages began to finally take on form. He had to get her mad enough to attack, get her in close so that when Mila popped open the lid the shadow would be sucked back into the darkness.

"I will consume you both," she whispered, a terrible, shivery sound that filled the room like killing frost, making his pulse stutter from the unbearable cold wafting out of it.

Frenzy desperately wanted to turn around, look to see that Mila now had the object in hand, but to do that would give away their endgame. Focusing all his fury into the shadow, he leered.

"Death is master of his own destiny. You cannot touch me unless *I* will it."

Clenching his jaw, he took a step closer, stomach filling with fury that the damned creature wasn't taking the bait. She stood in the doorway still, fully formed as she'd been in his apartment.

The eyes had appeared all over her, blinking and gazing back at him and Mila mournfully. Cocking her head, the slit where the mouth should have been opened and a terrible peal of laughter issued forth. It was a dry, sandpaper kind of sound that rubbed against his body abrasively.

"Fool me once, shame on you." She drifted closer, but her body was continuing to swell. Become round and oblong, pulling and stretching like a ball of taffy. "I know the truth, reaper. I am no fool. The queen has given her my box." The slit stretched apart into a macabre version of a grin. "She means to destroy me. It will not happen."

With a flick of her wrist, a shot of black bolted from her palm, and then he heard Mila's cry. Frenzy twirled just as the box flew to the other side of the room well out of their reach.

Bounding back to his woman, he grabbed her, tugging her close to his side. "Frenzy, I..." she stuttered, and he hushed her with a kiss to her temple.

"Not your fault," he murmured.

"How touching." The giant mass of shadow continued to spread throughout every corner of the room, laughing as it went. "Did you know, death, that I have a talent?" she asked in a breathless sort of wonder.

Mila trembled beneath his touch and he knew he'd been a fool to believe they could so easily bring a creature of the wild hunt down.

But he hadn't lost hope; he couldn't. Because the only way to protect his woman was to destroy this creature. He wouldn't lose her, not like this. Not ever. He'd lost love once and it'd almost ruined him. But he knew Mila's death would be one he'd never return from.

"What is your talent, you stupid piece of shite?" Mila growled, and though she trembled still in his arms, Frenzy now knew it wasn't from fear, but from fury.

Hissing, the shadow swirled all her attention on the slight woman in his arms. A rumbling sound tore from his lips as several sets of eyes focused on Mila alone.

"To give you what you crave most," she whispered, and then the air became dense. A strange shimmering sprang up between them, like a heat wave rippling on hot asphalt.

Suddenly Adrianna stood there. Brown curls piled high atop her head as the amber eyes that'd haunted him for centuries turned in his direction. She was nude, and he knew this was how she'd looked the night she'd been murdered by the Earl's valet.

"Why weren't you there, Frenzy? Why?" Her haunting whisper echoed through his skull.

Swallowing hard, telling himself this must be a mirage, he turned his head to the side, trying to blink away the image. But Adrianna wouldn't let him, floating toward him. A shocking trail of cold traveled up his wrist and forearm, and across his bicep in a familiar caress.

He shuddered, remembering how she'd loved to touch him in such a manner. How that touch would signal a precursor for more.

A strange noise vibrated in his ear. A low pitched sort of humming, distracting and unfamiliar. But Adrianna wouldn't let him focus on it, because her hands were now on his face and her velvety lips were so close to his own.

"Why weren't you there, Frenzy? Why?" Luminous amber eyes ensnared him and his breathing increased.

Where was he? What had he been doing? Those two

thoughts kept hammering at his skull because something important was happening, something he knew he should be focused on. But all he could see was Adrianna. All he could smell was the soft scent of roses perfuming her body.

"Adrianna." A choked cry dropped off his tongue.

Her smile was wide and radiant. "My darling," she cooed. "Why did you abandon me? Why did you leave me to him?" A visible tremble rippled through her.

Frenzy sensed something was wrong. Sensed the bindings of a spell encapsulating him. This wasn't real.

But she was crying. "Adrianna, do not cry. I came to you, I did."

"Oh, Frenzy, what did you do?" she sobbed, and the fight to hang on left him. He'd never been able to handle seeing her cry. Not then, not now.

Holding his arms out to her, he fell headlong into the memories.

Chapter 15

Mila gasped as she witnessed Frenzy's slow descent into madness. He was talking to thin air, holding out his arms and shushing softly, over and over again.

"What have you done to him?" she growled, twirling on the advancing shadow, whose eyes twinkled with mirth.

Opaque eyes turned back toward her. "I've given him his heart's desire."

Adrenaline speeding thick and hot all throughout her, Mila tried to shield Frenzy from the shadow's gaze as best she could. "I am his heart's desire. He told me. He bonded with me. We've become one."

The shadow scoffed as the slit of her mouth curled upward into a snarl. "Is that what you think? You poor, pathetic soul. What he sees now is his Adrianna." She practically purred the name.

It was like a punch to Mila's gut, because she'd seen the vision. Seen the love shining in Frenzy's eyes for that woman. The woman he felt such guilt for, the one for whose murder he blamed himself.

"No." She shook her head, trying in vain to deny it.

The shadow tossed her head back. "You truly are a worthless creature, aren't you?"

Being stubborn, she lifted her chin high as she tried to hang on to Frenzy's arm, but he kept tugging it away from her, following the invisible Adrianna around the room.

"A vision can only work if the soul desires it to be so," the shadow taunted.

Heat prickled the corners of Mila's eyes because a horrible realization was dawning on her. She didn't trust the shadow as far as she could toss it, but she'd known how torn up Frenzy was about Adrianna's death, how the nagging feeling was always in the back of her mind that he cared more for the ghost of Adrianna than he ever had for her.

"The bastard is correct," the shadow continued. "I cannot kill him. Death controls life, but," she hissed, undulating her neck like a hypnotic cobra, "I could not get to you with death in the way. This isn't hard, little seer. It won't even hurt. Won't you come to me?"

The cadence of her voice, the dulcet, shivery tone of it, it did something to Mila. Washed away the fear hammering away inside her veins. Made her claws retract and the panicking need for flight or fight dissipate.

And now when she stared at the shadow, she didn't see a nightmarish sight of sagging skin and a slit for a mouth. Instead, there was a voluptuous woman garbed in a diaphanous gown of midnight, with long black hair hanging well past her waist, full, plump lips and a curvaceous figure. She was beautiful and exotic and Mila began to wonder how it was that she'd always feared this creature.

"Do you not want to see your gran? Your mum again, little seer?" The shadow curved her finger in a beckoning gesture, luring her further in.

Throat squeezing tight, and not trusting herself to speak, Mila could only nod. And like magic they appeared before her just as they'd last been.

Gran was wearing a blue slip dress that fell past her knees. Her snow-white hair pulled up into a fashionable bun. Kind, crinkly brown eyes smiled back at her. "Ach, wee one, 'tis good ta see you again," she said, and it dragged tears to Mila's eyes, made her throat clog up.

Taking a stuttering breath, Mila nodded. "And you, Gran."

"Mila," her mum's sweet, sweet voice echoed through Mila's head. Salt-and-pepper hair was swept back into a ponytail. Her jeans and red blouse hugged her slim body to perfection. Her mum had always been conscious of appearance, practical, but beautiful in a classic and timeless way.

"Mum!" she squealed and let the tears drop finally. "I thought I'd never see you two again. After that night, when the shadow…" Just saying the name caused her heart to pound again and an awful nagging to prick away at her.

"Nay, lass, nay." Gran held up a soothing hand and, stepping in to Mila, she wrapped frail arms around her neck, breaking her out in an immediate wash of goose bumps. "The shadow isna so bad as all that. She's been good to us. She only wants what's best for the—"

A strange sensation began filling Mila's limbs, like she was slowly being leached of energy. The first faint fluttering of tiredness filled her bones. She shook her head. "But I thought you said to stay away from the shadow, that it would kill us all. I saw you die, Mum. Saw it take you up in its tentacles and suck you dry. I saw—"

Gran's smile was sweet, full of joy and suppressed laughter. "A vision, lass. Only a vision. It wasn't truth. The shadow's been protecting us. Guiding us, teaching us how to properly use our powers to their fullest potential."

Head beginning to feel a little fuzzy, Mila tried to understand what her gran was saying. How was it possible? All her life her mum and gran had warned her to never let the shadow get her. Now they were saying that it was okay?

Why was it so hard to focus? Vision blurring slightly, she shook her head as her stomach began to churn with something close to anxiety. But how? Why? Wasn't this what she'd always wanted? Her gran and her mum back again? Their love, their arms wrapped around her one last time?

"Mum?"

"Hmm?" Eyes so similar to her own smiled up at her. "Yes, lovie?"

"Is Da still alive?" Why had she asked that question? She'd wanted to ask her mum for a hug, wanted to ask her if she loved her, not that. Not about Da. But something was bothering her, nagging at her.

"Of course he is, love." She tsked as if Mila were a silly thing. "He lives in Ireland, as you well know."

She blinked, because it wasn't true. If these were the true spirits of her relatives, they should know that.

Heart raging in her ears, the vision of gran and mum wavered. "Mum," she said softly.

"Yes?"

Suddenly, as if listening to noise through a tunnel, she heard a horrible slurping noise, a buzzing that drowned out the happy smiles on her family's faces.

"Da's dead."

Mum's smile wilted, the beautiful amber eyes became hard as cut glass, and then Gran burst out with a horrible, grating sound of laughter.

* * *

Frenzy had his arms wrapped around Adrianna, inhaling her scent of roses, when another scent intruded. Fresh earth and a sharp burst of frost. It was powerful and all-consuming and filled his heart with such need that Adrianna wavered in his arms.

Her wide eyes grew large. "Frenzy?" She clutched at his back. "Where are you going? Don't leave me, don't leave me. You cannot leave me!" she snarled.

And all at once he knew this wasn't his Adrianna. His Adrianna was gone and buried. He'd mourned her loss, he'd let her go. He'd moved on and fallen in love with the woman who shared his soul.

"Mila," he whispered, and it was like someone took a hammer to a sheet of glass.

The ghost in his arms shattered into a ball of light. All at once the cabin was restored, as was the reality of their situation.

The shadow was stretched throughout every crevice of the one-room cabin. Pulsing tentacles of darkness were wrapped around his lover's body, one shoved down her throat as a glimmering, golden radiance emanated from within Mila's mouth.

The creature was pulling out her soul.

"Mila!" he cried, rushing toward her.

But the shadow was everywhere. It hissed as it looked up at him with glowing red eyes. "You should have stayed down, reaper! Now you'll get to watch her die." And then a thick wave slammed into him, tossing him against the farthest wall and knocking the air out of his lungs.

Panting, he grabbed hold of his chest as the pain radiated like a spider's web throughout his limbs. The darkness held him down in a choking, punishing grip.

At first Mila wasn't struggling, she was lax in the creature's arms, but after a second he began to notice her twitching and jerking, as if coming to her senses. The shadow returned its attention back to her, letting off some of the pressure bearing down on him.

Knowing he didn't have much time, he frantically searched around for something, anything, to distract it, when he spotted the box, lying not ten inches in front of him.

He couldn't move too fast; if he did he feared the shadow

would become aware of what he was trying to do. Inching his fingers painfully slow across the floor, he felt like it took an eternity rather than the few seconds it did to latch on to the cold piece of wood.

Clutching it in his hands, it dawned on him: it was finally over. All he had to do was open the box.

Snapping it open with fumbling fingers, he shoved the box into the bit of shadow that held him pinned to the ground.

Nothing happened.

The lid was open; the wood was still cold. Fear slammed a tight fist into his gut.

And as much as he wanted to roar to the heavens and go insane with his need to reach his woman, he shoved the panic down and tried to think it through. Lise had insisted many times that Mila had to be the one to do it. Maybe the magic within the box would only respond to the touch of a seer.

The thought gave him hope. Not much, but enough to realize that maybe there was still a chance.

Frenzy winced as Mila's screams cut through his skull. Her eyes were open and she was crying as she struggled to free herself of the shadow's hold.

"Mila!" he roared again.

This time she turned her eyes to him. They were wide and frantic.

The sight was horrible, and one that would live with him forever. He saw her clutched tight to the shadow, a good five feet off the ground as a thick, shadowy tentacle snaked deeper and deeper down her throat.

He was going to lose her. Trying to wiggle himself free of the shadow's absolute hold and not being able to, no matter how hard he tried or how he maneuvered, he knew there was only one way. He'd not be able to hand the box to Mila himself, nor could he throw it—the shadow could snatch it out of the air or swat it out of his reach.

He'd have to send it through a rift in time and into her hands directly. He'd never done anything like this before, and it made his hands slick with sweat, his throat dry, and his fingers numb. What if it didn't work? They'd traveled through time to get here; Lise had fixed the tampering the queen had done, but what if he couldn't do it?

Mila twitched, her fight was growing weaker.

Knowing he had no other recourse and, running out of time, he tore open a rift in the fabric of time and shoved the box inside. Squeezing his eyes shut, he focused all his energy on sending it directly into her hands.

He pictured the tunnel—the endless expanse of swirling blue and silver, the dimensions of the box, the color—pictured the lid open, pictured him slicing through the fabric of time right in front of Mila's hands.

Frenzy focused all of himself into that image, going into a trancelike state as he stared at the space in front of Mila's hands, willing the box to appear, willing the shadow's demise.

Blood trickled down his nose as his body began to convulsively jerk. To open a tear in time he had to physically do it: be there, slice his hand through the rift.

He couldn't do that this time, but if he didn't make it happen

Mila would die. His beautiful, wild woman. Closing his eyes, he willed everything within him to do it.

With one final gasp, a giant rift tore open in a blinding flash of blue around Mila's hands. At first his heart sank because nothing appeared, and just as his vision threatened to give out, he saw the black box.

Then the room spun and he passed out.

* * *

It took a second for her muddled brain to process what'd just happened. There'd been a blinding flash of blue, and she'd felt something hard. But unlike all the other times, when it'd been cold, this time the box was blazing hot.

A visible ripple moved through the shadow as it seemed to suddenly become aware of what Mila held.

Her strength almost gone, Mila slammed the box into the heart of darkness.

A keening cry echoed like an unholy scream all around them. A wash of blinding ivory poured like molten metal through the shadow, tearing holes into the fabric of its being.

It immediately let her go. She dropped with a loud thunk to the floor below, body trembling and coated in sweat.

Hair plastered to the sides of her neck, she could barely see, her vision was so cloudy. Nothing mattered to her now except getting to Frenzy's side. But her legs were weak, so she dragged herself along the floor, feeling by touch along the way for his body.

The shadow had very nearly drained her.

The room shook like an earthquake was ripping through it. Wherever the white light touched the shadow burned away. It was gathering into its body, forming a tight ball as it strove to get away from the incinerating light.

Her knee bumped into something hard but soft. With a gravel-filled cry, she gathered Frenzy into her arms, resting his head on her knees as she petted his hair over and over. "Baby, baby, can you hear me? I'm all right, I'm okay," she whispered lovingly, never wanting to let him go.

His body was nice and warm, his breathing even. Hopefully he was okay. Bending over, she peppered his face with kisses, so grateful to be alive, to be with him.

"I love you, Frenzy. No matter what, I don't care if you still love Adrianna more. I don't care. You're all I want, and I'm never going to—"

"Love Adrianna more?" he groaned, finally opening a molten silver eye.

With a cry of joy, she swept in, gathering his lips to hers. Everything inside her hurt—every bone, every organ, it all throbbed. Hell, even the blood moving through her veins hurt, but he was alive and so was she, and right now, that was all that mattered.

With a low moan, he gently pulled her away. "Mila, it almost killed you. I didn't think it would work, didn't think I'd save you…"

A final piercing scream blasted through the room, a swirling tempest of wind exploded the windows, pinging shards of glass against their bodies.

With a hiss, he tucked Mila into his body, shielding her as best he could. Finally, there was silence. Heavy and full.

"Is it over?" she whispered.

Almost afraid to believe it, Frenzy looked around. The box was sitting on the floor. The lid was shut, but now it gleamed a bright, almost fluorescent white.

Kissing the crown of her head, he said, "I think it is."

Not ready to let her go, but knowing she'd want to see it for herself, he helped her sit up. Her face was a mass of scratches. She should have healed quickly because of the blood she'd drunk from him not even an hour ago. But the shadow had taken so much from her. Her skin was ashen, her hair limp.

"What are those glowing things all over the floor?" she whispered, cutting off his inspection of her.

Frowning, he looked to where she pointed, and his bony hand immediately throbbed. She must have sensed it, because she glanced down at it where it rested on the crook of her elbow. There were at least ten glowing golden blobs.

"Those are the souls it had trapped within it," he said softly.

She sucked in a sharp breath. "My…my gran and mum?"

Rubbing his brow, knowing he'd have to attend to those souls soon, he nodded. "I'm sure they're there."

Scooting back on her knees, she crawled over to one of the orbs and stared down at it longingly. "Which ones, Frenzy?"

Every muscle in his body ached as he slowly worked his way to his feet. Coming to rest beside her, he kneeled, resting his arms on his lap. "Do you really want to know?"

Turning to him, eyes so wide and earnest, he couldn't refrain from tucking a strand of hair behind her ear. Wanting to touch her so badly, to wrap her in his arms and hold on to her for eternity.

She nodded and locked her small hand around his wrist. "Aye."

Smiling, because he loved her brogue, loved when he'd see the sparkle of excitement dance in her eyes, loved when she moaned and breathed his name…in short, he loved everything about this woman.

"Then come here," he ordered, holding out his bony hand for hers.

She didn't hesitate, simply slipped her hand into his and together they reached into the first orb.

A memory surfaced of a chubby, freckle-faced child as she danced through a field of sunflowers. A woman in a sundress stood on the curve of the hill, shading her eyes with a loving look tugging on her full, plump lips.

"Mila, you'll ruin your dress," the woman admonished with a smile in her words.

The beautiful little girl twirled in the field, holding her arms out to her side as she skipped back to her mother. "I love you, Mum," the little girl whispered as she jumped into her arms and planted a big, wet kiss onto the corner of her mum's cheek.

The woman laughed and hugged her tighter. "As I will always love you, my wild little hellion."

The image faded, but continued to echo with the glow and warmth of so much love. Mila sobbed and Frenzy tugged her into his side.

"Does she know I'm here?" she hiccupped, peering into Frenzy's eyes with hope shining in her own.

Patting her back, he kissed her head. "Souls know, love. They know."

Giving him a weepy smile, she nodded. "She said good-bye, didn't she?"

Swallowing the tears clogging his own throat, he nodded.

Running her fingers lovingly across the orb one final time, she nodded. "Take them home, Frenzy."

Standing, bringing her up with him, he was hesitant to let her go even though he knew the danger was passed.

"Do you want to come with me?" he asked.

"I can go?"

* * *

Nuzzling the side of her face, inhaling her heady scent deep into his lungs, he poured out his heart. "Mila, I've never loved *anyone*," he stressed, "the way I love you. I've never split my soul with another. We can only do that once. When a reaper finds his mate, his true mate, he is bonded to her for an eternity. You are all I want, all I'll ever want. When the shadow showed me Adrianna, I did not stay in the vision because I loved her. I stayed because I was telling her good-bye. I let her go."

Her tiny little sobs pierced his heart. Her nails dug into his back and it was a sharp, sizzling pain, but it also felt good. Because he was alive and so was she, and that was all he wanted.

"I love you, Frenzy. More than my own life. More than anything."

Rubbing his knuckles along her cheekbone, he shook his head. "I wish you hadn't traded yourself to the queen. I'm so sorry, Mila. Fifteen years of servitude—"

"Is nothing when you have an eternity," she finished for him, liquid amber eyes hypnotizing him. "I would do it all over again to make sure I never lose you. I've fought alone for so long. I'm tired. I don't want to be alone anymore. I just want you, Frenzy."

Heart so full it felt it might burst from his chest, he took her lips in a slow lingering kiss. When they finally came up for air, she laughed.

"I'm finally home, Frenzy. No matter where I go or who I'm with, as long as you're there, I'm home."

They didn't speak again until after they'd taken the souls to their afterlife. The final soul was actually the remnants of Mila the shadow had managed to suck out before being destroyed. It'd slipped back into her body with the happy joy of a puppy greeting her master.

In the cabin they made slow, beautiful love. Their eyes speaking louder than any words about their bond and affection. Pledging themselves to each other eternally.

Later, as the moon was full in the sky and they lay entwined in one another's arms, they talked about the night. About the death of the shadow.

"You know, the only thing that keeps bothering me," he said, "is why it didn't work when I tried to use it on her."

Mila chuckled, trailing her fingers along the ridges of his abdomen. "Maybe there are some mysteries in life that'll never be explained."

It might have bothered him, if it mattered. But Mila was right, there were some things in life that well enough was well enough.

"I love you, woman," he growled, rolling on top of her, letting her feel the hardness of his body once again.

Her eyes widened and her sultry laugh filled all the empty places in his soul. "I love you too, death. Forever and ever and ever..."

Epilogue

W ell, we must say, sister"—Clarion turned a wide smile onto Lise—"you have done well with death. Already we feel the balance of good and evil aligning. The world is returning to what it once was. The threat of war recedes more and more each day."

Lise nodded. "Death only needed a little nudge. That is all."

"But I do wonder"—Clarion's fat raven-colored curls bobbed around her oval face attractively—"why the box did not work for Frenzy. I am curious, if he is not."

Lise shrugged. "The answer was in the wood itself. Decades ago when I gave the box to the queen, I'd sealed a drop of seer blood into the tree the box had been hewn from. In fact, I'd sealed Mila's blood into it."

Clarion frowned. "You traveled time, then?"

Lise merely lifted a brow, a smug little smile lacing the corners of her lips. "It was the only way to ensure the queen could not destroy the creature herself."

Clarion's laughter echoed through the pearlescent chamber.

"Oh, sister, that was too clever. If the queen had been able to do away with her creation, then she would never have worked out a deal with the lovely vampire hybrid."

"Exactly. She would have killed the shadow and taken Mila herself. At least like this she was forced to work out a deal, one that I could seal and ensure would never be broken. After fifteen years Mila will be free and out from under the thumb of that wretched queen, and she and her redheaded beau will live happily ever after."

Clarion clapped her hands. Lise really was quite clever when she wanted to be.

Nodding, she turned to go.

"Wait, sister, you've only just arrived. Leaving already?"

"Club X will not run itself, sister dear." And with a wink she returned back to the land she loved. Being a fate was fun, but her true calling was living among the wild and the wicked. Lise had found her home and she'd fight the devil himself to keep *it*, and her children, safe.

"Round two goes to me, Queenie," she whispered into the night, laughing when an unmistakable growl of annoyance sprang from The Morrigan's lips.

This fight was far from over, and Lise had never had so much fun...

See the next page for an excerpt from the first book in Marie Hall's Eternal Lovers series

Death's Lover

Chapter 1

Eve Philips gripped her husband's arm tighter as they walked across the sidewalk to the mall entrance. She hadn't felt good this morning; she'd been haunted by bad dreams all night long. Dreams of blood and violence and gore. She'd screamed herself awake, clinging to her husband with a vague unsettling feeling. But as dreams often do, the intensity of it faded until now all that was left was a lingering echo of it and an annoying headache.

It was almost Christmas, and she and her husband had a shopping date planned. She refused to wuss out now over some stupid dreams. Still, the unease of this morning lingered in the darkest corners of her mind. Usually she could just shake these things. Maybe it was just the old, burned coffee the java shack had served her this morning. Either way, she really wanted to stop stressing about it. There were too many other real things to worry about.

Like the fact that in three days her coven would be required to vote on the fate of a werewolf who'd been caught stabbing his human wife. No matter that his wife had tried to kill him first with the aid of a warlock's spell. Humans demanded the supernatural folk—or "supers," as they preferred to be called—governed themselves as swiftly and brutally as possible, especially when the crime involved one of their own. That was the life of a witch, especially one who chose to live in a city in as much turmoil as San Francisco. Still, there was no other place in the world she'd rather be.

By congressional act, California had granted the first and only place that the *others* could come out of hiding and live as they truly were. Werewolves no longer had to hide in tunnels, vampires could roam the streets freely at night, and witches could practice their craft without fear of retribution by the normals. That was ten years ago, and she'd never looked back.

Not to say that it was one big love fest. A snake could shed its skin several times in a lifetime, but that would never change its true essence. In the end a snake would always remain a snake. Just as a vampire could not help but feed, or a werewolf would go mad by light of the full moon.

Having so many volatile and sometimes dangerous groups in such close proximity practically begged for the violence to occur.

But she accepted it and moved on, because freedom was worth any price. Glancing around, she inhaled the sharp nip of the wind. It was a cloudless, gray day. The type that made her want to curl up in front of a roaring fire with a steaming cup of chamomile, cocooned against her husband's body.

She didn't notice the small rut in the road and stepped down hard. Muddy water splashed up her leg. A large black gob of goo landed square on her bloodred pumps.

"Damn it!"

Michael glanced down. One side of his mouth curled into a half-formed grin. She growled and picked up a dead leaf to scrape off the nasty mixture.

"I don't even want to know what that was." He laughed.

Eve stood and glared at her husband's smiling face. Turning her nose in the air, she dropped the leaf with disgust and walked away.

"Honey." He grabbed her hand and chuckled. "You gotta admit…it was pretty funny."

"Ha-ha. I'm just howling with laughter." She pointed a finger to her deadpan face. "This is me in hysterics."

Michael hugged her and slowly she smiled, never really that mad to begin with, but loving to be a little dramatic all the same.

"Why does that only ever happen to me?"

"Because you're just so cute, the goddess had to give you some sort of flaw."

She nailed him with a glare and then sighed with exasperation when he refused to look at her. Michael refused to be ruffled today.

The mall was appropriately decorated: a large Christmas tree sat guard to the entrance, festive lights hung swag from one light post to the next, and there was, of course, the melee of people shoving against her at a constant, repetitive pace with barely an apology to be gained. She sighed. To say she had a love-hate relationship with the holidays was putting it mildly.

But Michael had been acting secretive all day, alluding to some great gift she'd find under the tree come Yule. In truth, her husband's enthusiasm for life was contagious. She wouldn't miss the annual last-minute shopping for the world, though she'd never tell him that.

"Michael," she grumbled, "let's go home. It's freezing. My feet hurt, and…" She paused, trying to think of the next excuse to come up with.

He only smiled as expected. "Love you, shrew."

She rolled her eyes, trying desperately not to snort with laughter.

Then, as if the weather felt some need to remind her just how cold it was—and that she had no freaking business being out in the first place—she was blasted with a sweep of frigid air up her trench coat.

She shivered. "Stupid weatherman. I should hex his ass. He said temperatures of sixty."

Michael's lips twitched. "When are you gonna learn that *were* don't know his ass from his head? The man's worthless. Call a toad a toad and a bad weatherman a bad weatherman. Period."

She nodded. "Hear, hear."

Ten minutes later Eve fingered a delicate gold-and-emerald butterfly brooch. "Baby, do you think Tamryn would like this?"

He glanced up from browsing at a case of black pearl necklaces she'd considered buying for her sister. "Sure. I guess."

She laughed. "'I guess'? The standard male answer for everything, right? Why do I even bother?" She caught the heavily made-up clerk's eye and nodded.

The blonde glided over in a sea of expensive perfume and sent a blatantly lustful smile in Michael's direction. Eve hid her laughter under a pursed lip and raised brow. "The butterfly," she prompted and handed the lady a fifty.

Michael grinned and encircled Eve's waist from behind, laying his head on her shoulder. A soft lock of his doe-brown hair brushed the side of her neck. She swept the hair aside and sighed.

"You just love it when that happens, don't you?"

"What?" he asked in a rush of innocence.

"'What?'" she mimicked. "You're too gorgeous for your own good."

Throaty laughter spilled from his lips as he swayed with her in time to the strains of "Jingle Bell Rock" floating through the overcrowded department store.

Eve snuggled deeper into his arms.

Michael nuzzled the side of her neck.

Her whole body tightened up in reaction to his touch. Even after five years of marriage he still had the power to make her heart flutter and her knees tremble.

"Michael," she whispered.

"Hmm?" He placed a gentle kiss on the nape of her neck.

Goose bumps skimmed along her forearms. "I'm ovulating."

He went still for a split second then nipped her earlobe. His large hand framed her stomach. "Let's go make babies, then."

Her lip twitched, and she wiggled her bottom against him. Michael growled low in his throat and pinned her arms to her sides, holding her still. "Eve," he warned.

She turned and draped her arms over his neck. "What?"

He dragged her closer, a mischievous twinkle in his emerald-green eyes. "Imp. You're lucky I'm wearing a coat long enough…"

"Excuse me." A strained voice interrupted them.

She turned. The sales clerk held her purchase and change in one hand. Her narrowed eyes and curled lip were too much for Eve to ignore.

Taking the bag, and without missing a beat, Eve leaned forward just enough to part her button-down shirt at the collar, causing her pentagram to swing free from between her breasts. "He ain't on the market, babe."

The clerk, obviously human, turned deathly white. No human liked to tangle with the dark arts. And though that wasn't what Eve did by any means, the blonde didn't know it, and Eve sure as heck wasn't going to correct her assumption. Judging by the reaction, the threat had done its job.

With a smile and a jaunty wave, she turned on her heel and marched off.

Michael held out his arm. "What in the world did you say to her, Eve?" She didn't miss the tinge of humor lacing his voice.

She just grinned. "What? And give you a bigger head than you've already got? I don't think so."

He chuckled and grabbed her hand in his, caressing her knuckle with the pad of his thumb. Laughter glittered in his eyes. Then he became serious and turned her face to look directly at him. "I love you."

The way he said it made her shiver. One of those freaky moments in time that made her wonder if there was some sort of sixth sense involved. Then she thought of the dream again and the visions of death.

Her smile slipped for a millisecond. She always tried to be aware of the signs and the environment around her. What if she was being purposefully ignorant? Ignoring the obvious? What if that dream really was a warning?

Don't make more out of this than what it is. Everything's fine.

Pushing the neurotic fears to the back of her mind, she gave him a crooked smile. "I know, Mikey. And I thank the goddess every day for you."

* * *

Cian waited within shadow just outside the entrance to the mall; the mortals he'd been sent to harvest should appear soon. Keeping his back to the crowd, he stood in such a way so that he had a clear view of the door as pedestrians filed and in out of the busy shopping plaza.

Using his essence, he transformed himself into an ordinary guy, hardly worth a second glance. Through all the years of using this guise, he'd never once been remembered. Right now, he needed people to look past him, not see the peculiarities that branded him not quite human. Unfortunately he couldn't go fully invisible until the harvest time came upon him.

His hair turned a drab brown, short and barely reaching his collar, his eyes much the same color. The process happened so fast, no one even had time to react at all.

Staring at his gloved hand, he waited for the next step of his transformation to take place. He didn't have to wait long. A shock, like a burst of flame, ran down his arm and into his hand, turning him from man to monster. Fire traveled his veins, making him grunt with a momentary flash of pain. He hissed and snatched off his left glove, making sure he was well within shadow. The day was so drab and gray that unless he did something obvious, like flash the crowd, no one would turn his way.

He clenched his hand, studying the bones of his fingers. For an outsider, to look at the transformation would seem surreal. Above the wrist he was man—flesh and blood. But when the change overcame him, and it was time to harvest souls, the hand turned to a design of the macabre. The flesh, muscle, and tendon literally faded from sight.

Human depictions always had the grim reapers wearing the traditional black cowl with a sickle in their skeletal grip. In truth, reapers were as normal as man. You could pass them on the street, commenting on their remarkable beauty, little knowing that beneath the white smile and ever-present gloves lurked the killer of legend.

A small, noisy crowd of humans walked toward him. Shoving his hand into his pocket, he leaned against the wall and waited; it wouldn't be much longer now.

After centuries of doing this job, he'd learned patience, the art of stealth, and the endless waiting game of death. For such a vital and intricate part of life, the actual moment of death could be unbelievably boring.

Several minutes later, an electrical rush of power surged through his body when a couple walked out. A man and a raven-haired witch. He felt her power ripple through the air like a powerful ocean current. The man, though, exhibited no energy, which meant he was fully mortal. The man grabbed the witch around the waist, pulling her close for a quick embrace.

Cian's pulse pounded when she smiled. It was a good smile, the kind that made him want to return it, to see her do it again just so he could have the enjoyment of gazing on that kind of radiant and rare pure joy.

The man hopped in front of her and grabbed her hands, toying with her fingers. Her laughter was a rich, lilting sound, deep and throaty, hot and sexy, and for the first time in his life, Cian wondered what it might be like to have a woman look at him that way. He envied mortals in some ways, specifically the way they could enjoy life, short as it was, and how they loved one another. He couldn't think of anyone who'd look so happy to see him.

Those thoughts were jerked from him as the final phase of his transformation washed through his body. A charge, like static energy, traveled through his pores, his blood, and in seconds he'd gone completely invisible. Only able to be seen by those straddling the line between life and death, he strolled purposefully toward the car garage.

Today's scenario would be no different than the thousands of others he'd seen through the years. He could see it in his mind, like an image on a television screen. A carload of teenagers barreling through the garage, the interior of the car heavily laced with the thick stench of cannabis. The driver was laughing, blaring the Ozzy tune "Crazy Train," unaware that soon he'd be indicted for two counts of vehicular homicide.

Cian often wondered at times like these why the humans couldn't feel it. The end of their lifeline, the disturbance in the air, death; for him it was like the blast of trumpets, loud and hard to ignore.

Turning his attention back to the couple, he waited. The man popped open the trunk of a green sedan, laid down his packages, and flashed the witch a smile. She stood by the hood of the car, her midnight curls blowing in the stiff wind.

The faint rumble of an approaching engine echoed eerily through the garage. The vibrations traveled through the soles of his feet. *Soon. It'll all be over soon.*

For a crazy second he wanted to scream at them. *Move. Get out of the way.* But he held his tongue. He wouldn't interfere; that was the single most important rule of the reaper. His skeletal hand twitched, and he yanked it out of his pocket. No mistakes.

The car made a sharp left around a concrete post in the garage and swerved headlong toward the couple with a loud, echoing cry of rubber.

For Cian the scene was agonizingly slow, each detail sharp and clear, as if it were taking minutes, though in truth it would be done within seven seconds.

When they finally noticed, it was already too late.

The witch's golden eyes grew wide in her face. Blood rushed from her skin, leaving her a pasty white. Her hands covered her mouth as a scream of raw fear flew from her lips. "Michael!"

The smile on the man's face died. He turned—unable to run for cover, to hide from his fate. She ran forward, arms outstretched, and tried to pull the man toward her.

Metal exploded against flesh. The sickening crunch of bone and tearing muscle warred with the scream of tires braking. The man was dragged under the car. She was flung aside, her limbs at odd proportions.

Cian's heart clenched painfully when he saw her ravaged body lying so helpless on the ground. She looked like a morbid porcelain doll. Beautiful and broken.

Blood spattered everywhere. All over the windshield. Even on the neighboring vehicles in the next three slots. The overwhelming metallic stench was all around.

The car squealed to a halt, slamming against the side of the sedan. The shattering of glass echoed through the garage with an eerie finality. It was done; their bodies slowly dying, their souls waiting only for him to harvest and carry on to the appropriate afterlife.

The driver, a pimply-faced redhead emerged. "Oh no! No!" He sang the litany over and over. He ran a trembling hand through his hair and glanced up. A family in the next row over stared back in openmouthed shock.

"Get back in the car, Derek!" the girl in the passenger seat screamed.

The wind picked up flurries of snow, enclosing them in winter's peaceful embrace. An ironic scene, at odds with the gruesome sight of death before him.

The kid jumped back in his car and squealed off with one last *bump-bump* in his wake.

Cian closed the gap between himself and the victims. First the male. The man's face had been nearly sheared off. His forehead was cracked open and a constant stream of blood gushed from the wound. Kneeling, Cian extended his skeletal hand, ready to harvest the soul and carry it safely to the afterlife.

The man moaned and opened green eyes glittering with pain. He didn't question why Cian was kneeling over him; instead he parted ruptured lips and croaked, "Save my wife."

Cian glanced over at her prostrate form for a brief second and then shook his head with a sad, bitter twist to his lips. He'd seen many broken bodies in the past, never feeling more than quiet detachment. But seeing her now, hearing the wet gurgle of her breaths, it was like razor-sharp spikes driving through his heart.

He closed his eyes, chanting over and over in his mind: *This is the order to life. Without order there would be chaos. To prevent the chaos there must always be order.*

Taking a deep breath, he plowed on, finishing what he'd started. "Find your peace, human..." *For us both.* Then he gently caressed the man's exposed cheek.

The light of death filled the man's eyes, and a single tear slipped down his cheek. The mask of pain relaxed, and a soft blue mist exploded from the caved-in chest—the soul pulsed with energy and differing shades of blue.

A glowing portal of brilliant white opened before him. The melodic song of a bubbling brook and rustling grass momentarily made Cian forget—forget the pain and loneliness.

The soul glided toward the light. It shimmered and glowed as it stepped through the portal. Then it was gone. The light went too, and with it the temporary peace Cian had sought his entire existence.

One left. The thought was a needle stabbing into his brain. He tried to remain clinical and study her not as a victim, but as a task and a duty to fulfill.

She wasn't in nearly as bad a shape as her husband had been. Both legs were broken at the hips. One foot was pointed north, the other south. Besides the obvious injuries, she also suffered a ruptured spleen and would soon die from internal bleeding.

Short, shallow breathing turned his gaze to her face. Thin and heart-shaped with full pink lips and almond-shaped eyes.

His hands trembled; something was causing him to hesitate, a strange feeling he had no name for. What was it? Curiosity maybe? Something about the witch tugged at his normally detached feelings about death and life. *Do it. You must. Take her from this misery.*

Her eyes snapped open. The lioness gaze ensnared him. Her bloody hand grabbed his fleshy one and his world turned upside down. Instantly images and thoughts came to him. The face of her husband, a sensation of overwhelming, heartrending love. The pain. The fear. The hope. Her hope exploded inside him like a seedling shooting through black earth.

His brows dipped, and his breathing spiked. He continued to

share her emotions. He bit the inside of his lip, and the bitter taste of blood pooled on his tongue as he fought off the onslaught. He'd known upon first seeing her that she was a witch, had sensed her energy, but her powers were intense. He'd never come across a projecting empath as powerful as she was.

Cian took slow breaths and pushed his will against her own in an attempt to extricate himself from her furious assault. His will was like talons ripping and clawing at her insides; the back blast resonated through him. He reeled from it but couldn't block himself off. She whimpered, moans spilled from her lips, and still she fought him.

He could break her wrist, force her to let him go. Force her to end the emotional battering. So why wasn't he doing that?

Because he couldn't. Because for the first time in an eternity she was making him *feel*—not just her pain, but her desperation for life. Emotions he'd never felt before. It was all so confusing, and yet…he'd never felt more alive. All his life he'd walked around in a daze. Moving from one soul to another, not living, just existing. For the first time, he wanted. He felt. Because of her, and he'd betrayed her in the worse possible way.

Her eyes, glazed with pain, held his own. Defying him to take her life. She wanted to live.

Another shot of emotions slammed him. They felt like churning waves of angry sea crashing against him, stripping the flesh from his bones. Her anger beat at him, clawed at his throat with desperation.

Right then he made a decision. In defiance of his queen, the ruler of the reapers, he let her live.

About the Author

Marie Hall has always had a dangerous fascination for creatures that go bump in the night. And mermaids. And, of course, faeries. Trolls. Unicorns. Shapeshifters. Vampires. Scottish brogues. Kilts. Beefy arms. Ummm…bad boys! Especially the sexy ones. Which is probably why she married one.

On top of that, she's a confirmed foodie; she nearly went to culinary school and then figured out she could save a ton of money if she just watched food shows religiously. She's a self-proclaimed master chef, certified deep-sea dolphin trainer, finder of leprechauns' gold at the end of the rainbow, and rumor has it she keeps the troll king locked away in her basement. All of which is untrue (except for the cooking part—she loves cooking); however, she does have an incredibly active imagination and loves to share her crazy thoughts with the world!

If you want to see what new creations she's got up her sleeve, check out her blog:

www.MarieHallWrites.blogspot.com